Being an author has a... dream. But it was only wh... during her final year at universi... he realised how soon she wanted that dream to become a reality. So she got serious about her writing, and now writes books she wants to see in the world, featuring people who look like her, for a living. When she's not writing she's spending time with her husband and dogs in Cape Town, South Africa. She admits that this is a perfect life, and is grateful for it.

Though her name is frequently on bestseller lists, **Allison Leigh**'s high point as a writer is hearing from readers that they laughed, cried or lost sleep while reading her books. She credits her family with great patience for the time she's parked at her computer, and for blessing her with the kind of love she wants her readers to share with the characters living in the pages of her books. Contact her at allisonleigh.com.

SURPRISE BABY, SECOND CHANCE

THERESE BEHARRIE

SHOW ME A HERO

ALLISON LEIGH

MILLS & BOON

First Published in Great Britain 2018
by Mills & Boon, an imprint of HarperCollinsPublishers,
1 London Bridge Street, London, SE1 9GF

Surprise Baby, Second Chance © 2018 Therese Beharrie
Show Me a Hero © 2018 Allison Lee Johnson

ISBN: 978-0-263-26518-7

0818

MIX
Paper from
responsible sources
FSC™ C007454

FSC
www.fsc.org

SURPRISE BABY, SECOND CHANCE

THERESE BEHARRIE

Grant.
Thank you for keeping me steady through my anxieties.

My ROSA Typewriter Club.
I'm so lucky to have found you both.
Thank you for believing in me.
Always remember how much I believe in you.

And Megan.

Thank you for your patience with me.
You've taught me so much. I can't wait for the rest of our books together—sorry, I couldn't resist!

CHAPTER ONE

ROSA SPENCER HAD two options.

One: she could get back into the taxi that had brought her to the house she was currently standing in front of.

Two: she could walk into that house and face the man she'd left four months ago without any explanation.

Her husband.

When the purr of the car grew distant behind her she took a deep breath. Her chance of escape now gone, she straightened her shoulders and walked down the pathway that led to the front door of the Spencers' holiday home.

It could have been worse, she considered. She could have bumped into Aaron somewhere in Cape Town, where she'd been staying since she'd left him. And since they'd lived together over a thousand kilometres away in Johannesburg, Rosa would have been unprepared to see him.

Since she worked from home most days, she would have probably been wearing the not-quite-pyjamas-but-might-as-well-be outfit she usually wore when she ventured out of the house during the week. Her hair would have been a mess, curls spiralling everywhere—or piled on top of her head—and her face would have been clear of make-up.

Exposed, she thought. Vulnerable.

At least now she was prepared to see him.

Her gold dress revealed generous cleavage and cinched at her waist with a thin belt. Its skirt was long, loose, though it had a slit up to mid-thigh—stopping just before her shape-wear began—to reveal a leg that was strong and toned: one of her best assets.

Her dress made her feel confident—after all, what was the point of being a designer if she couldn't make clothes that did?—as did the mass of curls around her face, and the make-up she'd had done before she'd got onto the private plane her mother-in-law had sent for her.

She hadn't seen Liana Spencer in the four months since she'd left Aaron either. And perhaps that was part of the reason Rosa had agreed to attend a birthday party that would put her face to face with the man she'd walked away from.

The other reason was because of her own mother. And the birthday parties Violet Lang would never get to celebrate.

Rosa took another breath, clinging to the confidence she'd fought for with her dress. It was a pivotal part of the armour she'd created when she'd realised she'd be seeing Aaron again.

She needed the armour to cloak the shivering in the base of her stomach. The erratic beating of her heart. The combination of the two was so familiar that she didn't think she'd ever truly lived without it. Though that hadn't stopped her from running from it all her life.

The door of the house was open when she got there and Rosa slipped inside, thinking that it would be easier than to announce her arrival by ringing the bell. There was nothing to indicate a celebration on the first floor—just the usual tasteful but obviously expensive furniture and décor—though that wasn't surprising. Liana usually went for lavish, which meant the top floor. The one where the walls were made entirely of glass.

It offered guests an exceptional view of the sea that surrounded Mariner's Island just off the coast of Cape Town. Of the waves that crashed against the rocks that were scattered at the beach just a few metres from the Spencer house. And of the small town and airport that stood only a short distance away from the house too.

Rosa held her breath as she got to the top of the stairs, and then pushed open the door before she lost her nerve.

And immediately told herself that she should have escaped when she had the chance.

There was no party on this floor. Instead, it looked like it usually did when there were no events planned. There was a living area and a bed on one side of the room—the bathroom being the only section of the floor with privacy—and a dining area and kitchen on the other side.

There was an open space between the two sides as if whoever had designed the room had decided to give the Spencers an area to be free in.

But in that open space stood her husband. *Only* her husband.

And the last thing Rosa thought of was freedom.

His back was to her, and she thought that she still had the chance to escape. He didn't know that she was there. If she left he wouldn't ever have to know. What harm would it do?

Except that when she turned back to the door it was closed. And when she looked over her shoulder to see if he'd noticed her she saw that Aaron was now facing her, an unreadable expression on his face.

'Running?'

'N-no.' *Be confident.*

His mouth lifted into a half-smile. 'No?' he asked in a faintly mocking tone.

Her face went hot. The shivering intensified. Her heart rate rocketed. But, despite that, she was able to offer him a firm, 'No'.

'Okay,' he replied in a voice that told her he didn't believe her. And why would he? Hadn't she run from him before? Without the decency to explain why? Hadn't the anxiety of that decision kept her up night after night?

Guilt shimmered through her.

She ignored it.

But ignoring it meant that her brain had to focus on something else. And—as it usually did—it chose his face.

Her eyes feasted on what her memories hadn't done justice to over the last four months. His dark hair, dark brows, the not-quite-chocolate colour of his skin. The mixture of his Indian and African heritage had created an arresting face, his features not unlike those Rosa had seen on movie stars.

But his face had more than just good looks. It spoke of the cool, calm demeanour that had always exasperated her even as it drew her in. He rarely let his emotions out of wherever he kept them, so they seldom claimed the planes of his face.

Except when he and Rosa were having a conversation about their feelings. Or when they were making love. There'd been nothing *but* emotion on his face then.

'Where is everybody?' she asked in a hoarse voice.

Aaron slid his hands into his pockets, making his biceps bulge slightly under the material of his suit jacket. Her breath taunted her as it slipped out of her lungs. As it reminded her that it wasn't only Aaron's face that she was attracted to.

It was his muscular body. It was how much taller than her he was. It was his broad shoulders, the strength of his legs, of everything in between.

He'd always been thrilled by the curves of her body. But his hands were large enough, strong enough, that she'd always thought he wouldn't have wanted her as much if her curves hadn't been as generous.

Aaron took a step towards her.

Which was no reason for her to move back.

But she did.

'Well, if I'm right—and I probably am—everyone's here who's supposed to be.'

'I don't understand. It's just you and...' She trailed off, her heart thudding. 'Did you—did you do this?'

'Oh, no,' Aaron replied, and took another step towards

her. This time she managed to keep her feet in place. 'Why would I want to see the wife who left me with no explanation?'

'Great. Then I'll go.'

She turned to the door again, ignoring her confusion. She'd figure it out when she was off the island that reminded her so much of her husband.

The island where he'd taken her months after her mother had died. Where he'd got down on one knee. Where he'd told her he couldn't imagine life without her.

Where they'd spent time after their wedding. Lounging in the sun at the beach. Lazily enjoying each other's bodies as only newlyweds could.

Where they'd taken holidays. When life had become too much for her and Aaron had surprised her with a trip away.

The island where he'd held her, comforted her, loved her on the bed that stood in the corner, its memories haunting her. Overwhelming her.

Yes, she'd figure it all out when she was away from the island. And far, *far* away from her husband.

A hand pressed against the door before she could open it. She swallowed and then turned back to face him.

Her heart sprinted now. Her body prickled. The scent of his masculine cologne filled her senses. Memories, sharp and intimate, could no longer be held back.

Again, she tried to ignore them. But it was becoming harder to do.

'Why are you stopping me from leaving?' she managed in a steady voice.

'Did you think you were just going to walk in here, see me, and then…leave?'

'I thought I was attending your mother's sixtieth birthday party.'

'Which I would have been at too.'

'And we would have seen each other there, yes. But you're the only one here. I've seen you. Now I want to leave.'

'Just like that?'

'Just like that.'

He inched closer. 'You're not the slightest bit curious about why you and I are alone here?'

'Sure I am. But I'm also pretty sure I can figure it out on my way to the airport.'

'The airport?' His lips curved into a smile. 'Honey, the airport's closed.'

'No,' she said after a beat. 'No, it can't be. I just got off a plane. Your mother said it would be waiting for me when I was done here.'

His smile faded. 'She lied. Your flight is likely to be the last one until Monday. The airport's closed this weekend.'

Panic thickened in her throat. '*All* weekend?'

'Don't sound so surprised, Rosa,' he said mildly. 'You know Mariner's Island doesn't work the way the rest of the world does.'

'Yes, but…but it was a *private* plane. Yours.'

'It still needs somewhere to take off from. To land at. And since the airport's closed we won't have that until Monday.'

She ducked under his arm, put distance between them. But it didn't make breathing any easier. 'So…what? Your mother just decided to leave her guests stranded here until Monday?'

'Not guests,' he corrected. 'Just you and me.'

'Did you know about this?'

'No.'

'Then how did you not suspect something was off when the main route off the island would only be viable again on *Monday*?'

'She told me that the party would be going on for most of the weekend.'

'And you *believed* her?'

'Yes,' he said coldly. 'It's not unusual for one of my mother's parties to continue for an entire weekend. You know that.'

'Okay,' she said, and lifted the curls off her forehead with a shaky hand. 'Okay, fine.' Her hand dropped. 'Then I'll take a boat home.'

'It's too late to get one tonight.'

'I know,' she said through clenched teeth. 'I'll take one tomorrow morning.'

'There's a storm warning for tomorrow. Starting tonight, actually.'

She looked beyond the glass walls, saw the dark clouds rolling in. Her stomach tumbled. 'That's fine.'

'It'll be a rough storm, Rosa. It's anticipated to last until tomorrow evening at least. Do you still want to take a boat?'

'Yes.'

He laughed softly. 'You're so determined to get away from me you'll take an almost two-hour boat ride in a storm? Even though you get sick when the water is calm?'

She hesitated. 'I'll be fine.'

His half-smile mocked her. 'I'm sure you will be.'

He was right, she thought, and hated herself for admitting it. Hated him for being right.

Except that what she felt in that moment was anything *but* hate.

Confusion, yes. How had this happened? Had Liana really orchestrated this on purpose?

Guilt, of course. She'd walked away from him. From their relationship. She hadn't even said goodbye.

Anger, *absolutely*. She *hated* feeling trapped. It reminded her of her childhood. Of being caught in her mother's world.

But hate? No, she thought, her eyes settling on Aaron again. There was no hate.

'Why are you so calm?'

'I'm not,' he replied in a tone that gave no indication that he wasn't. 'But I know my mother. And I know this scheme is probably well-thought-out. Much like the first time we met. Or don't you remember?' His voice was soft, urgent. 'Have you run away from the memories too, Rosa?'

She didn't reply. There was no reply she could give. She couldn't tell him that she hadn't been running away from him, not really, but *saving* him. From the anxiety, the stress, the worry of being with someone who was terrified of losing the health of their mind, their body.

Rosa had spent her life looking after someone like that. She knew the anxiety, the stress, the worry of it. She knew the guilt when the fear became a reality.

She'd saved him, she thought again. She'd saved him from going through what she'd gone through with her mother's hypochondria. She'd saved him from having to take care of another person. From having it break him.

The moment she'd felt that lump in her breast, she'd known she couldn't put him through all of that. So she'd walked away. Had tried to move on.

But the memories wouldn't let her. No, the memories were always, *always* there.

'Great,' Rosa said loudly. 'No one's here.'

But that didn't make sense. Her mother had told her there was a Christmas ball for cancer patients that night. Had asked Rosa to be her partner at the ball.

Of course, Rosa had agreed. Her father wasn't in Cape Town, though she doubted he would have agreed to accompany her mother even if he had been. Irritation bristled over her, but she forced her attention to the matter at hand. She'd spent enough of her time being annoyed at her father.

The room was decorated as if there was supposed to be a ball. A large crystal chandelier hung in the middle of the ceiling, white draping flowing from it to different spots on the walls. It lit the space with soft light, brightened only by the small Christmas trees in each corner of the room that had been adorned with twinkling lights.

There was only one table at the end of the room, standing next to the largest Christmas tree Rosa had ever seen, with champagne, canapés and desserts spread across it.

'Am I early?' Rosa wondered out loud again.

But, like the first time, she got no response. Throwing her hands up, she turned to try and find someone who could explain what was happening. As she took a step towards the door, it opened and her breathing did something strange when a man joined her in the room.

'Who are you?' she blurted out.

He lifted an eyebrow. 'Aaron Spencer. Who are you?'

'Rosa Lang.' She swallowed. How had the air around her suddenly become so charged? 'I'm, um, here for the Christmas ball...'

'Me too.' His eyes lazily scanned the room. 'Either we're really early or—'

'Or our mothers have decided to play a game on us,' Rosa said, his name suddenly registering with her.

He was Liana Spencer's son. Rosa had only met the woman a few times during her mother's group chemotherapy sessions but she'd been charmed. Not only by the woman's energy—which she envied greatly—but because she'd done an amazing job at keeping Rosa's mother's energy up, despite the fact that she was going through chemo too.

Liana had been vocal about wanting Rosa to meet her son, and Violet had tried to get Rosa to agree to it just as passionately. The dress Liana had sent her—along with the make-up, hair and car she'd arranged—began to make more sense. And seeing Aaron now had Rosa regretting that she'd resisted an introduction for such a long time...

'I wouldn't put it past my mother,' Aaron replied darkly. It sent a shiver down her spine. But she didn't know if that was because of what he'd said or the fact that she felt inexplicably drawn to him. Even though he didn't seem quite as enamoured.

'This does seem like an excessive prank though.'

'My mother's speciality.'

'Really?' She tilted her head and, for once, let herself lean into what she wanted to do, refusing to give the doubt that followed her around constantly any footing. 'How about we have a glass of champagne and you can tell me all about it?'

She wasn't sure how long he studied her. But when his lips curved into a smile—when his expression turned from reserved into one she couldn't describe but *felt*, deep in her stomach—she knew she would have waited an eternity for it. And thought that—just maybe—he was drawn to her too...

'I remember,' Rosa said softly. 'It was a hospital Christmas ball. Or so we thought. Our mothers told us they wanted us to go with them. That they'd meet us there because they wanted to have dinner before. But there was no hospital Christmas ball. Just a party for two that our mothers had arranged so that we could meet.'

There was a tenderness on Rosa's face that didn't fit with the woman who'd left him four months ago. An indulgence too, though he suspected that was for her mother who'd passed away a year after that incident. And for his mother, who Rosa still had a soft spot for, despite what she'd seen Liana put him through over the years.

Aaron clenched his jaw. The emotion might have been misleading but her actions hadn't been. She'd left him without a word. Without a phone call. Without a note. He'd got home from work one day to find her clothes gone. She'd taken nothing else, and he'd had to face living in the house they'd furnished together—the home they'd *built* together—alone.

'I imagine my mother wanted this to be much the same,' Aaron said curtly. 'She forces us to be alone together but, instead of starting to date this time, we work things out.'

'But it's not like before,' she denied. 'There actually was a ball then. Sure, no one else was there, but there was food and drink, and the place had been decorated for a party. This—' she gestured around them '—is so far away from that.'

'But she sent you a dress again?' He tried to keep what seeing her in that dress did to him out of his voice.

'No. I designed this one.'

'You've never made anything like this for yourself before.'

'I know. It was…a special occasion. Your mom's sixtieth birthday,' she added quickly. But it was too late. He'd already figured out that she'd made the dress because of him.

He wasn't sure if he was pleased or annoyed by the fact. He'd been trying to get her to make something for herself for years. Now, when they were…whatever they were, she'd chosen to listen to him.

Perhaps that was why she'd left. Because he'd been holding her back. He'd add it to the list of possibilities. A list that spoke loudly—accusingly—of his faults.

'I'm sure she would have if you hadn't told her you'd sort yourself out,' he said to distract himself. 'And she arranged the plane for you. And the car to get you here. She's a regular old fairy godmother,' he added dryly.

'No. No,' she said again. 'That can't be it. She wouldn't have arranged all of this just to play at being a fairy godmother.'

'She did it before. When we met.'

'That was just as much my mom as it was yours.'

'Somehow, I think my mother had more to do with it.' His shoulders tightened. 'She likes to think she doesn't live in the real world. And now, with this, she gets to play the perfect role. The good guy. The fairy godmother. To orchestrate a happy ever after.'

'For you and me?'

'Who else?' he asked sharply, hating the surprise in her voice. She winced, stepped back, brushed at her hair again. It spiralled around her face in that free and slightly wild way her curls dictated.

'You're saying your mother tricked us into being here together because she wants us to…reconcile?' He nodded. 'Why?'

'I don't know,' he said sarcastically. 'Maybe because we were happily married until I got home one day to find you'd disappeared?' She blanched. 'Or maybe I'd fooled myself into believing we were happy.'

She bit her lip, looked away. 'Did she tell you that she wanted us to have a happy ever after?'

He gritted his teeth, then forced himself to relax. Control was key. 'Not directly. But she's been urging me to contact you for the last four months.' He cocked his head. 'How did *she* contact you?'

'My…email. I've been checking my emails.'

Tension vibrated between them. As did the unspoken words.

I've been checking my emails. I just haven't replied to yours.

'I was always going to attend her birthday, Aaron,' Rosa said softly. 'You know this is about more than your mother. More than you and me.'

He did. Rosa's mother had made his mother promise to celebrate each birthday with vigour. A reminder that they'd lived. That they'd had a *life*.

That had been a deathbed promise.

It angered him even more that his mother would use her birthday as an opportunity for her scheme. In all the years she'd manipulated situations—in all the years she'd blamed

her 'zest for life' for interfering in other people's lives—
she'd never done anything this...*conniving*.

And in all the years since he'd taken responsibility for
Liana since he'd realised she wouldn't take responsibility
herself, Aaron had never felt more betrayed.

Or perhaps the betrayal he felt about Rosa leaving was
intensifying his reaction.

Whatever it was, he wouldn't allow it to control him any
more. He walked to the door...and cursed when he found
it locked.

CHAPTER TWO

'WHAT?' ROSA ASKED, anxiety pounding with her heart. 'What is it?'

'It's locked.'

'It's—what?' She strode past him and tried the handle of the door. It turned, but no amount of pressure made it open. 'No,' she said, shaking her head. 'This is not happening. We are *not* locked in here. There must be some mistake.'

Panic spurred her movements and she reached into the clutch she'd forgotten was in her hand. She took her phone out. 'I have signal!' she said triumphantly. 'Only a few bars, but it should work. Who should I call?'

'I suppose we could try the police.' His calm voice was a stark contrast to the atmosphere around them.

'Do you have the number?'

'No.'

She stared at him. 'How do you not have the number of the police?'

'It's on my phone. It's dead,' he said, nodding in the direction of the table where it lay.

'You didn't charge it,' she said with a sigh. It was something he did—or didn't do—regularly. Which had driven her crazy on good days. This day had been anything but good.

But if he was going to pretend to be calm—if he was going to pretend he wasn't freaking out when she knew that he was—she could too.

'Okay, so we don't have the number for the police station. I'm assuming that covers all emergency services?' He nodded. 'I guess we better hope that nothing happens during this storm,' she muttered, and scanned her contacts for the number she was looking for.

As if in response to her words, a streak of lightning whipped across the sky. It was closely followed by booms of thunder. Rosa closed her eyes and brought the phone to her ear.

'Liana, we're locked in,' Rosa said the moment she heard Liana's voice—distant, crackling—on the phone.

'Rosa?'

'Yes, it's Rosa. Aaron and I are trapped on the top floor of the house.'

'What?' Static dulled the sound of Liana's voice even more. 'Did you get to the house safely?'

'I'm fine. But we're locked in, so we can't get off the top floor.'

Liana didn't reply and Rosa looked at the phone to see if they'd been cut off, but the call was still ongoing.

'Here, let me try,' Aaron said and she handed him the phone. And bit back the response that *him* speaking to his mother couldn't magically make the connection better.

'Mom? We're locked on the top floor of the house. Hello? *Hello?*'

Rosa waited as Aaron fell silent, and then he looked at the display on the phone and sighed. 'It cut off. I don't think she got any of that.'

'We could try someone else—'

She broke off when thunder echoed again, this time followed by a vicious flash of lightning. And then everything went dark.

'Aaron?'

'Yeah, I'm here.'

Her panic ebbed somewhat with the steadiness of his voice. 'Does this mean what I think it means?'

'Yeah, the power went out.' She heard movement, and then the light of her phone shone between them. 'The generator should be kicking in soon though.'

Silence spread between them as they waited.

And relief took the place of tension when the lights flickered on again.

'I think we're going to be stuck here for a while,' Aaron said after a moment.

'We could just try calling someone again.'

'Who?'

'Look up the number for the police,' she snapped. Sucked in a breath. Told herself her confident façade was slipping. Ignored the voice in her head telling her it had slipped a long time ago.

Aaron didn't reply and tapped on the screen of the phone. Then he looked up. 'There's no signal. It must have something to do with the electricity being out.'

'That's impossible. We can't *not* have a connection.'

'It's Mariner's Island,' he said simply, as though it explained everything.

And, if she were honest with herself, it did. Mariner's Island was tiny. The locals who lived and worked there did so for the sake of tourism. And it was the perfect tourist destination. In the summer. When the demands on power and the likelihood of storms were low.

There was a reason the airport had closed over the weekend. A reason the lights had gone out. The island thrived during summer, but survived during winter.

A clap of thunder punctuated her thoughts and she turned in time to see another flash of lightning streak across the sky. She badly wanted to try the door again, but when she turned back she saw Aaron watching her. And if she tried the door again she would be proving him right. She would be proving to him that she *was* running. She would look like a fool.

She didn't want to look like a fool. A fool desperate not to be in the same room with the husband she'd left.

With the husband she still loved.

* * *

Again, Aaron found himself enthralled by the emotion on her face. She looked torn, though he didn't know between what.

It wasn't the ideal situation, them being locked in this room together. But it was what it was. And, since the storm was probably going to keep the good folk of Mariner's Island in their homes, no one would be saving them for a while.

They'd have to accept that fact and do the best that they could.

It almost seemed as if he were okay with it. As if being alone with the woman who'd left him wouldn't remind him of all the reasons he'd given himself for why she'd left.

His reluctance to be spontaneous. His caution surrounding their lives. How he always had to clean up the messes his mother created. How he did so without a word.

She hadn't seemed to mind any of it before. But then she'd left, so what did he know?

'You should turn your phone off.'

'What? Why?'

'Preserve the battery.' He took off his jacket, loosened his tie. Threw them both over the couch. 'We're not calling anyone for a while, but we'll have to do so tomorrow.'

'But what if someone tries to contact us?'

'No one is going to contact us.'

He opened the top button of his shirt, and then narrowed his eyes when he saw two suitcases in the corner of the room. He'd known something was up when he'd got to the top floor and saw that it hadn't been set up for a party. Instead, it looked as it usually did when they visited normally.

Perhaps that had dulled his suspicions. He'd thought his mother had wanted them to share a meal, or that they'd meet there before going to the actual party.

He should have known better.

The pieces had only fallen into place when he'd seen

Rosa. And he'd barely managed to see the whole picture those pieces painted when he'd been battling the emotion at seeing her again.

He walked over to the cases and laid them both on the bed. The first held men's clothing. The second, women's.

'Is that *lingerie*?'

His lips twitched. 'Yes.'

She'd come over from where she'd been standing on the opposite side of the bed and now began to throw the offending items out of the case. 'Well, at least there are some other things here too.' She paused. 'Did your mother pack this?'

He shrugged.

'The other things—' she pulled out a casual-looking dress, holding it between her index finger and thumb '—are less... seductive, I suppose. But I don't think any of them would fit me.' She frowned. 'If it was your mother, this makes no sense. She knows what size I am.'

'Maybe the selection was meant to seduce anyway.' He fought to steady his voice. 'You'd be able to wear that, but it would be tighter than what you're used to. Or more uncomfortable. So you'd—'

'Be encouraged to wear the lingerie?'

'I was going to say you'd look different.' He said the words deliberately now, determined not to show her how the conversation was messing with his head.

'There's nothing wrong with how I usually dress.'

'No,' he agreed.

'So...what? Tighter, more uncomfortable—*different*— clothing would seduce you? And then we'd reunite.' She said the last words under her breath, as though saying them to herself. 'There isn't anything I can wear here that's appropriate for this.' She gestured around them.

'I don't think my mother intended this.'

'Us being trapped?'

He nodded. 'She probably wanted us to go out and enjoy

the island like we have in the past.' He let that sit for a moment. 'You're free to use whatever she's packed for me.'

'It'll probably only be jeans and shirts.'

You could wear the lingerie, if you like.

The words seared his brain. Out loud, he said, 'You're welcome to help yourself.'

He walked to the other side of the room, as though somehow the distance would keep him from remembering her in lingerie. And what had happened after he'd seen her in lingerie. It would do nothing for his need for control to remember that.

He eyed the alcohol his mother had left on the counter of the kitchen—at least she'd done *that*—and reached for the rum and soda water, adding ice from the freezer. He was sipping it when he faced her again, but her back was towards him and the memories he'd tried to suppress struggled free, even though he couldn't see her front.

But he didn't need to.

Because, from where he stood, he could see the strong curve of her shoulders, the sweeping slope of her neck. He'd only have to press a kiss there, have his tongue join, and she would moan. She'd grab his hands as his mouth did its work and pull them around her, over her breasts, encouraging him to touch them…

He gritted his teeth. Reminded himself—again—that he needed to be in control. But his reaction wasn't a surprise. His attraction to Rosa had always goaded him in this way. When he'd first seen her—her curves, the curls around her face, the golden-brown of her skin—it had kicked him in the gut.

He'd managed to ignore it for a full year, and only because both their mothers had been going through chemotherapy and acting on his attraction had seemed inappropriate. But their year of friendship hadn't been enough for him.

And their chemistry had constantly reminded him of its presence.

Stalking him. Mocking him.

It was why control was so important now. He couldn't act on his attraction this time. He couldn't show Rosa how much she'd hurt him when she'd left. And how shaken he was to see her again. He'd only just begun to face the fact that the morning she'd left might have been the last time he'd ever see her…

Control meant that he had a plan. And plans were how he lived his life. How he made sure his law firm remained successful. How he tried to make sure his mother hadn't created another problem for him to fix.

He hadn't had a plan in his marriage, and he'd wondered if that had contributed to how—and why—it had ended so abruptly.

Or had his need to plan been the cause of its end?

He took a long drag from his drink and shook the feelings away. He might not know if his plans—his need for control—had contributed to Rosa leaving, but having a plan was the only way he'd survive the night.

Now he just had to come up with one.

CHAPTER THREE

'DO YOU HAVE any intention of offering me a drink?' Rosa asked when she turned back and saw Aaron sipping from a glass. It was filled with golden liquid, the kind she was pretty sure would help steady the nerves fluttering in her stomach.

'What do you want?' he asked flatly.

She almost winced. 'Whatever you're having is fine.'

He nodded and went about making her drink. She walked towards him cautiously and then busied herself with putting the bottles from the counter into the cabinet beneath. It wasn't necessary, but it was a way to keep her hands busy. Especially since something about his expression made her want to do something remarkably different with her hands.

Or was that because the clothing—the lingerie—had reminded her of all the times she'd *wanted* to seduce him? Of all the times it had worked?

Her hands shook and she waited for them to steady before she packed the last bottle away.

'You don't have to do that.'

'I know.'

But I was thinking about all the times we made love and I needed a distraction.

'Do you think your mother left something for us to eat?'

'Try the fridge.'

She did, though she wasn't hungry. Again, it was just because she wanted something to do. To distract from the ache in her body. From the ache in her heart.

She found the fridge fully stocked.

'How nice of her,' Rosa said wryly. Her patience with Liana had dropped dramatically after the seductive clothing thing. And now, finding the fridge filled with food, she couldn't deny that Liana had planned this any more.

She'd indulged Liana over the years she'd got to know the woman. Understandably, she thought, considering Liana's history with her mother. With *her*, during Violet's declining health. And…after.

But Rosa had let that influence her view of Liana's actions. Actions that Rosa had condoned by not speaking out. She wouldn't let that happen again—once they got out of their current situation.

'It's full?'

'Yeah.' The hairs on her neck stood when Aaron moved in behind her to look for himself. 'There's this dish—' she took it out, handed it to him—anything to get him away from her '—which I assume is something readymade for this evening. And the rest is ingredients to make meals. Eggs, vegetables, that sort of thing.'

'There was some meat in the freezer.'

Rosa closed the fridge. 'She's thought of everything, hasn't she?'

'She generally does,' Aaron said and handed her the drink. She braced herself for the contact, but it didn't help. A spark flared anyway. She'd never really been able to come to terms with the attraction she felt for him. That she'd felt for him since day one.

Or with your love for him, a voice whispered in her head, reminding her of why she'd had to leave—before either of those things had tempted her into staying.

Staying wouldn't have done either of them any good.

'She just doesn't think about consequences.'

'Oh, I think she knows.' She removed the foil that covered the top of the dish and found a rice and chicken meal of some kind. She took out two plates and, without asking him if he wanted any, dished portions for both of them. 'That there are consequences, I mean.'

'But she never stops to consider *what* those consequences might be.' His voice was steady, but there was frustration there. He'd never been able to hide it completely when he was talking about his mother. 'You know how many times I've had to deal with consequences that weren't favourable. Like the time she gave her car to a guy she met at a conference she attended.'

Rosa nodded. 'She thought it would be easier for him to get to his job in the city if he had a car. And that would make sure he didn't lose his job, and that he'd be able to look after his family.'

'Instead, the man *still* lost his job because *he couldn't drive*, and he ended up selling the car, which then got him into trouble with the police because she hadn't transferred the car into his name.'

'And you had to sort it all out,' she said softly. The microwave sounded, and she handed Aaron the heated plate before putting in her own. 'I'm sorry, ba—'

She stopped herself. She'd been about to call him 'baby'. And it wouldn't have been like the 'honey' he'd called her when she'd first tried to leave. No, that had been said sardonically. This? This would have been said lovingly. Endearingly.

It was because of the routine she'd slipped into. Dishing for him, heating his food. Normal parts of what had been their life before. But that life was gone. She'd walked away from it. It didn't matter why or how—she *had*. Which meant accepting that she couldn't just *slip* back into routine.

The microwave finished heating her food and she used it as an excuse to turn her back to him. To ignore the emotion that was swirling inside her.

'You didn't change,' he said into the silence that had settled in the room. She took her plate and drink to the couch and tried to figure out how to sit down without the slit revealing her leg.

'No,' she replied after a moment, and then gave up and lowered to the seat. She set her food on the coffee table in front of them, covered as much leg as she could and then took a long sip of the drink before she answered him. 'As I predicted, there were only a couple of shirts in there and jeans. The jeans wouldn't fit me.'

He settled at the opposite end of the couch. 'You could have worn one of the shirts.'

She lifted a brow. 'And that wouldn't have been…distracting?'

'What you're wearing now isn't?'

His eyes lowered to the leg she'd been trying to cover, and then moved up to her cleavage.

'I'll go change,' she said in a hoarse voice, setting her drink down.

'No, you don't have to.'

His gaze lifted to her face, though his expression didn't do anything to help the flush that was slowly making its way through her body.

'It's probably for the best.'

'Are you afraid I'll do something neither of us wants?'

'No.'

Because both of us would want it.

'I just think it would be better for us not to…cross any boundaries.'

'Are there boundaries?' he asked casually, though she wasn't fooled by it. She could hear the danger beneath the façade. 'I didn't realise a married couple had boundaries.'

'That's not quite what we are now, though.'

'No? Did I miss the divorce papers you sent to me while you were in Cape Town?'

Bile churned in her stomach. 'There are no divorce papers.' She frowned. 'You knew where I was?'

He nodded. 'I needed to make sure you were okay.'

She closed her eyes. 'I'm sorry. I didn't think—'

'That I'd want to know that you were alive?'

'I took my clothes. I thought—' She broke off as shame filled her. 'I should have let you know.'

A chill swept over her as she took in his blank expression. 'You said we aren't *quite* married, but you haven't asked for a divorce.' He stopped, though she clearly heard the *yet* he hadn't said. 'Which is it, Rosa?'

And, though his expression was still clear of emotion, the danger in his voice was coming out in full now. She swallowed and reached for her drink again.

'I don't want to get into this,' she said after she'd taken another healthy sip. She'd need a refill soon if she went on like this.

'You can't get out of it. We're stuck here.'

'I know.' Couldn't forget it if she tried. 'I also know that if we start talking about this stuff, being trapped here is going to be a lot harder than it needs to be.'

'Stuff,' he repeated softly. Her eyes met his and she saw the anger there. 'Is that what you call leaving me after five years of being together? After three years of marriage?'

'I call it life,' she replied sharply. 'Life happened, and I had to go.' She stood. 'There's no point in rehashing it now.'

He stood with her, and the body she'd always loved cast a shadow over her. 'Where are you going to go, Rosa?' he asked. 'There's nowhere to run. This room is open-plan. The only other room is the bathroom, and even then you wouldn't be able to stay there for ever.'

She took a step back. Lowered to the couch slowly. 'You're taking too much joy from this.'

'This isn't joy.' He sat back down, though his body didn't relax. She nearly rolled her eyes. What did he think he was going to have to do? Tackle her if she tried to get past him?

'What would you call it then?'

'Satisfaction. Karma.'

'Karma?' she said with a bark of laughter. 'I didn't re-alise you believed in karma.'

'I didn't. Until today. Now. When it's become clear how much you want to run from this—from me—and can't.'

Now she did roll her eyes. 'And what are *you* paying for? What did *you* do that was so bad that you deserve to be locked in a room with the wife who left you?'

His features tightened. 'Maybe I don't believe in karma then.'

'Sounds like you're taking the easy way out.'

'Or like I'm doing whatever the hell suits me.' His voice was hard, and surprise pressed her to ask what she'd said that had upset him.

But she didn't. She didn't deserve to know.

'Doing whatever the hell suits you *does* sound like you're enjoying this.'

'Maybe I am. Hard to tell since I've forced myself not to feel anything since you left.'

And there it was. The honesty, the vulnerability that had always seeped past the coolness he showed the world. The emotion that showed her how deeply he cared, even when he pretended he didn't.

It had always managed to penetrate whatever wall she'd put up with him. Or whatever wall he'd put up to make her believe he didn't feel. But he did. Which made her actions so much worse.

She'd done many stupid things in her life. Most of them because she'd wanted to find out who she was after giving so much of herself to her mother.

Like dropping out of college because she didn't think they were teaching her what she needed to know about design.

Like moving out when she was tired of being responsible for her mother's mental health.

Like ignoring her mother's phone calls for almost two

months after she moved out, because she thought Violet was trying to manipulate her into coming back home. When really her mother had been calling to tell her about her cancer.

She hadn't thought anything about her relationship with Aaron had been stupid. At least she hadn't until she'd found the lump. Until it had reminded her of how stupid she'd been by choosing not to be tested for breast cancer when her mother's doctors had advised it.

And suddenly all the uncertainty she'd battled with in the past about her decisions had returned. Maybe they'd never really gone away. And the disaster scenario of what that lump could mean had echoed her mother's own anxieties so closely that it had reminded Rosa that she was her mother's child.

It would have been selfish of her to stay. To put Aaron through what she'd gone through with her mother. To put him through anything that would cause him to suffer as he had when his mother had been ill.

'Maybe that's for the best,' she told him, kicking off her shoes. 'If we don't feel anything, we don't get hurt. And since we're already in this situation—' she waved between them '—committing ourselves to not getting hurt doesn't sound so bad, does it?'

He stared at her. 'Are you...are you serious?'

'Yes,' she said, and lifted the plate she'd set on the table, resting it on her lap as she leaned back into the couch. 'Doesn't it sound appealing to you? Us not hurting each other?'

'Is that why you left? Because I hurt you?'

She toyed with the food on her plate. 'No,' she said, lifting her gaze to his. 'You didn't hurt me.'

'Then why did you leave?'

'Because I would be hurting you by staying.'

'Why?' But she shook her head. 'Rosa, you can't just

tell me something like that and not give me *anything* else.'
Still, she didn't answer him. He clenched his jaw. 'You don't
think you're hurting me now? With *this*?'

'I know I am.'

'And that doesn't mean anything to you?'

'It…can't.'

He wanted to shout. To demand answers from her. But
that would only keep her from talking to him.

And he needed her to talk to him. He needed to know
why she was saying things his wife never would have said.
The Rosa he'd married would never have given up on anything. She would never have settled for backing away from
the possibility of pain when there was a possibility for joy.

Or perhaps this was karma, like he'd said. Maybe this
was *his* karma. For not acting with reason when it came to
Rosa. She'd only been twenty-three when they'd married.
He'd been twenty-six. Older. Wiser.

At least old enough to know that she might not have
been ready to marry him. She'd still been grieving for her
mother when he'd proposed. Her decision might not have
been entirely thought through.

But as he thought back to the moment he'd proposed he
couldn't remember any hesitation from Rosa…

He wanted everything to be perfect. Simple but perfect.
That was his plan. And, since only he and Rosa were on the
beach in front of the house on Mariner's Island, there'd be no
one but himself to blame if everything didn't go perfectly.

He took a deep breath and Rosa looked up at him. 'Are
you okay?'

'Yeah.'

'You're sure?' Her brow furrowed. 'Because you've been
quiet since we got here. I mean, quieter than usual.'

She gave him a small smile and his heart tumbled. Even
her smile could make his heart trip over itself. No wonder

he was proposing to her when he'd never thought he'd get married.

'I'm thinking.'

'About?'

'This. Us.'

'Really?' She pressed in closer at his side when the wind nipped at their skin. It was cooler than he would have liked, but he supposed that was what he got by wanting to propose just as the sun was going down on an autumn day. 'And what have you come up with?'

'You're amazing.'

His feet stopped, though they weren't close to the place where he'd planned on proposing. This was good enough. Waves were crashing at their feet. Sand around them. The sun shining over them as though it approved of his actions.

Besides, none of that mattered anyway. Not any more. All that mattered was her. And that he couldn't imagine another moment going by without knowing that she'd one day be his wife.

'Well, yeah,' she said with a smile that faded when she saw his expression. 'What's wrong?'

'I have something for you.'

'Okay.' Confusion lined every feature of her beautiful face, but there was trust in her eyes. He hoped he would never betray that trust. 'Aaron?' she asked quietly after a moment. 'Are you going to tell me what it is?'

Instead of replying, he stepped back from her and removed the rose petals he'd been keeping in his pocket. It had been a silly idea, he thought now as the confusion intensified on her face. But it was too late to stop now.

He cleared his throat. 'I got these from the house.'

'You stole...petals from the garden?' Her lips curved. 'Just petals? Not the actual flowers?'

He smiled. 'I wanted to take a picture of you standing in a shower of petals.'

'Aaron,' she said after a moment. 'You realise you're being weird, right?'

His smile widened. But he only nodded. She let out a frustrated sigh. 'Okay, fine. Should I just—' She cupped her hands and mimicked throwing the petals into the air.

'Yes. But throw them over your shoulder.' He handed her the petals, careful to protect them from the wind. 'So, turn your back to me while I get the camera ready.'

There was impatience in her eyes now, but she didn't say anything. Only turned her back to him. She was indulging him, he thought. Because that was who she was. Always putting him first, even when she didn't understand why.

He took the ring from his pocket and took another deep breath. And then he got down on one knee and said, 'I'm ready.'

She threw the petals into the sky and turned, a smile on her face for the picture she'd thought he was about to take. At first the confusion returned. Her eyes searched for where she'd thought he'd be as the petals swirled around them. Then, as they were carried up and away by the wind, her gaze lowered, settling on him.

She sucked in her breath and then, on an exhale, said his name. The surprise had turned into something deeper, more meaningful, as she did. And suddenly all the fear, all the uncertainty disappeared.

It was going to be perfect.

That was the last thing he thought before telling her why he wanted to spend the rest of his life with her.

No, he thought as he closed his eyes briefly. There had been no hesitation when Rosa had accepted his proposal.

But hadn't his mother shown him that he would need to take responsibility for others at some time in his life? So why hadn't he realised Rosa might have needed that from him too?

But now that he thought about it, he wondered if it was because he *had* been responsible when it came Rosa. He'd promised her mother that he would look after her. And, since he'd loved her so damn much, marriage had seemed like the perfect way to do it.

But maybe *that* had been his mistake.

Or maybe *he* was the mistake…

'Okay,' he said curtly, ripping himself out of the web his memories had caught him in. 'Do you want another drink?'

She blinked at him, and then silently nodded and handed him her glass. He deliberately brushed his fingers against hers as he took it, and saw the slight shake of her hand as she drew it back to her lap.

He turned away from her, satisfaction pouring through him. Whatever it was that she was going through—whatever it was that *they* were going through—he hadn't made up their attraction. And that attraction had come from their feelings for one another.

Perhaps he'd made one too many mistakes with Rosa. Heaven knew he had with his mother, so it might not have been different with his wife. But at least he could make sure Rosa didn't forget that they were drawn to one another. Something neither of them had ever been able to deny.

And then what? an inner voice asked as he poured their drinks. Would they just become hyperaware of their attraction, since their feelings were seemingly out of bounds, and then let it fizzle out between them?

There was no way that was happening. And if they acted on it…what would that mean for him? For them? Would she just walk away from him again? Would he just let her go?

An uncomfortable feeling stirred in his stomach and he walked back to her, setting her glass down on the table to avoid any more touching. He had no idea what he wanted to achieve with her. With his marriage. And he'd never thought he would be in the position to have to worry about it.

He'd thought he'd done everything right in his life. He'd looked after a mother who hadn't cared about looking after herself. About looking after him. He'd got a stable job. Succeeded in it. He'd fallen in love—though it had been unplanned—and he'd married.

And still everything had gone wrong.

Though, if he was being honest with himself, perhaps that had started when his mother had been diagnosed with cancer and he'd realised the extent of his mistakes.

Now, the fear that had grown in the past four months pulsed in his chest. Had him facing the fact that everyone in his life who was supposed to love him had left him. His mother. His father. And now Rosa…

He couldn't deny that he was the problem any more.

CHAPTER FOUR

'So, WHAT HAVE you been doing these last four months?'

Somehow, she managed to keep her tone innocent. As if she wasn't asking because she desperately wanted a glimpse into the life he'd made without her.

It was veering into dangerous territory, that question, and yet it was the safest thing Rosa could think to ask. Something mundane. Something that didn't have anything to do with what they'd been talking about before.

Feelings. Emotions. Their relationship.

But the expression on his face told her that perhaps the question wasn't as safe as she'd thought. Still, he answered her.

'Work.'

'Work?' When he didn't offer more, she pressed. 'What about work? New clients?'

'New clients.'

She bit back a sigh. 'And?'

'We're expanding.'

'Oh.'

Expanding? He'd never spoken about the desire to expand before. His law firm was one of the most prestigious family practices in Gauteng. He had wealthy clientele, made sure his firm helped those in need, and he'd always spoken about how content he'd been. Proud, even. So why was he expanding?

She waited for him to offer an explanation. He didn't. And she didn't have the courage to ask him. Not when she would have known if she'd just *stayed*.

'You?'

Her gaze sprang to his. She hadn't expected him to engage. 'I've been working on a new line. Evening gowns.'

'Like the one you're wearing.'

'Exactly like the one I'm wearing. For women like me.'

His eyes swept over her, heating her body with the faint desire she saw on his face. He was controlling it well, she thought. He never had before. She'd always known when Aaron desired her. It would start with a look in his eyes— much more ardent than what she saw there now—and then he'd say something seductive and follow his words with actions.

She'd loved those times. Loved how unapologetic they had been. How freeing. And since they both had problems with being free—no matter how much she pretended that she didn't—those moments were special.

And now she'd lost them.

'It'll be popular.'

'I hope so.' She paused. 'I did a sample line. I've been promoting it on the website for the past month, and it's got some great feedback. I might even do a showcase.'

'I told you it would be great.'

'You did.'

Neither of them mentioned that for years he'd been telling her that she needed to make clothes for herself. For others like her. But that wasn't why she'd got into fashion. At least, not at first. She loved colours, patterns, prints. She loved how bold they could be, or how understated. She loved the contrast of them—the lines, the shapes.

She hadn't wanted to confine herself when she'd started out. She'd wanted to experiment, to explore, to learn about everything. And, because she had, she now had momentum after being labelled a fresh and exciting young designer. Enough that she could finally design the clothes she wanted to. For women who looked like her. Who were bigger. Who weren't conventionally curvy.

She'd shared all her worries, her fears, her excitement with Aaron. And she wanted nothing more than to tell him about the challenges, the joys she'd had creating this new line now.

But the brokenness between them didn't lend itself to that discussion.

Her heart sank and her eyes slid closed.

How had her *safe* question led to *this*?

Watching her was going to be the only way he'd figure out what was going on in her head. It was clear she wasn't going to tell him. And, since he hadn't exactly been forthcoming himself, he could hardly ask her what was causing the turmoil on her face.

But he couldn't be forthcoming. How was he supposed to tell her that his expansion plans had started the moment his mother had informed him of where Rosa was? He hadn't been interested in finding her…at least, that was what he'd told himself. But then he'd received Liana's email telling him Rosa was in Cape Town.

And suddenly he was planning to expand his firm to Cape Town.

How was he supposed to tell her all that?

'Oh, look,' she said softly, her gaze shifting to behind him. The pain had subsided from her face—had been replaced by wonder—tempting him to keep looking at her.

Dutifully—though reluctantly—he followed her gaze and saw that she was watching the rain. He didn't know what she found so fascinating about it. Sure, it was coming down hard, fast and every now and then a flash of lightning would streak through it. But still, it looked like rain to him. Regular old rain.

And yet when he looked back to Rosa's face he could have sworn she had just seen the first real unicorn.

She got up and walked in her beautiful gown to the glass

doors, laying a hand on them as though somehow that would allow her to touch the rain. It was surprisingly tender, but he refuted that description almost immediately. What he was witnessing wasn't *tender*. How could his wife watching the rain be tender?

But he couldn't get the word out of his mind as she spent a few more minutes there. Then she walked to the light switch in the kitchen and turned it off. The entire room went dark and she murmured, 'Just for a moment,' before returning to her place at the door.

He still wasn't sure what was so special about it. About watching the rain in the dark. But her reaction had cast a spell around him. And now he was walking towards her, stopping next to her and watching the rain pour from the sky in torrents.

'I don't think I've ever seen a storm more beautiful,' she said softly from beside him.

'An exaggeration,' he commented with a half-smile.

She laughed. Looked up at him with twinkling eyes. 'Of course it is. But I like to think that I use my opportunities to exaggerate for effect. Is it working?' she asked with a wink.

His smile widened and, though his heart was still broken from her leaving, and his mind was still lapping up every piece of information she'd given as to why, as they looked at each other, he was caught by her.

He told himself it was the part of him that wanted things to go back to the way they'd been before. The part that mourned because it was no longer an option. Not with how things had shifted between them. Not when that shift had confirmed that they were no longer the same people they'd been before she'd left.

And still he was caught by her.

By her brown eyes, and the twinkle that was slowly turning into something else as the seconds ticked by. By the angles of her face—some soft, some sharp, all beautiful.

He didn't know why he still felt so drawn to the woman beside him when she wasn't the woman he'd fallen in love with any more. Or was it himself he didn't recognise? He'd spent the four months since she'd left racking his brain for answers about what had gone wrong. And what he'd come up with had forced him to see himself in a new light. A dim one that made him prickly because it spoke of things he'd ignored for most of his life.

'Why do you still make me feel like this?'

He hadn't realised he'd spoken until her eyes widened. His gaze dipped to her mouth as she sucked her bottom lip between her teeth. It instantly had his body responding, and he took a step towards her—

And then suddenly there was a blast of cold air on him and Rosa was on the balcony in the rain.

'Rosa! What are you doing?'

But she turned her back to him and was now opening her palms to the rain, spreading her fingers as though she wanted to catch the drops, but at the same time wanted them to fall through her fingers.

'Rosa!' he said again when she didn't answer him. But it was no use. She didn't give any indication that she'd heard him.

He cursed and then took off his shoes and stepped out onto the balcony with her, hissing out his breath when the ice-cold drops immediately drenched his skin.

Her eyes fluttered open when he stopped next to her, and he clearly saw the shock in them. 'What are you *doing*?'

'The same thing as you, apparently,' he said through clenched teeth. 'Care to explain why we're out getting soaked in the rain?'

'I didn't think you'd—' She broke off, the expression on her face frustratingly appealing. Damn it. How was that possible when their lives were such a mess?

'Rosa,' he growled.

'I wanted to get out of that room,' she said. 'I wanted to breathe in proper fresh air and not the stifling air in *that* room.'

'That room is over one hundred and fifty square metres.'

'You know that's not what I meant,' she snapped. 'I just felt…trapped. With you. In there.'

'You felt trapped with me,' he repeated.

'No, not like that,' she said. 'I felt… It's just that room. And the fact that resisting you—resisting us—is so *hard*. Everything between us is suddenly so hard.' She let out a sound that sounded suspiciously like a sob. 'Mostly I feel trapped by what I did to us.' She closed her eyes and when she opened them again he felt the pain there as acutely as if it were in his own body. 'I threw what we had away.'

He took a step forward, the desire to take her into his arms, to comfort her compelling him. But then he stopped and told himself that he couldn't comfort her when he didn't know why. That he couldn't comfort her when, by all rights, she was supposed to be comforting him.

She'd left *him* behind. She'd hurt *him*.

And yet there he was, outside, soaking wet in the rain because of *her*.

He moved back. Ignored the flash of hurt in her eyes.

'We're going to get sick if we stay out here,' he said after a moment.

'So go back inside,' she mumbled miserably.

It was a stark reminder that she hadn't asked him to come outside in the rain with her. And it would be logical to listen to her and go back inside.

Instead, he sighed and held his ground. Tried to commit the experience to memory. He suspected that some day he'd want—no, *need*—to remember this moment, however nonsensical it appeared to be.

To remember how she looked with her curls weighed down by the rainwater, the make-up she wore smudged dramatically on her face. How her one-of-a-kind dress clung to her beautiful body, reminding him of all that he'd had.

To remember how this—standing on a balcony while it poured with rain—spoke of her spirit. The passion, the spontaneity. How he'd never consider doing something like this and yet somehow he found it endearing.

Heaven only knew why he wanted to remember it. Because the feelings that accompanied it *gutted* him. The longing, the regret. The disappointment. Heaven only knew why he was thinking about how incredibly beautiful she was when empirical evidence should have made him think otherwise.

'Why are you looking at me like that?' she demanded.

The misery, the pain in her voice had disappeared. Had been replaced with the passion he was used to.

'Like what?'

'Like *that*,' she told him, without giving any more indication of what she meant. 'You know what you're doing.'

Was he that obvious? 'I'm waiting for you to decide to go inside.'

She stepped closer to him. 'No, you weren't.'

'You'll get sick.'

'And you won't?' He lifted his shoulders in response. She took another step forward. 'You're not helping me feel any less trapped than I already do, Aaron.'

Again, he shrugged. Again, she took a step forward.

'And you're not as unaffected by all this as you're pretending.'

'What are you doing?' he asked, clasping her wrist just before her hand reached his face. Somehow, she'd closed the distance between them as she'd said her last words without him noticing.

'I'm trying to show you that you're not as aloof as you believe,' she said, and dropped her hand with a triumphant smile. 'I told you.'

He didn't reply. He couldn't do so without telling her that she was right—unaffected was the *last* thing he felt. But he showed her. Slid an arm around her waist and hauled her against him.

'Maybe you're right,' he said, his voice slightly breathless, though measured, he thought. But he could be wrong. Hell, he could have been imitating the President of South Africa right then and he wouldn't have known. 'Maybe I was thinking about the first time we kissed.' He dipped his head lower. 'You remember.'

It wasn't a question. And the way her breath quickened— the way her hand shook as she wiped the rain from her brow—confirmed it.

'Aaron, wait!'

He turned back just in time to see Rosa running towards him. His stomach flipped as it always did when he saw her. And he steeled himself against it. He couldn't fall into the attraction. He hadn't for the last year. He could survive whatever she was running to tell him.

'Would you give me a lift home?' she asked breathlessly when she reached him. As she asked—as he nodded—a menacing boom sounded in the sky before rain began pouring down on them.

'Here, get in,' he said, starting towards the passenger's side of the car. But she put a hand on his chest before he could make any progress, and he held his breath.

Control. Steel.

'No,' she replied tiredly. She leaned back against his car, dropping her hand and lifting her head to the sky. 'No, this is exactly what I need.'

'To be drenched in rain?'

She laughed huskily and need pierced him. 'No. Just... a break.'

'Hard day?'

'Isn't every day?'

She glanced back at the hospital where her mother was staying overnight. His mother had a chemo session but she'd left the book she'd wanted to read at home. And since Rosa's mother—Liana's usual companion—had started a new course of treatment, she wasn't in Liana's session to keep her company.

And because Liana knew Aaron would do anything to make what she was going through easier, she'd asked him to fetch her book.

'But today was particularly hard,' Rosa continued with a sigh. 'I had to meet a deadline for a couple of designs. And my creativity hasn't exactly been flowing over the last few months.'

'I'm sorry.'

'It's okay.' She smiled at him, and then something shifted. He didn't know what it was, but he felt it. It had need vibrating through him again.

'We should go,' he said hoarsely, clenching a fist to keep from touching her.

'What if I'm not ready to go?'

'I'll wait until you are.'

Now, he saw the change. Her eyes darkened. Her lips parted. And he realised how his words had sounded.

'Rosa—'

'No, Aaron,' she said softly, taking a step closer. 'I don't want to—' She broke off. Shook her head. And when her gaze rested on him again, he saw heat there. 'I'm too tired to keep myself from wanting this.'

In two quick movements she gripped the front of his shirt and kissed him.

'It was outside the hospital,' he continued, the memory and his words weaving the web tighter around them. 'On a rainy day, just like this. You were exhausted after a deadline, but you still came to visit your mother in hospital.' He brushed a thumb over her lips, feeling the shiver the action caused go through them both.

'You asked me to take you home, and for the first time you let me see that you were attracted to me. And then you closed the space between us and told me you were too tired to run from it.'

She was trembling now, though he couldn't tell if it was because of the rain or the memory. It didn't stop him.

'And then you stood on your toes and pressed your lips—'

He stopped when she took an abrupt step back, breaking the spell.

'You're going from "I don't want anything to do with you" to *this*?'

'I wasn't the one who said they didn't want anything to do with the other,' he replied gruffly, forcing himself to take control again. Now, he took a step back and the railing pressed into his back.

'I know that was me. I wanted space. Why won't you give it to me?'

'I didn't plan for us to be locked in together.'

'But you won't even give me a moment to be alone. Why?'

He didn't answer.

'I'm fine out here. Alone,' she said again with a clenched jaw. 'I just wanted some…space. I wanted to feel the rain. I wanted to stop feeling trapped.' She turned away from him, but not before he saw a flash of vulnerability in her eyes. 'You should go inside before we say something to hurt one another even more. '

'So you *are* hurt?'

She shook her head and took another step away from him. Aaron immediately got a strange feeling in his stomach. A familiar feeling. Hollow, sick. The kind of feeling that usually preceded his mother telling him she'd done something stupid. Or him getting the call that confirmed that she had.

Except now he wasn't sure how to understand it. He didn't think Rosa had done something wrong. And if she had he was sure she'd be able to figure it out herself. Unless...

'Are you in trouble?'

'What?' She turned slightly to him. 'No.'

'You don't have to lie to me.'

'I'm not.' But she shifted in a way that made him think that she was. The feeling in his stomach tightened.

'Rosa—'

'Go back inside, Aaron.'

For a moment he considered it. But then he realised he didn't *want* to go back inside. She'd pushed him away before. Then, he didn't have a say in it. If he let her push him away now, he'd be having a say. And he'd be saying that he didn't care about her.

He might not know where they stood with each other, but he *did* know that not caring wasn't the message he wanted to give.

He took a step forward.

CHAPTER FIVE

'Rosa.'

'Go back inside, Aaron.'

'Not until you tell me what's going on with you.'

How many times would she have to tell him that it was nothing? That nothing was wrong? Would she have to keep convincing him? She wasn't sure she could. And her impulsive decision to come outside in the rain was fast becoming one of her worst ones.

She'd just wanted some space, like she'd told him. And she'd wanted to breathe something other than the tension in the air between them.

Now she was sopping wet, the rain finally penetrating her skin. She was cold. She was miserable. And yes, she was in pain. She didn't want things to be the way they were between them. But what choice did she have?

She was doing this for the good of them. She was doing it for *him*. Why couldn't he just leave her alone to do that in peace?

She turned to him now, took in his appearance. He was as soaked as she was, and yet he gave no indication of it. She'd always admired how at home he seemed to be in his body. How he owned the space around it, even though he was taller, stronger, more intimidating than most. He never seemed out of place. Even here, in the rain, soaked to the core, no doubt, he looked as if he belonged.

With me, she thought, and nearly sobbed.

'Let's go back inside then,' she managed quietly, and walked past him before realising she would soak the entire floor if she went in wearing her dress.

The small carpet at the door would probably soak up

some of it. But the rest of the floor would not escape un-scathed. Forcing herself to be practical, she undid the ties of her dress at her waist. And then she dropped it to the floor before stepping out of it.

She refused to look back. Knew what her actions would seem like, and after what had happened outside...

She was just being practical, she thought again as she turned on the lights and went to the bathroom for towels. When she handed one to Aaron his expression was un-readable.

But the silence between them flirted with the tension that was still there. Wooing it. Courting it. Reminding them of what would have happened at any other time had she stood in front of him in shapewear that clung to the curves of her body.

It was the dress kind that plunged at her breasts and stopped mid-thigh, and hastily she patted down the water from her body before picking up her soaking dress and flee-ing to the safety of the bathroom.

She released an unsteady breath when she got there and then squeezed the excess water from her dress, wincing at the destruction it didn't deserve. Making the best of the sit-uation, she hung it over the door and then stepped into the shower. She made quick work of it, knowing that the door was open a smidge now because of the dress. She didn't want to take any more chances with Aaron.

Not that he'd cross that boundary. Not when his control was back in place after what had happened on the balcony. It was stupid to feel disappointed, she admonished herself, and reached for another towel—there seemed to be plenty of them, fortunately—and then tied it around herself before opening the door widely.

And walking right into Aaron.

His hands reached out to steady her, though her own hands had immediately lifted to his chest to steady herself.

Only then did she notice that her face was directly in line with his chest. That fact wasn't a surprise. He was significantly taller than her.

No, the surprise was that his chest was bare.

She blinked. Stepped back. And then saw that he wore only the towel she'd given him around his waist.

Her mind went haywire. Memories overwhelmed her. Suddenly she was thinking about all the times she would have jumped into those arms, wrapped her legs around his waist, kissed him. And how those kisses would have turned into something more urgent as soon as she had.

Her breathing went shallow and she told herself to step around him. To ignore how his body hadn't changed. How the contours of his muscles were still as defined, as deep. How his shoulders were still strong, still broad. How his torso was still ripped.

She loved his body. Loved how big and strong he was. How he could pick her up, carry her around and not lose so much as a breath as he did.

Like the time she'd teased him about not wanting to accompany him to some event. He'd threatened to carry her there and, when she'd goaded him, had made good on the threat, though the event hadn't been for hours.

He'd picked her up and tossed her over his shoulder. She'd complained, squirmed, called him a caveman for doing it. But she'd loved it. And when he'd set her down she'd given him a playful punch to the chest before launching herself into his arms and—

'Excuse me.'

His deep voice interrupted the memories and she nodded. Stepped around him. And let out a sigh of relief when some of the tension inside her cooled.

She figured out her clothing options quickly. She'd have to wear the lingerie Liana had packed for her as underwear and, since none of the other clothing would be comfortable, she'd wear one of Aaron's shirts over it.

She was buttoning up the shirt when Aaron emerged from the bathroom, again in nothing but that towel.

Her heart started to thud. She forced herself to focus on something else.

'I'm going to try the kitchen and hope your mother left coffee.' That was something else, she thought gratefully. 'Would you like some?'

He nodded and she walked away as fast as she could. Fortunately, Liana had left coffee and she busied herself with the task. But her mind wandered and, since she didn't want to slip back into memories, she thought about why she'd stepped out into the rain in the first place.

She'd felt claustrophobic. And plagued by the connection she and Aaron had shared. The rain had offered an alternative. An escape. It had seemed like a perfectly logical thing to do at the time. And yet it wasn't.

She'd made too many decisions like that in her life. Because she'd wanted to test herself. To see how those spontaneous decisions made her feel.

It was a form of control, she thought. The only kind she'd had. She'd been lost in the world of her mother's anxiety for the longest time, and those spontaneous decisions had been a reprieve. Even though some of them had been stupid. Even though some of them had got her into trouble. They were *her* decisions. And when she made them, for the briefest of moments she felt free.

But freedom had come at a price. And that price had been—when she'd felt that lump in her breast in the shower—leaving her husband.

Because that lump had made her think she had cancer. And how could she put Aaron through that again when she didn't think he'd fully recovered from his mother's illness?

Especially when hers could have been prevented if she'd just made the right decision when she'd had the chance.

But, like so many other moments in her life, she didn't know what the right decision would be. Uncertainty clouded every one she'd made. Even running away to protect Aaron seemed uncertain. And now, as she thought about it, her stomach turned, her heart thudded at the doubt...

'It always used to drive me crazy, how quiet you were,' she heard herself say suddenly. She closed her eyes, told herself it would be better to speak—even if she was speaking about things she should leave in the past—than to let her mind go down that path again.

'I know.'

She whirled around, then shook her head. 'You always know.'

He was wearing jeans and a shirt, though somehow he looked just as gorgeous as he had in his suit. Perhaps because he hadn't buttoned the shirt up entirely, and she could see his collarbone, the start of his chest...

'Not always,' he responded quietly. 'But this, you told me. Too many times to count.'

He walked to the couch, sank down on it with a fatigue she'd rarely seen him show. Her fault, she thought. And added the guilt to the sky-high pile she already had when it came to him.

She sighed. 'You should have told me to stop harassing you.'

'You weren't harassing me.'

She set his coffee on the table and took a seat on a different couch. 'It didn't bother you?'

'How could it? You said it to me before we got together. I can't fault you for something I knew about when we met.'

It was ridiculous to feel tears prick at her eyes, and she took a gulp from her coffee—burning her tongue in the process—to hide it from him. But she'd been reminded of how unselfishly Aaron had loved her.

He wasn't like her father. He would have accepted her anxiety about her health. He would have supported her decision not to get screened for breast cancer. He wouldn't have given up on their relationship, like her father had on his marriage. But she couldn't be sure.

She'd often asked herself why her mother hadn't left her father because of his lack of support. The only answer she had come up with was that her mother had been scared. And that that fear had been rooted in selfishness. Violet hadn't wanted to go through her illness alone. And her marriage—even the illusion of it—prevented that.

But Aaron didn't deserve that. Again, Rosa thought that it would have been selfish for her to stay. To do what her mother had done. And it would have been worse for Aaron because he wouldn't check out like her father had. Worse still because he'd already been through so much.

The decision seemed clear now, though she knew it wasn't. Not when she looked into his eyes. Not when she saw the pain there.

'I didn't mean to drive you crazy.' Aaron spoke so softly Rosa almost thought she'd imagined it.

'I loved it,' she said immediately. 'Not in that moment, of course, because your quietness would always make me run my mouth off about something.' *Like now.* She stared down into her cup. 'But I loved it.'

'But…it annoyed you.'

'No. Driving me crazy and annoying me are two different things. You being okay with things being quiet between us? That drove me crazy. You taking my car to work without telling me? *That* was annoying.'

His lips curved. 'It was more economical.'

'Sure, Mr Big-Shot Lawyer.' She rolled her eyes. 'You were thinking about being *economical*.'

'I was.'

'No, what you were thinking was that my car would help make some of your clients feel more comfortable. Which, after I got through my annoyance at finding myself with your massive SUV when I had to go into town where the parking spaces are minuscule, I'd forgive you for.'

'You always did forgive quickly.'

'Not always,' she said softly.

'Rosa?' She looked up. 'What did I do? What couldn't you forgive?'

CHAPTER SIX

'IT WASN'T YOU,' she replied after the longest time. Her heart ached at the look on his face.

'You keep saying that, but how can I believe you?'

'Because it's true.' She set her cup on the table and went to sit next to him, drawing his hands into her own. 'It wasn't you. It was—' She broke off, closed her eyes. Could she tell him she couldn't forgive herself? 'It was me. It *is* me.'

'No,' he said. 'No, it's not. It has to be me. It's always me.'

She opened her mouth as he pulled his hands from hers and stood, staring at him. But no words came out.

'Wh...what do you mean?' she said when she managed to get over her surprise.

'Nothing.'

'No,' she said standing. 'That definitely meant something. What are you talking about, Aaron?'

When she joined him in front of the glass door—just as they'd stood earlier, watching the rain—she felt his entire body tense. She lifted a hand to comfort him, then dropped it, hating how uncertain things had become between them.

He didn't answer her question but she had to make him see that it hadn't been him. And the words spilled from her mouth before she could stop them.

'I found a lump in my breast.'

Aaron immediately snapped out of his self-indulgent moodiness. 'What? When? Are you okay?'

'Yes. I'm fine.' But she crossed her arms over her breasts, her hands on her shoulders. Her self-protective stance. 'It was just over four months ago.'

'Before you left?' She nodded. 'Why didn't you tell me?'

Her eyes lifted to his, but he didn't know what he saw there. It killed him. Just as he feared his lack of oxygen would if he didn't catch his breath soon.

'Because it turned out to be nothing.'

That wasn't the reason, but he let it slide. It was more information than he'd thought he'd get. And when finally he'd caught his breath he asked, 'What was it?'

'A milk duct.'

He lifted his eyebrows as the air swept out of his lungs again. 'A milk duct?' he rasped. 'As in—'

'No! No,' she said with a shake of her head. 'Not a baby, no. It was just something that happened. Hormonal.'

He nodded. Tried to figure out why he felt so…disappointed. Was it because she wasn't pregnant? Or because she'd gone through this hellish ordeal and hadn't told him about it?

'You should have said something.' He left his spot at the door and headed for the drink he hadn't finished earlier. He downed it, ignoring his coffee.

'I didn't want to worry you.'

He turned around. 'Were *you* worried?'

Confusion spread across her features. 'Yes.'

'Then you should have told me. When you're worried, I should be worried too. That was the marriage *I* signed up for.'

'Yes, but sharing my concerns about—' she threw her hands up '—my career isn't the same as sharing my concerns about my health.'

'Why not?'

'I don't know. This is more important.'

'And you didn't want to share something important with me?'

'No, Aaron, come on. I didn't mean it like that.'

'How did you mean it?' She didn't answer him and he

nodded. 'Maybe it's better if you and I just don't talk and get some sleep. You can take the bed. I'll take the couch.'

He spread the throw that hung over the couch over it. Not because he wanted to sleep there—he almost laughed aloud at the prospect of sleeping when things were like this between them—but because he wanted her to realise he didn't want to talk any more.

Everything she'd said tore his broken heart into more pieces. He could almost feel the shredded parts floating around in his chest, reminding him that he hadn't done enough in their marriage. That he hadn't managed to get her to trust him. To tell him about the *important* things.

She sighed and then switched off the lights again. Moments later, he heard her settle on the bed and he settled on the couch himself. His body barely fitted, but he wouldn't take the bed if she was there. It gave him some sort of sick satisfaction that she'd be aware of his discomfort.

Or was that sick feeling a result of what she'd just told him?

He'd been there when his mother had found her lump—had stayed with her right until the moment they'd told her she was in remission—and he knew what havoc it wreaked.

Granted, his mother wasn't entirely the best example of responding to anything with grace. He knew Rosa would be. Or perhaps not, since she hadn't told him about it. Since she'd run.

Still, he wished he could have helped her through it. After what her mother had gone through— after it had led to her death—he could only imagine how terrified she'd been.

And yet she hadn't told him.

No matter what Rosa said, he knew that had something to do with him. His mother had blamed him for everything since his birth. The fact that things hadn't worked out with his father. The fact that his father had walked away from them...

Never mind that he'd never even met the man who'd supposedly left his mother because of *him*.

'I can hear you thinking,' Rosa called over to him. It had been something she'd say to him in bed often, right before they went to sleep. Except then, she'd turn over and force him to talk about it. And he would, because he'd wanted to share it with her.

Now, he didn't.

'You're not going to say anything, are you?' she said a bit softer, though he still heard her. 'I'm sorry, Aaron. I didn't mean to hurt your feelings. It's just… You know my parents didn't have the most conventional relationship. They didn't share things with one another.'

'We weren't like that,' he heard himself say.

'I know we weren't. But that's because—' he heard rustling, and assumed that she was now sitting up '—we weren't like them.'

'Now we are?'

'Now…things have changed.'

'Because you found a lump in your breast.'

'Yes.' Silence followed her words, but he waited. 'You already went through all that with your mother. I didn't want you to have to go through that with me too.'

He frowned, and then sat up. His eyes had adjusted to the dark and he could see the silhouette of her on the bed. She was sitting up, like he'd thought, and had drawn her legs to her chest, her arms around them, her head resting on her knees. He'd found her like that before. Once, when her mother had just died. And again on each anniversary of her mother's death.

He still couldn't resist it. Even though, as he walked to her, as he sat down next to her on the bed, he told himself he needed to.

'I can't imagine how scared you must have been,' he said softly. 'I wish you'd told me.'

'But—'

'I know you didn't want me to worry. And now I know that you were also thinking about what happened with my mother. But you shouldn't have. You should have thought of us first. Of yourself too.' He paused, struggling to figure out how to tell her what he'd thought she already knew. 'We're…stronger together. No matter what we face, we're stronger facing it together.'

'You don't mean that.'

'I do. Why is that so hard for you to believe?'

'Because I was you, Aaron. And I didn't feel the way you claim to feel now.'

'What do you mean?' Aaron asked her in that quiet, steady way he had. And since his quiet, steady presence had already calmed her, she answered him.

'I didn't ask to be my mother's emotional support when she got sick.' She stopped and wondered if he'd know what she meant by that. That she was talking about her mother's mental illness *and* her cancer.

But her mother's mental illness wasn't a subject she'd ever wanted to talk about—it had been too difficult— though she had mentioned it to him once. But could she expect him to remember something she'd only mentioned once?

She shook the doubt away. 'But I had no choice. My father…was useless with that kind of thing—' *with everything that she'd gone through* '—and my brothers used excuse after excuse to keep from dealing with my mother's illness. Or emotions. Or anything beyond their own lives.' She rolled her eyes at that, much like she had to their faces. 'I was forced into being her carer, and I didn't want to do that to you.'

'I took my vows seriously.'

'But you don't know how… You don't know until you know.'

His hand engulfed hers. 'I do know,' he told her. 'I made those vows intentionally. I'd be there for you in sickness and in health.'

'My parents made those vows too,' she responded quietly. 'And look where that got them.'

'They weren't us.'

'It's not that simple.'

He didn't reply. Only drew her into his arms and slid down so that they were lying together on the bed.

She didn't want this. She didn't want to be reminded of how good it felt to share her worries with him. How good it felt to lie there in his strong arms and let him take that burden from her.

But she stayed there and, for the first time in months, felt herself relax.

CHAPTER SEVEN

THE RAIN HAD calmed slightly when Aaron opened his eyes. It was barely light, and it took him a moment to figure out that he'd fallen asleep. Rosa stirred against him, reminding him of how *she'd* fallen asleep first the night before.

He hadn't had the heart to move her then, and now, though he knew he should, he didn't move. She was still sleeping, but it wouldn't be long before she woke up. It was her habit to wake as the sun came up. She'd check to see if he was still in bed with her. If he was, she'd snuggle against him and go back to sleep. If he wasn't, she'd go find him. Miserable, sleepy, she'd creep into his lap, complaining that if he hadn't been working she'd have been able to sleep longer.

It had been one of her endearing qualities. Much like the fact that she couldn't deal with quiet—his preferred state—so she'd keep talking until he'd answer her.

Things had been good between them. But he could see the cracks clearly now. Her running instead of turning to him when she'd found that lump had been the first sign of it. The last four months—and the last twelve hours—had highlighted the others.

All of which seemed to lead to the same conclusion: she didn't want *them*. She didn't want *him*.

He got up, the thought making him too anxious to continue lying still beside her. He'd never given much thought to being unwanted, though his mother had reminded him of it often enough that he should have.

There were days when she'd told him he was a surprise. Others when she'd call him an accident. It was only when she was feeling terrible about herself that she'd call him a mistake.

But he'd brushed it off. It had been easy to do when he'd been raised by his nanny—a kind woman who his mother's rich family had been able to afford. So the idiosyncrasies of the woman who'd showed up twice a day to say good morning and goodnight to him hadn't really mattered.

And since he'd never met his father, he hadn't cared about that either. His needs had been taken care of. His nanny had been there when he was younger. His mother had become more of a permanent fixture in his life when he got older. And when she'd got sick it had jolted him into realising she was the only family he had.

He hadn't needed anything else until he'd met Rosa. Until he'd married her. Until she'd left. And he'd realised how, despite believing otherwise, being unwanted had affected him.

He went about his morning routine as usual. His mother had thought of practicalities like toothbrushes and toothpaste, fortunately—hell, he'd take what he could at this point—and when he was done he went to the kitchen to make coffee.

'Coffee?' he asked when he heard a rustling behind him.

He made another cup after her sleepy, 'Yes, please,' and by the time he was done she'd emerged from the bathroom looking adorably mussed from sleep.

The shirt she wore was creased, her hair piled on the top of her head. It took less than a minute for his body to react to how much of her legs the shirt now revealed.

He took a steadying breath as he set her cup on the table and then moved to watch the rain through the glass doors. It was easier to do that than to watch her. Than to want her.

Than to need her.

'It's better today,' she said softly from behind him. He grunted in response. The annoyance of the situation was catching up with him now.

Sure, that's it, a voice in his head mocked him.

'We're back to this now, are we?' she said after another few moments of silence. He took a sip of his coffee in response. Pretended not to hear her frustrated sigh.

'Aaron—'

'I'm sorry that you had to go through what you did,' he said, turning to her. 'I'm sorry that you felt you couldn't share that with me. Whatever your reasons were,' he added. 'But clearly we have different opinions on this relationship. Now mine is finally catching up to yours.'

Being locked in that room was torture.

She'd thought it before, when she hadn't alienated her only company. Well, she considered, at least not to the extent that she'd alienated him now. And she wasn't even sure how she'd done it. They'd been on okay terms when she'd fallen asleep. Then, when she'd woken up, she'd found Aaron as aloof as always.

Except he hadn't really ever been aloof with her. With other people, yes. But her? No. Being the recipient of it made her heart ache.

And now she'd also have to live with the silence she'd complained about earlier. For an indefinite amount of time. Within the first hour she was antsy. And then antsy turned into bored. She was desperate to run out in the rain again. But she didn't. Because she was a mature, responsible adult who wouldn't deal with her feelings by doing something that stupid. Again.

Instead, she went to the bed since Aaron had claimed the couch. The bedding was rumpled, the indentation of their bodies still there…

'We have to leave this room at some point,' Rosa said, snuggling into the warmth of Aaron's body. He made a non-committal noise, tightening his arm around her, his free hand lightly trailing up and down her arm. 'We're on honeymoon. We should be going to the beach. Exploring the town. Showing off our love to the world.' He didn't reply. She sighed. 'Fine. For food then, at the very least.'

'We don't need food.'

'Really?' she replied dryly. 'You don't think we're going to need fuel if we want to stay here?'

The side of his mouth lifted. 'I suppose you have a good point there.'

'I know,' she said with a laugh. 'Honestly, I'm not sure how we've survived so long without it.'

He looked down at her, his eyes alight with desire and amusement. 'Probably like this.'

His lips were on hers before she could stop him. And then so was his body, the weight of it a comforting and intoxicating pressure on her aching skin.

Suddenly, all thought of food fled from her mind. Suddenly, she didn't want to stop…

She sucked in her breath at the memory. Brief as it had been, it had stung. It had reminded her of the good times she and Aaron had shared. Not only in their marriage in general, but there, in the very room they were trapped in. On the very bed she was looking at.

And she'd given up on that. On them. Because she'd made the wrong decision a long time ago. Because, even now, she didn't know how to make the right one.

Desperate to escape from her thoughts, she began searching through the drawers of the bedside tables, hoping to find paper so she could work on a design that would keep her mind busy.

But, almost as quickly as she'd been swept into that memory of her and Aaron, she was drawn into another memory. This time, though, instead of paper she'd found a picture of her mother, holding the flowers they'd both been named after, smiling up at the camera.

The air left her lungs and her legs crumbled. She sagged down onto the bed.

'Rosa?'

His voice was behind her. She hadn't realised he was so close. The bed dipped next to her. His hand covered the one she'd let fall to her lap.

'I didn't realise your mom had this picture,' she said absently. 'It's the one I put next to my mom's hospital bed. A reminder of the flowers we'd been named for. Forces of nature. Symbols of life.'

She smiled. 'I forgot this picture existed.' She traced her mother's smiling face with a finger. 'She looked so happy here. She was pregnant with me, so it was before she got sick.'

'Long before the cancer.'

'No, I meant the hypochondria.' She set the picture on top of the bedside table. Tilted her head as she looked at it. It had been a long time since she'd seen that smile on her mother's face.

'Your mom was a hypochondriac?'

His question lulled her out of the memories, and she quickly realised what she'd told him.

'Yes,' she forced herself to say lightly, and got up. Away from him. 'I told you that.'

'I'm sure I would have remembered if you had.'

'I told you at the funeral.' Her stomach cramped. 'You asked me why people kept telling me how sorry they were that this had actually become something.'

He swore softly. 'I forgot about it.'

'I know.'

'You didn't remind me either. I don't think you've ever spoken about it.'

'No,' she replied with a thin smile. 'I didn't.'

She walked away, towards the door that showed the light shower that was coming down now. She wanted to escape, but it wasn't from the room any more. Or from him. It was from the memories.

From the reminder of how often she'd held her breath, waiting for her mother to tell her how the rash she'd got from being out in the sun was skin cancer. Or how her headaches were a brain tumour.

Rosa's life had revolved around her mother's anxiety. And that anxiety had spilled over into her own life. Rosa had never been free to do what she wanted to, too afraid that her mother would need her.

It had been easier not to make plans. She'd told herself that, and yet she'd still wanted to do things. And the tension between wanting and telling herself that she shouldn't, that she couldn't, had constantly churned in her stomach.

So she'd done spontaneous things. Things she'd wanted to do. She'd chosen to seize the moment because she hadn't known when those moments would be snatched away from her.

And they would inevitably be snatched from her. And she'd mourn the loss of her freedom even as she'd wondered whether she should have done those things in the first place.

'It hurt you.'

The quiet words said from behind her had tears prickling in her eyes. 'It doesn't matter,' she said. Except that it came out in a whisper, which didn't make it sound like it didn't matter. 'It's over now.'

He moved next to her and she thought about how often they'd stood there, like that, since they'd arrived.

'What was it like?'

She shook her head, fully intending not to answer that question. Which was why, when the words came spilling out of her mouth, it was so surprising.

'Difficult. My mother had always been anxious. But i

was okay, for the most part, because she could deal with it.'
She paused. 'I don't know what changed that. I don't know
why she suddenly started obsessing about her health. But
by then I'd had already taken on the role of soother. I don't
have any memory that wasn't somehow affected by it.'

She blew out a breath. 'People use that term so easily.
Hypochondriac. I remember a friend of mine calling a colleague a hypochondriac because she'd take sick leave often.
And I found myself asking her whether she knew what that
really meant.'

She stepped away from the door now, and began pacing.
'It was terrible, and I felt so bad afterwards. Because her
explanation was so pathetic, and didn't come close to what
it's really like. How the person can feel themselves suffering. Or how they can see themselves dying. The panic, the
anxiety. How they can never truly believe that things are
going to be okay. How they can't fully enjoy life because
one day they believe life is going to destroy them.'

She didn't mention what it was like for the people around
the hypochondriac. How they'd constantly be waiting for the
anxiety, for the panic to come. How that would make *them*
anxious and panicked. How they'd doubt themselves. Had
they handled it properly? Had they done the right thing to
help? Had they helped at all?

How, even after the person was gone, they'd still feel
the effects of it.

She stopped when her legs went weak and bent over,
waiting for it to get better. And when it did she stood, and
saw the conflicting emotions on Aaron's face. He wanted
to help her and yet he didn't know if he could.

Her own fault.

'I'm sorry—I didn't mean to go on about it.'

'I asked.'

'I shouldn't have spilled it all out on you like that.'

She walked to the couch, sank down on it.

'You should have,' he said when he took the seat opposite her. 'You should have told me sooner.'

'Apparently there's a lot I should have told you.' She gave him a wry smile. 'And with all my talking too, I hadn't told you any of it.'

'It's part of the reason you left.'

She stiffened, her heart racing. 'What do you mean?'

'There's a reason why, with all your talking, you didn't tell me about your mother. Or open up about it,' he said quietly when she opened her mouth to protest. 'It's probably why you didn't tell me about the lump in your breast either.'

'No,' she denied. But she'd started shaking. He was awfully close to the truth.

'Yes,' he told her. 'You've had to be brave for your mother for so long. You don't know how not to be.'

CHAPTER EIGHT

ROSA RELEASED A sharp breath and nodded. 'I suppose you're right.'

And yet, somehow, Aaron felt as if he'd got it wrong. Not entirely, he thought, looking at the pensive expression on her face. But there was relief there too, which made him think that there was something else.

'You should be able to talk with me. Or you should have been able to talk with me,' he corrected himself when that annoying voice in his head reminded him that they were no longer together.

'I've made a lot of mistakes with you,' she admitted softly, and his chest tightened.

'I know. I'm sorry.'

'Why are you apologising?'

'Some of those mistakes were my fault.'

He threaded his fingers together, braced his arms on his thighs, but he refused to drop his head like he wanted to. No, he would face her. He would face the mistakes that he'd made. Especially now, after hearing about her mother's issues.

He hadn't known before. Or, more accurately, he hadn't been paying enough attention. He vaguely remembered her mentioning her mother's hypochondria but, since he'd only ever heard it used in the way she'd described her colleague using it, he hadn't thought much of it until now.

He should have. He should have been more attentive. He should have done his part for her.

'I don't understand how my mistakes could have been your fault.'

'I shouldn't have let you make them.'

Her eyes narrowed. '*Let me?* I don't think that's the correct phrase.'

'I don't mean it that way.'

'Then how *do* you mean it?'

He opened his mouth to explain, and yet every explanation he could think of sounded wrong. And exactly the way she'd thought he'd meant it.

'I was…older than you when we married,' he tried eventually. 'I should have…helped you.'

'Helped me…with what?'

'Helped you see that perhaps marrying me wasn't the best idea.'

Her expression twisted into one that would have been charming had the words he'd just said not turned his heart inside out.

'I…' She blew out a breath. 'No, Aaron. That's not one of the mistakes I was talking about.' She pushed up from her seat now, sat down next to him, curling her legs under her. 'It wasn't a mistake marrying you.' She closed her eyes. 'At least, not for the reasons you mean.'

'But it *was* a mistake.'

She let out a breath again and leaned forward, taking his hand. 'I don't remember ever being happier than that moment you proposed to me. It was like…a light in a terrible darkness that I couldn't get out of. You helped me get out of it.'

'You were grieving for your mother.' He didn't know why he was still speaking. About his fears. About all the things he'd realised since she'd walked into the room. Since she'd left four months ago. 'I should have given you more time.'

'So why didn't you?'

'Because I—'

'What?' she prompted softly when he broke off and didn't continue. 'Because you what?'

'Because I made a promise to your mother to take care of you.' There was a stunned silence, and then her hand left his. He turned to her. 'She didn't ask me to marry you. Just to make sure you'd be okay. It seemed like a natural thing to do because I loved you. And I wanted to live my life in case... Before it was too late.'

She didn't respond. Instead, she shifted back and stared blankly at her hands in her lap.

'Rosa—'

'No—' she cut him off in a hoarse voice '—you just told me one hell of a thing. I need... I need time.'

'Okay.'

He watched helplessly as she stood and began pacing again. He couldn't say more than he had. Nor could he do anything to make her feel better. So he watched. And waited.

'How do I know?' she asked suddenly. 'How do I know that your proposal wasn't just because of my mother?'

'We'd been dating over a year before I proposed.'

'So what?' She stopped in front of him and rested her hands on her hips. 'So what, Aaron? It was a *year*. Sure, we were friends for a year before that. But what does it matter? We spent most of our time together at the hospital. Can we even call that dating?'

'We got to know each other during that time,' he replied measuredly. 'You got a job designing clothes without any qualifications when you were nineteen. Now you're an incredible success.'

'Because of your mother.'

'My mother might have helped spur it along with her connections, but you got your foot in the door by yourself.'

She clenched her jaw. 'Those are facts. I shared facts with you.'

'I learnt that your drive got you to where you were. And that drive came from a passion to create. That creating calms your mind. That it helps you make sense of things.' Her expression turned softer, and feeling hopeful, he continued. 'I know that your family life was hard. That your father and brothers were hopeless with your mother's disease—and now I realise how deep that goes—but that it taught you to be strong. Brave.'

'Too brave,' she offered with a smile.

'Only when it comes to trusting the person you agreed to spend the rest of your life with.' Silence pulsed between them, reminding them that they were no longer in that place. But neither of them addressed it. 'Besides, I bought the ring I gave you long before your mother spoke to me.'

Her hands curled into fists, but not before he saw that she was still wearing her ring. He wasn't sure how he'd missed that, but the fact had hope beating in his heart, healing some of the pain there.

'You're lying.'

'I had the ring made the day after you showed me how to dance.'

She stared at him. Shook her head. 'Now I *know* you're lying.'

He smiled. 'I'm not.'

'But that went *terribly*.'

'Only because your instruction ability left much to be desired.'

'*Excuse me?*' she said. 'I'm a *terrific* teacher. The entire reason we were able to do our wedding dance was because of me.'

'You, and the dance instructor I hired to show me how to do the steps after each of our lessons.'

She gasped. 'You did *not*.'

His smile widened. 'I did.'

She stared at him a while longer and then shook her head. 'This is a betrayal.'

'Apparently,' he replied, amused. 'Because you've forgotten the reason I mentioned the dancing in the first place.'

'Firstly—' she lifted a finger '—I taught you to dance

out of the goodness of my heart. The reason it went so badly
was because you have two left feet. Secondly—' a second
finger lifted '—I didn't *want* to teach you our wedding
dance. I remembered how badly it went the first time. The
only reason I did it was because I didn't want you to look
silly when we danced in front of all your fancy colleagues.
Though now, of course,' she muttered darkly, 'I wish I'd
left you to embarrass yourself. And thirdly—' a third finger lifted, and then she threw both hands in the air '—why
on earth would that make you want to marry me?'

He stood now, ignoring the way her eyes widened when
he took her hand and put it on his shoulder, before resting
one hand on her waist and taking her other hand in his.

'Because,' he said as he started swaying, 'I could smell
your perfume when we did. It made me realise I'd be okay
if that was the only scent I'd smell for the rest of my life.
And having you in my arms made me think that I'd be okay
if that was the only thing I could feel for the rest of my life.'
He pulled her closer until her body was pressed against his.
Something akin to belonging washed over him. 'I also loved
how hard you tried to make me think you weren't annoyed
with me. And that smile you'd give me every time I'd step
on your toes.'

'You're doing pretty great now.'

'That's because I always knew how to dance,' he said
with a crooked smile. Felt it widen when she frowned at him.

'But the instructor?'

'Didn't exist.'

'I don't understand.'

'It's simple, really,' he said, and stopped moving. 'I'd
lie about anything if it gave me an opportunity to do this.'

He lowered his lips onto hers.

She'd seen it coming. In the way his eyes had first softened, then heated. She could have stopped it. Should have.

Instead, she closed her eyes and let herself be swept away by her husband's kiss.

Oh, how she'd missed it. The way his lips knew how to move against hers. The way his tongue knew how to tangle with hers. It sent shivers down her spine just as intensely as it had the first time he'd kissed her. The butterflies were there too, as was a need she hadn't known could exist inside her. As was a want she didn't think would ever go away.

His arms tightened around her. Pulling her in. Keeping her safe. She could feel the strength in them and then in his hands, when they moved from her waist, down over her butt, squeezing gently before coming back up over her hips.

Her body shuddered under his touch. Her breath hitched as he deepened the kiss. As his hands moved up over the sides of her breasts to take her face in his hands. He was being gentle, sweet, and she would have protested against it—against the control she knew it required from him—if she wasn't so desperate for the taste of him.

As it was, her hands couldn't stay still. They slid over the grooves of his muscles. His back, his shoulders, his arms. Down between them, over his chest. His abdomen trembled under her touch when her hands lowered, and she felt the effect she had on him press against her stomach.

'Wait,' he said, gently pulling away from her. Which was strange, she thought, a bit dazed, since the expression on his face was fierce, obviously pained, and far from gentle. 'I can't do this with you.'

'Do what?'

'This.' His hands tightened slightly on her arms and then he took a step back. Controlled, she thought again, and a violent wave of resentment washed over her.

'You were the one who started this, Aaron,' she said in a low voice.

'It was…a mistake.'

He walked away from her and the pain that spasmed in her chest was so intense she thought her heart had broken.

'I'll add it to the list, I suppose.'

'Another thing that's my fault.'

'Oh, stop that,' she snapped. Hurt and anger had done dangerous things to her patience. 'Nothing that happened between us is your fault. I married you because I wanted to. I left you because I had to. That's it. End of story. I'm not your mother, Aaron. You don't have to take responsibility for me. Or for something that you didn't cause.'

CHAPTER NINE

'IT'S NOT THE SAME.'

'Isn't it?' she shot back. 'Because that's what I'm hearing right now.'

Aaron couldn't describe the emotions going through him. It was a mixture of desire and annoyance. Anger and frustration. All because of her. He shook his head.

'I'm not going to have this conversation with you.'

'What else are you going to do?' she exclaimed. 'Walk out through the locked door?'

'It won't be locked for long,' he said, and made the kind of spur-of-the-moment decision he'd warned himself against. He walked to the door and then took a couple of steps back. Enough so he could plough through it.

'Aaron?' There was panic in her voice. 'What are you doing? Aaron,' she said again when he didn't answer. When he began to move forward, she shouted, 'No!'

It wasn't that she'd shouted at him. It was more the complete panic in her tone that stopped him. A few seconds later, she was standing in front of the door, her back against it, arms spread out, shielding the door with her body.

'Are you out of your mind?' she said in a shaky voice. 'You can't break down this door.'

'Why not?'

'What would happen if it didn't work?' she demanded. 'You would no doubt hurt yourself, and there's absolutely nothing in here that would help me look after you.' Her chest was heaving. 'I wouldn't be able to call for an ambulance, and who knows how long it'll be until we get out of here?'

'Careful,' he said quietly. Dangerously. 'You almost sound like you care.'

'I *do* care,' she said through clenched teeth. 'I wish I didn't, but I do.'

'Then what's the real reason you left?'

'Because I found a lump in my breast. Because I immediately thought I had cancer. Because I remembered a doctor had told me that I should get screened for breast cancer. Because, in some stupid, misguided cling to independence, I decided against it.' She sucked in air. Continued. 'Because I thought about how my life would change while I went through chemotherapy. Because I knew I couldn't put you through that again.' Her voice caught at the end and he cursed himself for forcing her to speak.

'Rosa—'

'I told the doctor that my mother had cancer, that I hadn't been screened for it, and they gave me all the tests. I sat through the whole process fearing the worst and in the end there was nothing. *Nothing.*'

She lifted her hand and let it fall on her last word. 'So I'd insisted, and imagined it all, and there was nothing.' Her eyes shone when she lifted them to his. 'Just like my mother.'

And suddenly Aaron understood why it had affected her so badly. And why she really had left because of the lump. With quick steps he pulled her into his arms and held her as her body shook.

He closed his eyes. Told himself he was an absolute jerk for pushing. And when the shaking subsided he pulled back and saw that her eyes were dry. That it hadn't been tears at all, just…shaking.

'You're not like your mother.'

'You don't know that.'

'I know it just as well as I know that you're not like *my* mother either.'

'And where does that get us?' she asked, pulling away from him now. 'We still have a broken relationship.'

'Because you were scared about having cancer.'

She stared at him and then shook her head sadly. 'No. No, that's not it at all.'

'Tell me then,' he said urgently, an unknown fear compelling his words. 'Tell me what I'm not understanding.'

'I don't want to be in a relationship with anyone, Aaron. That's why I shouldn't have married you. That's why I left.'

How could she have hurt him more than she already had?

She hadn't thought it possible, and yet here she was, watching the hope on his face transform into something uglier. And then his expression went blank, his calm façade back in place.

She hated it.

'I'll file the divorce papers as soon as I get home.'

'No, Aaron—'

'No, what?' he said almost conversationally. 'You don't want to be divorced? Because that's the reality of our situation, Rosa. You don't want to be in a relationship with anyone. You made that clear four months ago. You've made it clear now.'

'But… I don't want to be divorced either,' she replied lamely.

'You have to make a decision,' he said coldly now. The tone she'd heard him use with opposing council. 'You can't have it both ways. If you want to fix this, we'll make that decision together and try our best to fix it. If you don't, I file for divorce when I get back and we end this. Either or. Not both.'

She bit her lip when he turned away from her, the tears she'd resisted earlier threatening to spill over now.

But a sound at the door distracted her. She took a step back automatically, felt Aaron approach, placing himself between her and the door. Seconds later, a red-faced man was standing in front of them.

'Aaron and Rosa Spencer?'

'Yes,' Aaron answered.

'Sergeant Downing.' He showed them his badge. 'Liana Spencer—your mother?—called to say that there might be some trouble here. Was she right?'

Rosa heard the hesitation in the man's voice and for the first time realised how it must look to him. Aaron was wearing a wrinkled shirt and jeans, barefoot, and she wore only his shirt. It looked less like the captive situation he'd thought he'd be stepping into and more like an invasion of privacy.

'She was right,' Aaron replied. Cool. Collected. Always. Though he'd stepped in front of her, blocking her from the sergeant's view. 'The door was locked. We couldn't get out.'

'Not locked.' Rosa peered from behind Aaron to see the sergeant lift his hand to his chin. 'It was jammed and I had to use some force, but it opened.'

'So…no one locked us in?' Rosa asked softly. Aaron stiffened in front of her.

'No, ma'am.'

'And the electricity?' Aaron asked.

'We're working on it.' Sergeant Downing frowned. 'Your mother told us she was worried about you and to check. She told me about the spare key she left with the security company down the street.' He paused. 'The only reason I knew to check up here—' his face went red '—was because I… er…heard voices.'

Rosa could only imagine what those voices must have sounded like to an outsider.

'Thank you, Sergeant.'

Aaron didn't move from where he stood, didn't offer the hand she knew he would have if he wasn't still protecting her. Her heart swelled, though she wasn't sure how. She was certain it had broken.

'We couldn't contact you, and with the storm… We thought we'd be stuck here all weekend.'

'You're welcome,' Sergeant Downing replied. 'Well,

then, the rain's calmed somewhat, but it's still pretty bad out there so I should be off. There's bound to be another emergency somewhere. A missing dog or something.' He winked at them and only then did Rosa noticed the shimmer of raindrops on his coat. 'You two try to stay out of trouble for the next twenty-four hours.'

'Twenty-four?' Rosa spoke again, almost without noticing that she had. 'Will the storm be continuing until tomorrow?'

'That's the expectation, though you know what the weather's like on this side of the world.' He paused. 'I know this is probably a much better place to ride out this weather—and since I'm a police officer I'm supposed to tell you that you should stay inside until it gets better outside—but this weekend is our annual heritage celebration.'

'In winter?'

'Yeah,' Sergeant Downing said with an indulgent smile. 'We don't get many visitors this time of year, and our founders rocked up here on the fifteenth of this month, so we celebrate. It's nothing major—just some food, some wine, some music inside city hall—but we'd love to have you.'

'We won't—'

'Thank you so much, Sergeant Downing,' Rosa spoke over Aaron. Again, she felt him stiffen. 'We appreciate the invitation. And your assistance.'

'It's fine. And, while I'm here, I'll write down my number in case things get rough again.' He took out a notepad and pen and wrote quickly before handing Aaron the paper. 'Things should be up and running again in a few hours at best—by the end of the day at worst—so you should be able to call. Otherwise, I'll see you in the city.'

He nodded at them and a few moments later they were alone.

'I'd better go down and make sure he locks up,' Aaron said.

'Do you want to go?' she asked instead of replying.

'Do I want to go to the heritage celebration?' he asked, and then shook his head. 'I can think of better things to do.'

'Like spend your time here, alone with me?'

His expression grew stony. 'You're more than welcome to go.'

'How?'

'Take my car.'

She lifted her brows. 'So you really won't go with me?'

'Rosa, I've told you where I stand. You're on the side that doesn't allow me to go with you.'

He left the room before she could reply.

She wasn't on the top floor when Aaron returned. Which was fine, he told himself, because he was tired of whatever was happening between them.

He wondered if his mother had given any thought to the havoc her plan would wreak. Liana hadn't known why Rosa had left him—*he* certainly hadn't, so she didn't find out from him, at least. Though now that he knew she'd been in contact with Rosa, perhaps his wife *had* told Liana why she'd left...

He dismissed it almost instantly. His mother would have told him if she'd known what had happened. It would have been an opportunity to tell him where he'd gone wrong, and she'd never be able to resist that.

He couldn't describe his relationship with his mother. Liana had kept him at a distance for most of his life. And then she'd got sick and things had changed between them. Probably because *he'd* been determined to change things between them, and he acknowledged that he'd bridged the gap more than she ever had.

But watching her suffer the way she had... His stomach turned just thinking of it. It had been enough to ignore the fact that she hadn't wanted the reconciliation as much as he had. It had been enough to move his life to Cape Town until she got better.

Maybe it was time to face the truth—that his mother still

didn't want the relationship he'd tried to forge with her. Perhaps, this weekend, she'd wanted him to face the fact that the end of his marriage had been his fault. Or perhaps she'd been trying to fix it. Which, if that was true, would have been ironic since he'd been cleaning up *her* mistakes his entire life.

I'm not your mother, Aaron. You don't have to take responsibility for me. Or for something that you didn't cause.

He sat down heavily on the couch, clutching the glass of rum he'd poured for himself, Rosa's words echoing in his head. Maybe he *was* conflating the two issues. Rosa and his mother were nothing alike. And Rosa was right. She had a mind of her own. And she'd never expected him to clean up after her. She'd always taken responsibility for what she'd done, even if what she'd done had been spur-of-the-moment.

'Aaron?'

When he looked up Rosa was hovering in the doorway, wearing fitted jeans and his shirt, which she'd paired with ankle boots. 'Where'd you get the clothes?'

'I found some things I left behind the last time we were here.' She shifted her weight from one foot to the other. Was she remembering how different things had been the last time they were there? 'The shoes are your mother's.'

'No top?'

Her cheeks turned pink. 'No.'

He frowned at her reaction, but didn't ask her about it.

'I'm going to go into town. Are you—' She broke off, cleared her throat. 'You're sure you don't want to come along?' He shook his head. 'Okay. Right. Fine.' She paused. 'Well, I'll try to find somewhere else to stay then.' Her gaze met his. 'Since there's a line in the sand now.' She stepped back and then nodded. 'Take care of yourself, Aaron. I'll make sure your car gets back to you in one piece.'

And then she was gone. Seconds later he heard the garage door opening and then closing again. He didn't move.

Just kept wondering if this really would be the last time he'd see his wife.

If it was, it would be his fault. He'd been the one who'd drawn a line in the sand. Who'd given them sides to stand on. He was the one who'd told her that she needed to decide between saving or ending their marriage.

Really, it had been selfish. Because he'd hoped that his ultimatum would force her into letting him in. She had—a little. She'd told him about her mother's illness, how she'd thought she was becoming like her mother when she'd found that lump.

But it was so obvious that she *wasn't* like her mother.

Why hadn't she believed him?

And what had she meant when she'd said she shouldn't be in a relationship with anyone?

Clearly, she'd been right when she'd told him he didn't get it. He didn't. He didn't understand how she could claim that marrying him had *and* hadn't been a mistake. He didn't know how she could say she didn't blame him and yet not want to be with him.

It was hopelessly messy. He hated it. Hated how much it reflected the messiness of his mother's life.

With a sigh, he went downstairs to try to find the suitcase he'd brought with him when he'd thought he'd be staying at the house for the weekend. He found it in the room he and Rosa had shared when they'd been there last. He ignored the memories that threatened and was on his way to the shower so he could change when he glanced into the closet Rosa had used the last time they'd been there.

She was right. There were extra clothes of hers there. Including three or four long-sleeved tops, any of which she could have worn out that night.

So why had she worn his shirt?

CHAPTER TEN

ROSA PULLED IN to the city hall's car park with a sigh of relief. Sergeant Downing hadn't been joking when he'd said it was still pretty bad outside. She'd driven forty the entire way, praying that she wouldn't bump into anything since the visibility was so bad.

Which was probably for the best. She didn't want to be reminded of all the things she and Aaron had done together on the island in happier times.

Things hadn't ended particularly well between them now, but she hoped that he'd realise her leaving hadn't been his fault. Though she didn't think that was the case. She'd botched the explanation. Partly because she couldn't say that she was a *hypochondriac*. Not out loud. She could barely think it. The other part was because she didn't think he'd respond well to her saying she'd done it for his own good.

So, really, she'd given him all that she could.

Her fingers shook as she unbuttoned Aaron's shirt. It was pathetic, lying to him about why she was wearing it. Especially since he could so easily figure out that it *was* a lie. But she didn't care.

The shirt would remind her of the last day they'd spent together. Even if it wasn't exactly his, she could still smell him on it. Remnants of sleeping together the previous night, which proved that he'd held her while they'd slept.

She pulled it off, held it to her chest for a moment, and then folded it neatly and set it on the passenger seat. Then she pulled at the long-sleeved top she'd put on under Aaron's shirt and hurried into the hall, her handbag the only protection she had against the rain.

She worried she'd made a mistake when she walked in

and saw only unfamiliar faces, though that feeling in itself was familiar. It had accompanied all of her spur-of-the-moment decisions. And when Sergeant Downing had told her about this event, right after she and Aaron had had such an immense argument, it had seemed like the perfect escape.

And since that was what she did—ran, escaped—she'd come.

She shook the water off her clutch and then walked further into the room as though she belonged.

'Ms Spencer?'

She whirled around, felt a genuine smile on her lips when she saw Sergeant Downing. 'I hope you meant it when you invited me.'

'Of course,' he replied with a smile. He was handsome, she noticed for the first time. He had short curls on his head, dimples on either side of his mouth that became more pronounced when he smiled. If she hadn't been so entirely enthralled by her husband, she might have been interested.

'This place is pretty big for such a small town.'

'Yeah.' He stuffed his hands into his pockets, looked around. 'It's meant to hold the entire town. We're about six thousand, so it has to be pretty big.'

'It's lovely,' she said, taking in the hall.

It was decorated informally, with stands throughout the room that held food and other goodies. A makeshift bar stood against the wall on one side. There was an elevated platform on the other side, where children chased each other and screamed, and parents soothed and chatted in groups.

The windows were high—almost at the roof—and were spattered with rain, though they provided enough light for the room that the fairy lights that had been haphazardly draped throughout weren't entirely necessary.

'You have generators here?'

'Yep.' He lifted his shoulders. 'City hall is also the designated safe venue for disasters.' He gave her a chagrined smile. 'Small town.'

'Oh, no, I love it. Apart, you know, from the fact that I was locked in a room with my husband for a day because we couldn't make any calls.'

He laughed. 'Speaking of your husband…'

'He's not coming,' she said, her body stiffening. 'He's tired, and me being out the house is giving him the chance to…rest.'

He studied her but only nodded. 'Shall we get something to drink?'

Relieved, she said, 'Sure.'

She followed him to the bar but, when she saw that there was a hot drinks stand right next to it, pivoted and ordered a hot chocolate instead of the alcohol she'd first wanted. Sergeant Downing seemed well-liked by the town—certainly well known, though in a town of six thousand that was expected—and when he began to introduce her as 'Ms Spencer' she automatically corrected him.

'It's Rosa,' she said while she took the hand of the elderly woman who'd handed her the drink.

'That's a lovely name,' the elderly woman—Doreen—said.

'Thank you. I was actually named after my mom's favourite flower. It's a tradition in our family. For the daughters, at least.'

'How lovely.' Doreen beamed. 'It's almost like our Charles over here.'

Rosa glanced over just in time to see Sergeant Downing wince. She cocked an eyebrow. '*Charles?*'

'He was named after his mother's favourite royal,' Doreen offered enthusiastically.

Both her eyebrows rose.

'My mother's always been unique,' Sergeant Downing told her grimly. 'Thanks for that, Doreen.'

'It's a pleasure.'

Rosa laughed. 'Thanks for the hot chocolate, Charles.'

'Charlie,' he replied with a smile. 'You're welcome.'

The whole encounter made some of the sadness that inevitably came when she spoke about her mother ease. Which was strange, considering that she barely spoke about her mother outside of her family. Hell, she barely spoke about her mother *in* her family.

Her father and brothers' lives had pretty much gone on as usual after her mother had died. They lived in Mossel Bay, a small town on the Garden Route in the Western Cape. She'd grown up there, and had then gone to Cape Town when she'd started college. And then, when she'd dropped out, she'd started working for a commercial chain as an intern, before working up to a junior and then senior designer, with help from Liana's connections.

She'd only gone home a couple of times since she'd left for college. The first to pick her mother up and take her to Cape Town so that she could help take care of her as she went through her treatment. Her father and brothers would visit once a month, sometimes twice, which was hopelessly too few times, and yet every time she'd told them that they'd told her they had their own lives to live.

And so that had been that. Even after her mother had died, and Rosa had gone home to pack up her mother's things, it had been Aaron who had been by her side, helping her through it all.

Her brothers hadn't been interested. Her older brother had just started his own business and was more interested in Aaron's legal advice than their mother's belongings. And her younger brother had just got married to someone Rosa had only met once, and he'd been no help whatsoever.

And as for her father… Well, he'd been living a life separate from his wife for a long time by then. Now, of course, he was living with the title of 'widower' and enjoying the attention.

No, Rosa thought again. She hadn't been able to talk about her mother in the longest time. She hadn't wanted to bring it up with Aaron because… Well, because she hadn't wanted to remind him of how terrible their experience with cancer had been.

It had been long after his mother had gone into remission and her mother had passed away that Aaron had relaxed. She'd only then realised how negatively he'd been affected by it all. He'd finally started eating properly. He'd smiled more. He wouldn't toss and turn as much at night.

She hadn't wanted him to slip back into the person he'd been before. Hadn't wanted that for herself either. So she'd left. Protected him from going back. And felt *herself* revert as she did. She'd been foolish to believe it was possible for her to do otherwise when her life was still shadowed by what she'd gone through with her mother.

'Rosa?'

She blinked and then offered a smile to Charlie when she saw his questioning look. 'Sorry. It's been a rough morning. What did I miss?'

He gave her a sympathetic look. 'I don't think I'm going to be making your day any easier, I'm afraid.' He hesitated. 'Your husband managed to get hold of me just now. He says he has your phone, and asked whether I could pick it up for you.'

Aaron was waiting at the front door when Sergeant Downing rang the doorbell. There was surprise on the man's face when Aaron opened the door almost immediately after the bell sounded.

'Hi,' the sergeant said cautiously. 'You called.'

'Yes. Thank you for coming.'

'Rosa insisted.'

Aaron paused as he reached for Rosa's phone on the table next to the door. 'You spoke with her?'

The man's face turned a light shade of red. 'Yeah. I was with her when I got the call.'

Now Aaron turned to face the man fully. 'You were with my wife when you got my call,' he repeated.

'Not like that,' Sergeant Downing said quickly. And then he straightened his shoulders. 'I was the one who invited her. Both of you,' he added. 'And when I saw you weren't with her…' He trailed off. 'Well, I didn't want her to feel alone. Like she was amongst strangers.'

'She was. Is.'

'Yes, but she didn't have to be.'

Aaron considered it for all of a minute. 'You're right. I should probably come back with you. I'll give Rosa the phone myself, and make sure that she isn't amongst strangers any more.'

CHAPTER ELEVEN

ROSA SMILED WHEN she saw Charlie walk through the door of the hall, but the smile froze in place when she saw Aaron following closely behind him.

'What is it, dear?' Doreen asked worriedly when she turned back to Rosa with an outstretched hand that Rosa was meant to supply with a cup of hot water.

'Nothing,' she said, and quickly turned to pour the hot water from the dispenser. She cursed quietly when she saw her hand shaking and told herself to stay steady when she turned back to Doreen. 'Sorry about that,' she murmured, and kept her eyes on the woman who was now making tea for a customer.

After Charlie had left, Rosa had wondered around aimlessly until deciding that her mind would be put to better use if she was working. So she'd asked Doreen if she could help, and had been doing so for the last twenty minutes.

But suddenly working with hot liquids didn't seem like such a great idea.

'Charles, you're back,' Doreen exclaimed, and Rosa was forced to look up and into her husband's eyes.

They were steady as they met hers, as if he hadn't an hour ago told her he'd be filing their divorce papers when he got home.

'I didn't realise you were picking up my phone *and* my husband, Charlie,' Rosa said, pleased with how calm she sounded.

'Your husband?' Doreen exclaimed—the woman really only seemed to have one way of speaking. 'I thought you were here with our Charles.'

'No, Doreen,' Charlie interrupted quickly. 'We're not

here together. I actually invited Rosa and her husband, Aaron, to come here this evening when I was on a call to their house.'

'Which house is that?'

'The Spencer property off Main.'

'You're Liana Spencer's son?' Doreen asked, her voice raised even higher.

'Yes, ma'am,' Aaron replied with a nod.

'Why, son, let me give you a hug.' Doreen walked around the table and made good on her word. Rosa's lips twitched. Her husband didn't feel comfortable with public displays of affection, let alone displays with *strangers*. It was kind of adorable to watch.

The older woman's head barely reached Aaron's chest and she gave him an unexpectedly tight squeeze. Rosa hadn't imagined the woman's body had had the strength to give it.

'Thank you,' Aaron said when Doreen pulled back, and Rosa didn't bother trying to hide her smile.

'No, dear, that was me saying thank you to you.' Doreen dug into the front of her apron and pulled out a crumpled tissue which she pressed to her face. 'Your mother let me and my boys—all three of them, and their wives and my seven grandkids—stay in that house for a month after the place we'd all been staying in burnt down.'

'That was the Spencer place?' Charlie asked now, interest alight on his face. 'Yeah, I remember. I'd forgotten about it.'

'We didn't have any money to spend on staying somewhere else, and we lost everything in that fire. The insurance was giving us a hard time—' Doreen cut off, sniffled. 'And then one day, out of the blue while I was talking to someone in the grocery store, your mom came by and told me she'd heard what had happened and that we could stay in her house until we found something else.'

'Where did she go?' Aaron asked after a moment.

'Not sure. She was gone by the time we got there, and she didn't once check in with us.' Doreen pressed the tissue under both eyes before stuffing it back into her apron. 'Of course, that didn't mean we took advantage. I made sure that house stayed spick and span. And that nothing broke, even though all the grandkids are under ten.'

Aaron's eye twitched. 'I appreciate that, ma'am.'

'Your mother is a good woman, boy.' Doreen reached up and patted Aaron's cheek. 'Now, if you want anything from me or my boys, you can have it for free. Make sure they know it's you and that I told you that, and they won't give you any trouble.' She cocked her head. 'They're good boys too.'

The only thing Aaron had wanted to hear less than an old woman telling him she'd thought Sergeant Downing and Rosa were on a date was that his mother was a good person.

'Bet you didn't expect that,' Rosa said when they finally managed to escape the woman. The sergeant had wisely found someone else to engage with.

'No.' He led them to a less populated area in the corner of the hall. 'You seem to be having a good time here.'

'It's been okay.' They took two empty seats and, for the first time, Aaron noticed she wasn't wearing his shirt.

'You've changed your clothes.'

She looked down. Immediately colour spread over her cheeks. 'I...yes.'

'The shirt?'

'Is in the car.'

'I thought you didn't have anything else to wear?'

She shrugged, which would have annoyed him if he hadn't already known that she'd had something else to wear. And maybe that was part of the reason he'd decided to accompany Sergeant Downing. Because she'd seemed to... want something of him.

Though the tinge of jealousy at Sergeant Downing's words and the panic that had risen with the D-word had contributed to his decision too.

'You know that's technically not my shirt.' She made a non-committal noise. He almost smiled. 'So you stole it for nothing.'

'I didn't steal it.' She looked over at him and something on his face made her roll her eyes. 'You're teasing me.'

'I'm asking.'

'I didn't steal it,' she said again. 'I…kept it. As a memento.'

'Of what?'

'This weekend.'

'It's been terrible.'

She laughed. That sound had always weakened something inside him. And he realised that she hadn't laughed nearly as much as he'd have liked since they'd been on the island.

'You're right,' she answered. 'But… If this was going to be the last time you and I spend any time together, I wanted to remember it.'

'Even if it was terrible?'

'Even if it was terrible.'

'Why?' he asked after a moment.

'Because it hasn't always been terrible,' she replied, surprising him with her answer. 'We were happy.'

'Yeah, we were.'

'The way things ended,' she said suddenly, her eyes meeting his. The emotion there stole his breath. 'It had nothing to do with the way things were, okay?'

'I'm not sure I can believe that.'

'You have to.' She reached out, took his hand. 'I told you. All of it… It's my fault. I'm the reason things ended badly. Me. It has nothing to do with you.'

'You felt like you had to leave.'

'It's not that simple.'

'It is to me.'

He turned his hand over so that their fingers intertwined.

'I know you see things in black and white.' Her gaze was on their hands. 'If something went wrong between us, it's because someone did something wrong. But...that isn't what happened here.'

'Maybe,' he said. 'But you said it was a mistake marrying me.'

'Only because I shouldn't have put you in this position in the first place.'

'This is—was—a marriage, Rosa. You didn't put me in any position. I chose to be here. We both did.'

'But I shouldn't have.' Her words were soft. Insistent. 'You deserve more than this. You deserve more than *me*.'

His grip tightened on hers as surprise fluttered through him. 'That's not true.'

'It is.'

She blinked and stared ahead at the crowds of people, though he didn't think she saw any of them. And suddenly he thought how strange it was that they were sitting here, in the corner of a hall in a small town, surrounded by strangers, having the kind of conciliatory discussion they hadn't been able to have when they'd been alone.

'I might turn out just like her, Aaron.' She said it so softly he thought he'd imagined the words. 'I might turn out to be exactly like my mother.'

'You won't.'

She turned to him, the smile on her lips unbearably sad. 'You don't know that. The cancer scare...it could be the first of many. Or it could lead to actual cancer.'

'Because she had it?'

'Yes.' She paused. 'And because I refused to take the test to screen for it after she died.'

Silence slithered between them. He wanted to break it.

To keep the momentum of their conversation—her honesty—going. But his mind was still processing what she'd said. He couldn't think what to say to keep the silence from choking them.

He saw her more clearly now. Understood the extent of the terror she must have gone through. The blame she'd taken on herself. Her cancer scare took on a deeper meaning. Again, he wished he could have been there. Didn't understand why she hadn't turned to him.

'Why did you refuse?'

She lifted her shoulders. 'I'm not sure.'

But he could see that that was a lie. She knew why she hadn't taken that test. She just wasn't ready to talk about it. Pain drenched his heart.

'Did your mother ever see someone about...' He trailed off, unsure of whether she'd answer. But she didn't seem to mind.

'Sometimes. When it got really bad I'd be able to talk her into seeing a psychologist.'

'Did it help?'

'For as long as she went.' She paused. 'But when she got to that point—when she actually decided to go—it had already got so bad that she had no choice but to acknowledge something was wrong.' She wrapped one arm around herself, held her chin up with the other. 'The therapy would help, then she wouldn't experience such intense symptoms for long enough that she could convince herself that she was fine.' Her eyes met his. 'It was a vicious cycle.'

He nodded. 'And you...?'

'Have I seen someone?' She laughed dryly and dropped the hand at her chin. 'No. That would entail admitting something was wrong.' The laughter sobered. 'No, I'm too much like my mother to let that happen.'

'You've already told me,' he reminded her softly.

'Only because I wanted you to know that none of this—'

she waved a hand between them '—is because of you. And, trust me, it was hard enough telling you.'

He knew it had been. Which was why it meant so much to him. Even if there were some things she was still keeping from him.

Hope began to bandage some of the pieces of his heart together again. Perhaps foolishly. But his black and white view of things told him that they'd identified the problem. And, since they had, maybe they could find the solution...

'We should probably stop being so antisocial,' he said suddenly.

She blinked. 'What?'

'Let's go talk to your friend.' He stood, held out a hand to help her up.

'My friend—Charlie?' He nodded, and was proud that he managed to keep himself from rolling his eyes. 'Why?'

'Because when I walked in here you looked happy to see him.'

She gave him a strange look, but took his hand and stood. 'You're not going to try and get on his good side and then beat him up, are you?'

He smiled. 'No.' Though that wasn't a bad idea.

'I'm not sure I trust this change in attitude.'

'You should,' he said, serious now. 'You need happy. If happy means you talk to a man and the old woman who believes that the two of you should be together, then that's what we'll do.'

She stared at him and then a smile crinkled her eyes. It hit him as hard as her laugh had. More, when she reached a hand up to his cheek and stood on her toes to press a kiss to his lips.

'I knew I didn't deserve you,' she said softly, the smile fading. And then she took his hand. 'Come on. Let me introduce you to some new friends.'

CHAPTER TWELVE

ROSA HAD THOUGHT that the term 'new friends' would cause Aaron to give up his appeasing mood and run far, far away.

Except it hadn't. In fact, right at that moment, she was watching him engage in a conversation with Charlie about some legal show they both happened to enjoy.

Of course, for Aaron that meant that he said one sentence—sometimes that sentence would take the form of a single word—and letting Charlie speak several others before he spoke again.

It was charming—though it drove her crazy when it was directed at her. But since it wasn't now—and since he was engaging for her sake—she found it extra charming. Found *him* extra charming.

She'd been talking to another friend of Charlie's while said engaging was happening, but the woman had excused herself minutes ago, leaving Rosa to witness Charlie and Aaron's conversation. But it also gave her time to think. To consider what it meant that she'd told him the truth of why she'd left and he hadn't reacted the way she'd expected.

Except now that she'd told him, and had seen his reaction, she wasn't sure what her expectation had been. Had she thought he would agree to end things between them because she might be ill like her mother? Or had she expected him to stay, to support her, and *that* had been what she'd feared?

She didn't know. Both seemed equally fearsome to her now. Both seemed like valid arguments.

Because of what she'd been through with her mother, she still couldn't make a decision to save her life. Literally. She didn't want that for Aaron. Nor did she want him to go back to being afraid of life, of love because his life had taught him to be. Because the people in his life—because almost losing his mother—had forced him to protect himself.

Aaron's eyes met hers and he gave her a small, indulgent smile. Something swelled inside her. Guilt, she thought. Because, by leaving, she hadn't proven to Aaron that living and loving were worth it. Danger, too. Because something swelling inside her meant that she wanted to.

'Rosa, you've never watched *City Blue*?'

Her eyes flickered up to Charlie's, her mind taking a moment to play catch-up before she shook her head. 'No. Legal dramas are more Aaron's thing.'

'And what's your thing? *South Africa's Next Top Model*?' Charlie asked with a wry grin, but her gaze had already met Aaron's and they were both smiling when she answered.

'Yes, actually.'

Charlie looked between them. 'You're serious?'

'Rosa's a designer,' Aaron said. 'Shows like *South Africa's Next Top Model* are like drugs to her. Either she gets ideas for her new designs or she gets to picture herself designing the clothes the models wear.'

Charlie blinked, though Rosa couldn't tell whether it was because that was the most that Aaron had said during their conversation, or because he was surprised by the information her husband had supplied.

'I immediately regret my dismissive comment now,' Charlie said, rubbing a hand over the back of his neck.

'Don't worry,' Rosa said with a chuckle. 'It takes more than that to offend me.'

As she said it, the lights in the room flickered. Moments later, a woman walked into the hall and announced that the electrical grid was up and running one hundred per cent again.

'Storm's calming too,' Charlie said, looking up at the windows. There was barely a beat between his words and his radio crackling. He spoke in quick, short sentences and, by the time he was done, he offered them an apologetic smile.

'Duty calls. It was lovely meeting you both.' He shook their hands. 'When are you guys leaving?'

'Monday,' Aaron answered.

Charlie nodded. 'Well, shout if you need any more help. Though I wouldn't recommend shutting yourselves in rooms any more, okay?'

He gave them a quick smile before walking off, leaving a strange, not quite awkward but not easy silence behind him.

'We should probably get back too,' Aaron said finally.

'And I should find somewhere else to stay.' But she didn't move.

'You know you don't have to.'

Her gaze met his. 'You're...okay with having me there?'

He nodded. She bit her lip and wondered what she would be getting herself into if she agreed to go back to the house with him.

Danger.

Except not going back with him would be throwing away the progress they'd made that evening. She wasn't sure why that progress was suddenly so important—what did it matter, if she still intended to leave him when this was all over?—but it had her nodding and handing him the keys to the car.

They made the trip back to the house silently and when they pulled into the garage Rosa held her breath. She didn't know what to expect from him. Didn't know what *he* expected. And holding her breath seemed to help still the sudden drastic beating of her heart. And the sudden trembling anxiety in her stomach.

'We should go in.'

She forced herself to breathe. 'Yes.'

Silence pulsed between them for another few moments, and then he turned to her. 'How does a movie night sound?'

* * *

It was like old times. Which was probably a thought he should steer away from, especially since old times hadn't involved Rosa pressed against one side of the couch with him at the other.

Old times would have her curled up against him. Old times would have meant they wouldn't be resisting the electricity sparking between them. If it *had* been old times, Aaron would have pulled Rosa into his lap ages ago and done something constructive—something enjoyable—with the restless energy flowing through his veins.

But it *wasn't* old times. Though there *was* something between them now that hadn't been there before. He couldn't put his finger on what. Couldn't place how he felt about it. Or how the divorce discussion they'd had earlier had contributed to it.

How it had shifted something inside him. As though that something was desperately shunning even the *thought* of ending their marriage.

So he sat there, ignoring it all, pretending to watch the movie.

An explosion went off onscreen—the final one, thankfully—and the movie ended with a close-up of the hero and heroine kissing.

He rolled his eyes.

'You didn't like it?' Rosa asked with a slanted smile.

'I've seen better.'

'Yeah?' That smile was still in place. 'Like… *City Blue*?'

'Movies,' he clarified. '*City Blue* is a series.'

'And it doesn't compare?'

'It's much better than this.'

'Oh.' Her smile widened now, and his heart rate slowly increased.

'You're teasing me.'

'How can you tell?'

His lips curved. 'I've missed this.'

He cursed mentally when the easiness of their banter dissipated and her smile faded.

'Me too,' she replied softly after a few moments, and when their eyes met he swore he felt fire ignite between them.

Suddenly, he was reminded of that kiss they'd shared earlier. How it had been comfortable but had displaced something inside him. How it had soothed him just as it had spurred him on.

His fingers curled into his palms as he remembered how soft her skin had felt under them. As he remembered the way her curves felt. Slopes and indents and bumps unique to her that made his body ache and his heart race.

'Maybe…' she said hoarsely, before standing up slowly. She cleared her throat. 'Maybe I should make some tea.'

'The only kitchen that's stocked is the one on the top floor.' His voice was surprisingly steady.

'Okay. Just don't let the door shut behind us.'

She left him without checking that he was following and, a little helplessly, he did. He worried when a voice in his head questioned whether he'd follow her anywhere. Felt alarm when his heart told him he would.

Run, he told himself. It would be best to run, to get away from the temptation of her. But his feet kept following. And his eyes ran over the curves his hands had only just remembered touching.

She had swapped her jeans for pyjama pants he'd found in his cupboard, though she'd kept the top she'd worn earlier. The pants were baggy, ill-fitting, and yet he could picture the lower half of her body so clearly she might as well have been naked.

He shook his head and stayed at the door when they reached the top floor. He leaned against the wall. Watched her go through the motions of making tea.

'I didn't mean you have to stand there like a stalker,' she told him after putting on the kettle.

'I'm keeping the door from shutting.'

'Which I'd appreciate more if you didn't look like a creep doing it.'

He shifted his body. 'Better?'

Her lips curved. 'Was that your attempt at making yourself less creep-like?'

He smiled. 'It didn't work?'

She laughed. 'Not as well as I think you think it did.'

They smiled at each other, and then she drew her bottom lip between her teeth and turned away.

'Rosa?' he asked softly.

'It's nothing,' she replied. And then the click of the kettle went off and she sighed. 'I just… I keep thinking about what Doreen said about your mother. About how she did good things sometimes.'

He stiffened. 'What about it?'

'Well, don't you think that maybe this is one of those things?' She poured the water into two mugs, avoiding his eyes.

'I don't know what you mean.'

'You do.' Now she did meet his eyes, but she looked away just as quickly and replaced the kettle on its stand. 'But, since you're probably going to keep pretending you don't, I'll tell you.' She stirred the contents of the mugs before removing the teabags and adding milk. 'Bringing us together this weekend. Forcing us to talk.'

'She might have brought us here together, but she didn't force us to talk.'

'We both know it would have happened.'

'Not in the way it has.'

She walked to him with the two mugs, handed him his before switching off the lights. Everything went dark except for the stars in the sky, clear now that the rain had stopped.

'It really is beautiful up here,' she said after a moment. He looked around the room his mother had designed with an architect and grudgingly agreed.

'Better now that we're not trapped.'

'Yes,' she said, turning back to him. His eyes had adjusted to the darkness, allowing him to see her half-smile. His heart shuddered as their eyes held, and then she looked away. 'We should get back down before our tea gets cold.'

'You don't want to have it up here?'

'And have you stalk me while I drink it?' She smiled. 'No, thank you.'

His lips curved as he followed her down the stairs, careful not to spill the tea. She led them to the living area on the first floor. It was pretty here too, he thought, taking in the tasteful décor, the view of the beach through the windows.

His family had owned this house for decades, though his mother had made a lot of changes over the years. Some—like the top floor and the décor on the current floor—he'd agreed with. Others—like the incredibly excessive water feature she'd installed in the garden—she should have let go.

'I get that the talking is us,' she told him. Her expression was careful, and he wondered what she saw in his face when he hadn't realised she'd been watching him. 'But would we have talked if your mother hadn't tricked us into being here?'

He didn't reply immediately. 'I know that sometimes she means well.' It was almost painful to admit. 'But this—you and I—and Doreen... Those cases are few out of many.'

'Don't they count?'

He gripped the mug between his hands. 'My mother hopes for the best when she does things. She doesn't think them through.' He stilled. 'Those people she invited to live here could have been criminals. They could have taken everything in here. Or worse.'

He tried to relax his jaw, and then continued carefully.

'You have to think about the consequences of your actions. That's how life works.'

'Speaking as someone who can act without thinking about consequences,' she said slowly, 'I think you need to give her a break.'

'You might act impulsively sometimes, Rosa, but you don't expect other people to bear the brunt of those decisions.'

'Sometimes I do,' she said quietly. 'I have. With you.'

CHAPTER THIRTEEN

'WHAT DO YOU MEAN?' There was an urgency in the question that had the answer spilling from her lips.

'Things would have been different for us if I'd had that test done.'

'How?'

'I wouldn't have worried as much about the lump. I wouldn't have felt as though I had to leave to protect you from it. From me.' She rubbed her arms. 'I wouldn't have doubted my decisions. Every one of them, since my mother died.' She laughed breathlessly. 'Since long before it, actually. But then it was for different reasons.' She shook her head, hoping her words made sense to him. She took a breath. 'We wouldn't be here if I'd had that test done.'

'Wouldn't we?'

It was the only comment he made. She'd ripped her heart out to tell him that—and that was all he said.

Not that she could blame him. He was right. Their relationship would have taken this turn eventually. There'd been too many things left unsaid between them. Too many cracks in their foundation. Neither of them had noticed it before. But it would have come out eventually. And their relationship would have crumbled down around them, just as it had now.

'I'm tired of hoping with my mother.'

'What?'

'It started when I was so young I can't remember anything other than the hope.' Something unreadable crossed his face. 'But, as I got older, I realised that I'd keep hoping, even when she'd prove to me that it wasn't worth the pain. Like when she got sick. I hoped she'd change.'

Understanding he was offering her something with this, she nodded. 'But she didn't.'

He shook his head. 'It wasn't that I was hoping for too much. I just wanted her to change her behaviour so I wouldn't have to keep fixing things for her. And—' he hesitated '—I wanted her to be there for me like I'd been there for her.' He paused. 'I put my life on hold when she found out she had cancer. It made me realise how much the fact that she was my mother meant to me, however complicated our relationship was. But even a life-changing event like cancer couldn't make *her* change.' Another pause. 'She used her *birthday* to manipulate us, knowing how important it would be to you.' He shook his head again. 'It's not as easy to forgive her as you've made it seem.'

She wondered what he would say if she told him that this was part of why she'd left. He'd never told her this before, but it had clarified things for her. Because she'd sensed some of how he felt. Enough to understand that Aaron would have put his life on hold for her too, if she'd had cancer.

And if she'd had cancer she would have become the person she'd been running from her entire life. Anxious, bitter. Terrified of death. She would have become her mother.

The lump had catapulted her in that direction anyway. Had awoken the seed of fear she hadn't known had been buried inside her. But it had grown so quickly Rosa had known she couldn't stay. She couldn't let him see her become her mother. She couldn't let him go through that pain. Because now, hearing him say this… It made her fully appreciate how painful it would have been for him to be at her side.

'Aaron—'

'We should get to bed,' he said, not meeting her eyes. He set his mug down, his tea untouched.

'You don't want to—' She broke off when he sent her a beseeching look, and she nodded. He'd given her enough.

He didn't want to talk about it any more. And, if she were honest with herself, neither did she.

'It's probably for the best to get to bed. To finally get a decent night's sleep.'

'You didn't sleep well last night?' he asked in a wry tone that sounded forced.

'It'll go better tonight, I'm sure.' After the briefest hesitation, she leaned over and brushed a kiss on his forehead. 'I'm sorry. For all of it.' She left before he could reply.

As she climbed into bed she heard Aaron's footsteps pass her door. When the sound stopped, she held her breath, anticipation fluttering through her. But then the footsteps continued, and she blew out the air she'd been holding in her lungs.

She wasn't sure why she'd reacted that way. Or what she would have done if Aaron had entered her room.

No, she thought, shutting her eyes. She knew *exactly* what she would have done.

And that was part of the problem.

When the sun woke Rosa the next morning, she wasn't surprised. Cape Town was famous for its unpredictable weather. And, since Mariner's Island was only thirty kilometres from Cape Town, the weather was pretty much the same there too.

Which was great, she mused, since the restlessness she'd felt the night before—when she'd thought Aaron might be coming into her room to seduce her—was still with her. But sunshine meant escape. And, right now, escape meant going for a run on the beach.

It wasn't ideal running gear, she mused as she looked at herself in the mirror. Most of what she was wearing had come from Liana's closet and, since her mother-in-law was smaller than her, the outfit wasn't quite appropriate for a run.

But the tank top would keep her boobs in place, and she'd

replaced her ridiculous lace underwear with Liana's yoga tights. Again, not ideal, but it would have to do. Though she breathed a sigh of relief when she found a long, loose T-shirt of her own that would cover most of it.

When she'd tied her running shoes—Liana's—she stepped out of the room and made her way to the front door.

'Rosa?'

She spun around, her heart racing when she saw Aaron on the couch in the front room. His shirt was only half buttoned, revealing smooth muscular skin. It stopped just below his crotch, which she hadn't noticed before. Perhaps because, before, he'd been wearing *pants*.

She cleared her throat. 'You slept here last night?'

He lifted a hand to his hair and she fought to keep her eyes on his face. 'Yeah. None of the bedrooms were…comfortable.'

She nodded. 'I'm…er…going for a run.'

'A run?' He arched a brow. 'That bad, huh?'

She managed a smile. 'Just some restless energy.'

'Up for some company?'

She shook her head. 'It won't be for long.'

'Okay.'

Though his expression was unreadable, something in his tone gave her pause. And then it hit her. He hadn't been *uncomfortable*. He'd been watching out for her. He'd slept in the front room because he'd thought *that she might leave*.

Guilt knocked the breath from her and she forced herself out of the door before she did something about it.

He kept himself busy. Which was exactly what he'd done when she'd left the last time—so he wouldn't go crazy.

Now, though, it seemed ridiculous. He'd seen what she was wearing. And she'd left without any of her things. She wasn't *leaving*, leaving. Besides, where would she go? It was Sunday; the airport was still closed. She couldn't escape Mariner's Island even if she wanted to.

He clenched his jaw and continued preparing their breakfast. Ignored the voice that mocked him for being so desperate about not letting his wife leave him that he'd slept on the couch.

When he heard the front door open, the air began to move more easily in and out of his lungs. He made coffee and, by the time she came upstairs after a shower, had a cup ready for her.

'Did it work?' he asked as he handed her the cup. Her mouth curved. So, she wasn't going to pretend she didn't know what he was talking about.

'A little.'

'You were gone a while.'

'I was coming back.'

'I know.'

But something pulsed between them that confirmed she knew he hadn't been sure of it.

'How is it outside?'

She quirked a brow. 'Are we talking about the weather now?'

A faint smile claimed his lips as he nodded. 'Unless you have something else you want to talk about?'

'Oh, no,' she said dryly. 'The weather's fine. It's cool, with a south-easterly wind. Not quite swimming weather, folks.'

His smile widened. 'You sound exactly like her.'

'Cherry du Pont,' she said with a smile. 'The weather woman we listened to every morning for years.' She lifted a shoulder. 'I should hope I know what she sounds like.'

'Have you been listening to her by yourself?'

He wasn't sure what had made him ask it. And when she tilted her head, studied him, he was sure she didn't want to answer it. Surprise fluttered through him when she did.

'Some days. When I felt—' her eyes swept away from him '—when I felt lonely, or missed you.' She shifted away from the table, went to the glass door overlooking the beach. 'Most days, actually,' she continued. 'But then I'd force myself out of it, and start working. I managed to do an entire line that way.'

She gave him a cheeky smile over her shoulder and looked back at the beach before he could smile back. Good thing, as he wasn't going to smile back. No, he felt as if he could barely move, could barely *think* over her words echoing in his head.

When I...missed you... Most days...

He wanted to ask her why she hadn't come back then. Didn't she think they could be saved? Didn't she think that whatever she was going through they could go through *together*?

'It was because of you that I did it,' she said, breaking through his thoughts.

He cleared his throat. 'What was because of me?'

'The line.' She turned back now and walked to the stack of French toast he'd made earlier. She put two slices on a plate and squeezed honey over it.

'What does the line have to do with me?'

She looked at him and he saw understanding flood her eyes. She knew what her words had done to him. Perhaps that was why she kept talking.

'The line. For bigger women.' She went to the couch with her coffee and her toast.

He stacked his own plate with toast and bacon, and then went to sit opposite her. 'Why now?'

'I don't know.'

'Rosa.'

She looked at him. 'It's not an easy reason.'

His stomach clenched. 'Tell me.'

'I don't think—'

'Rosa,' he said again. He injected as much patience as he could into his tone, and unspoken words passed between them.

Tell me.

You won't like it.

Tell me anyway.

'I guess… Well, at first it was practical. And the reasons that had kept me from doing it were no longer much of an issue. Being a prominent lawyer's wife had done wonders for my own designs. And the people who wore them because of your mother.' She gave him a smile that was marked by sadness. 'Anyway, it seemed like the right time to do it.'

'At first,' he said quietly. 'You said at first.'

'And you would pick up on that, wouldn't you?' she asked in the same tone. But she nodded. 'It also…made me feel close to you.'

Surprise and emotion punched his heart. He nodded. 'Okay.'

'Okay,' she repeated, though it wasn't a question. And that was the last thing either of them said for a while.

They started eating in silence and by the time they'd finished their meal he realised it was his turn. He debated what would be the best way to tell her. Began speaking before he'd fully decided.

'The expansion,' he said, setting down his plate. 'It's a firm in Cape Town.'

'Cape Town?'

He nodded. 'Frank's been nagging me for a while. It seemed like the right time.'

They'd both used that phrase to explain what they'd been doing while they'd been away from one another. And now that Aaron had said it he realised that the 'right time' merely meant that they'd needed to occupy their time. With things that felt like work but reminded them of each other.

'In hindsight, maybe going for a run wasn't such a good

idea,' Rosa said suddenly. He turned in time to see her set down her empty cup and plate and push back her hair. Her face was a bit pale and when she looked at him her eyes were dim.

'You're not feeling well?'

'I feel...off.' She shifted to the front of her seat. 'Though that could be because I went for a jog. It's...been a while.' She gave him a weak smile.

'You should rest.'

'Maybe,' she replied with a frown. And then she stood and when he saw that she wasn't entirely steady he moved beside her and told her to lean on him.

'This is probably an overreaction.' He grunted in response. 'I'm fine, really.'

He looked over at her as he led her to the bed. 'You're tired.'

'So are you.'

He grunted again.

'We're not letting each other sleep very well, are we?'

'You're going to sleep now.'

'That sounds like a threat.'

'It is.' But he smiled at her and said softly, 'Get some sleep.'

'Okay.'

He watched as she settled down. Felt an ache in his heart that he'd ignored for months but couldn't any more. He didn't know how long he sat at the edge of the bed, making sure she was okay. But when he shifted to leave he felt a hand on his forearm.

Her eyes were still closed when he looked back, but her grip on his arm was firm. And after a short moment of deliberation he let himself relax beside her.

A mistake, he knew instantly. There were boundaries, as she'd said, and he wanted now, more than ever, to keep those boundaries. He understood them. Because they didn't know where they stood with one another. *He* didn't know.

And, he considered as he held his breath as Rosa snuggled back against him, he didn't think she did either.

What he needed to do was get up and go downstairs. He needed to put distance between them. So that when, the next day, they left and went back to the separate lives they'd forged for themselves it wouldn't hurt as much.

And he thought it might not. Now that he knew the circumstances of why she'd left, he realised that it had less to do with him and more to do with her. Logically. Except it still *felt* as if it was to do with him. Just like he'd thought it was for every moment of those last four months.

Since he couldn't stop himself from feeling it, he figured there must be some truth in it, regardless of what she said. And, honestly, he couldn't blame her.

CHAPTER FOURTEEN

WHEN ROSA WOKE it wasn't entirely dark, but it wasn't light either. She took some time to realise that she'd slept most of the day away, and it was now dusk.

But it seemed the sleep had done its work. The fatigue she'd felt earlier had lifted somewhat and she didn't feel as listless. It wasn't a surprise that she'd felt that way. She had stepped into the rain like a fool—and she swore she'd feel the effects of that soon—and she hadn't slept well over the last two nights.

She should thank Aaron for forcing her to sleep, she thought, and then started when there was a movement next to her.

Her breath whooshed from her lungs. It was *Aaron*. Aaron was *sleeping beside her*. She searched her mind for any memory of how that had come to be, and nearly groaned when she remembered grabbing his arm as she'd fallen asleep.

It had been a reflex, and she hadn't meant much by it. No, she thought with a silent groan. That was a lie. Her sleepy self had just had the courage to do what she couldn't when she was awake.

Cling to him. Ask him not to leave her.

It was ridiculous, she told herself as she shifted so that she could see him better. She'd left him. And for good reasons too. Though, for the life of her, at that moment Rosa couldn't remember one of those reasons.

Her hand had lifted without her noticing it and now her fingers were tracing his forehead, down the side of his cheek. Her thumb brushed over his lips and her heart thudded at the memories of what those lips had done to her.

Moreover, it craved the healing those lips had done. How they'd kissed away her tears when her mother had died. How they'd comforted her as he'd kissed her temple at her mother's funeral.

She'd got through so much because he'd been there for her. Those lips, kissing, comforting, yes, but because of *him*. Because of his presence. Because of his steadfastness.

She blinked at the tears that burned in her eyes and her hand lowered. Over the curve of his Adam's apple, into the cleft at the base of his neck. Her fingers fluttered over the collarbone on each side, before resting between them. He wore another shirt, though this one was flannel, the kind she knew he wore on casual occasions.

The top buttons were open and she saw her fingers shake more as they scooped down to the edge of the skin that those buttons revealed. It was just enough for her to see the slope between his pecs, and she remembered all the times she'd rested her head there, listening to his heart, being calmed by it.

Without thinking about it, she undid another button and was about to slide her hand in, so that she could feel his heart again—so that she could have that calmness again—when his fingers closed over hers.

She sucked in her breath, felt her skin flush with the embarrassment of being caught caressing the man she'd left while he was sleeping.

'What are you doing?' His voice was husky, sexy, sending a shiver down her spine.

'Nothing,' she replied, breathier than she wanted.

'It didn't feel like nothing.' His eyes opened and she nearly gasped at the need she saw there. At that intense look in his eyes that had always meant one thing.

Resist.

But she could feel herself falling.

'It…wasn't nothing,' she said helplessly. She tugged at the hand he held in his grip, but he wouldn't let go.

'What was it?'

'Memories,' she whispered, giving up now. She flattened her hand under his, let her fingers spread across his chest.

'Of…us?'

'Of you. And how often you've made me feel…better than I should.'

'When?'

'Always.'

'That can't be true.'

'It is.' She took a breath and shifted up so that their eyes were in line with one another's. 'You know now that I didn't leave because of you.'

His eyes darkened and his other arm went around her waist, pressing her closer to him. It was seduction, though she didn't understand how it could be.

'No.'

'Aaron—'

'Rosa.' His expression was serious and she stopped herself from interrupting him, knowing that he needed to speak. 'You left because there was something about me that you didn't want.'

'I left because I didn't want you to see how broken I was,' she corrected him softly, and used her free hand to press against his cheek. 'I didn't want you to be me and I didn't want me to be—'

'Your mother.'

'Yes.'

'You didn't have to leave,' he said after a moment.

'I know. And if I'd told you whatever I was feeling you would have told me that too. But I know you. And I know that you're…committed to making things better for other people.'

'I'm committed to you,' he replied simply. 'You're my wife.'

'And that's why I had to leave. I didn't want you to have to…to have to be responsible for me too. To take care of me when you shouldn't have to.'

'That's what you thought?' He pushed himself up against the pillows. 'You thought that this—us—would somehow end up being like the relationship between me and my mother?'

'I didn't at the time,' she admitted softly. 'Up until last night, I don't think I did. I thought I was doing it because I was saving you from something. Protecting you from being me in the relationship I had with my mother. But I see now that part of it was just trying to keep you from… from being *you*.'

His face tightened and a pain she didn't understand shone in his eyes. 'I'm sorry.'

'Why are you apologising?' she demanded, unsteady from the emotion.

'I've made you cry.' His hand lifted to brush the tears from her cheeks.

She blew out a breath. 'That wasn't you.'

'Hard to convince me of that when you're crying in my arms while talking to me.' He smiled, but it wasn't the easy smile he usually gave her. And it…bothered her.

'Aaron, it's never you.' She moved again, and this time she propped her head on his chest, on her hands, and looked him in the eye. 'You're the best thing that's ever happened to me.'

He nodded, though she didn't think he believed her. She was about to open her mouth to try and make him understand again when he looked beyond her and a more genuine smile claimed his lips.

'We might just have weathered a bad storm on Mariner's Island, but that won't keep the locals from celebrating.'

She followed his gaze and sat up with a gasp when she saw the fireworks go off on the beach. Though it was some distance away, they could see it clearly and the silence as they watched made the tension following their conversation settle.

She leaned back against him and sighed with pleasure at the simplicity of the moment. Somewhere in her mind she thought that perhaps she hadn't only been tracing the shape of his face, letting the memories wash over her when he'd been sleeping. No, now she thought that she'd been memorising it. Just like she was memorising that very moment so she could go back to it some day.

And with that thought something loosened inside her and, though her mind told her it was a terrible decision, she ignored it. Much like she ignored every warning it would give her when she was about to do something rash. When she was about to do something possibly stupid.

'You never needed an excuse, you know,' she said, turning to him and moving until she was sitting on her knees facing him.

'For what?' he asked carefully.

'To kiss me.'

His eyes went hot. Seduction, she thought again. 'You mean I don't have to dance with you to kiss you?'

'Yes.'

'Okay.' But he didn't move.

She cleared her throat. 'That was an invitation.'

'I know.'

'So…?'

He shook his head. 'You don't need an excuse either. If you want me to kiss you, you're going to have to do it yourself.'

She understood why he wanted that from her. He wanted her to make the decision. He wanted her to cross the line. Which was fair, she considered. He'd kissed her the first time, when they'd been dancing. And she'd been the one who had put the line there in the first place.

With an exaggerated sigh, she leaned forward and slid a hand behind his head. 'Just like our first kiss,' she whispered as she brought her lips closer to his. 'Seems like I have to do everything myself.'

And then they were kissing—falling—and it didn't matter who'd started it, only that they had.

He hated himself for what he was about to do. Hated it because he'd slept on a couch the night before to prevent *her* from doing it. But he didn't have a choice. And though the voice in his head told him that that was a lie—that it was an excuse and he *did* have a choice—he was going to do it anyway.

With one last look at Rosa sleeping naked beside him—accepting the longing, the guilt—Aaron got up and made a few calls. Then he packed everything he'd brought with him and forced himself to leave the house without saying goodbye to her.

She'd understand, he told himself as he got into his car and drove away from the house—from his wife. She'd understand that he couldn't deal with what had just happened between them. What he saw now had been inevitable from the moment he'd seen her—in that gold dress, in her sexy shapewear, in his shirt, her jeans, that running gear.

From their *kiss*.

But she'd understand that he couldn't deal with the intimacy, the passion, the *love* that had been clear in what they'd just done. That he didn't want any of it to be spoilt by a discussion of what would happen next.

So he'd left.

It was Monday morning—early, yes, but the airport would be open—so he *could* leave. He'd called his plane and, though it would take some time for it to get there, he'd rather wait at the airport than at the house. With the prospect of Rosa waking up. Realising what was happening. The inevitable confrontation. The inevitable conversation…

He was trying to avoid all that. For both of them. He would be saving them both from the pain, the heartache.

So why did he still hate himself for doing it?

CHAPTER FIFTEEN

IT HAS BEEN a month since Aaron had left her alone in that bed. A month since they'd made love. A month since she'd woken up to find herself naked and alone.

The last thing Rosa wanted was to be in Aaron's office now, *especially* thinking of that weekend. It made the fact that *he'd* left *her* this time worse than when she'd left him.

At least that was what she told herself.

But she *had* to think of it in that way. In *any* way that would make her feel better about the turn her life had taken in the last month. If she'd had a choice, she'd still be in Cape Town. Safe, away from Aaron. She'd still be working on her line. On her life.

Instead, she was in Johannesburg, in her husband's office—*the husband who'd left her alone and naked after they'd made love*—waiting for him so that she could tell him her news and return to that life she'd created for herself in Cape Town.

Her stomach tumbled when she thought that that might not happen after she told Aaron her news.

The door opened, distracting her as Aaron entered the room. Just as handsome as ever, she thought. More so when he was surprised. She almost smiled at his widened eyes. At the way he tensed.

Good.

And then her stomach heaved in a way that had nothing to do with nerves, and she gritted her teeth. She would do this without throwing up. She couldn't give him that power too.

'Rosa,' he said in a calm tone, but she heard the subtle quaking. 'What are you doing here?'

Fairly certain the contents of her stomach were back where they belonged, she replied, 'I've come to see you, darling husband.' She stood up—dramatic flair had always made her feel more confident. 'At least that was what I told your secretary. Turns out he still believes we're a married couple.'

'Of course he still believes it,' he said in a low voice, closing the door behind him. He set his briefcase on the chair next to the door and walked directly to his bar. 'That's what we are.'

'Could have fooled me,' she said through her teeth. 'I didn't realise married couples left each other naked after a passionate night of reconciliation without so much as a word.'

His skin darkened slightly. 'Don't.'

'Why not?'

'You're not as innocent as you're making it seem.'

He took a healthy sip of the alcohol. Jealousy stirred inside her. She would have liked to have something to dull her nerves before she told him. Hell, she would have liked to dull everything inside her. Except, in her current state, she couldn't.

Which brought her back to the real reason she was there.

'Fortunately, I'm not here to discuss the tit-for-tat turn our marriage has taken,' she said swiftly. She walked around the desk, stood closer to the door. Closer to escape when she needed it.

'Then why are you here?'

'Because it seems our—' she swallowed and told herself it would be best just to get it out '—because our night together has led to a...consequence.'

'What con—?' He cut himself off, his eyes lowering to her stomach, and she resisted an urge to put her hand on her abdomen. She wasn't sure where that urge had come from. She'd been strangely detached from the news that there was a life growing inside her since she'd found out. Detached. Alone. The way that life had come to be—how *that* had ended—was the only explanation she could think of for why she felt that way. Or the only explanation she *allowed* herself to think of.

'Are you...' he started, and then his voice faded before he cleared his throat. 'Are you telling me you're pregnant, Rosa?'

'Yes.'

She straightened her shoulders. Drew up her spine. This was the reason she'd worn another one of her designs. Confidence. Courage. This time it came in the form of high-waisted pants and a blue shirt.

'How...how... Are you sure?'

She'd rarely seen her husband so frazzled. 'I've taken multiple pregnancy tests.' And had hated herself for it. It seemed like something her mother would have done. 'And had it confirmed by my GP. It's still early, as you can imagine. But it's there.'

'But...how did this happen?'

'I wasn't taking the Pill any more. It didn't seem necessary.'

He made a disbelieving noise. It felt as if he'd slapped her. '*What?*'

'I didn't say anything,' he snapped, and began to pace the length of the room.

'No, you didn't,' she said. 'But that sound you made implied something. Almost as if getting pregnant was some kind of plan. As if the unwilling and unknowing part I played in your mother's misguided fairy tale plan was meant to end up like *this*.'

Her stomach turned again and she held up a finger when he opened his mouth, pressing her other hand to her own mouth. The wave of nausea had barely passed before another took its place and she strode to the door of his bathroom—

thank heaven it was adjoined to Aaron's office—barely making it to the toilet in time to empty her stomach.

Which was strange, she thought as she heaved, since the only thing she'd managed to choke down that morning was a dry piece of toast and black rooibos tea. But there it went, followed by a few extra lurches of her stomach.

She flushed the toilet and sank down to the floor. It was refreshingly cool, though a moment later she felt an even colder cloth pressed to her forehead. She knew it was him before she opened her eyes. Saw the concern—and something else she couldn't place—on his face.

'I'm fine,' she said and tried to stand, incredibly aware of the fact that she hadn't rinsed her mouth. Steady hands helped her up and, exhausted, she couldn't summon the energy to be annoyed at his assistance.

She'd expected it, hadn't she? It was part of why she'd left him in the first place. Because she hadn't wanted this to be her life—to be his—if she were sick like her mother.

Ignoring the irony that had brought them to this point anyway, she asked him to get her handbag. And when he left gave herself a moment to take a quick breath before she washed her face and patted it down with the dry end of the towel he'd given her.

She was pale, she thought as she looked at herself in the mirror. The skin under her eyes looked bruised, and the light brown of her hair somehow looked darker because of it.

But she told herself not to be too concerned about it. She'd already been there, worrying about all the possibilities that had made her look and feel that way. It had pushed her into making an appointment with a psychologist, but then she'd missed her period and postponed *that* appointment in lieu for one with her GP.

Aaron returned with her handbag, and thankfully gave her space when she rummaged around in it to find the travel toothbrush and toothpaste she'd started carrying when throwing up had become the norm.

She made quick work of it, and then took another breath before walking out to face Aaron again.

'Better?' he asked in a clipped tone. She frowned. How had she possibly annoyed him by throwing up?

'For now,' she answered mildly. 'You?'

His expression darkened, and there was a long pause before he said, 'I'm sorry. I shouldn't have reacted that way.'

'You didn't really react. Besides when you implied that I somehow tricked you into making me pregnant.' At his look, she shrugged. 'You know that's how you made it seem. And, if I recall, you were as much into the activity that got us here as I was.'

Though she hadn't thought it possible, he looked even more peeved than he'd been before. Not that it surprised her. She was purposely being contrary, but it was the only way she could cope with what was happening. And again, she'd give herself permission to do just about anything if it helped her cope.

'Does this mean you're not accepting my apology?' he asked quietly, and she lifted her shoulders. 'Rosa,' he said more insistently now, and she blew out a breath.

'Yes. Fine. I accept your apology.'

He folded his arms and leaned against his desk, looking at her evenly. Back to being in control, she thought, resenting it.

'What did you hope to achieve by coming here today?' he asked.

She frowned. 'I didn't hope to achieve anything. I just came to let you know.'

'You came all the way to Johannesburg to let me know that you're pregnant?'

'Yes. Or would you have liked that information over the phone?'

He didn't react to her sarcasm. 'Thank you for coming to tell me in person.' He paused. 'But I suppose what I'm actually asking is whether this was a planned trip, or whether it was spur-of-the-moment?'

It *had* been spur-of-the-moment, something she'd convinced herself to do before she lost the nerve. So she'd booked the ticket, put on the sample suit she'd made for her line, and now she was here.

But she wouldn't tell him that.

'I came here to tell you that you're going to be a father,' she said, and saw that he wasn't as unaffected as he was pretending to be. 'Other than that… Well, no, I suppose I didn't know what else *to* achieve.'

'But you didn't think you were going to tell me and then just leave?'

Her heart started thudding, reminding her of when he'd said something similar when she'd first arrived at the house on Mariner's Island. 'I know we have to talk about things.'

'Yes,' he agreed. 'But more than that, Rosa. We're going to have to fix this marriage.'

She inhaled sharply, and then let the air out between her teeth before she replied.

'That's a high expectation from someone who didn't have any intention of doing that a month ago.'

'Did you?' he asked softly, the haughtiness of her statement not putting him off. In fact, it did the exact opposite. It told him that she was scared. And he'd contributed to that fear by leaving.

'Did I what?'

'Did you have any intention of fixing things between us after we slept together?'

She opened her mouth and then cleared her throat. It was enough of an answer. Enough that he didn't need her to say anything else.

'So I was right to make it easier on the both of us by leaving.'

'Oh, is that why you did it?' Her eyebrows rose. 'I thought you left because you wanted to make me know how it felt to be the one left behind.'

'I'm not that vindictive.'

'I didn't think so either. But I had to wonder. Karma, and all that.' She was throwing his words from the first night on the island back at him. Then she abruptly changed the topic. 'Your mother called me.'

'You...you didn't tell her?'

'No. I didn't answer, actually. And then she sent an email saying she hadn't heard from you since you got back. Asked me whether that was some form of payback. Karma?' she asked lightly.

Annoyance bristled through him. 'You know better than to listen to my mother.'

'She's right about some things, Aaron,' she said. 'She was right to bring us to that island.'

'Look where that got us.'

Her hand shifted, moving towards her stomach before she jerked it back. Something about the movement irked him. 'Yes, we're in a...situation now, but this situation is proof that we couldn't just walk away from things and hope to never face them again.'

'I didn't walk away f—'

'First?' she interrupted him. 'Yes, I know I did that. And I know that I was wrong to do that, especially without any explanation.' She bit her lip, and then blew out another breath. 'I saw that on Mariner's Island when we were talking. And I realised that I should have told you about what I was going through so that, at the very least, we were on the same page.'

Why was she being so calm now? He almost preferred the haughtiness.

'So you would have tried to fix things between us?'

'No,' she said after a moment. 'But I would have tried to make you understand why I couldn't. So that when we walked away from one another I'd be able to move forward with a clear conscience. We both would.'

'Is that what you want to do now?' he forced himself to ask. Was proud of how he'd managed to ask it without revealing the emotion that was choking him.

'Partly, yes. We have even more reason to be on the same page now. Without the past clouding things.'

'What does that mean, Rosa?' He pushed off from the table. Took a step closer to her. 'What do *you* really mean?'

'We can't fix this,' she said stiffly. 'So maybe your idea of ending things—of filing for divorce—was for the best.'

CHAPTER SIXTEEN

HE WASN'T EMOTIONALLY prepared to hear that Rosa wanted a divorce. Hell, he wasn't emotionally prepared for *anything* that had happened in his office since he'd walked in and found her there.

He'd been on somewhat of a high when he'd got there too. The case he was working on was a particularly dirty one. The husband had more than enough money and power to force his wife into divorcing him quietly. And he would have succeeded too, if Aaron had agreed to be *his* lawyer.

But the moment Aaron had met the man he'd known no measure of money or power could make Aaron represent him. Instead, he'd reached out to the man's wife and had offered to take on her case pro bono.

It had been a rocky ride—would be for some time—but that day the judge had ruled on custody. And since the husband was the ass Aaron thought he was, he'd gone for full custody based solely on the fact that his wife wanted the kids. But that day the wife had won. *They'd* won. And it had felt *damn* good.

Until he'd seen the wife he'd walked out on a month ago, found out she was pregnant and that now she wanted a divorce.

It was his own fault. He'd mentioned it before. And that had set the events in motion that had culminated in their night of passion.

But she *was* right. Things were hanging mid-air between them, and they couldn't live like that for ever. Particularly not if they were going to raise a child together.

A child.

He pushed the thought aside and told himself it wasn't

the time to think about that. Or to remember how disappointed he'd been when she'd told him about the milk duct in her breast—the lump—and that that hadn't meant she was pregnant.

One problem at a time.

Since he'd had an appointment shortly after Rosa had dropped her bombshell, he'd had to deal with work first. But they'd arranged to have dinner together that night. So they could talk about *getting on the same page*.

She was already there when he arrived, and he fought the feeling of nostalgia at seeing her there. The restaurant had been his suggestion—it was the first one that had come to mind. Unfortunately, it was also one they'd been to often when they were together. And often she'd be waiting for him to get there.

Except then she'd had a smile on her face. Her expression would be open, warm, as soon as she saw him. That was not the case now. His heart took a tumble when he saw her wary expression. The tightness, the nerves. He'd done that, he thought again, and then forced it aside and took his seat.

'You came,' she said after a moment.

'You thought I wouldn't?'

'I…wasn't sure. After what happened today.'

'We don't have many choices any more, Rosa. You and I are in this together, whether you like it or not.'

She winced, but nodded. She was still pale, and when the waiter took their drinks order she asked for black tea and water. Not her usual.

'How are you feeling?'

Her eyes lifted. 'Fine.' They were tired. And he knew that she was lying.

'Rosa.'

'What?'

'If we're going to have this conversation, then we should be honest.'

Colour flooded her cheeks but she nodded. 'It hasn't been the best experience.'

'Obviously you're suffering from morning sickness.'

'Obviously,' she repeated dryly. 'And I'm tired. Even when I wake up. Par for the course.' She lifted her shoulders, but the gesture looked heavy and a sympathy he didn't understand pooled in his belly. A fear too.

He frowned. 'I'm sorry.'

She opened her mouth and then caught him off-guard with the smile that formed there. 'I was going to say it's not your fault, but then I realised it's at least fifty per cent your fault.'

His lips curved. 'I suppose.'

Her gaze suddenly sharpened, and then she released a breath. 'It is yours.'

It took him a moment to figure out how to reply. 'I didn't think it wasn't.'

She nodded. 'I know some... Well, thank you for not doubting that.'

'Things might not be in the best state between us,' he said stiffly, 'but I don't suddenly think that you've changed.'

'And changing would be sleeping with someone else?'

The air was charged, but he couldn't tell if it was because of her words or because of the way things were between them.

'Changing would be lying to me.'

And she'd never done that, he thought, seeing the confirmation of it on her face. At least there was that. They'd had honesty between them for the longest time. And if somehow that had changed it was just as much his fault as it was hers.

It might very well have been his fault alone.

'I'm sorry,' he said after the waiter brought their drinks. He waved the man away when he mentioned food, seeing Rosa recoil at the suggestion. 'I shouldn't have left you the way that I did.'

'Why did you?'

'I already told you.'

'You told me that you left because I was going to leave.' She was watching him closely. He shifted. 'I don't believe that, Aaron.'

'You should. It's the truth.'

'Not the whole truth.' She paused. 'If you've changed your mind about being honest…'

He clenched his teeth and then reached for his drink, which thankfully had alcohol in it. He nearly hissed as the liquid burnt down his throat and then he pushed it aside, no longer interested in the courage it offered.

Fake courage, he thought, since he still had to steel himself to answer her question.

'It seemed easier.' He didn't look at her. 'And what we shared…was special. To me, at least.' He paused. 'I knew that whatever we'd say to each other about it would spoil that, and I didn't want that memory to be destroyed. So I left.'

She took a long time to answer him. Because of that, he forced himself to look at her face. Her expression was unreadable, though her hands trembled slightly as she put some sugar into the tea in front of her, stirring the liquid much longer than it required.

'You're right,' she said eventually. 'It would have.' The stirring stopped. 'But then, I don't think you leaving the next day did much different.'

She lifted her eyes and their gazes met. Clashed. But in them Aaron saw the acknowledgement that what they'd shared *had* been special. He didn't know if the effect that had on his heart was good or bad, all things considered.

'I'm sorry.'

She lifted her hand, as if to brush his apology away, and then dropped it again with a nod. 'Okay. It's in the past. Let's move on.'

There was an expectant pause after those words, as if she were waiting for him to say something that would do just that. Except he couldn't. Not immediately. His thoughts were too closely linked to the past. His feelings too.

He fought through.

The child.

'What are we going to do about the baby?'

She'd lifted her cup to her lips, but lowered it slowly after his question. Still, her hand shook. He resisted the urge to lean over and grip it.

'We're going to have it.' He nodded. He hadn't been concerned about that. He knew where they both stood on that issue. 'But, other than that, I… I don't know.'

Her grip tightened on the cup and he watched as she forcibly relaxed it.

'So let's take it one step at a time,' he said slowly. The temptation to make the decisions for her—to take the pain of it away from her—was strong. 'Your pregnancy.'

'Yes.' She blew out a breath.

'Where do you want to live during that time?'

'I…haven't thought about it. I have a flat in Cape Town. I suppose I'll live there.'

Panic reared its head, but he reined it in. 'Okay. Do you have friends out there?'

She gave him a strange look. 'Yeah, a few.'

'So they'd be able to help you through…this.'

'I suppose. I mean—' She broke off. 'It's not their responsibility.' He waited as she processed it, and then she sighed. 'Not this again.'

'What?'

'You know what, Aaron.' She pushed away her cup. 'You're trying to make me think that this—that I am your responsibility. I thought we were over that. I'm not your responsibility. I make my own choices.'

'I didn't say that you don't,' he replied with a calmness

he didn't feel. Her words spoke to that inexplicable fear he'd had since seeing her on the ground after she'd thrown up at his office. After she'd told him how poorly she was feeling now. 'But didn't you tell me that I'm at least fifty per cent responsible for this?'

She narrowed her eyes. 'I hate that you're a lawyer.'

He smiled thinly.

'So, what?' she asked, wishing with all her might that she could wipe that smile off his face. 'You're saying that you want me to move back here? To go through my pregnancy here?'

'It's an option.'

'No. No, it's not.' She shook her head, and then rested it in her hands when the movement caused her head to spin. She shut her eyes, and then opened them again in time to see a drop of water fall onto the tablecloth.

She lifted one hand to her face and realised that the water was coming from her eyes. Was she crying? Damn it, she thought, and pushed her chair back, determined to make it to the bathroom before it became obvious.

But her head spun again when she stood, and pure panic went through her when she thought she'd fall down in the middle of the restaurant. But steady hands caught her and soon she was leaning against a rock-solid body.

'I'm fine,' she said but it sounded faint, even to her.

He didn't say anything, only lowered her back into her chair. Then he gestured for the waiter.

'What are you doing?' she asked through the spinning. 'We're not done yet.'

'No,' he agreed, his face etched with concern. 'But we'll continue some other time. You need rest.'

'There is no other time,' she said and closed her eyes. When he didn't reply, she opened them again. He was watching her with an expression that told her he wouldn't indulge her, and then he was speaking to the waiter and settling the bill.

Soon he was helping her up and out of the restaurant.

She wanted to pull away and tell him that she could walk by herself. But she wasn't sure that was the truth. The last thing she wanted was to fall down and make herself look even more of the fool. It was bad enough that she was basically being carried out of the restaurant.

'You can call me a taxi,' she said when they got outside. The air was crisp, and it helped to clear her head.

'You can ride with me.'

She debated wasting her energy on arguing with him, and then nodded. 'Fine. I'm at the Elegance Hotel.'

'You'll stay with me.'

'Aaron—'

'It's just one night,' he said, cutting off her protest. 'For one night you can stop fighting and just come home.'

Home. It sounded amazing, even though she wasn't entirely sure where home was any more. And perhaps it was because that made her think of her mother and sadness rolled over her in waves. Or perhaps it was because he'd been referring to *their* home and longing and nostalgia went through her.

Or perhaps it was just because his face was twisted in an expression she'd never seen on him before. And the concern—the only emotion she could identify in that expression—was as strong as on the day he'd been beside her when she'd buried her mother.

Whatever it was—all of it, most likely—it had her agreeing.

'My flight leaves tomorrow evening.'

His expression tightened, but he nodded. 'Fine.'

'Fine,' she repeated as she got into his car. And then she closed her eyes and wished she were anywhere in the world but there.

CHAPTER SEVENTEEN

AARON COULDN'T HELP the ripple of anger that went through him as he remembered how helpless Rosa had looked at that restaurant. It took him some time to realise the cause, and even then he could only put his finger on one small thing: the fact that he'd let things go too far.

He shouldn't have slept with her. He knew that and yet, every time he thought back to the day it had happened, he didn't see how he could have avoided it.

They'd somehow woven a spell around themselves that weekend. Though he didn't know how that spell had gone from hurt and accusation to a deeper understanding of their issues. Their fears.

What had been missing in their marriage to make them end up like that? It had gone so wrong, and he'd thought things had been *good* between them. But clearly there'd been layers they'd barely explored.

Those questions had kept him up at night, and each time the buck had stopped with him. And he'd been forced to realise that he'd been doing something wrong. That maybe his approach of keeping his thoughts, his feelings to himself until Rosa extracted them from him had been wrong.

He'd got it wrong. Again.

He still felt the stirring of anger when he pulled into his driveway, though now it was tainted with guilt that tightened in his stomach. He took a breath and then got out of the car, moving to the other side so that he could carry Rosa into the house.

But she was already opening her door when he got there. The look in her eyes had anger and guilt spinning in his body again, making tracks he didn't think would ever go away.

Her gaze met his, and there was a recognition there that was replaced so quickly with caution that it did nothing for the way the emotions churned inside him.

'I can walk.'

He didn't reply. Instead, he stepped aside and waited for her to get out, standing close enough that if she needed him he'd be there. It sounded like a metaphor of some kind, but he couldn't find the energy to figure it out.

She staggered slightly when she stood, and she braced herself with a hand against his chest. And then she looked at her hand, removed it and straightened.

'Thank you,' she mumbled. He made a non-committal noise in response. He waited for her to walk in front of him, and then followed. He didn't bother guiding her. He'd driven to their house; she knew her way around.

He watched as she left her handbag on the kitchen counter, kicked off her shoes and took off her jacket, hanging it on the coat rack. It was so familiar his heart stuttered, nearly stopped. He needed to get a grip.

But then, it *was* his fault. He'd been the one to bring her here. And then she went straight to the couch, sat there gingerly, and he knew he'd made the right decision.

'What can I get you?'

'Nothing.' Then she shook her head. 'Actually, I didn't get to finish my tea, and that's about all I can keep down these days.'

He nodded and went to the kitchen to make her tea. He made himself a cup of coffee, thinking that he'd had enough to drink, though a part of him disagreed.

He handed her the tea and then sat down on the adjacent couch. There was a moment of silence, when he thought they were both thinking about how weird it was. The last time they'd been there together, they'd been happy. Or not, he thought, reminding himself that the last time they'd been there together, she'd left.

His hands tightened on the coffee mug.

'I really would have been okay,' she said into the silence.

He acknowledged her words with a nod. She bit the side of her lip, held the mug between her hands.

'Thank you.'

'You're welcome.'

More silence. They should go to bed, he thought. But now, with her there, going to bed didn't feel right. Not to the bed they'd shared, and not to any of the other rooms in the house. Because she was there. She should be with him. In his bed. In *their* bed.

He hadn't spent much time there in the four months she'd been gone. He'd worked late, stayed at the office as long as he could stay awake. And when he did come home he'd sleep on the couch she was now sitting on, unable to go to their bedroom alone.

When he'd returned from Mariner's Island, he'd tried. Told himself that he had to, since *he* was the one who'd made the decision to leave now. But when he hadn't been able to sleep for the fifth night in a row, he'd realised that he hadn't made that decision at all. That it hadn't been a decision. More, it had been a defensive move. He'd leave before she left him. Again.

The thought made him nauseous.

'I'll think about staying here.' She broke the silence again. 'Which was probably your plan all along.'

'My plan would have involved more than you just staying here,' he told her. 'But I appreciate it.'

'You knew I'd agree. You've been much too quiet...'

The corner of his mouth lifted. 'It's not that easy.'

'No.' She sighed. 'But you're right. I don't have people there. Not like I do here.'

'Then why did you go there?'

If she was surprised by the question, she didn't show it. 'I didn't really have much of a plan when I left here.'

'Spur of the moment.'

Now her lips her curved. 'Partly. But mostly it was me

trying to run from what scared me most. Then,' she added almost as an afterthought, and he watched again as her hand lifted, almost moving to her stomach, and then dropping back to the mug again.

'And now?' he asked softly, compelled by her gesture.

'Now I have much more to fear.' The vulnerability in her eyes when she met his gaze knocked the breath from his lungs.

'You don't have to be scared of it. Of this.'

'Of course I do. There's so much we don't know. And this wasn't planned—'

'Isn't that when you work best?'

'Not with this. Not ever, really.' She frowned. 'I don't do the unplanned because I don't want a plan. I like plans. But for most of my life, plans haven't worked out. Or they involved things I wanted to do but that my mother's illness…' She trailed off. 'I had to be flexible. Or rebellious.'

'And…marrying me?' He forced himself to say it. 'Were you being rebellious?'

She didn't say anything for long enough that he thought their conversation was over. He was about to stand up, excuse himself when she started speaking.

'I've done a lot that I've called spontaneous. I probably would have continued calling it that if it hadn't been for our conversations. On the island. Now.' She ran a finger over the rim of her cup. 'The right word would probably be rebellious. Because that's what I was.' She lifted her eyes to his. 'Small moments of rebellion against the fact that I couldn't control so much of what was happening in my life.'

He breathed in slowly, deliberately letting the air in and out of his lungs. If he didn't, he'd probably pass out waiting for her to speak.

'Because of it, whatever I chose to do felt wrong. Whether I did it for myself or for my mother.' Her gaze fell again. 'If I did it for myself, guilt and uncertainty followed me. If I did it for my mother, it…wouldn't change anything. She'd still be sick.' She paused. 'Even after she died, I was rebelling. I didn't get the test because of it. And now I have to live with the guilt and uncertainty of that decision.'

She took a breath. 'I did things that weren't planned. Rebelled. But marrying you—loving you—was never part of that.'

The air he inhaled grew thicker, though by all rights it should have been easier to breathe. She'd told him their relationship hadn't been a mistake. Yes, things had fallen apart towards the end, but at the beginning things had been good. So why didn't that make him feel any better?

Maybe it was because all he could think about was how she'd told him she'd left because of *him*. Because of who he was.

He'd thought about that often over the past five months. Had figured it was the reason his mother hadn't responded to his efforts to make a better relationship with her too. It was probably why his father—

No. That made no sense. He didn't know his father. His father didn't know him.

His father not being around had nothing to do with him.

Except maybe it did.

'Aaron?'

It was messing with him. This whole thing was messing with him.

'It's been a rough day,' he said gruffly. 'We should get some rest.'

She opened her mouth, but then nodded. 'I'll take one of the spare bedrooms.'

'No. Take the main bedroom.'

'That's not—'

'Rosa,' he said firmly. 'Take the main bedroom.'

She let out a breath. 'Okay. I'll see you in the morning.'

She disappeared around the corner to the passage that led to the bedroom, and Aaron waited until he heard the click of the door before moving. But, instead of walking to the room he'd planned on spending the night in, he went to the sliding door, opening it to let the fresh winter air in.

He stepped outside onto the deck that gave him a perfect view of the dam the houses in their security estate had been built around. He'd known he wanted to live there the moment he'd seen it. And when one of his clients who knew the owner of the security estate had given him the details, Aaron had jumped at the opportunity to buy a property.

Months later, it had been his and Rosa's.

His and Rosa's. He'd taken that fact for granted. He'd believed that they were going to be a unit, a him-and-her-for-ever. But he'd been sorely mistaken. He realised now how often that happened. How he'd ignored it to protect himself.

He'd been mistaken when he'd thought his mother would change after recovering from cancer. That she'd be more responsible. That she'd begin to value her only son.

He'd been mistaken when he'd thought his wife would be with him for ever. When he'd believed that she hadn't left because of him—as she'd led him to believe in the early part of their visit on the island.

He'd been mistaken when he'd slept with her. When he'd been so overcome by the love he still had for her that he'd let his feelings cloud his judgement.

And now he was here—so raw that he felt as if he were made entirely of abused nerve-endings. What was wrong with him that the people in his life didn't want him? What more could he do to make them love him as much as he loved them?

He hung his head as the pain crawled through him. As it ripped its nails down him as on a chalkboard.

Because the answer was simple. He *couldn't* do anything more. Because nothing he did would change who he was. And who he was wasn't enough.

CHAPTER EIGHTEEN

IT FELT GOOD. That was the first thing Rosa thought when she woke up. Being home, waking up in her own bed… It felt good. The only thing that was missing was Aaron.

Her second thought was she was going to throw up, followed closely by the fact that she needed to get to the bathroom. She scrambled to it and made it just in time. After a solid fifteen-minute heaving session—her record so far—she brushed her teeth and stumbled into the shower.

The motions of it were so familiar that she had to close her eyes against the tears that burned. Hormones, she told herself. The intense nostalgia—the even more intense regret—were hormones.

It was the only way she could comfort herself. The only way she could lean away from the doubt. She had to believe she'd done the right thing. She *had* to.

She went back to bed after her shower, collapsing there in only her towel. The sun was shining through the glass wall opposite the bed when she clicked to clear the glass, and she almost groaned aloud when its rays hit her body, warming her skin.

She loved the light, the sun in the mornings. Loved the view of the water rippling out on the dam. She'd missed it. Hadn't realised how much until right that very moment.

Almost as much as you missed the man you shared it with.

A knock on the door interrupted her thoughts.

'Come in,' she called as she sat up. She had no energy for modesty, and was glad when Aaron's face didn't change from its usual unreadable expression when he saw her.

But her heart did soften when she saw that he had a tray with him, and that it held the usual delights for a pregnant woman. Dry toast—butter on the side as an option—and black tea.

'I wasn't sure if you were awake.'

'You didn't hear the retching noises?' she asked wryly, accepting the tray from him.

'No.' He paused. 'Were they bad?'

'No worse, no better.' She took a tentative bite of the toast and, when her stomach didn't recoil after swallowing, took another. 'Though I am beginning to feel like I'm on some cruel reality TV show where this is a delicacy.' She lifted the toast.

'*Torture*—the new show where people who love food are forced to eat only dry toast.'

She smirked, though his words had been said with a straight face. 'Sounds like a winner to me.'

Silence followed her words, and Aaron walked to the window, staring out with his hands in his pockets. He was wearing jeans and a flannel shirt again, and she studied him as she chewed the toast mechanically.

Something about his movements—his posture—worried her. Maybe she shouldn't have mentioned her morning sickness. She knew things like that bothered him.

'I'm sorry. I didn't mean to upset you.'

'You haven't.'

'No?'

He turned. 'Why do you think that you have?'

'Because…' It sounded silly now that she had to say it aloud. She took a breath. 'I know this is difficult for you.'

'What?'

'Seeing me like this.'

'Why?'

'You know why.'

'No, Rosa. I don't think I do.' He walked back to the bed and sat at its edge. 'Tell me.'

She set her unfinished toast aside and took another breath. 'Seeing me sick. It must bother you.'

'It does. But that's because I…care for you,' he finished slowly.

'And because it reminds you of your mother.'

He frowned. 'What?'

'You can't tell me watching me throw up, feeding me this—' she gestured to the toast '—doesn't remind you of how things were when your mother was ill. My mother suffered like that too,' she reminded him softly after a moment. 'I know this is…similar to the reaction to chemo. And that it must be difficult for you.'

Emotion kidnapped his once unreadable expression. It felt like an apt description when Rosa knew he wouldn't have willingly allowed his emotions to show. Nor would he have wanted her to witness it. When he met her gaze, there was a realisation there that stole her breath.

'When you found that lump—when you left—you were thinking about this?'

'I told you that.'

'No, you didn't. Not like this.' He stood. Ran his hand over his head. 'You were worried that if you'd had cancer it would remind me too much of my mother.'

She had to tell him the truth. They were long past the point where she could deny it. She nodded. 'I was protecting you.'

'From myself?'

'From…hurting like you did.' She blinked, surprised at the tears prickling her eyes. 'I saw what your mother's illness did to you. Only realised how bad it was when you started coming out of it. I couldn't do that to you, Aaron. It would have been my fault if I had too, because I chose not to get that test and—'

'And what?' he interrupted. 'If you'd got that test, the result would have changed things?'

'Yes.'

'If it had been negative, maybe. What if it had been positive?'

She had an answer for him. Of course she did. She'd thought all this through. She'd known that not taking that test had been a mistake. Had known it as soon as she'd found that lump.

But when she didn't have the words to offer him, she realised that she'd been fooling herself. That taking that test would have only changed things if, like Aaron had said, the result had been negative. There was no way she'd have been able to stay if it had been positive.

He was right. It wouldn't have changed things.

'I... I need to take a walk,' she said suddenly. 'I need some fresh air.'

He didn't answer immediately, and then he gave her a curt nod. 'I'll come with you.'

'No.'

'Last night you almost fell over in a restaurant. I'm coming with you. Thirty minutes.'

He left before she could respond, and she sucked in air as the door closed behind him. Hoped that somehow the oxygen would make her feel better about what she'd just discovered.

There was no more running from it. She had to face things now. Not only for her own sake, but for the sake of her child. Because she was having a *baby*. And that baby was dependent on *her*.

Her heart stumbled at that, and fear joined tenderness as she finally let herself acknowledge she was going to be a *mother*. She forced herself to breathe, to let air into her body again. And then, when she'd managed that, forced herself to think about her reaction.

This had all started with her own mother. All the things in her life could somehow be traced back to Violet. Rosa's decisions had been dictated by her mother's anxiety, by her illness, and then by her death. She feared making decisions because she could never figure out whether they were right. Because she'd always been torn between what she wanted to do and what she thought she should do. And that was so closely tied to her mother too.

Was it any wonder thinking about becoming a mother herself had caused her to react so strongly?

But when would she stop using that as an excuse? When would she face that *she* made her own decisions now? That *she* lived with the consequences of them?

It didn't matter what her decisions were, she always had to live with the consequences. Good, bad, she had to face them. She was facing them now. The aftermath of leaving her husband. Of conceiving a child with him.

And that last part she couldn't blame on her mother. No, *that* had all been her.

The realisation jolted her. Made her realise the extent of the excuses she'd been making for herself. Her indecisiveness had come from fear—had led to her anxieties—because she hadn't known how to live her life outside of her mother's world.

But, without her realising it, she *had* been living outside of her mother's world. She'd made a life with Aaron outside of it. But she'd left him because she'd blurred the lines between her mother's world and the one she'd created for herself. And it was time that she stopped doing that.

She could no longer use her mother's disease as an excuse not to live her life. She could no longer let it weigh down—or dictate—her decisions. She couldn't let the fear of what had happened to her mother—what might happen to her—turn her into the parent her mother had been.

She took a deep breath as tension tightened in her body. She might know these things now, but living them… That was an entirely different thing.

* * *

They were walking in silence.

He wanted to say something to break it, but nothing he thought up seemed good enough. So he waited for her to say something. Waited for her to save him from his thoughts.

They were taunting him. Chiding him. Had kept him awake all night. And now he had the added complication of knowing what she'd meant when she'd said she'd left because of who he was.

It stripped him of every illusion he'd had about himself. And he didn't know how to face it.

'I've missed this,' she said softly, closing her eyes and opening her arms to the sun.

It was so typically Rosa that his heart ached in his chest. Her eyes met his and something jumped in the air between them. And then he looked away, kept his gaze ahead of him, and heard her sigh next to him.

'Don't you get tired of it?'

'What?'

'Thinking so much.'

He almost smiled. 'Always.'

'Then why do you do it?'

'You're saying there's a way *not* to think?'

'Yep.'

'I don't think that's true.'

'Really?' The challenge in her voice made him look over. 'Because I've been known not to think, Aaron. And I have to say I'm pretty good at it.'

Now, he did smile. 'Sure.'

'Remember when I called out that guy who was acting like a complete ass at your end-of-year function?'

'My top paying client,' he offered dryly.

She grimaced. 'Sorry about that. But at least I wasn't thinking.'

'Oh, you were thinking. You just weren't thinking about the consequences.'

There was a beat between them, and he realised that that was exactly what he'd said about his mother. He opened his mouth to take it back, but she was speaking before he could.

'I was thinking that no amount of money should entitle you to treat other people like they're less than you.'

'I think my employees would disagree with you.'

'But *you* didn't,' she challenged. 'You were annoyed at losing him. And yes, I'll give you that. You had the right to be. But you didn't disagree with me. And, if I recall,' she added, 'you replaced him pretty quickly with the guy who helped us get this amazing place.'

She did a twirl with her hands out at her sides. He looked around lazily, enjoying her energy, since it seemed she'd lost some of the fatigue that she'd greeted him with that morning. In fact, he hadn't seen her like this since...since before she'd left.

Neighbours greeted them as they walked, and he nodded while Rosa waved. It was the kind of neighbourhood where people worked from home. Or ran their companies from home, he corrected himself as he took in the borderline mansion properties.

'Hey,' she said suddenly. 'Aren't you supposed to be at work?'

'I pushed my meetings for today.'

'No court?'

'Not today.' He paused. 'The mid-year function is tonight.'

She stilled beside him. 'Are you going?'

'What time is your flight?'

'Seven.'

'It begins at six-thirty.' He considered. 'I probably won't attend then.'

'You're their boss, Aaron. You can't not go.'

'I have more important things to deal with.'

'Like dropping me at the airport?' He nodded. 'No, that isn't as important as this. This…this sets the tone for the rest of the year. And it's been a rough one.' As if he needed a reminder. 'Some might even say it sets *the bar* for your company.' She nudged her shoulder against his.

He chuckled, surprising himself. Though a voice told him he shouldn't be surprised. This was exactly why he'd fallen for Rosa. Because during the worst of times—the most hectic of times—she could make him laugh.

'You have to go,' she insisted softly.

'And who's going to take care of you, Rosa?' he replied.

He'd meant who was going to take her to the airport, but instead the question came out more sombrely than he'd intended. But he realised then that he'd meant the question. And he wanted to know the answer.

Because, since the night before, he'd realised one thing: he was no longer the right person for the job.

CHAPTER NINETEEN

ROSA DIDN'T KNOW how to answer him. Her instinctive response had been that she could take care of herself. But that didn't seem like the best option any more. Not when she wasn't the only one she needed to think about.

Her hand immediately went to her stomach, and she gripped her shirt there. She felt his gaze on her before her eyes caught his, and again something shifted between them. She opened her mouth, but thunder boomed above them and they both looked up.

The sun of that morning was gone and the clouds were now an ominous grey.

'Why does it feel like everywhere we go there's a storm brewing?'

'A metaphor for the way things are between us?'

'Aaron...' She stopped when she saw the smile on his face. Felt her own follow. 'Was that a *joke*?'

'I've been known to make them,' he replied seriously, and her smile grew.

'Really? By who?'

'Everyone.' He looked up when the thunder boomed again, and held out his hand as they turned back. She took it without saying a word. She *deserved* this, she thought. She deserved this short period that had somehow turned light-hearted. That had somehow turned into a normal day for them.

'Everyone?'

'Everyone. I'll probably get the mid-year award for office jokester tonight.'

She snorted. 'Maybe...*if* everyone who used to work there has been fired and replaced by a bunch of morticians.'

'Are you saying I'm not funny?'

'No. I'm just saying that there are funnier people in the world.' She paused. 'In the country. The city. This conversation.'

She laughed when he sent her a look, and the rest of the walk was in companionable silence. She hadn't expected it, but she was enjoying it.

Though she shouldn't be, she thought. She *had* to speak with him. She had to share what she'd realised earlier that morning. It would entail putting her cards on the table. All of them. Except now, there seemed to be more cards than what she'd started with. Cards she hadn't expected.

Ones that held his laughing face, or the serious expression he'd had when he'd been trying to convince her he was funny. Ones that held that quiet, caring look he'd had when he'd asked her about who would look after her, or the annoyed expression he'd had when she'd said she'd been fine and obviously hadn't been.

Cards that reminded her how in love she still was with her husband.

They arrived at the house just as the sky opened and rain poured down. She settled into the couch as Aaron put on a fire, and felt the tension build as she prepared to be honest with him.

'How are you feeling?' he asked when he sat beside her.

'Okay.'

'Are you sure?'

Something in his voice had her frowning. 'Yeah, why?'

'Because I've been thinking,' he said softly, and her breath caught when she met his gaze. 'And I don't want to think any more.'

In a few quick movements she was on his lap, his mouth on hers.

He shouldn't have done it. And if he had been thinking properly he wouldn't have. But, as he'd told Rosa, he was tired of thinking.

He didn't want to think about how her leaving that evening sat heavily on his chest. Or how he couldn't stop thinking that he needed to convince her to stay. How he couldn't stop wanting to help take care of her, even when he might not be the best person to do so.

He didn't want to think about how close taking care of her and taking responsibility for her were. Or how much that reminded him of his mother.

He didn't want to think about the baby.

He didn't want to think about being a father.

He didn't want to think about *his* father.

He only wanted to kiss her.

And so he had.

She made a soft sound in her throat when their lips met, and it vibrated through him as his mouth moved against hers. As he savoured the taste of her—a fire, a sweetness, a combination of the two that made no sense unless he was kissing her and tasting it for himself.

She shifted so that her legs were on either side of his and tilted her head, both movements allowing their tongues to sweep deeper, allowing their connection to become more passionate.

She kissed without reservation. Without the heaviness that had always weighed each of his actions. The only time he did anything without reservation was when he was with her. When he was kissing her. Because then the only thing that mattered was that he was kissing her.

And that was the only thing he thought about.

About their lips moving in sync, and their tongues taking and giving. About the stirrings in his body, of his heart. Even in this physical act—in the touches, caresses—there was emotion. Memories. Reminders of why he'd fallen for her, and how hard. Reminders of what they'd shared and, now, of what they'd created. Together. Always together.

They were better together.

He fell into the kiss when that made him want to think again, and let his hands roam over the curves of her. He couldn't get enough. Of kneading the fullness beneath her skin. Of the bumps there, the faint feel of her stretch marks beneath his fingers. It had never been enough. It never would be. And so he took, letting his hands speak for him. Letting his touch, his kiss, say what he couldn't.

And when she pulled back, her chest rising and falling quickly, he let his hands linger on her hips, ready to take, to give when she gave the word.

But when her eyes met his he knew that that wouldn't happen. No, the anguish there, the agitation told him so.

'I made a mistake,' she whispered as tears filled her eyes. 'I made a mistake and I don't know how to fix it.'

Let me fix it for you, he thought, but didn't say. Instead, he lifted a hand to her face and let his heart take the lead. For once. 'What mistake?' She shook her head and he took a breath. 'The baby?'

'No.' A tear fell down her cheek and he brushed it away. 'No, not the baby. You.' His throat closed. His breathing stopped. And then she said, 'I shouldn't have left you, Aaron.'

A long time passed as his lungs figured out how to work again.

'How... Why...?'

It was all he could manage.

'I was scared. And I realise that now because I'm just as terrified. More.' She squeezed her eyes shut and more tears spilled onto her cheeks. 'I left because I thought I was protecting you. But I was just deciding for you.' She wiped her tears away, and his hand fell back down to his lap.

'I have an anxiety problem. Struggling to make decisions—being unable to trust them—is only a part of that. Another is being afraid I'm going to get sick like my mother did. That I'll suffer with being unable to trust my body. That some day it'll betray me anyway.' Her voice had lowered to a whisper again. 'I'm scared, Aaron. I'm scared that this baby will be born into the same kind of world I was born into. That he or she might go through what I went through. That because of me—like me—they'll worry excessively about things they don't have control over too.'

Her eyes lifted to his, the lashes stuck together because of her tears. 'I'm scared that you'll become indifferent to me like my father was to my mother. That this—' she gestured between them '—will never happen again once you realise that the uncertainty, the anxiety—the *sickness*—might not go away. That you'll stop caring.'

She'd barely finished before he pulled her closer, tightening his hold on her. He understood now that leaving him, *protecting* him, had been her way of trying to prevent that he'd stop caring for her.

He hoped that his embrace told her she didn't have to worry. That he would always care for her. That he'd be there for her whether she was sick or not. And that their kid would be too.

But he knew that this time actions weren't enough. So he loosened his hold and, when she pulled back, took her hands in his.

'You're right. You did make this decision for me and it wasn't the right one.' He paused. 'I know that part of the reason you left was because you thought you were protecting me. But I don't need protection. Not from this.'

'But—'

'Rosa,' he interrupted. 'My mother's sickness hit me so hard because…our relationship was difficult. Finding out she had cancer made me realise she was my only family. So I fought for that.' He took a breath. 'I lost some of myself because of it. I can see that now. But you helped me find that part of myself again. Because of that, I *can* be there for you. Through whatever happens.'

He struggled for his next words, unsure of how to make her see what he saw. 'Everything that happened with your mother was…terrible. But you chose to stay. Even though it was difficult, and you sacrificed a lot because of it,' he said when she opened her mouth to protest. 'Even though now you're still living with the effects of it. You stayed because your mother meant something to you. There's nothing wrong with that.'

She blinked, and another tear made its way down her cheek. It fell, dropping to his lap before either of them could brush it away.

He wanted to say more. He wanted to tell her that she meant the world to him. That he'd asked her to marry him because she did, and that he'd stand by her side for ever—that he was strong enough to—because that was what he'd vowed to do on their wedding day.

But he couldn't make that promise to her. How could he stand by her side for ever when he knew he wasn't enough for her? When his genes carried things like his mother's flightiness? With his father's disregard for family?

And how the *hell* was he supposed to be a father when the only thing he knew about fathers was that they *weren't* there?

'Aaron?' she asked with a frown. 'What is it?'

The doorbell rang before he could answer.

CHAPTER TWENTY

'YOU HAVEN'T BEEN answering my calls,' Liana said as she brushed past Aaron. She stopped when she saw Rosa on the couch, and then her face split into a smile. 'And if this is the reason, I suppose I'll forgive you.' In three steps she was in front of Rosa, pulling her into a hug. 'It's lovely to see you, darling.'

'Liana,' Rosa said with a smile. Forced, since she was suddenly feeling queasy again, and it was only partly because of her pregnancy. At least she didn't have one of those faces that stayed blotchy for long after crying. 'It's lovely seeing you too. Though I was hoping to see you a month ago. At your birthday party, which turned out to be a ruse.'

Rosa caught Aaron's look of surprise before focusing her attention back on Liana. She had the decency to look guilty.

'It's in the past now, isn't it?'

'Not quite,' she muttered, and then shook her head at Liana's questioning look. 'I wasn't able to give you your gift.'

'Oh, you know that gifts aren't necessary,' Liana said, and then waved a hand. 'Do you have it here?'

'No. I sent it by courier though. It should have been delivered by now.'

'Oh, I haven't been to the house in a while,' Liana replied vaguely, and Rosa wondered whether she should ask. But then, since Liana was there, she figured they'd find out about it soon enough. The expression on Aaron's face told her he figured the same thing.

'How long have you been here, darling?' Liana settled on the couch.

'Just since yesterday.'

Liana frowned. 'But I thought you two...' She trailed off,

likely realising that she was opening herself up to another attack by mentioning the island reunion she'd tricked them into. 'Well, then,' she said instead. 'Why haven't you been answering my calls since you got back, Aaron?'

'I was afraid you wanted something,' he replied. 'Since you're here, I suppose I'm right.'

Liana's brows lifted and Rosa felt the surprise echo in her chest. This wasn't the Aaron who dealt with his mother with resignation. Which confirmed her suspicions that something was wrong.

'I didn't realise I was such a burden,' Liana said with a huff. She didn't mean the words, Rosa knew. Liana was more self-aware than she gave herself credit for. She knew her actions burdened Aaron. Though Rosa didn't think she knew how much they hurt him.

'I'm sorry,' Aaron replied curtly. 'You're here for a visit. Do you want me to make some tea? Coffee?'

Liana's expression turned pensive, and Rosa almost smiled at how smoothly Aaron was handling his mother. They all knew now that if Liana said she wasn't there for a visit, she'd expose her lie. So Liana wouldn't come clean, though at some point she'd find a way for Aaron to fix whatever she'd done.

Again, Rosa thought about how blind she'd been to Liana's manipulations. And how much it must have bothered Aaron. How much it must have *hurt* him. But he hadn't shared any of that hurt with her because he'd known how much Liana had meant to her. That was just the kind of man he was.

Rosa would always thank the heavens that Liana had decided Cape Town held the best chances for her recovery. She would always be grateful because it had meant that Liana had been able to make the end of her mother's life better. Liana had done so much for her, for Violet, and Rosa would always love her for it.

But perhaps it was time for her to take her husband's side.

'No, thank you, darling,' Liana said. 'I was just making sure that you were still alive, really. I didn't know what to think after you stopped replying to my messages.'

'I've been busy.'

'Yes. Well.' Liana paused. 'Since you're alive and well, I suppose I can leave. Rosa, it was really lovely to see you. And—' Liana hesitated slightly '—does this mean that I'll be seeing you again in the future?'

'Always,' Rosa answered honestly, and then made a split-second decision. 'Though I was wondering… What are your plans for the rest of the day?' She saw Aaron step forward—to protest, she thought—but ignored him. 'Aaron has a function this evening and I don't have anything to wear. Would you mind taking me to find something appropriate?'

Liana clasped her hands together. '*Of course* I will. I can have Alonso drive us to the boutique immediately. I'll call Kitty. She'll have a couple of dresses waiting when we get there.'

Almost vibrating with glee, Liana took out her phone and went to make her phone calls in the kitchen. When Rosa moved to follow, Aaron caught her arm.

'What are you doing?'

'Being your wife,' she replied simply. 'And doing it the way I should have a long time ago.'

His grip tightened slightly. 'What does that mean?'

'I'm going to accompany you to your function tonight.' It was the easiest explanation.

'What about your flight?'

'I'll change it.'

Or cancel it.

'Rosa,' he breathed, and her name was a warning now.

'Don't worry,' she said, and stood on her toes to give him a kiss. When she pulled back, she saw Liana watching them with a smug smile. 'Ready?' Rosa asked her mother-in-law, and she nodded. 'See you later,' she told Aaron, and ignored his confusion as she picked up her handbag and followed Liana out of the door.

Rosa had never been a schemer, but when she'd left with his mother that afternoon she'd *definitely* been scheming.

If her answer about why she was doing it was anything to go by, she was scheming for him. And he couldn't figure out what that meant. Or how it made him feel.

All he knew was that her scheming wasn't like his mother's scheming. He trusted that, even if the very fact that she *was* scheming worried him. But Rosa was nothing like his mother. Especially since his mother had never, *ever* done any of her scheming for him.

No, he corrected himself immediately. She had. She was the reason he and Rosa were in this situation in the first place. How had he forgotten that? But then, that made it one scheme for him out of *hundreds* of schemes for other people. So perhaps this one had really only been for Rosa's sake.

He paced the floor, waiting for Rosa to return, and realised why the fact that his mother didn't scheme for him bothered him so much. Because if his mother was going to scheme for him, he wished she'd done so a long time ago.

Like when he'd been younger, and had still cared about growing up in a happy family. When he'd wanted a father, and needed a mother. But none of her schemes had done that. Which told him that she wasn't interested in scheming for him.

Because she'd never wanted him.

Just like his father had never wanted him. And just like he'd thought Rosa had felt when she'd left him.

Now that she was back—now that she'd told him why she'd left—he had to figure out how to get over all the flaws he'd discovered in himself when he'd been trying to figure out why she'd gone.

It left him feeling hopeless. As if he couldn't be a good son, a good husband, a good *father*, no matter how hard he tried.

He choked back the emotion when the door rattled and Rosa walked in. And then a different kind of emotion settled inside him, soothing what had been there before, though he knew it shouldn't.

She wore a royal-blue gown. It had a high neckline adorned with an amazing piece of jewellery, and then creased at one side of her waist before flowing down regally to the floor. The bold necklace was accompanied by matching earrings that he spotted through the spiral of curls around her face.

The colour contrast—the blue of her dress, the bronze of her skin—was striking, and his breath went heavy in his lungs, as if weighed down by her beauty. He'd always been struck by that beauty. It had knocked him down, and then out, and he'd never fully been able to get up again.

It was no different now.

'Are you going to say anything?' she said softly after a moment. Only then did he realise he was gawking at her.

'I…yes. Sorry.' He shook his head. 'You look amazing.'

A small smile played on her lips. 'Thank you.'

'You meant for me to react this way.'

The smile widened. 'Well, I was hoping.' And then faded. 'Just like now I'm hoping that I don't end up being sick in this dress.'

He took a step forward. 'Is there anything I can do?'

'To keep me from throwing up?' She smiled kindly. 'No. But I appreciate the attempt. I'm just going to have to…well, hope.' She paused. 'How are you doing?'

'Fine. Good.' He frowned. 'Why?'

'I haven't seen you all afternoon. Is it a crime to check in?'

'No. But you're checking in for a reason.'

She gave him a look that told him she had no intention

of sharing that reason. He bit back a sigh. 'How were things with my mother?'

'Fine. I gave her the opportunity to play fairy godmother with me. Willingly, this time.' She tilted her head. 'Honestly, she loved it. The dress, and then the shoes.' She swept the dress from her leg—nearly stopping his heart as he realised the dress had a slit and he could ogle her leg freely—revealing a shoe that sparkled up at him. She let the dress go. 'Plus, she was thrilled that her plan to get us back together had worked.'

'And you let her believe that.' The dry comment wasn't meant as a question.

'No, actually, I didn't. I told her that she needed to think about her actions. That she wasn't a real fairy, which meant those actions had consequences. And that those consequences affected you.'

He couldn't formulate a reply.

'You're welcome,' she said with a smirk.

'I… I don't know what to say.'

'I just told you you're welcome. You don't have to say anything.'

'Why?' he asked, when his mind still couldn't grasp what was happening.

'Because someone needed to tell her.' She paused. 'I didn't tell my mother that her actions were affecting me. I expected her to know somehow, or I wished… I wished my father would say something. But he didn't, and she didn't, and now—' She broke off on a slow exhale of air. 'I wish I'd said something to her. Maybe our relationship would have changed. Maybe I wouldn't have felt the way that I do now.'

Her eyes had gone distant with the memories, but when she looked at him they cleared. 'So I thought that if I said something to your mother it might make a difference.'

'Did it?'

'She was surprised to hear it.' She bit her lip. The first

show of uncertainty. 'She didn't expect anyone to call her out on it.'

'I never did.'

'I know.' She gave him a small sad smile. 'You just did what it took to make it go away. And while I get that—I did it too—it's not going to be as easy to do when the baby gets here. And your mother needs to know that.'

'You told her about the baby?'

'No. I just said that we're working things out, and that that means we have to have boundaries.'

'And she agreed?'

'We'll have to see.' The uncertainty was back. 'Did I... did I overstep?'

'No.' He moved forward and kissed her forehead. 'No, you didn't.' He paused. 'Thank you.'

'You're welcome,' she said again, and rested her head on his chest.

The movement should have comforted him, but instead it sent a ripple through his already unsettled feelings. He wasn't upset by what she'd done, but he also didn't know why she'd done it. Or why it felt as if another weight had been added to what he was already carrying on his shoulders.

CHAPTER TWENTY-ONE

HE WASN'T UPSET with her.

He'd told her he wasn't, and the way he engaged with her seemed to suggest the same. But he'd been distracted on the way to the hotel that was hosting his function. And his usual collected demeanour seemed frazzled.

His colleagues had noticed too. At one point, his partner Frank had spoken about the expansion and Aaron had just looked at him. Had just *stared*. And then he'd asked Frank to repeat the question, and Frank had shot her a look of concern before replying.

Rosa was worried. She was also beginning to think Aaron's strange mood had something to do with her. He'd been that way since they'd kissed that afternoon, and she'd broken down in his lap and spilled her deepest, darkest fears to him. Maybe he regretted what he'd said now.

If he did, would it affect how comforted she'd felt because of what he'd said?

She smiled at one of Aaron's colleagues, accepting their curiosity as a part of the event. She didn't imagine her absence over the past five months had gone unnoticed. And then the previous day she'd shown up at his office and now she was attending the company function.

It was too good to pass up, and so she forgave the people who looked at her as if somehow that would give them the answers they were hoping for.

She focused her attention back on Aaron, but now he was preparing to give his speech for the evening, and he'd gone even quieter. Her chest ached and her stomach rolled, and she pleaded with the new life growing inside her to give her an evening without throwing up. If she did throw up it would no doubt give the people who were looking at her the answers they wanted.

So perhaps they were right to stare at her.

Thankfully, she made it through Aaron's speech. Smart, concise, motivating. He was an excellent boss, she thought, and would make an excellent father.

But was he still interested in being an excellent husband?

The evening moved into a more casual phase after Aaron's speech. The band began to play, the alcohol began to kick in and people were moving to the dance floor. Aaron had been intercepted by one of his employees on his way back to the table, which made it easier for Rosa to excuse herself.

She made her way to the bathroom and then, when she saw the queue to the ladies' room of the venue, pivoted and went to the elevator. She almost pressed for the first floor, but then someone might have the same idea as her, so she pressed for the third floor instead.

It was the top floor of the hotel, and she thanked the heavens when she was able to make it there and locate a bathroom before anyone else saw her. She was also grateful that her baby had allowed her to close the door of the stall before she or he demanded that Rosa be sick.

There was more in her stomach than usual, since she'd felt obliged to eat some of the meal they'd served to avoid suspicion, which made the experience longer and more unpleasant. When she straightened her head started to spin, and she had to spend even more time in the stall to make sure she wouldn't fall over when she exited.

It was all of thirty minutes later by the time she left the bathroom—breath fresh and make-up fixed, thanks to the contents of her bag—and she knew that Aaron would be worried about her. But she still felt a little clammy, and she eyed the door to the balcony before deciding that fresh air might help steady her.

She didn't know what the sound was at first when she

got there. Thought it was in her head, the harsh, unsteady breaths. But when her eyes adjusted she saw a shadow in the corner.

She blinked, realised it was a person sitting hunched on the floor, and was about to leave when she realised that that person was her husband.

He couldn't breathe.

It was the damn tie, and the shirt, and the suit jacket. And though his brain was fuzzy and there were a million thoughts going through his mind—or none—some part of it knew he couldn't throw off all his clothes. So he threw off his jacket, loosened his tie, opened his top button and tried to breathe.

The attempt sounded ragged to his own ears. He was dimly aware of someone else on the balcony and, though he wanted to, he couldn't bring himself to care. If his employees saw him like this it would break something he didn't think could be fixed.

He didn't care.

If Frank saw him it would put their partnership at risk.

He didn't care.

And yet, when he felt the person crouch down in front of him and he lifted his head and looked directly into Rosa's eyes, he found himself caring.

'Rosa,' he rasped. Why did his voice sound so strange?

'It's okay, baby,' she said, settling some of the spinning happening inside him. 'It's okay. You're okay.'

As she wrapped her arms around him he wanted to tell her that it didn't feel as if he was okay. That his head hurt with all the thoughts, and his lungs felt as if they couldn't hold the air he was breathing.

But the thoughts he'd believed so coherent in his mind came out as a garbled mess of air and words. Her hold tightened on him but her voice stayed calm and after some time had passed—he didn't know how long—he looked up at her, and followed her instructions to breathe.

'In,' she told him, 'and out.' She smiled. 'See, you're doing it. Just keep breathing. Inhale on a count to five, exhale on a count to five. You've got this, baby. You can do this. I know you can do this.'

He didn't know how long it took before he believed her. Or how long after he believed her that his breathing actually reflected it. And when he was still—when he felt his mind and body still—she was on her knees and somehow he was cradled in her arms.

'I'm sorry,' he said quietly. She pulled back, her eyes sweeping across his face, and then she shook her head.

'What are you apologising for?'

'That…that you had to see this.' The words were more helpless than he'd intended, and only succeeded in making him feel even more of a fool.

'If by "this" you mean whatever happened out here, don't apologise.' She shifted, and it tugged him out of whatever was going on in his head. The position she was in must have been uncomfortable, and he wasn't sure how long she'd been sitting there like that.

He helped ease her off her knees and then pulled her forward so that she sat on his lap. She didn't protest, just lifted a hand and swept hair from his forehead.

'You don't have to apologise, Aaron,' she said again, her hand now playing with his hair.

'You shouldn't have—'

'Do you think I wanted you to see me after I threw up yesterday?' She clenched her jaw, and then relaxed it again. After taking a breath, she continued. 'Or have you witness what my anxiety is doing to me? What it *could* do to me?' She lifted her shoulders. 'I've run away—hid—from you before because I didn't want you to see that. But you showed me that was wrong.' She paused, as if she were letting her words sink in. 'Talk to me. Let me in.'

Her words shook him. And again he realised how complicated her decision to leave had been.

But he'd just had a panic attack. The first he'd ever had, and he didn't know where it had come from. He needed time to process that. And what she'd told him. He couldn't find the right words to explain that to her.

'Okay,' she said when the silence stretched. 'Tell me what happened before you came up here.'

'I… I was just talking with Lee about—' He broke off when he realised Rosa would learn nothing about what had caused him to react like that from a discussion he'd had with one of his associates.

Because his panic attack had had nothing to do with what he'd been talking about with Lee. At some point during the conversation his head had started spinning and it had felt as if he couldn't get enough air into his lungs. And his mind…

He'd been thinking about all the promises he'd wanted to make to Rosa, but that he'd never be able to keep.

And about how he couldn't keep lying to her. About how she had the right to know that he wasn't worthy to be her husband. He was barely worthy of being a father to their child.

'Aaron—' her soft voice interrupted his thoughts '—talk to me.'

He looked into her eyes and could only see the things he couldn't give her. 'I can't be there for you, Rosa. Not in the way you need.'

Her heart dipped almost as violently as it had when she'd seen him in that corner. It was still bruised from holding her stoic, strong husband in her arms as he shook, as he struggled for air. It could barely bear the weight of him telling her now he couldn't be there for her.

'I'll get it under control,' she said, her voice just above a whisper. 'No,' she said almost immediately. 'I don't know if I have what my mother had. I don't know if I'm a hypochondriac. Or about the cancer. So I'll get it diagnosed. I'll see a psychologist, and get screened for the breast cancer gene. I'll keep my anxieties in check. I'm already trying,' she added, desperation fuelling her words. 'I go to the doctor if I feel off, and it almost always *is* something. It isn't in my head.'

The last words were said in a whisper, and her hands reached for his, gripping them tightly. 'I'll fix it, Aaron. Just don't…don't leave me.'

'Rosa,' he said, his voice shaking. But it wasn't from whatever had happened to him. No, it was because of what she'd just told him and she immediately felt guilt crush her.

'I'm sorry. I'm being selfish. I'm being…' The words drifted and she felt tears follow them down her cheeks. 'I'm sorry.'

'I wasn't talking about that,' he replied, and he let go of one of her hands and slid an arm around her waist. 'I should have thought you might think that.' His expression softened. 'That's another part of why you left, isn't it? You thought I'd leave you too. Like your dad did with your mom.'

Not trusting herself to speak, she pursed her lips. Nodded.

'I won't,' he said softly. Firmly. 'Not because of that. Not because of you.' He pressed a kiss to her lips that calmed some of the frantic beating of her heart. 'It's because of me, Rosa. It's always because of me.'

'That's what happened earlier.' Somehow her reaction had made him see the reasons for his own more clearly. 'I was thinking about how I wanted to promise you I'd always be there for you.' He took a breath. Wondered how, over the last month, he'd shared more with her—had delved more into his emotions—than he ever had before.

'Lee's been working on a case where a mother who desperately wants custody of her kids won't get it.' And now that he thought about it—now that his brain was steadier—he realised his discussion with Lee had contributed to his reaction after all. 'She promised them they'd be able to live with her, but her two jobs won't make that possible. She broke down in Lee's office because she'd have to break that promise to them.'

The more he spoke, the clearer it became. 'It's not fair. She works two jobs to make sure that they have everything they want. Except her.' He paused. 'And because of that broken promise they're going to spend their lives not trusting her.'

'Aaron, it's not the same thing—'

'No,' he interrupted. 'That's not what...' He blew out a breath. 'What happened here was partly because of the promise I couldn't make to you, and partly because those kids... They're going to wonder if *they* were the reason that promise was broken. If they did something wrong, or if she really wanted them in the first place.' Emotion, strong and heavy, sat in his chest. 'They're going to be angry with her at first, and then they're going to feel responsible for making sure she believes their existence was worth it.' He looked at her. 'It'll make them take responsibility for things they shouldn't have to. It'll affect their entire lives. And everything that goes wrong from this point in their lives will make them wonder if it was their fault.'

'Like if their wives leave.'

'Yes.'

'Even when it's clear their wives have problems, fears of their own, that contributed to why they left?'

How did she always see what he couldn't say? 'Yes.'

'And at what point do they start believing that there's

nothing wrong with them? That their wives love them more than anyone else in the world, and that they would do anything to make them believe that?'

'I'm broken,' Aaron said, and the pain in his chest agreed with him. 'You saw that. You left because of it.'

'But you've shown me that I was wrong, Aaron. The way you've dealt with all this.' She made a vague gesture towards her stomach. 'And with your mom today.' She paused. 'What you said to me this afternoon. You've grown. I just didn't see it.'

'Or you did, and—'

'No, Aaron. I was wrong. Scared.'

'But my mom took so little interest in me, and my dad… He wasn't even there.'

'That's more about them than it is about you,' she said gently. 'You've learnt that with me this past month.' She squeezed his hand. 'It doesn't mean you're the one who's broken. And if you are… Well, then, all of us are.'

'But your mother and father didn't leave—' He broke off with a shake of his head. 'I'm sorry. I wasn't thinking.'

'No, it's okay.' She leaned back against the railing, making him think about how ridiculous they must look. Her in her beautiful gown, and him in his tux. Broken, shaken, on the floor of a balcony.

'I don't think I ever thought that there might have been something wrong with *me* because my parents…were who they were. Are, I guess, in the case of my dad. Not until I found that lump and freaked out.' She lifted a hand to his face now. 'I understand why you feel this way. And now, with the baby on the way, why it's an issue.'

'Because I'm going to be a terrible father?'

'What? No!' She straightened. 'I meant it made you think of your parents. Of your father. No,' she said again. 'You're going to be a terrific father.'

'I don't know if I can believe that.' He was so tired of

saying it, and yet it haunted him so that he couldn't do anything *but* say it.

'Well, I'm telling you.' She paused. 'I know your relationship with your mother is…difficult. And unfair. But she's done a pretty decent job of teaching you how to be responsible.' She wrinkled her nose. 'Silver linings.'

'Yes, I know how to be responsible. I've been responsible my whole life. But look where that got me.' He felt helpless saying it. And, despite what she'd told him, he couldn't believe her. He couldn't believe that he'd be good for them. For her and the baby.

'I'm having a panic attack during a work function, Rosa. I can't face that I'm going to be a father. The responsibility is…easy. I'll look after the child. I'll be there, which is more than what my mom and dad did.' He paused. 'But what is responsibility going to teach this child? That I *have* to love them?'

'Is that how you feel?'

He shrugged. 'I don't know.'

Silence followed his words and, though he knew she would never say it, he sensed that he'd hurt her with his answer. Felt it confirmed when she drew herself up and tried to stand. He helped as much as he could, and was already standing when she turned back to him.

'You have to figure this out, Aaron,' she told him softly, kindly, though he'd hurt her. 'We—me and your baby—don't want to feel like you're just there for us out of some warped sense of responsibility.'

'I wouldn't be.'

'No? There isn't a part of you that feels like the only reason you're open to getting back together again is because I'm pregnant?'

'I… I didn't realise that was on the table.'

She laughed lightly. Mockingly now. 'You didn't realise that getting back together was an option? Not when I sat on your lap and kissed you back? When I fell apart and told you enough to help you put me back together again?' Any pretence of humour left her face. 'You didn't think me speaking with your mother, me staying here to accompany you tonight, that *any* of that meant I wanted to get back together again?'

'I... I didn't want to hope. After what happened,' he finished lamely.

'After I left.' He nodded, and she sighed. 'Maybe I was stupid for thinking that we'd be able to move past this.' She lifted a hand to her forehead. 'Or maybe we just need to clear it up.' She straightened her shoulders. 'You know why I left. And I know where I went wrong in making that decision.' She paused. 'I'm going to manage my anxiety. Or do my best to try. You said you'd be there for me.' He nodded. 'Did you mean that as the mother of your child, or as your wife?'

He hesitated only briefly. 'Both.'

She gave him a sad smile. 'If this is going to work we have to be honest,' she said, reminding him of his words at the restaurant the night before. But he didn't respond. Couldn't, since he was still trying to figure out what had happened that had got them to this point.

Hope and guilt made a potent shot, he thought, and wondered why he'd downed it.

'Aaron... I want to stay married to you. I love you—' her eyes went glossy as she said the words '—and I'll always regret how stupid I was to leave you instead of opening up to you. But this whole experience has taught me that there were things that we were going through by ourselves that we shouldn't have gone through alone. That we should have shared.'

She blew out a breath. 'So maybe, in some weird way this was a good thing.' She went silent, her face pensive and then she shook her head. 'But we know what we know

now. And the actions of the past have brought us here, to make this decision. So, if you want me—' her voice broke and she cleared her throat '—you're going to have to move past what happened and—' she threw up her hands '—and hope again. Because, right now, I'm choosing you again. Not because of the baby. Because of *me*. Because I love you, and I was foolish to believe that I could go through life without you.'

She stepped forward, laid a hand on his cheek. 'But I will, if you can't choose me too. If you don't *want* to be responsible for me and our child. Because that's what it is, isn't it?' She didn't wait for an answer. 'Wanting to be responsible for someone instead of feeling like you *have* to be. Can you say that about us?'

He opened his mouth to agree, to tell her how much he wanted their lives to go back to being how they'd been before. But he knew that he couldn't. Because, as she'd said, they knew what they knew now. And the things he knew about himself worried him more than anything he'd found out about her.

He couldn't be sure that he *wanted* to be responsible for them. Couldn't be sure because he didn't know what *wanting* to be responsible looked like. His entire life had been spent doing things he *had* to do. Except for Rosa. He'd wanted her, but now even that had felt like a compulsion of sorts.

Had he felt obliged to be with her because that had been what their sick mothers had wanted? What her mother had asked of him? Or had it been the attraction, the heat, that had dictated their relationship? Their love?

Her eyes filled again as the silence grew. Her hand dropped and she hung her head. He wanted to comfort her, to draw her in and promise that he'd made a mistake.

He couldn't.

When she looked up at him again her eyes were clear,

though there was still that unbearable sadness in them. She lifted up onto her toes, put both hands on his cheeks and kissed him.

It tasted like goodbye, and somehow that taste felt familiar to him. He found himself swept away by it. Felt the emptiness fill him when she pulled away. Felt his hands go to her hips as she lowered to her feet again. As he kissed her forehead.

He didn't know how long they stood like that, but he knew he'd remember for ever what happened next.

'Be happy,' she said hoarsely. 'Find out what that means to you and go for it. I'll be in touch about the baby. We can figure things out once you've had time to…' Her voice faded and it was a few seconds later when she said, 'When you've had time.'

And then she was gone.

CHAPTER TWENTY-TWO

'AND YOU DON'T think it's normal?' The delicate older woman waited patiently for Rosa's reply, and Rosa took a deep breath, preparing herself to answer the question honestly.

She had been the one who'd decided to make good on her promise to get her anxieties under control. She might not have a husband to do it for—she swallowed at the pain that quaked through her body—but she had a child. Or she would have a child. And since her anxiety had spiked since she'd returned to Cape Town the week before, she'd finally decided to go to the psychologist.

'Normal?' Rosa asked. 'The fact that I worry incessantly about what's happening in my body? That I can't trust it?'

'Yes,' Dr Spar replied. 'You don't think, after what your mother went through, it's normal to have your concerns?'

'Well, I suppose that's why I'm here. Because it's normal coming from where I come from.' She bit her lip. 'But the worrying extends to my decisions. And I can't trust them either.'

'Which bothers you?'

'It's affected my life.'

Dr Spar nodded. 'Have you thought about how not trusting yourself might have come from your mother being unable to trust herself?'

'Not quite so specifically. But I know my indecisiveness, or struggling to trust my decisions... I know that's because of my mother.'

'You told me that you didn't want to use your mother as an excuse for your actions any more.'

'That doesn't mean I magically know how to stop doing that.'

'Except being here of your own accord—for your child—means that you have, in some way. Can you see that?'

She lifted a shoulder. 'Maybe.'

'You struggle with it.'

'With seeing that I'm not my mother?' Rosa asked.

'Yes,' Dr Spar replied. 'But also with seeing yourself for who you are.' She paused. 'You're not your mother, Rosa. You can see where your fears and anxieties come from. And you're facing them. Do you think your mother could do that?'

Rosa shook her head silently as she thought it through. The rest of the appointment passed in a blur after that. It had been her second appointment—the first had been spent sharing what Rosa thought she needed help with—but already she knew that it was helping.

She wasn't foolish enough to think she was cured. She was still anxious. Still doubted herself. And she still couldn't bring herself to be screened for the breast cancer gene, though she was using her pregnancy as an excuse for that. So she made her subsequent appointments and patted her stomach as she walked out of the building.

We're going to get through this, pumpkin, she told her baby silently.

She bit her lip and tried to push past the tears that always seemed to be close by recently. Partly because she'd been worrying about what kind of mother she would be. Worrying that she'd be similar to *her* mother. But having Dr Spar point out how differently she'd reacted to her anxieties compared to her mother had made her feel better.

As she headed home she told herself that it was okay that she didn't want to be like her mother. That she wasn't betraying her mother by wanting that. She'd loved her mother. She wouldn't have put herself through what she had for Violet if she hadn't.

But that didn't negate the difficult experience Rosa ha

had with Violet. No, that experience and that love could co-exist. And there was nothing wrong with Rosa not wanting her child to live in a world where it did.

It was harder to convince herself that the other part of what had brought her to tears recently was okay. The fact that her child would grow up without his or her parents being together. Especially because Rosa knew how much she'd contributed to that fact.

Her decisions had brought her to this point. Long before she'd found that lump too. And now she knew she'd always fear inheriting her mother's hypochondria. The anxiety, the mistrust of her body, of her decisions, would stay with her.

But she could deal with that. She'd fight for her mental health just as hard as she'd fight for her physical health. Even though that battle would probably extend throughout her life.

She wouldn't let it control her life, her actions. Not any more. She would continue her therapy and learn how to manage it. Learn how to look after herself properly. And see who she really was.

But before she'd got to that point she *had* let it control her life, her actions, her decisions, and she couldn't ignore that she had a part in breaking up her marriage.

She hadn't spoken with Aaron since that night at his work function. She didn't think she was strong enough yet. Not for that. She'd left immediately after that conversation with him. She'd gone back to the house, not particularly caring about what people would say about her departure; she'd packed and had been at the airport an hour later.

The whole thing had cost her a fortune, and there had been no fairy godmother to pick up her tab. But then, her life with Aaron felt like a made-up tale to her now anyway. The clock had struck twelve on her—her carriage had turned back into a pumpkin and she'd turned back into a normal woman with no prince at her side.

'But we don't need a prince, do we, pumpkin?' she murmured softly, laying her hand on her stomach. Ignoring the voice that said, *Liar*.

She *did* need a prince. *Her* prince. But the clock had struck twelve.

She choked back the grief.

It had been two weeks since he'd last seen her. Two weeks without a phone call or message. Of course, he'd gone without either for much longer. But things were different now. Because of the child, he told himself. Because she was pregnant.

Was she okay? Was the baby okay? How was she feeling?

Those questions—and variations of them—had plagued him since she'd left. And he could have got the answers to them with one simple phone call.

That was how he knew he was lying to himself. Things weren't different between them because she was pregnant. At least, not *only* because she was pregnant. They were also different because things had changed between them. Things had become more intense.

He missed her. He missed sharing with her. Regretted how rarely that had happened when they'd been happily married.

Happily.

He didn't think he could use that word any more. Not knowing what he knew now. Not considering the depths their relationship had sunk to before he'd been stupid enough to let her go.

He took leave from work when he realised his usual strategy of throwing himself into his cases was no longer effective. And if he'd managed to pass off his colleagues' concerns when he'd returned to their function that night two weeks before without Rosa, he wouldn't be able to now

He *never* took leave. And he'd had to convince Frank that he was fine.

But he wasn't.

He spent his days on menial manual tasks. He went to the gym, ran. Fixed things in the house that needed fixing. At some point he found himself at the hardware store purchasing wood, and when he'd got home he'd started building a treehouse. He hadn't given it much thought, had just done it, and he'd been halfway through when he'd realised he was building a treehouse.

Anything to avoid your problems, a voice in his head told him mockingly. But he didn't think he was avoiding his problems. No, he was avoiding his *mistakes*. Because if how miserable he was without Rosa was any indication, he *had* made a mistake. And he didn't know how to fix it.

Which was why he was now at his mother's house.

He had a key, but he didn't want to use it. He'd dodged whatever his mother had wanted because of Rosa the last time, and he hadn't heard from her since. But that didn't mean that he wouldn't. For all he knew, he could be walking into another family staying at his mom's house.

His mind had created such a convincing picture of it that he was mildly surprised when he found his mother alone.

'So, this is the reason for the weather today,' his mother said when she saw him. She stared pointedly out at the rain through the windows before meeting his eyes again. 'You're visiting me.'

'Yes.' He wasn't in the mood for dramatics, though he understood the sentiment. 'I wanted to talk to you.'

'I assumed so, yes. Something to drink?'

When he shook his head she asked for tea from the housekeeper, who'd been hovering in the room since she'd opened the door for Aaron.

When they were alone, Aaron continued, 'What's wrong with me?'

'What?'

'Why didn't my father want me?'

To his mother's credit, she didn't look nearly as surprised as he'd thought she would. Though she did get up and start pacing. When she finally answered him, she had taken her seat again.

'It wasn't you. It was me.' There was pain in her eyes that he had never seen before. 'Your father didn't want *me*.'

'He walked away from his son.'

'Because he didn't want to have a child with me.' She cleared her throat. 'Because he was married.'

'He was…' Aaron couldn't quite process the words, though he'd half repeated them. It took time, during which his mother's tea had been brought and now sat untouched on the table in front of her. 'You slept with a married man?'

'I didn't know he was married when we met.' Liana looked out of the window as she spoke. 'It was a one-time thing too. And when I found out I was pregnant it was hard to find him. The only reason I could was because I had money. Which, thankfully, he didn't know about.'

'He was a one-night stand?' he asked slowly. 'You didn't know him?'

'I was young, Aaron,' she said coolly. 'It was a mistake.'

'You mean *I* was mistake.'

'I've said that in the past, yes.' She looked at him now and her expression softened. 'Though I doubt I meant it. I was just…angry. At myself for making such poor decisions. At you for—' she took a breath '—for reminding me that I should have been responsible.'

'Because I was responsible.'

'Yes.' She brushed a non-existent hair from her face. 'Even though I knew responsibility was your coping mechanism. Responsibility and control.' She smiled sadly. 'Because your mother was irresponsible and out of control.'

'Is that…' He closed his eyes. Opened them. 'Is that why you didn't want to spend time with me when I was younger?'

Her lips pursed. 'I wouldn't have made a good mother. You didn't need me around.'

'I did,' he disagreed softly.

'No, you didn't. Look what's happened to your life since I've been around.'

'It didn't have to be like that. After you got sick—'

'You tried to salvage our relationship,' she interrupted. 'But I saw what that cost you, Aaron.' Her breath shuddered through her lips. 'I said that your father was a one-time mistake, but I've made so many more. I forced you to become someone you shouldn't have had to be. I hurt you beyond measure. I've made you doubt your worth. I'm… I'm sorry.'

He didn't know where her candour was coming from. Didn't know what to do with the emotions it caused inside him. What he *did* know was that his mother's apology meant something to him. That it shifted something inside him.

'You didn't deserve us as parents,' she interrupted his thoughts softly. 'You're a good child. And you have been better to me than I deserved. And your father…' She sighed. 'He's missed out on getting to know you. But that wasn't because of you. That was only because of the circumstances you were born into.'

'Thank you.'

'You don't have to thank me. I should have done this for you a long time ago.'

'Be honest?'

'Yes. And not punished you for my actions. My mistakes.' She leaned forward. '*I* should have been responsible for *you*. Because you were my child, yes, but also because I love you.' She cleared her throat. 'I shouldn't have hurt you the way I have. I should have put you first. I'm sorry.'

'Mom—'

'I knew she'd be good for you,' she interrupted. 'I didn't realise she'd be good for *us*.'

His heart began to sprint. 'Rosa?'

'Of course. She told me all this, you know.' He nodded. 'And she said you'd come here soon. To prepare myself.'

Though his mother's honesty began to make sense now, the reason why surprised him. Again, something shifted inside him. Again, he thought about the mistakes he'd made.

'I see a bit of myself in her.' His eyes lifted and she met his gaze. 'Is that why you're here, and not with her?'

'How—'

'I keep track of my family,' Liana said.

'You knew she was here when you visited me a few weeks ago.'

She nodded. 'I promised Violet that I would look out for Rosa too.'

And yet he was beginning to think that Rosa looked out for them more than they ever had for her.

'She's not like you.'

'No,' Liana agreed. 'She's better. And she's shown you that being spontaneous doesn't have to be a bad thing.' She paused. 'Perhaps she'll help you to let go a little.'

He didn't reply immediately, his mind racing. And finally, when he looked at his mother again, there was a knowing glint in her eyes.

CHAPTER TWENTY-THREE

'WHY DID I decide to live on the top floor of this stupid building?' Rosa wondered out loud, speaking to no one in particular. The elevator of her building had broken. She was almost seven weeks pregnant, and so tired she was barely able to lift a hand to her face, let alone her feet up three floors.

And so she sank down next to the broken elevator, ignoring the looks of the other residents as they easily made the journey up the stairs. She sighed, leaned her head against the wall and closed her eyes.

She was probably going to get mugged. Her handbag was on her lap. The bags from her grocery haul sprawled around her. Toast and tea, ginger biscuits and prenatal vitamins—the extent of what her stomach would hold. And then there were the sample dresses that she'd had to get for her show in two weeks' time.

Why she'd decided to showcase her new line during her first trimester she'd question for ever.

Because you're desperate to prove that you can move forward with your life without your husband by your side?

She groaned, and pleaded with her thoughts to stop bringing Aaron up. It happened too often for her liking, at the most inopportune times—

'Rosa?'

And now she was hearing his voice. She opened her eyes with a soft curse, and then felt them widen when she saw Aaron right in front of her, crouching down with a concerned look on his face.

'Are you okay?'

She frowned and then reached out, touched his face, to make sure he was really there.

'*Aaron?*'

'Rosa,' he said again, his voice firm. 'Are you okay?'

'If you're really here…' She paused, gave him a moment to confirm it.

There was slight amusement on his face when he nodded.

'Yes, I'm fine.' She straightened now. 'What are you doing here?'

'What are you doing on the floor?' he countered. There was a beat of silence while they both waited for the other to answer, and then she sighed.

'The elevator's broken, and I'm too tired to climb the stairs.'

'That's it?'

'Nauseous, dizzy too. But yes, that's it.'

'So you sat on the floor of an apartment complex?'

She pulled a face. 'I would have moved eventually.' She blew out a breath. 'And yes, I know it's disgusting and I was putting myself in danger, but—'

She broke off when he placed the grocery bags in her one hand, slid her handbag over her shoulder and put the garment bags in her other hand.

'What are you—?'

Again, she broke off. This time, though, it was because he'd scooped her into his arms, holding her as she held the bags easily.

'You're not going to carry me up three floors.' He answered her by turning to the stairwell and doing just that. 'Aaron, you don't have to do this. I'm fine. Just let me down—'

'Are you going to complain the whole way?' he asked, pausing to look down at her. He didn't even sound out of breath, she thought, and cursed him silently for always doing the kind of thing that made her swoon.

'No,' she answered sullenly, and his lips curved. 'It's not funny.'

'No,' he agreed, and kept walking.

Rosa told herself not to get too excited by the fact that he was there. It was probably for the sake of the baby, and she pushed back against the guilt that swelled up inside her. She should have called him, as she'd said she would, and given him an update. But there was no update. She still felt crappy. She still wished that things were different between them.

She couldn't bring herself to call since she didn't trust what she would say. She'd told him she could live without him that night, but her courage had faltered terribly since she'd left Johannesburg.

Besides, what was wrong with his phone? He could have called her too.

Happy with that, and ready to defend herself if she had to, she barely noticed that they'd reached her floor until he stopped in front of her door and set her down gently.

She stared at him. 'How did you know this was my apartment?'

'My mom.'

Rosa's forehead creased. 'Your mother? How did she... Is that how you knew I was in Cape Town the first time?'

He nodded. 'She always knows where her family is. Her words, not mine,' he said with a shrug when her face twisted into a questioning look.

The day was becoming stranger and, since she didn't want to waste her already limited energy on arguing about something that wasn't worth it, she merely nodded. She handed him the garment bags and reached for the key in her handbag to open the door.

He was still holding the garment bags as he walked in and looked around. She closed the door and tried not to fidget. She lived there, but nothing about the flat was hers.

She'd rented it furnished. The quirky colours, odd furniture and weird paintings weren't her choices.

In fact, they'd almost deterred her before she'd remembered the flat had a view of Table Mountain and was located close to the factory that made her designs. She'd realised then that those were her only two priorities.

'Are these for your show?' he asked when she took the bags from him. She didn't bother asking him how he knew.

'Yep.'

'Can I see them?'

'Why would you want to?' she asked tiredly. 'You didn't come all the way here to look at the clothes I designed.'

'No,' he agreed again, and she nearly sighed. Why did he have to be so damn amicable?

'So why did you? Come, I mean.'

'To fight,' he answered slowly.

'What are you fighting for?' she asked after a stunned silence. He'd expected some version of that question, though it was still a punch to the gut.

'You.'

She stared at him. 'There's nothing beyond "you"?'

'I...' He took a deep breath, and then plunged. 'No, there is. I'm sorry, Rosa. For...everything. You shouldn't be here. You should be home. You should be with me.' He gave her a moment to process. 'It's my fault that you're not.'

Her expression remained unreadable. 'How does this change things?'

'I'm here, aren't I?' It came out in a surlier tone than he'd intended. And of course she picked up on it.

'Really? You're annoyed because you're here? Aaron, you've barely said anything beyond *I'm sorry*. And I appreciate your apology, I do, but what am I supposed to do with it? Things haven't changed, which means you're probably here because you think it's what you should do.'

'No,' he said after a moment. 'I'm here because I'm… choosing to be. And because I didn't think about it. I just booked a flight and came here right after I spoke with my mother.'

'You…spoke with your mother?' she asked slowly, before shaking her head. 'No, wait, you *just* booked a flight?'

He clenched his teeth, and then forced himself to relax. 'I was being spontaneous.' He hissed out a breath. 'So yes, I suppose I am annoyed to be here. I'm annoyed that I don't have anything better for you than *I'm sorry*. Because that's what happens when I don't have a plan.'

'But you're here,' she said softly. 'And that means something.'

The emotion in her eyes told him that it did. And suddenly all the uncertainty didn't feel so overwhelming.

'Tell me about the visit to your mother,' she urged softly, when silence took over the room.

'I asked her about… Well, I asked her about my father. And about her.' He cleared his throat. 'About why they didn't want me.'

'And she told you it wasn't you.'

'Yes.' She always knew. 'He was married.'

'Oh, Aaron.' She took a step forward, and then stopped. 'I'm sorry.'

'Don't be,' he said, his heart aching at her hesitation. 'It made me realise that the things I've believed about myself, about my life, weren't entirely correct.'

'And you're okay with that?'

He thought about it. 'No. I don't think I will be for a long time. But I have answers now, and they'll help me figure it out. That's enough for now.' He paused. 'I think that's why you leaving—why all of this—hit me so hard. Because I thought all of it was me. Because I didn't have answers.'

'But you know better now,' she said. 'You have answers.'

'Yes.' He cleared his throat. 'She told me you told her I'd come.'

'A guess,' she said, but angled her face as if she didn't want him to see her expression.

'No, it wasn't a guess.' He walked towards her, stopping only a few metres away. 'You know me. How?'

She laughed hoarsely. 'You're my husband.'

'And you're my wife.' He stepped closer. 'Yet somehow I didn't realise how important that was until you walked away from me. When I saw you again, and I couldn't keep my heart or body from you. And when you told me you were pregnant—'

He sucked in air. Let it out slowly.

'My mother told me she should have been responsible for me because I was her child. But also…because she loved me.' He closed the distance between them now. 'And I love you, Rosa. Being responsible for you and our child… It's because I *want* to be. I'm choosing you.' He lifted his hand, brushed a finger across her lips. 'No matter what happens in my life, Rosa, I always end up choosing you.'

She sucked her lip between her teeth and then blew out a breath. 'You really know how to sweep a woman off her feet, don't you?'

His lips curved. 'I'm only interested in sweeping one woman off her feet.' His hand dropped to her waist. 'You have questions.'

'So many,' she said on a little outburst of air. 'But I also have to tell you… I've been seeing someone about my anxiety.'

'Has it been helping?' he asked carefully.

'Yes. But it's not just going to go away.'

'I know.' He took her hand. Squeezed. And let go.

'And I haven't done the test yet.'

'The screening?' She nodded. 'Can you do it while you're pregnant?'

'I... I haven't seen a doctor about it, so I don't know for sure. But I wanted you to know, so that—'

'I can be there for you if and when you choose to go?'

Her mouth opened, and then she swallowed. 'I'm going to do it.'

'Okay.'

'So there's no *if*.'

'Okay.'

Her brow furrowed. 'You're really okay with all this?'

'They're your decisions, Rosa. I'll support you, no matter what you decide. And we'll deal with the consequences of whichever decision you make.'

Her eyes filled. 'Thank you.' Seconds later, she said, 'You mean it, don't you?'

'Yes.'

'You're choosing it. You're choosing me.'

'Rosa, I had a heart-to-heart with my mother about my father, and her actions in the past.' He stroked her hair. 'And then I flew here on the spur of the moment with only my mother's word that you'd be here. I have no clothes, no toiletries, no place to stay. I only have you.'

'But—'

'I don't want to waste my life like my parents did,' he interrupted. 'Their choices—the fact that I'm here—were a series of mistakes. And yes, we've made mistakes too. But *we* were never a mistake.'

His hands moved to her waist again, and tightened there. 'And, if you'll have me, I'll believe that nothing that's brought us here has been a mistake either.'

Now he placed a hand on her abdomen and felt his entire body warm when she covered his hand with both of hers.

'I still love you, Rosa,' he said again, quietly. 'I've never stopped—'

He was silenced by her lips on his. It was a long, sweet kiss, free from the anguish that had plagued them for longer than either of them knew. Only when the doorbell rang did they come up for air.

'I'm not expecting anyone,' Rosa said breathlessly as she moved to open the door. He caught her waist.

'I am.'

'What? Who?'

'I…ordered some camellias.' He swallowed. 'I remember you said you liked them. I know they're not your favourite, but they're sometimes called the rose of winter.' He waited nervously but she didn't say anything. 'If we have a daughter,' he added quickly, 'the name would be perfect to fit into your family's tradition. Because yours is Rosa, and she was conceived in—'

Again, she silenced him with a kiss. Tears glistened on her face when she drew back. 'I… I can't tell you how much that…' She stopped, offering him a watery smile. 'Thank you.' She laid her head on his chest. 'I love you, Aaron.' She paused. 'We're going to figure it all out, aren't we?'

He kissed the top of her head. 'Together.'

She looked up at him and smiled. 'Together.'

* * * * *

SHOW ME
A HERO

ALLISON LEIGH

For my family.

Chapter One

The house was nineteen-point-six miles outside of town.

"Incredible," Ali Templeton muttered under her breath when she pulled up in front of the dated-looking two-story building that sat on a small knoll in what seemed like the middle of nowhere.

Only nineteen-point-six miles.

She exhaled and pushed open the door of her cruiser, sticking one sturdy boot out onto the frozen red earth. She was on personal time and probably shouldn't be using the vehicle assigned to her by the department. It would be one more reason for her sergeant to give her grief, but her own little pickup truck was in the shop, and would be remaining there until she could scrabble together the money to pay for the new transmission it needed.

She zipped up her jacket against the whistling wind

as she studied the house in front of her. Sgt. Gowler had been annoyed with her ever since she stopped dating his son, so she was used to it by now. What was one more reprimand?

Discovering that Grant Cooper was living just nineteen-point-six miles outside of her very own hometown was either the height of irony, or the proof that she wasn't much of a cop, just like Sgt. Gowler seemed to think.

Not that she was here for professional reasons.

Not exactly.

Her bangs blew into her face, obscuring her view, and she shoved her sunglasses up onto the top of her head to keep her hair out of her eyes. She should never have impetuously cut the bangs. It was taking forever for them to grow long enough to stay contained in the bun she had to wear because Gowler was a stickler for regulations.

She'd been out to this abandoned ranch once before. Just over a year ago. Then, it had been at the behest of a single mom at her wit's end over the wild crowd her fifteen-year-old son had fallen in with. Alongside one of the county's deputy sheriffs, she'd rounded up Trevor and the rest of the kids, boarded up the broken windows that had allowed them access to the vacant house and hauled the kids back home to their parents.

There were still no animals in the fields. But now the sheets of plywood were gone. All the windows were intact. And though there was no sign of any vehicles, there was a thin stream of smoke coming from the chimney that she hoped meant the man she sought was actually inside.

When she went up the weathered porch steps, they creaked ominously, as if they hadn't borne the weight of a human being in about half a century. Jabbing her gloved finger against the doorbell didn't elicit any response, so she tugged off the glove, balled her fingers into a fist and pounded loudly on the door. A shelf of snow slid off the roof, landing with a plop next to her feet.

She wasn't going to take it as a bad sign. The snow could just have easily landed on her head.

She swiped the pile sideways with her boot until it fell off the side of the small porch, and knocked again, a little more gently this time. Even if he didn't answer the door, she wasn't going to give up.

Not now that she'd finally found him.

She glanced at her watch. She couldn't afford to be too long before she reported in, or Gowler really would have a legitimate reason to be all over her case. But she'd just discovered where Grant Cooper was and she wasn't taking any chances. She knocked on the door again, then glanced over her shoulder, scanning the landscape around the house. It looked even more desolate than it had when she'd rousted the weed-smoking teenagers.

But then again, it was the middle of January. In the middle of Wyoming.

"Come on." She lifted her hand to knock again, but the door was yanked open from the inside, startling her enough that she fell back a step.

Annoyed with herself, she stiffened her shoulders and looked up into the face of the man who stood there.

Six feet tall. A lean 170. Dark-haired. Dark-browed, dark-bearded. Her brain automatically categorized the details that she'd only seen in a photo in his DMV record.

When she got to the eyes, though?

She felt her brain short-circuit.

Not blue.

Not green.

Aqua.

Entirely heart-stopping, even though they *were* glaring at her.

"I can't believe I finally found you," she blurted.

His lips thinned. "It's my only one." He shoved something into her hands. "Now get off my property." Before she could blink, he slammed the door shut. Right in her face.

She was too stunned to react.

At first.

But annoyance quickly hit and she pounded on the door again, using the spine of the hardback book he'd pushed into her hand. It served one good purpose at least—it made an effective door-knocker.

It didn't matter to her if he turned out to be as strange as a three-dollar bill. She wasn't going to just turn around and leave because he hadn't greeted her with a big smile and howdy-do.

So she banged with the book and pulled out her badge with her other hand. "Mr. Cooper, open the door," she said loudly. "I'm not going away until we've had a chance to speak." She banged again. "Open up!"

The door was yanked open again. "If Chelsea sent you—"

Ali did the shoving this time and pushed her badge right in front of his face. "I'm Officer Templeton with the Braden Police Department, here on official business." She was definitely stretching the truth about that, but oh, well. "I don't know who Chelsea is, nor do I care, unless she has information about the whereabouts of Daisy Miranda."

Only because she was watching him closely did she catch the glint of surprise in his otherwise glowering expression.

"Are you Grant Cooper?"

He still looked like he wasn't going to answer and she wiggled her badge a little, even as she tried to make herself as physically imposing as five foot two could ever be.

"Yes," he admitted through his teeth.

"Then Daisy is your sister." The woman might be a rolling stone, never staying in one place for more than three or four months at a time, but she seemed to have tried to always maintain some sort of contact with her brother.

Which was the only reason Ali had found him right here at all. She'd literally followed a postcard to the man.

Nineteen-point-six miles. He'd been practically under her nose all this time.

His expression darkened even more. "My sister's name is *Karen Cooper*. Not Daisy Miranda."

But he'd recognized the name. Ali had seen it in his eyes. She wished they had a photo of Daisy. But she didn't. Just a general description provided by the people who'd known her during her brief stay in Braden. "Medium height. Slender. Red hair, green eyes? Maybe she married?"

His expression revealed his disbelief. "No way."

"Does she often use an alias? Are there other names she goes by?"

His lips were pressed together.

She let out a little breath of frustration. "If you think your silence will make me give up, you're wrong, Mr.

Cooper. Regardless of what she's calling herself these days, I'm looking for her. And I intend to find her."

"You and about a dozen others. If you're here because my sister owes somebody money, you're out of luck. You won't get it from me."

"This isn't about money."

"I don't care what it's about." He tried closing the door again, only to glare at her even harder when he couldn't because she'd quickly planted her heavy boot in the doorway.

"So you don't care about her abandoned baby?" Ordinarily, she would have cringed a little at her own bluntness, but these weren't ordinary circumstances.

This time she didn't have to look closely to see the shock that crossed his handsome face. He closed his aqua eyes for a second. Then he frowned and moved away from the doorway. But he didn't try shutting the door.

It was invitation enough for her and she stepped inside.

The interior of the house was only slightly less derelict than it had been when she'd confronted the teenagers. Then, the kids had been sprawled around on sleeping bags and tattered beach chairs. Now, only one piece of furniture remained in the main room—a couch that was presumably new, considering the thick plastic wrapped around it. It was pushed to one side of the square room and sat beneath a foggy-glassed wall mirror. A couple of packing boxes were stacked next to it, along with what appeared to be new, unfinished kitchen cabinets. On the other side of the room were gallon cans of paint along with paint rollers stacked atop a tarp. Clearly he was preparing to paint over the graffiti-covered walls.

The problems she and her sister were having with the Victorian they'd been restoring were owed strictly to the age and decline of the house. He had to deal with an old house *plus* neglect and outright vandalism.

He disappeared through a door near the paint cans and she followed, setting the thick book on top of one of the boxes as she passed the stack.

He was standing in the middle of the kitchen, seeming to stare at nothing at all.

He made no sign that he even recognized her presence. Chewing the inside of her cheek, she stepped around him to reach the sink against the cabinetless wall. When she'd been here before, the kitchen had had vile yellow cabinets and she wondered if he'd pulled them out in preparation for the new ones, or if it had been vandals.

The white enamel sink was still chipped, but it was no longer filled with cigarette ashes and discarded beer cans. In fact, it looked scrupulously clean. There was a dish drainer sitting on the bottom of the sink and she pulled one of the glasses from it. It was still damp from being recently washed, and she filled it with water.

He hadn't moved a muscle.

"Mr. Cooper, why don't you sit down?" She gestured to the round table wedged in the space between an avocado-green refrigerator and a tin-doored pantry cupboard.

He still didn't move.

His chambray shirtsleeves were rolled up his sinewy forearms and she cautiously touched his elbow through the cloth.

He jerked as if she'd prodded him with an electric rod and glared down at her.

She pushed the water glass toward him until he had

no choice but to take it. "Maybe this will help," she said calmly despite the distraction of his intensely colored eyes. "Would you mind if I sat?"

His eyebrows lowered as she pulled out one of the padded metal chairs without waiting for his answer. She sat on the edge of the yellow vinyl cushion, hoping he would follow suit.

She needed his cooperation. It would be easier to get that if she could get beyond his annoyance and his shock. In her experience, sitting together at someone's kitchen table was a step in the right direction.

After a brief hesitation, he pulled out a second chair. The metal legs scraped against the black-and-white checkered linoleum floor. He sat, and finally drank down half the water.

Then he set the glass in the middle of the table and sighed. He rested his forearms on the Formica and pressed his fingers together until the tips turned white around his short, neatly clipped fingernails. "I didn't know she'd had a baby," he said after a moment. His voice was low. Gruff. "Or that she was in Braden. We—" He broke off and cleared his throat, curling his fingers into fists. "We haven't spoken in a while."

Ali very nearly reached out to cover his hands with her own. Instead, she clasped them together in her lap just to be sure she kept them under control. She wanted to ask what his and his sister's connection was to Braden that they'd both ended up here during entirely different time frames. Braden was simply too small for it to be coincidental. But she held back that particular question for now. "How long is a while?"

His jaw shifted. "A while." He focused those unsettling eyes on her face. "How do you know this baby you're talking about is Karen's?"

She couldn't fudge the facts about that. "I don't know for certain that she is," she admitted. "Only that a child has been abandoned, and the evidence seems to point to her being Karen's."

"What evidence?"

An old-fashioned electric clock hung on the wall opposite them, above the stove. It was shaped like a black cat, with a long tail that swung right and left in time with the ticking hands of the clock face on the cat's belly. "There was an unsigned note left along with the infant. We believe your sister wrote it. Her wording was distinct."

His eyebrows rose slightly.

"'Jaxie, please take care of Layla for me.'" Ali recited the brief missive from memory.

Grant sat back in his chair. His expression turned annoyed again. "How does that tell you anything? Except the kid's name is Layla. You don't even know for sure that the author of the note is Layla's mother. You're just assuming."

"In the absence of any other information, it's the only assumption we have to make. Maybe Daisy isn't—"

"Karen."

"*Karen.* Maybe she isn't the baby's mother, but she clearly had some involvement with the child or she wouldn't have written the note."

"*If* she wrote the note. Do you even have proof of that? And who the hell is Jaxie?"

She glanced at the clock again. Gowler would take lateness even worse than he would her personal use of a department vehicle. God only knew what he would assign her to next. Janitorial, maybe. It was about the one thing he hadn't done. Yet. "Maybe I should start at the beginning."

He gave her a long look that seemed to say "you think?" "Maybe you should."

She suddenly felt too warm and unzipped her jacket. "An infant was left on the doorstep of a home owned by two brothers in Braden last month. The only identifying item left with the baby was the note. Unsigned, as I said. On common, white paper. No clear fingerprints. But the reference to Jaxie presumably meant Jaxon Swift, who is one of the occupants of the home. Mr. Swift owns a business in Braden and he had an employee for a short while named—" she inclined her head slightly "—Daisy Miranda, who was the only one who ever used that nickname for him. But she left Mr. Swift's employment more than a year ago and he hasn't heard from her since."

"So? The kid is his. Why else leave her for him? What's the problem?" His eyes looked cynical. "*Jaxie* doesn't want to take responsibility?"

"That was our assumption, too, at first. That he was the father, I mean. But DNA tests have already disproved his paternity. He's not Layla's father. The business Mr. Swift owns is a bar. Magic Jax. Karen was a cocktail waitress. Their uniforms are, um—"

"Skimpy?"

She hesitated. She'd been known to work as a cocktail waitress at Magic Jax a time or two for extra money. She was taking a few shifts right now to help get her car out of auto-shop jail. "Let's just say the outfits are closely fitted. Given the timing, it's unlikely that your sister was even pregnant when she quit working there. There are no records locally about Layla's birth, but we estimate she's now about three months old."

"So where is the baby?"

Ali kept herself from shifting. "The judge in charge

of her case has placed her temporarily with a local family while we investigate."

His lips twisted. "He's put her in foster care, you mean."

The term was accurate, but implied a formality and distance that wasn't the case at all, since it was Ali's own sister Maddie and her new husband, Lincoln Swift, who were providing the care. "Yes. A very good foster family. Can you give me any information about Karen's friends? If she was involved with a particular man?"

"No. I didn't even know she'd been here in Wyoming."

Ali waited a moment for him to explain further, but he didn't. And even though she tried to give him her best demanding stare, his gaze didn't shy away.

She was afraid that she was the one who came away feeling unsteady. She wasn't used to feeling unnerved by a man. Even an unreasonably handsome one.

Determined to get back on track, she reached into the inner pocket of her jacket and pulled out one of her business cards. They were generic cards for the police department, but she kept a small supply on which she'd added her badge number, email and phone number. "If there's anything that comes to you, anything at all, please consider calling me."

He didn't take the card. "So you can arrest her for abandoning her child?"

She thought about the sweet baby that she herself had rocked and played with and fallen for just like everyone else who'd come into Layla's orbit. It didn't really matter what had drawn this man and his nomadic sister to the same place at entirely different times.

What mattered was Layla.

She placed the card on the center of the table as she

stood. "So I can find a child's mother," she amended quietly.

He didn't respond. Didn't reach for the card.

She squelched a sigh. "Thank you for your time, Mr. Cooper." She turned to leave the kitchen.

"I haven't talked to Karen in nearly three years," he said abruptly.

She stopped and looked at him. She couldn't imagine not speaking with any one of her siblings for three days, much less three years. "That's a long time."

"You don't know Karen." He stood from the table and escorted her from the barren kitchen back through the nonlivable living room. "She's flighty. Irresponsible. Manipulative. But she wouldn't have done this." He opened the front door and a rush of bitterly cold wind swept inside. "She wouldn't have dumped off her baby."

"Not even if she was desperate?"

His lips tightened. "If she was that desperate, she would have let me know."

"Well…" Ali zipped up her jacket. Fortunately, her departmental SUV had good heating. She stuck out her hand, hoping to show him that she wasn't his adversary. "If you think of anything at all that might help us find her, please consider calling me."

He looked vaguely resigned. He briefly clasped her hand, then shoved his fingers in the front pockets of his jeans. "I won't think of anything."

She fought the urge to tuck away her own hand, because her palm was most definitely singing. "But if you do—"

"But if I do, I'll contact you."

It was the best she could do at the moment. Bringing up the subject of testing *his* DNA to help identify whether or not Karen, aka Daisy Miranda, was actually Layla's mother wouldn't get her anywhere. Not just yet. She didn't have to possess the kind of brilliant mind that had been bestowed on her siblings to recognize that particular fact. "Thank you." She barely took two steps out the front door when it closed solidly behind her.

She didn't look back, but let out a long, silent exhale that clouded visibly around her head as she went down the steps and headed to the SUV. At least she'd learned Daisy's real name.

Daisy Miranda might have seemed to have disappeared off the face of the earth.

But maybe Karen Cooper hadn't.

She pulled open the truck door and climbed inside, quickly turning on the ignition and the heat.

Only when she drove away did she finally rub her palm against the side of her pants until the tingling went away.

Grant Cooper watched the SUV until it was out of sight.

Then he turned on his heel and strode through the disaster zone that was the living room, heading back to the kitchen.

The sight of the book sitting on top of his packing crates stopped him.

He picked up the thick novel. Stared for a moment at the slick black cover featuring an embossed outline of a soldier. The author's name, T. C. Grant, was spelled out in gold and was as prominent as the title—*CCT Final Rules*.

He turned and threw the book—hard—across the room.

It bounced against the plaster wall, knocked a can of white paint onto its side and fell with a thud to the floor.

He still felt like punching something.

If not for Karen, he never would have written the damn book he'd just thrown. But what was a little signature forgery, which had locked him into writing a fourth *CCT Rules* book, compared to abandoning her own child?

He raked his fingers through his hair.

"She wouldn't do that," he muttered.

But his eyes caught in the old mirror hanging on the wall. And there was uncertainty in his reflection.

Karen would have *had* to have been desperate to do it. If he hadn't barred her from his life three years ago, she'd have come to him.

Just like she'd always come to him, expecting him to clean up the latest mess that she'd landed herself in.

Until that last, unforgiveable act, when she'd signed his name on the publishing contract he'd decided against accepting, he'd always been there for her.

She'd been crashing on his couch at the time, pitching the advantages of the contract as heavily as his publisher had been. It was his fault for leaving the unsigned contract right out on his desk where she'd had easy access to it. His fault for not even realizing the contract had disappeared, until he'd received it back, fully executed and with a handwritten note of "glad to see you came to your senses" attached. That's what he got for having an ex-wife for his publisher. He'd known immediately what Karen had done, then. Signed his name on the dotted line. Same as she'd used to sign their parents' names on school report cards.

It was easier to write the book than admit what she'd done. Courtesy of his ex-wife, Karen had walked away with a shopping spree for her part in "convincing" him to take the deal he'd admittedly been waffling over.

She'd never known that writing the book had taken everything he had left out of him. Because he'd drawn the line with her by then. No more cleaning up. No more paying off. He didn't want to hear from her. Didn't want her phone calls. Her text messages. Her emails. Not even the postcards she always mailed from the places she ended up on her never-ending quest to find her "perfect" life.

Didn't matter how many times Grant told her there was no such thing. His troubled sister was always on the hunt for it.

She'd even come to Wyoming, where she didn't have any connections at all except for the one that he had.

And now there was a baby. Supposedly hers.

He looked in the mirror.

It wasn't his reflection he saw, though. It was his sister's face when he'd told her to stay out of his life for good.

He looked away from the mirror. Sighed deeply.

"Hell, Karen. What have you done?"

Chapter Two

Grant didn't recognize her at first.

Which wasn't all that surprising, he supposed.

Instead of the shapeless navy blue police uniform covering her from neck to ankles, she wore a short red dress edged in black, which crossed tightly over her breasts to tie in a bow at her hip, and high-heeled black shoes. Her shapely legs peeked out below the snug hem that reached only a few inches past her butt.

He studied Officer Templeton over the rim of his beer as she made her way between tables, taking orders and picking up empties on her way toward the bar, where he was sitting in front of the taps. She didn't even glance his way when she got to the end of the bar, delivered her orders to the bartender and picked up a fresh set of drinks.

"Thanks, Marty," she said as she headed back out to the tables with her heavy tray balanced on one hand.

Grant's gaze followed the sway of her hips longer than was probably polite before he managed to pull it away.

The bartender was back at the taps, filling more beer mugs. He smiled wryly as he caught Grant's eyes. "Don't waste your time on that one," he advised. "The trips are hard to catch."

"Trips?"

"There are two more, look just like her. Identical triplets. Except one of them got married a couple weeks ago."

"I guess at least she got caught."

Marty grinned. "Yeah, by the richest guy in town. Lincoln Swift. His brother, Jax, owns this place."

Grant's interest was piqued a little more. Officer Templeton hadn't provided that particular piece of information. That her brother-in-law's *brother* owned the bar where Karen had worked. Or that she herself worked there, too. Because the police department didn't pay enough, or because of some other secret she harbored?

He glanced over his shoulder again. It was easy to follow Officer Templeton's progress around the dimly lit room. For one, the dress was like a bright red beacon. Then there was her hair. She didn't have it twisted back in a god-awful tight bun tonight; instead, it reached beyond her shoulders, a streaky mass of brown and blond waves that bounced as she walked.

Seymour would have taken one look at Officer Templeton and said she was sex on a stick.

If Seymour wasn't six feet under.

Grant looked back into his beer. He didn't want to think about Seymour Reid any more than he wanted to speculate about his sister and her baby. But Seymour had been on his mind ever since he'd gotten the invitation in the mail that afternoon.

It was for a ceremony a month from now, when Claudia, Seymour's widow, would accept the Distinguished Service Cross for her deceased husband. She'd included a handwritten note for Grant, imploring him to attend. Grant had been Seymour's best friend. He was godfather to their two children. Wouldn't he please, *please* come to North Carolina, where the ceremony was being held?

He dug his fingertips into his pounding temples. Unlike Grant, who'd been a combat controller with the US Air Force, Seymour had been army all the way. A Green Beret. He'd been a few years older than Grant, a hothead with the need to be a hero running in his veins. Grant had been attached to Sey's unit for more than half the time he'd served. When he'd gotten out of the air force nearly six years ago because he'd thought it would save his marriage, Seymour had warned him it wouldn't. At the time, Grant had warned Seymour that *his* marriage wouldn't survive *him* staying in.

But it turned out Seymour had been right.

As usual.

Grant and Chelsea had been divorced within a year.

At Seymour's funeral last year, Claudia's wedding ring had been firmly in place on her finger.

"Getcha another, bud?"

He realized Marty had spoken and looked at his now-empty mug. He hadn't even realized he'd finished the beer.

Which was a pretty good reason not to have another. "No thanks." He tossed enough cash on the bar to cover the drink and a tip, then pushed out of his seat and grabbed his coat from the empty bar stool next to him.

From the corner of his eye, he saw Officer Templeton bending over slightly as she cleared a table. How anyone as short as her could have legs that went on forever was beyond him. His ex-wife was nearly as tall as he was and her legs hadn't seemed that long.

He was almost to the door when the pretty police officer straightened and her gaze collided with his.

She looked surprised for about half a second, then dumped her round tray into the hands of one of her customers and started toward him, not stopping until she was two feet away. She propped her hands on her slender hips and gave him a steady look. "There are at least ten bars in this town. Yet you pick Magic Jax."

"So?"

She shrugged. "Don't expect me to believe it's coincidental. You wanted to see the place where Daisy worked."

"Karen. And interesting that you didn't mention you work here, too."

"It's temporary." Her dark eyes continued to boldly meet his. "Are you going to ask when you can meet your niece?"

He grimaced. "You don't know that she's my niece. You only think she is."

"Little lady, are we gonna get our cocktails anytime soon, or—"

She looked at the old guy wearing a ten-gallon hat who'd just interrupted them. "Squire Clay, I've warned you before. If you call me 'little lady' again, I'm not gonna let you off for speeding the next time I stop you."

The auburn-haired woman with Ten Gallon hid a snicker.

"You want your drinks right this second, go on over and get 'em from Marty," she told him.

Ten Gallon looked a little abashed. "Sorry, Ali," he muttered.

Seeming satisfied, Officer Templeton looked back at Grant. "It's a pretty good hunch," she continued as if there'd been no interruption at all. "If you're willing to provide a DNA sample, we could know for sure."

His DNA wouldn't prove squat, though he had no intention of telling her that. Particularly now that they'd become the focus of everyone inside the bar. The town had a whopping population of 5,000. Maybe. It was small, but that didn't mean there wasn't a chance he'd be recognized. And the last thing he wanted was a rabid *CCT Rules* fan showing up on his doorstep.

He'd had too much of that already. It was one of the reasons he'd taken refuge at the ranch that his biological grandparents had once owned. He'd picked it up for a song when it was auctioned off years ago, but he hadn't seriously entertained doing much of anything with it— especially living there himself.

At the time, he'd just taken perverse pleasure in being able to buy up the place where he'd never been welcomed while they'd been alive.

Now, it was in such bad disrepair that to stay there even temporarily, he'd been forced to make it habitable.

He wondered if Karen had stayed there, unbeknownst to him. If she was responsible for any of the graffiti or the holes in the walls.

He pushed away the thought and focused on the officer. "Ali. What's it short for?"

She hesitated, obviously caught off guard. "Alicia, but nobody ever calls me that." He'd been edging closer to the door, but she'd edged right along with him. "So, about that—"

Her first name hadn't been on the business card she'd left for him. "Ali fits you better than Alicia."

She gave him a look from beneath her just-from-bed sexy bangs. "Stop changing the subject, Mr. Cooper."

"Start talking about something else, then. Better yet—" he gestured toward the bar and Marty "—start doing the job for *Jaxie* that you conveniently didn't mention before."

"I told you. It's temporary."

"I don't care if it is or isn't. But it makes me wonder what other details you've left out."

She looked annoyed. "Mr. Cooper—"

"G'night, Officer Ali." He pushed open the door and headed out into the night.

Ali stifled a curse as she watched Grant Cooper flip up the collar of his coat before he strode across the street.

Then the door to Magic Jax swung closed, cutting off the sight of him as well as the flow of cold air.

That didn't stop her from feeling shivery, though.

"Ali, all your orders are backing up."

She smiled at the other cocktail waitress working that night. It wasn't Charlene's fault that Ali was more interested in chasing after Grant Cooper for information about his sister than she was delivering drinks. "Sorry about that, Charlene." She couldn't push Grant out of her mind, but she could at least do what she was being paid to do. She hurried over to the bar and began loading up a tray. "Marty, you work most nights, right?"

The bartender didn't stop polishing glasses with his towel. "Most."

"Has he been in here before? Grant Cooper?"

"That's the guy you were just talking to?" Marty shrugged. "He's been in a couple times."

"Recently?"

"Yeah, I guess. The last few weeks, anyway."

"He ask any questions?"

Marty smiled wryly. "Yeah, what've we got on tap."

"About something *other* than beer?"

He shook his head. "Nope. Why? What's the story?"

"No story. I was just curious."

"You're never *just* curious, little… Ali," Squire interjected, stopping next to the bar and handing her a twenty. Not too long ago, she'd learned that the prosperous rancher from Weaver was sort of her relative. "Gloria and I are headin' out now."

Ali held up the twenty-dollar bill between two fingers. "What's this?"

"Bribery. For next time you pull me over for speeding."

"I've got a better idea, Squire." She plucked the hat off his gray head and tucked the twenty into the hatband. "Just stop speeding."

He guffawed and clapped her on the back with one of his big, rough hands. "You're a good girl, Ali, even if you got that uppity shrew for a granny. Ya oughta be finding a husband like that sis of yours has now."

She shook her head. "Nobody left who's worth marrying, Squire, since you've been hitched to Gloria all these years."

Standing near the doorway, Gloria sniffed loudly. "You're welcome to the old coot, Ali," she called. "You just say the word."

"Eh, she needs a young buck like that fella she was just talkin' to." Squire winked at her as he headed toward his wife and the exit. "Someone who can keep up with her."

Ali chuckled as was expected of her, and picked up the heavy tray.

But the truth was, she was thirty years old. She'd been dating since she was sixteen, and in all that time, she'd never met a man she'd been inclined to marry. And even though there'd been all sorts of inclinations circling inside her since she'd met Grant Cooper, none of them were in the "proper" realm of marriage.

As for her thoughts of Grant inhabiting an improper realm? Now that was a whole different kettle of fish.

But it was a lot more important to get Grant Cooper on board when it came to finding his sister than it was to think about properly improper-ing him.

She finished delivering the drinks and returned to load up her tray again.

"You going to work again tomorrow night?" Marty had pulled out the schedule and set it next to the drink station.

She sighed. The thought of spending another five hours wearing high heels held no appeal whatsoever, particularly after spending eight hours on her feet doing traffic duty, which was Gowler's latest punishment for her. But she still needed to get her truck out of the shop. "Yeah. And probably the night after that, if I can."

Marty scribbled on the schedule with his pencil. "You got it, little lady."

She made a face and tossed a lemon curl at him. "Very funny."

"I thought so." He grinned. "So what *is* behind your curiosity with that guy, Grant? Been a while since you dumped Keith Gowler. You finally looking for some fresh flesh?"

"Don't be gross, Marty." She preferred not to think that she'd *dumped* Keith since they'd only dated a few weeks, but it was true she'd been the one to put the brakes on dating him. "Grant might be a link to Layla."

Looking surprised, Marty stopped what he was doing. Most everyone in town, and particularly those who worked at the bar, knew a baby had been abandoned on the Swift brothers' doorstep last month. "He's the baby's father?"

"Uncle. He's Daisy Miranda's brother."

He propped his elbows on the bar. "No kidding. First time he came in, he told me he was staying at the old Carmody place outside of town."

"I know that *now*, so don't rub it in, okay?" Ali had been to New Mexico, Colorado, Idaho and California— all on her own time and Linc's pennies—following the circuitous trail that Daisy Miranda had left in her wake after quitting her job at Magic Jax. What Ali had learned along the way was that there had been only two consistent things about Daisy. One—her inconsistency. And two—her habit of sending postcards to a man named Grant Cooper that were routinely marked "return to sender." But one of those postcards had gone against that trend. It had been returned to the post office right here in Braden with a label on it containing a forwarding address for a desolate ranch located nineteen-point-six miles outside of town.

"Did you ever meet the Carmodys?" Marty pulled a tray of clean glasses from the dishwasher and started emptying it. "Roger and Helen?"

Ali shook her head. "I don't recall, but I suppose our paths would have probably crossed somewhere along the way. Can't really live in Braden all your life and not have run into everyone else." She nabbed one of the glasses, filled it with water and gulped it down. She hadn't had time to eat between her shift at the police department and when she'd gone on duty at Magic Jax, and her stomach was growling in the worst way. "I assume you did." Since he knew their names and all.

"They went to the same church as my grandma. Helen died way before he did." He made a face. "I think they were as uptight as my grandma, too."

"Well, I don't know anything about that. But I do know the bank took back Roger Carmody's property about ten years ago and he was forced to move away. I did not know, until just this week, however, that it had been bought at auction by none other than Grant Cooper, who turns out to be the brother of Daisy Miranda. He never lived there, though. Until now. He's got his work cut out for him. Leaving it vacant all those years was just an invitation for vandals." She set her glass in the rack of dirty dishes. "He's here and claiming he doesn't know anything about his sister's whereabouts or her baby."

"You don't believe him?"

Did she? Ali picked up her loaded tray again. "I think it's a lot of coincidences."

"In other words, you don't believe him."

There was something about Grant Cooper that made her instinctively want to believe him.

Or maybe it was just those darned aqua eyes.

"It's too soon to tell, Marty. It's just too soon to tell."

Eighteen hours later, Ali was working her way along Central Avenue, trying to pretend her feet hadn't turned into blocks of ice despite her boots as she monitored the frost-rimmed parking meters lining the four blocks of the downtown area. Since it had been snowing steadily since that morning, she didn't feel particularly inclined to punish the folks who didn't want to keep running out to feed coins into the meters every ninety minutes. But she also knew if she didn't write at least a few parking tickets, Gowler would accuse her of being soft. And being "soft" wasn't going to earn her an opportunity to move up the ranks—assuming he ever forgave her for dumping his son.

So she kept tramping up and down the snowy street looking for the worst of the offenders. She pulled out her pad and halfheartedly wrote out a couple citations, tucking them beneath windshield wipers before shoving her cold hands back into her gloves.

When she reached the edge of the business district, she crossed the quiet street and started making her way back down the other side. For every two meters with time on the clock, there were two more that had expired. She tucked her nose farther into the knit scarf wound around her neck and kept walking.

"Templeton!"

She stiffened at the sound of her name and looked toward the source. Sgt. Gowler was standing on the sidewalk in front of the library. She stomped her feet in place on the sidewalk. "Yes, sir?"

"Know for a fact that meter you just passed is expired."

"By only a few minutes."

"Expired is expired."

She swallowed her retort and pulled her citation book out of her pocket again. "Yes, sir."

It was obvious that he intended to stand there and wait to make sure she did her duty. She turned back to the last vehicle and peeled off her thick glove again so she could write out the parking ticket. "Parking shmarking," she muttered under her breath.

If she had more than a few bucks in change to spare

she'd have carried it around in her pockets just to feed the dang meters herself. She tore the ticket off her pad and brushed the mound of snow off the windshield, then lifted the wiper enough to stick the ticket underneath it.

From the corner of her eye, she saw her boss go back inside the library.

Grumbling under her breath, she moved to the next expired meter next to a badly rusted truck. Her fingers were numb as she quickly marked the form and wrote in the license plate number. She yanked off the form and hurriedly shoved it under the wiper blade.

"You've gotta be kidding me."

She jerked up her head, looking toward the library again. But instead of Sgt. Gowler, this time it was Grant Cooper who'd come out onto the sidewalk.

He wore a dark jacket, unzipped, as if he was impervious to the weather that was currently making her long for life in the tropics. He had no scarf. Wore no gloves. Within seconds, his dark hair was dusted with snow. "I had ninety minutes on that thing," he said, pointing a long finger at the meter. "I haven't been in the library that long."

"The meters don't lie." She blew on her fingers, warming them a little before stuffing them back inside her glove. She wanted to tell him that if it was up to her, the meters wouldn't even exist on that street. They hadn't been updated in the past generation and the town had an old repair guy on standby just to keep them in operation. But she also didn't want her sergeant coming out again and seeing her flagrantly disregarding his instructions, either.

"Looks like you had a productive visit." She gestured at the stack of books he was carrying. The book he'd pushed into her hands when she'd shown up at his door wasn't far from her mind, though she'd paid no attention whatsoever to it at the time. "You must be a big reader."

He showed her one cover. "*Plumbing for Dummies*. Not exactly pleasure reading."

"Ah." She couldn't help a surprised laugh, as she shifted from one frozen stump to the other. "I actually need a copy of that one myself. My sisters and I own an old Victorian that we're restoring."

"Because you don't have enough to do, slinging drinks and doling out parking tickets?" He moved past her and tugged the ticket free. "How much is this gonna cost me?"

She started to point at the street sign nearby that warned of the fine for parking violations, only to realize that the surface of it was obscured by icy snow. "Fifty bucks. If you don't pay it by the date indicated on the ticket, the fine doubles. And it gets worse from there." Considering the state of his ranch house and the state of the vehicle, she hoped he got the message. Even if it was outrageously high, paying the parking fine on time was the simplest way to avoid owing even more money.

"Nice payback, Officer." The truck door screeched when he yanked it open and he tossed the ticket and his stack of books inside on the bench seat that was covered with a worn woven blanket. Maybe to keep his admittedly fine tushy warm or, if he was like Ali with her truck, to hide the rips and stains in the upholstery.

"Payback! For what?"

"Not cooperating as much as you wanted." He climbed into the truck and yanked the door closed with another protesting screech of metal.

She rapped her gloved knuckles on the window.

He looked as annoyed as she felt, but he rolled down

the window a few inches. His aqua eyes skated over her face. "Now what?"

"If I wanted payback," she said evenly, "I would also write you up for the broken taillight and the expired tags on this heap of rust. Instead, I'll just offer a friendly warning to get them taken care of as soon as possible."

"Or?"

"Or the next patrolman who gets stuck on traffic duty might not be so easygoing about it and you'll end up owing even more money that it doesn't look much like you can afford." She stepped back from the truck and smiled tightly. "Drive safe, now. I don't know what sort of conditions you were used to before coming to Wyoming, but the roads are treacherous in this kind of weather."

His lips thinned. He rolled up his window and cranked the engine. It started after a few tries, belching a cloud of black smoke from the tailpipe.

Ali winced and tucked her nose back into the protection of her knit scarf and watched him drive away.

Chapter Three

"**Y**ou should have let Cooper skate on the expired parking meter."

Ali set the mineral water and lime and the order of onion rings on the table in front of her sister Greer. If Magic Jax wasn't so busy, she'd have set herself down, too, in the seat opposite her. "I had to choose between citing Grant Cooper or getting skewered by my sergeant again. If Gowler has an actual reason to write me up, it'll be the first nail in my coffin with the department. And he only needs three nails."

"He's not going to fire the only female officer he's got," Greer countered. "Particularly if she's not guilty of anything more serious than letting a new resident off a minor infraction with a warning. Everyone else with the department does it from time to time. Why not you?"

"Everyone else doesn't make the mistake of dating his precious son, Madame Prosecutor. I am not taking any chances."

Greer gave her a look. "I'm a defense lawyer."

"Don't remind me." Greer was the oldest of the three triplets and worked with the public defender's office. Maddie was the middle triplet. The ultimate do-gooder, she was a social worker with family services. Because of her role there, the family court judge had agreed to let her be the temporary caregiver for Layla.

Ali gestured at the stack of files sitting on the table next to her sister's elbow. The public defender's office workload was so huge that they also had a rotating crew of private attorneys who took cases pro bono. "Always trying to get the people I arrest off with just a slap on the wrist."

"You do your job and I'll do mine. That's how it works. Gowler aside, you could have at least bargained a little with Cooper over the ticket. You catch more flies with honey, you know."

Ali didn't dare slip her toes out of her high-heeled shoes so she could wiggle some blood back into them. If she did, she feared she would never get her feet back into the shoes. And she really didn't want to hear Greer's advice at the moment. "You want anything else to go with those onion rings?"

"I shouldn't even be eating these." Greer plucked a ring from the basket. Magic Jax didn't provide a full menu, but they did offer the usual types of bar food. "But I'm starving. Came straight here from the office."

"If you change your mind, let me know." She grabbed her tray and headed back to the bar, picking up empty glasses along the way. It was even busier than it had been the night before. Part of that was because it was Friday night. A larger part, she figured, was because Jax himself was actually mixing drinks behind the bar. For as long as she'd been picking up shifts at Magic Jax, she could only recall a handful of times when he'd actually played bartender.

Every time he did, though, word seemed to spread and the ladies came in droves.

It wasn't surprising. Jaxon Swift was rich. He didn't take any part in the running of the family oil business like Linc did, but he was still part of Swift Oil. He was also as handsome as a blond devil and loved women just as much as they loved him. In short, nothing much had changed since he and Ali had been in high school together.

And now, thanks to Maddie marrying his brother, Linc, they were theoretically one big happy family.

She went behind the bar to rinse the empties and stack them in the dishwasher tray. "Busy night. I didn't expect it to be, considering the snow today," Ali said to her boss.

Jax took the lid off the blender and filled three hurricane glasses with the virulent pink daiquiris that the giggling college girls at table four had ordered. "Busy is the way I like it." He set the glasses on a tray, leaving Ali to top them with the requisite whipped cream and sliced strawberry. He glanced at his next order and reached for a bottle of wine with one hand and a bottle of gin with the other. "Keeps us all in business."

They both glanced toward the door as it opened and a flurry of snowflakes danced inside. A few more women hurried in and started shimmying out of their cold-weather gear. One wore a spaghetti-strapped blue sequin dress under her parka. The other had on a strapless red corset with rhinestone-studded jeans.

Both fluffed their hair as they focused on Jax behind the bar.

Ali had a hard time not rolling her eyes as she finished fanning one of the strawberry slices over a mound of cream. "I think I'm the only one here who's never wanted to date you," she told him.

He chuckled. "What about Greer?"

"Greer never dated anything except her textbooks. Besides, it would have been gross. You went out with Maddie."

He deftly poured two glasses of wine, set them on a tray for Charlene and tossed the empty bottle into the bin beneath the bar top. "Yeah, but she married my big brother." He shrugged and grinned. "No accounting for taste, sometimes." He quickly prepared a gin-and-grapefruit, shaking out the last few drops of grapefruit juice from the plastic pitcher before tossing it into the stainless-steel sink, and added the glass to Charlene's order. "No more grapefruit." Then he picked up a knife and finished prepping the last daiquiri while she fussed with her second one. "You're lagging, Ali."

She rolled her eyes as she picked up the tray and headed around the bar again. After delivering the drinks, she went over to the newcomers, who were still hovering near the entrance. She didn't recognize them. "Help you find a place to sit?"

One of them bit her deeply red lip. "We wanted the bar."

Ali looked over her shoulder. There were a half-dozen bar stools and all were occupied.

By women.

"You're welcome to wait, but I think it might be a while." She gestured at a two-top in the far corner. It, and one other just like it, were the only vacant tables in the place. "If you change your mind, just grab one of those over by the pool table." She barely paused as she spoke, since standing still for too long just reminded her how sore her feet were.

She made the rounds of her tables again and headed back to Jax with a fresh set of orders. Then she went into the small kitchen and dumped another bag of already breaded onion rings into one fryer basket and added similarly prepared chicken fingers to a second.

She left them bubbling merrily away in their vats of hot oil and nipped into the employee bathroom long enough to pee and wash her hands. Then it was back to the fryer, then to the drink station to fill some water glasses, and then out to see if Corset and Spaghetti had decided to forgo the coveted stools at the bar for a table.

They had, and she went to deliver water to them and collect their orders. "First time in?"

Corset nodded and fluffed her hair again. "We drove over from Weaver."

Ali lifted her eyebrows. The thirty-mile drive between Braden and Weaver was tedious even without snowy conditions. "Hope you're planning to spend the night in town. Probably going to be hard getting back there tonight. What can I get you?"

"Do you have a menu?"

Most people didn't bother asking. "Sure." She grabbed one from another table and returned with it. "It's a full bar, so we can make most any drink you want." She smiled. "Unless it takes fresh grapefruit juice. We ran out a few minutes ago." It was obvious to her that they weren't ready to make a decision since they were too busy ogling Jax. "I'll come back in a few minutes and check on you."

She headed back through the tables, only to stop short at the sight of her sergeant coming in. But then she straightened her shoulders. There was no rule against her working a second job, and plenty of the other guys did it to help supplement their public-servant wages. She headed toward him. "Good evening, sir. I'm afraid we've only got one table left—"

Gowler lifted his hand, cutting her off. His usual scowl was in place and he looked no more pleased to be there than she was pleased to see him. "Heard you were moonlighting here these days."

No matter what logic told her, she felt the alarm like a swift, oily wave inside her stomach. "Temporarily."

"Whatever," he said, dismissing her reply. She didn't even have time to draw a breath of relief before he plowed on. "Got a disabled vehicle out on the expressway. Need you to get on some real clothes and report for duty. Get things moving before we've got something worse on our hands."

The "expressway" was Gowler's favored term for the highway between Braden and Weaver. Mostly because it was in no way an express. The road was narrow. Winding. Just two lanes for most of the distance between the sister towns. And unfortunately, it was the site of increasingly frequent accidents. The more Weaver continued to grow—mostly because of people going there to work for Cee-Vid, an electronics and gaming manufacturer—the more people there were traveling back and forth between the sistering towns.

She stifled the "why me?" that hovered in her mind and nodded. She knew if Gowler had had a choice, he'd never have asked her to pull overtime. He hated when the excess pay screwed with his sacred budget. "I just need to let Jax know. He'll have to call in another cocktail waitress."

Gowler waved, looking impatient. But not even his mammoth-sized ego was large enough to think he could order her to do otherwise. Particularly where the Swift family was concerned. Swift Oil was integral to the town's existence. "Do what you've got to do. Then get your rear out to mile post seventeen." He turned on his boot heel and stomped back out the door.

Jax was a lot more understanding than Charlene when Ali broke the news that she had to leave. But then Jax wasn't the one who had to cover all the tables until he found someone else to come in at the last minute on a Friday night.

As she rang up her last set of orders, her gaze fell on Greer. The onion-ring basket was half-empty and she had files spread out all over her table. Greer didn't seem to be aware of anything going on around her as she bent her head over her work. Her dark hair was twisted up in one of her fancy chignons and the only movement she made was with her pen as she scrawled notes on a legal pad.

"Get Greer to fill in for an hour," Ali suggested to Jax.

She left him giving her sister a speculative look and went to the employee bathroom again to change back into the uniform she'd just changed out of only a few hours earlier. She was dog-tired and didn't really look forward to spending any time out on the dark, snowy highway. But there was one bright spot: she got to peel the high-heeled pumps that she had a hate-hate relationship with off her feet.

She rolled up the cocktail uniform and stuffed it in her carryall, pulled on her overcoat and headed out to the front again.

Greer spotted her and gave her the stink eye around Jax as he stood next to her table, clearly trying to talk her into emergency-waitressing for him. Ali smiled broadly as she headed out the exit. Greer would never be able to flat-out refuse their brother-in-law's brother. And in Ali's opinion, her legal-eagle sister could stand an hour or two slinging drinks like common folk.

The traffic was backed up so badly on the highway that it took Ali nearly an hour to work her way through it. She had to weave slowly between cars on both sides of the road with her beacon flashing before she got to the sight of the disabled truck. One of the county deputy sheriffs from Weaver was already on site, but it was obvious that he'd arrived only a few minutes before Ali had.

She grabbed a bright orange vest from her emergency kit and pulled it over her coat as she jogged across the headlight-illuminated road to where he'd set out flares. "Hey, Dave," she greeted when she got close enough to recognize Dave Ruiz. He was a longtime deputy with plenty of experience when it came to their expressway. Far more experience than she had, at any rate. "Miserable night for this particular pleasure, but nice to see you all the same."

Dave, wearing a similar vest, handed her a bundle of flares. "You, too, Ali." He gestured at the semi-trailer that was on its side, blocking both lanes of traffic. "Driver's cleared the debris from the hay bales he lost, but we're still waiting on the tow to get it back on its wheels."

If it hadn't been for the headlights and the glow of the flares, it would have been impossible to see much of anything. As it was, the lights reflecting off the falling snow made their task even harder. "At least this wasn't two miles up the road."

"Amen to that. We'd have had someone go off the curve for sure. All we have to deal with now are a bunch of pissed-off, impatient drivers." The deputy pointed at the toppled trailer. "If we could get some snow cleared away from that side of the trailer, we could redirect traffic one-by-one past the block."

She squinted at the vehicles crowded around them. "Going to have to get each side to give an inch or two."

He grunted. "Yep." He jerked his head. He was wearing a dark beanie, same as she was, and snow clung to it. "Already got a Good Samaritan working on our side to get 'em pulled back some. Busy night with the snowstorm, or we'd have more boots on the ground here."

"Help is help. I'll work on my side," she said. "Considering the angle of the trailer, might be easier if we started letting my side go through first."

"That was my thinking, too."

Happy that they were on the same page, she lit a flare and started working her way back along the highway, dropping the flares as she went to outline the improvised route.

When she was finished, she walked back along the line of bumper-to-bumper vehicles, telling each driver what the plan was and assuring them they were trying to get the road passable as quickly as they could. Her feet were cold again inside her boots, but at least they didn't ache the way they had in the high heels.

There was no room to use the plow on the front of her unit or Ruiz's, so she pulled the snow shovel she always carried from the back, headed over to the end of the long semitrailer and started attacking the berm that had built up from weeks of snowplows clearing the highway. It was a good four feet high, packed hard with ice and snow and dirt, and she was already breathless when someone carrying a pickax joined her.

"Fancy meeting this way."

She went still, peering at the tall figure. "Mr. Cooper?"

He had on a proper coat and gloves at least, though his head was still uncovered.

"Might as well make it Grant, Officer Ali." With a smooth motion, he swung the sharp tip of the pickax into the iced-over mound. "I'll break. You shovel."

It was too much effort to argue, particularly when the idea was a good one, and between the two of them, they managed to break down a car length's worth of snow and ice, shoving the clumps off into the ditch on the other side. The ditch wasn't terribly deep, but it could break an axle if a driver wasn't careful. They both moved farther along the berm and continued.

"You always carry a pickax around with you?"

"Doesn't everyone?"

"Your truck parked somewhere in this logjam?"

"'Bout a mile back on the other side."

"So you are capable of a straight answer." She stopped for a minute to catch her breath and rub the growing ache in the small of her back. She was in good shape, but this was a workout like none she'd had in a while. "Have business in Weaver?"

He, on the other hand, just kept swinging away with the pickax. The guy was like a machine. "My sister isn't in Weaver."

Too proud to let him make her look weak, she jabbed the tip of the shovel into the mess again and resumed pitching it off to the side. "That's not really what I asked."

After siccing Jax on Greer back at the bar, she was going to have to work hard to get her sister to let her use her sweet, claw-foot bathtub back at the house to-night. When she and her sisters had bought the place, they'd agreed to pay separately for the renovations to their own bedrooms and en suite bathrooms, but combine their funds to restore the rest.

A fine idea in theory.

Except that Ali's bathroom was still a work in progress. It had a plywood subfloor perpetually in wait for tile, a sink that worked most of the time and a shower that didn't. Since Maddie had moved in with Linc, Ali had taken to regularly using her shower. But a shower wasn't going to help her aches and pains anywhere near enough after tonight.

Greer, on the other hand, had immediately redone her bedroom and bath. In the entire house, it was the one haven from all that was broken or about to break down. And her claw-foot tub was seriously a thing of beauty.

"It's what you meant," Grant countered.

She didn't bother correcting him, since it was true. "You bought the Carmody place quite a few years ago."

The sharp tip of his pickax sliced cleanly through the snow and ice. "Your point?"

She possessed excellent peripheral vision. Which was handy, because she could watch him without seeming to watch him. "You left it vacant for a long time."

"No law against that." He moved farther along the berm, chipping away faster than she could shovel.

She clenched her teeth and sped up, even though her muscles protested. From behind the truck trailer, she heard engines revving up. Impatient drivers were starting to get a scent of freedom. Just to be safe, she left the shovel standing in the berm and walked back to the first car. The middle-aged driver—smoking his way through a pack of cigarettes if the butts sitting on the road were any indication—rolled down his window when she approached.

Smoke wafted out around her and she coughed once.

A lot of her fellow officers smoked, but she'd never understood the appeal.

She repeated what she'd told him once already. "I'll come back and let you know when it's safe to proceed. It's still gonna be a little while yet, I'm afraid."

He swore. "Little lady, I've got places to be."

She smiled, though she wanted to grind her teeth. "We all do, sir. Might want to consider preserving your gas a little if you can stand the chill—"

He swore again and rolled up the window, cutting her off. He did not turn off his engine.

She straightened, headed back to her shovel and pulled it from the snow. "Just another night in paradise," she muttered.

Already two yards farther than he had been, Grant paused. "Say something?"

He'd done such a good job of breaking up the berm that all she had to do was push the tip of the shovel against the road to plow the chunks off into the ditch. "You're pretty good at this. Had a lot of practice?"

He didn't answer.

"Naturally," she said under her breath.

They chipped and plowed for another few minutes when she saw Dave Ruiz signaling with his mag light. They'd cleared about thirty feet of iced-over berm.

"That's good enough to start," she told Grant, and his rhythmic swinging immediately ceased. He hooked the deadly tip of his pickax over his shoulder and headed off.

"Thank you," she called after him.

He didn't pause. Didn't look back. Merely lifted his left hand in acknowledgment.

The less he said about anything, the more curious she got.

The feminine side of her wished she wasn't so darn

predictable. The cop side of her just accepted the fact that she was always curious where all people were concerned. Not just enigmatic, aqua-eyed men.

She propped her shovel against an upturned wheel on the trailer as she walked back around it, stomped her feet hard against the road to make sure she still had *some* feeling in them and returned to the first car in the lineup. "I'm going to walk ahead of you until you're past the trailer," she told the driver. It wouldn't speed up the process any, but she wasn't taking any chances on an impatient man going off into the ditch and suing the department as a result.

And one by one, that's how she slowly cleared enough of the road on her side to allow traffic on Dave's side a chance of squeaking around the trailer.

Eventually, she was able to get back into her own SUV, crank up the heater and call in the progress as the traffic slowly crawled along the flare-lined path. About two hours after they'd started, three heavy-duty tow trucks arrived and they had to block off the road again from both sides to allow them space to get the semi back up on its wheels.

The only saving grace was that the snow stopped falling halfway through the mammoth task. But when it did, the temperature dropped another ten degrees and the wind—always pronounced, particularly along this highway cut into the hills—picked up.

But finally, the deed was done. The semi was hitched to the back of another tractor and was headed down the road to Braden. The highway returned to its usual quiet midwinter-night state. Dave and Ali congratulated each other on getting the job done without any collisions or injuries, and they all headed home.

When Ali finally made it there, she noticed Greer's

car parked in her half of the detached garage behind the house. In the kitchen, the slow cooker was sitting on the plywood counter. Stone-cold. Full of uncooked ingredients. Ali had forgotten to turn it on when she'd left the house this morning.

She clamped the lid back on top and left it. It wouldn't be any worse come morning and she could deal with it then.

She dragged herself up the narrow staircase and decided she was too tired to worry about waking up her sister to beg to use her fancy-ass bathroom. Instead, she turned on Maddie's shower and stripped once the bathroom was full of steam.

Then she *finally* stepped beneath the blessedly hot spray. She expected her mind to go blank as she stood there, unmoving, her eyes closed while the water rained down on her head. But she was wrong.

She kept thinking about Grant Cooper. Working beside her. Without being asked. Without complaint. Then just walking away.

She shivered, and realized the water was running cold. She shut it off, stepped out and wrapped a towel around her body. Then she wrapped another towel around her head, returned to her own bedroom, climbing in bed just like that, and pulled her quilt up to her ears.

She wasn't even able to enjoy the grateful thought that she didn't have to work the next day before she was out cold.

Chapter Four

Grant eyed the cardboard box sitting on the front porch.

He hadn't noticed it the night before when he'd finally gotten home after the mess on the highway. The bulb in the porch light fixture still didn't work even though he'd replaced it, and it was a wonder he hadn't tripped over the carton in the dark.

He didn't have to open the box to know what was in it. His publisher's logo was imprinted on the side. The address of his cabin in Oregon was crossed out. The address where he stood now had been marked over it in slashing black ink. Because, God forbid, his author copies of *CCT Final Rules* should have remained behind at the cabin, along with everything else he didn't want.

Just like Officer Ali Templeton, his ex-wife publisher had found him.

He grabbed the box and carried it inside, dumping it on the fireplace hearth.

He'd burn them right now, except he'd probably also end up burning down the entire house. Considering the overall condition of the place, he wasn't setting a match to anything in the fireplace until he got a chance to have the chimney inspected.

He knew he had electrical problems. The porch light was just one example. He also knew he had plumbing problems. The kitchen faucet only worked on hot. The shower in his bathroom upstairs only worked on cold, which meant he was out of luck because the bathtub in the bathroom downstairs was too damn short. He was also pretty sure he smelled something burning every time he turned on the furnace, which was why he wore a damn coat inside the house, even when he was sleeping.

He could make things a lot easier on himself by giving up the notion of living here.

He could go back to Oregon anytime he chose. Calling his place there a "cabin" was basically just a nod to the fact that it was located on a remote, forested ridge that overlooked the wild coastline. But it had plenty of amenities. All the electrical outlets there worked. His shower had eight jets, and they all produced hot water. He could also go to the condo in Los Angeles that had sat vacant for more than a year while he'd holed up in Oregon pulling words out by his teeth to finish writing the book he hadn't planned to write in the first place. And if he really wanted a different flavor, he'd never gotten rid of the New York brownstone that he and Chelsea had shared. When they'd gotten divorced, she'd moved into an apartment closer to her Manhattan office. He'd gone to Los Angeles, putting as much distance as he could between them.

Any one of those properties was by far better than

this run-down ranch house he'd decided to fix up himself. But he had no desire to go anywhere else.

He just wished the box of books hadn't found its way to him. It meant that he'd be hearing from his ex-wife sooner or later. Not because she harbored some emotional leftovers from their marriage, but because she still wouldn't accept his decision to quit writing.

She called it a waste. Accused him of being lazy. Lacking ambition.

His gaze landed on the ancient mirror on the wall. The image looking back at him seemed to smirk.

"Right." He grimaced. "That's what you get for being married to your publisher." He turned away. Nobody stood to make more money on another *CCT Rules* book than Chelsea did.

Not even him.

It was too cold inside the house to paint the walls. Besides, the holes in the plaster that he'd spent the previous evening patching were still damp. The gas stove in the kitchen worked—and he had even installed a couple of the cabinets now—but there was nothing in the refrigerator. That was what had driven him out the front door in the first place when he'd spotted the book shipment.

He went back outside and pulled the door closed behind him. Out of habit, he started to lock it, but didn't. If anyone wanted to break in to steal a couple gallons of paint, they probably needed them more than he did. If they stole the plastic-wrapped couch…well, he could order another one online the same way he had this one.

It had seemed necessary to put at least a few pieces of furniture in the house when he'd gotten here. He might not have unwrapped the couch yet, but he'd been using the mattress set from the first night it had been delivered.

He crossed the cold, hard ground between the house and the barn, following the path he'd shoveled yesterday morning. The snow had nearly filled it up again, but he didn't mind. Shoveling snow was mindless muscle work. Yeah, he had to concentrate harder than he wanted to in order to keep his brain from dwelling on anything other than where to pitch the next shovel of snow, but at least with the physical exertion and then the highway mess, he'd slept more than an hour at a stretch last night.

Instead of nightmares of Afghanistan, his fitful dreams had been about a chocolate-eyed brunette with blond streaks in her hair. And for once, the cold shower had been handy.

He pushed open the oversize, rolling barn door and studied the two vehicles inside. He'd bought the black SUV two months ago. It had every bell and whistle: the car salesman's fantasy sale. And it had gotten Grant from Oregon to Wyoming in perfect comfort.

Instead of heading to the SUV, he went to the rusted pickup. Why not? He'd bought the ranch lock, stock and barrel. That included whatever was left behind on the property. And the truck had definitely been left behind. He'd even found the faded title to it when he'd scrubbed the kitchen enough so that he didn't feel like he was still back in Afghanistan. It had been stuck to the bottom of one of the drawers, along with a newspaper ad for dial-up internet and a half-empty roll of hard candy.

The name on the title was Roger Carmody.

Grant knew Roger Carmody was dead. He had no living heirs. Except Grant, the illegitimate grandson Roger had made certain never used the Carmody name.

Grant had grown up knowing exactly who his biological family was. And he'd known that they didn't want him.

The same perverseness that had made Grant buy the property when it had gone to auction had motivated him to get the hunk of rust running. It was the same perverseness that had him getting behind the wheel and driving the truck now.

"Too bad, Rog," he muttered, cranking the key in the ignition. The engine sputtered a few times, but it started. Grant didn't consider himself a great mechanic, but he figured with enough tinkering, he'd get rid of the sputter, too. The same way he'd get the cold water going in the kitchen and the hot water in the shower. It just took time.

And all he had these days was time.

He drove out of the barn, closed the door behind him and then headed into town. The parking ticket Officer Ali had given him had fallen onto the floorboard on the passenger side and was fluttering in the blast of air from the heater.

It was still fluttering when he parked in front of the town's municipal building. He saw the parking sign and grimaced, checking his pockets for coins.

"There's free parking around the back of the building." An attractive woman bouncing a red-cheeked baby on her hip smiled at him from the sidewalk. Her eyes were friendly. Bright. "They just won't post a sign that says it. Silly if you ask me." She pointed. "Turn at that corner, then make another quick right. You can't miss the parking lot."

He pulled out his keys again. "Thanks."

"You bet." She turned, and her long dark ringlets bounced against the back of her coat as she pulled open the glass door of the municipal building and went inside.

He drove to the corner, made two rights and found a space in the parking lot. Ticket crumpled in his hand, he went into the building from the back. A guard directed him to the cashier's office and he joined the short line in front of the counter. The town wouldn't advertise the free parking in back of the municipal building, but it spared no expense on signs warning the line occupants to remain behind the wide yellow line painted on the floor until it was their turn to approach the cashier. Small-town idiosyncrasies at their best.

The woman with the ringlets and the baby was in front of him. Her eyes crinkled a little as she turned and smiled at him. She was older than he'd first thought. That wild brown hair was deceptive. Then the baby wrapped a hand in her hair and gave a merry yank that had her wincing, even though the smile in her eyes never dimmed.

It felt rude to stand there and not say something, considering her friendly smile. "Got quite a grip there," he said.

"I'll say." She flipped the rest of her hair around her other shoulder, trying to keep it away from the baby. "I ought to have learned by now." She realized the person in front of her had stepped up to the yellow line. Now only she and Grant were still in line. "You know what they're like, though."

He smiled noncommittally. What he knew about babies was somewhere between nothing and less than nothing. Being godfather to Seymour's twins didn't change that. He and Seymour had watched their baptism via Skype. Grant sent Claudia checks on their birthday and at Christmas so she could buy whatever she figured they needed. And unfailingly, within a few days, he received thank-you notes printed in their youthful handwriting.

The line moved forward and he automatically shuffled forward, too.

He never had to wonder what age Eva and Emi were.

They'd been born the same day their father saved Grant's life at Hunt Ridge. Eleven years ago. Covering Grant's body with his own while RPGs and machine-gun fire rained over them because Grant, with his specialized skills, couldn't be as easily replaced as Seymour.

If Grant had stayed in the service, would Seymour still be alive today?

He didn't have the answer to that. Never would.

And it haunted him. Morning. Noon. Night.

"Mom!"

His attention was yanked back to the present. The person working at the cashier's counter was none other than Officer Ali.

And she was looking at the lady in line in front of him. Calling her *Mom*.

"What're you doing here?"

"Paying the water bill." The woman jiggled the baby and pulled an envelope out of her purse as she moved to the counter. "I thought I'd mailed it, but I guess I forgot. What're *you* doing here? You're supposed to be off this weekend."

"Well, clearly, that didn't work out. Gowler called me in again 'cause Jerry's out with the flu." Officer Ali stood up from her chair to reach for the baby, but froze for a second when she spotted Grant standing behind the yellow line.

She wasn't wearing her police uniform or the short, figure-hugging red dress. This time she had on a thick pink sweater, and her hair—instead of being scraped back in a tight knot or flowing in a mass around her shoulders—was pulled back in a messy ponytail.

She was still looking at him, so he inclined his head slightly. "Officer Ali."

Her mother looked back at him with a surprised expression as she surrendered the baby to her daughter. "You know Ali." Her smile was suddenly even wider. "Well, now. Isn't that nice."

He held up the parking ticket between two fingers. "Depends on how you look at it," he said drily.

She chuckled. "Oh, well. Blame Growler. He's positively anal about some things."

"Mom!"

The woman took no notice of her daughter's horrified exclamation. "I'm Meredith. Ali's mother. And you are—?"

In the wrong place at the wrong time. "Grant," he answered.

"You're definitely a new face around here." Meredith's musical laugh fit the sparkle in her bright blue eyes. "And a handsome one, too. Is there a Mrs. Grant?"

"Mom!"

Noting Ali's reddened cheeks, Grant's mood suddenly lightened. "Who's Growler?"

"Gowler," Ali said through her teeth, "and with my luck, he's standing behind the wall, overhearing all of this."

"He's her sergeant," Meredith explained in a loud whisper. "He's been giving her a hard time ever since she dumped his—"

"Muh-ther!" The baby joined the game, too, letting out a loud, garbled squeal that didn't drown out Ali's pained exclamation.

Ali carried the baby around the counter and dumped her in her mother's arms. "Do you need a receipt for the payment?" She didn't wait for an answer. "No? Okay then." She went back behind the counter and looked at Grant without really looking at him. "Next!"

Instead of being upset at her daughter shutting her down, Meredith appeared as if she wanted to laugh more than ever. "Don't let Ali's bark scare you too much. She doesn't really bite."

Pity.

He looked Ali's way, having the good sense to keep the thought to himself. He may have been living like a hermit for the last year, but he still possessed some social sense. "I'll keep that in mind," he told her mother when she carried the baby out of the cashier's office.

Then it was just Officer Ali and him.

He stepped over the yellow line and approached the counter, setting down the crumpled ticket and flattening it beneath his palm. "You look like you need some sleep."

"Flattery won't get you out of the ticket." She tugged it free of his grasp. "I assume you're here to pay the fine?"

He pulled out his wallet. He'd used most of his cash on dinner at the grill in Weaver the night before, so he'd pay with his credit card. "I assume that's true?" he asked, tapping the corner of the card against the laminated Cash or Credit Only sign taped to the counter.

"Yes." She delicately pinched the edge of the credit card between thumb and forefinger as she took it from him and ran it through her machine. "I really would let you out of the fine if I could. You were a big help last night." Her lips suddenly rounded. "Oh," she murmured. She looked up at him. "I'm sorry. Your card was declined."

He frowned. "Try again."

She slid the card through the machine once more, then looked at him a moment later with the same expression. Embarrassment. Sympathy. "Do you have another method of payment?"

He held open his wallet so she could see the meager supply of single bills inside.

"Well—" she held out his card "—don't worry. You still have thirty days to pay the fine." She hesitated for a moment. "If you're looking for work, I can probably recommend a few places—"

"I'll keep it in mind." But he wasn't worried. Irritated? Yes. The card had a massive credit limit. After the money had started rolling in from his first *CCT Rules* book, banks had started throwing credit at him. He'd ignored nearly all the offers. His parents—the ones who *had* cared enough to give him their name after adopting him when he was ten—had been staunchly middle-class. They had passed on their pay-as-you-go mentality to him.

Karen, though, had never seemed to learn the same lesson. She'd just been a baby, already adopted by the Coopers when he'd officially joined the family. She'd never known any other family besides Cal and Talia Cooper. But she'd flown in the face of everything they'd tried to teach their children.

When she'd forged Grant's name on a contract, he'd been glad they hadn't been alive to see it.

He took the credit card back from Ali, making no effort to avoid brushing his fingers against hers, and enjoying more than he should the way she quickly curled them against her palm. But if he expected her dark eyes to shy away from his, he was wrong. "I'll come back with cash." There was a bank not too far away.

"Cashier's office closes at noon on Saturday."

He glanced at his watch. "Then I'll be back before noon."

"Templeton!"

She visibly stiffened and the dark circles under her eyes looked even more pronounced as she stared beyond Grant. He glanced behind him. A uniformed officer stood in the doorway. Except for the paunch he carried, the gray-haired man reminded Grant of one of the drill sergeants from when he'd gone through basic training.

"Yessir?"

"Mendez needs help finding something in the evidence locker."

Her expression didn't change much, but Grant saw the way the skin around her eyes tightened slightly. "I'll get on it."

Grant waited until the officer was gone. "Growler?"

"Gowler. And, yes. He's my sergeant." She set a desk bell on top of the counter, with instructions to ring for assistance, and handed Grant his ticket. She locked a drawer beneath the counter and came out from behind it.

He took in her faded blue jeans and heavy-duty leather work boots.

"Reminds me of a drill sergeant I had a long time ago. He was a royal pain in the ass."

She pressed her lips together, but a faint dimple showed in her pale cheek.

"Every time I see you, you're working one job or another."

"Everyone in the department has to put in their time covering the cashier's office."

"Even Gowler?"

"Theoretically, yes."

Grant lifted his eyebrows and her faint dimple deepened. They headed out into the tiled corridor that led to an information desk in front of a solid door and a long window. A kid sat there, wearing a stiffly pressed police uniform, reading something. He looked so wet-behind-the-ears that Grant was willing to bet it was a children's story. Through the window behind him, Grant could see a half-dozen desks, though only a few were occupied.

Everyone he saw was male, from the kid to the grizzled gray-bearded guy nodding off at another desk behind the window.

"Remember, you've got thirty days to pay the fine."

He'd be back in thirty minutes to pay the fine. "How many women work in the department?"

She looked surprised by the question. "Civilian employees or sworn officers?"

"Sworn."

She shrugged. "Just me."

"And civilian?"

"Darlene Dunworthy—we call her DeeDee—is the chief's secretary."

"That's it?"

"We're a small-town police department. We have fourteen officers and four civilian employees. And not a lot of turnover, so…" She shrugged again. "To use a cliché, it is what it is."

"Templeton!"

She sighed. "I'd better get back to the evidence locker before Sergeant Gowler has a stroke."

"Why's he got it in for you?"

"He doesn't." She made a face. "Well, he does. But he'll get over it. In time." She started to turn away again, only to hesitate. "Do you, ah…lunch? I mean, would you like to have lunch? My treat," she added quickly. "I can't fix the ticket for you, but it seems the least I can do after all the help you gave me last night."

"Or you're trying to sweeten me up to get more information about my sister."

Her eyes narrowed slightly, but the dimple in her cheek didn't go away. "Would it work?"

"We'll never know. I told you that I haven't heard from her in years. There's nothing helpful—"

A phone rang at the information desk, and the kid sitting there startled so badly he knocked his book on the floor. He picked it up and answered the phone.

"—I can tell you," Grant insisted. He lifted his hand. "Scout's honor."

"Were you a Boy Scout?"

"Um, Ali?" the young officer asked, turning red. "Sergeant Gowler says for me to tell you when you're finished flirting, to get your bu—ah, get yourself into his office."

"Great," she muttered, grimacing. "Thanks, Timmy." Then she looked up at Grant. "Sorry."

He was the one who was sorry. Gowler struck him as a jerk, but Grant was the one who'd delayed her.

"Lunch sounds good," he said, moving away from her. "Where?"

Surprise brightened her expression, but it didn't make the dark circles under her eyes disappear. "There's a coffee shop a couple blocks down from here. Josephine's. There's no sign but the name's painted on the front window. North side of the street." She pushed open the solid door next to the window. "My lunch break is at one o'clock."

"One o'clock it is. You can tell me more about Layla."

He hadn't expected to say those words. But he'd said 'em. Maybe the baby was his sister's. Maybe she wasn't. But he knew what it was like being the kid that nobody wanted. "And the foster family she's with."

Timmy—of course, the kid would have a kid's name—looked up from his book. Amazingly, it wasn't a children's book, but had a glossy cover that was way too familiar to Grant. It was a few years old. From when his pseudonym wasn't featured as prominently on the front cover as the title. When there wasn't a photograph of Grant on the back. "Didn't your mom have Layla with her when she came in?" With every word, Timmy's face turned redder.

Ali, though, just looked pained. She let the door to the police department close again.

To her credit, her gaze didn't shy away from Grant's.

"Quite a little detail you left out," he said evenly. He wasn't sure exactly what he felt, knowing that he'd been within touching distance of what was supposedly Karen's baby. "Your mother is fostering Layla?"

"No. My sister is. Mom was babysitting."

"A regular family affair."

"Look, I wasn't trying to hide it. But as you've said, we're only speculating that Dai—that Karen is Layla's mother. Which means you may or may not be the baby's uncle. And her—"

He lifted his hand. "Save it." Through the long window, he could see Gowler stomping around the desks, heading their way.

Her eyebrows drew together. "But—"

"You can explain at lunch."

She nodded quickly. "Yeah. Of course."

The door opened behind her. "Dammit to hell, Templeton! When I say jump, you say how high!"

Grant's jaw felt tight. "She was assisting me."

Pure suspicion filled Gowler's beady eyes, which looked him up and down. "And who are *you*?"

Ali took a step between them. As if to protect him. "This is Grant Cooper," she said quickly. "He's the citizen I told you about who helped us clear the highway last night."

Grant had survived a lot worse than small-town police sergeants puffed up on their own power. Ignoring Gowler was easy. A helluva lot easier than ignoring the odd sensation of having a pint-size police officer trying to protect *him*. "Josephine's at one," he said, then turned and headed back down the hall.

Chapter Five

Ali yanked open the door to the coffee shop and rushed inside. She was thirty minutes late and she half expected Grant to have given up.

But there he sat, in the far booth by the corner window.

Yesterday's snow had given way to clear skies and a winter sun that cast its unforgiving glare across the table. Combined with the sparkling snow outside, it was almost blindingly bright. There were no plates on the table. Just two sturdy white coffee cups, one sitting upside down on a saucer. Grant's long fingers were curled around the other.

Fortunately, she was starting to get used to the jolt she felt whenever she saw him. She figured the reaction would subside soon enough. Pulling off her coat, she crossed the nearly vacant coffee shop and slid onto the padded bench opposite him. "Sorry."

His aqua gaze flicked over her face. "For lying about who has my sister's kid, or for being late?"

She pulled off her scarf and piled it on top of the coat beside her. So much for the niceties. "Then you know your sister had a baby named Layla? You admit she's your niece?"

He spread his fingers. "You tell me, Officer Ali."

She swallowed a sigh. She didn't want to be back at square one with him, but it was her own fault if they were.

"You want more coffee?" She didn't wait for an answer, but slid out of the booth again and went over to the counter. From the pass-through between the kitchen and the front, she could see Josephine working at the grill, so Ali grabbed the coffee carafe from the burner and carried it back to the table. She filled his cup before turning up the second one and splashing coffee into it, too. "You need any cream or sugar?"

He gave her a look. "What do you do? Moonlight here, too?"

"Just habit." She took his nonanswer to mean he liked his coffee black, the same as she did, so she didn't bother to fetch the milk. She returned the carafe to the machine behind the counter and grabbed a basket of fresh rolls before coming back to the booth. "Josephine's rolls are great." She'd been looking forward to them ever since suggesting the coffee shop.

"Have you decided what you want?" She pulled one of the laminated menus from where they stood next to the salt and pepper shakers. "I've had everything on it. Well, everything except the liver and onions. Personally, I can't abide the stuff, but for those who can, it's supposed to be just as good as everything else. Which is very good, I mean." *Good grief, Ali. Just shut your mouth.*

She set down the menu on the table and grabbed her coffee, scalding her tongue when she took too fast a sip.

What was wrong with her? Greer and Maddie may have gotten the brains out of their trio, but Ali had gotten their mother's easy way with people. Old. Young. Female. Male. Okay, particularly male. And she'd never felt tongue-tied around a man. It was just…Grant.

And those damn aqua eyes.

She blew out a breath. "I didn't lie."

He didn't miss a beat. "You didn't present all the facts."

Yep. That was true. No denying it. "Layla is living with my sister Maddie and her husband, Linc."

"Lincoln Swift."

"Yes." She chewed the inside of her cheek. She strongly doubted that Grant would have had a reason to meet Linc, but stranger things did happen. Linc was unquestionably the richest guy in town and Grant was clearly in a different economic bracket—broke, like her. Probably worse than her, because she could use her credit card without it being declined. But none of the triplets had many nickels to rub together, primarily because they'd been feeding all of them into the house they'd bought.

They all loved the Victorian. But it was, unquestionably, a complete money pit.

And yet the wealthy Linc was now married to Ali's social-worker sister. "Do you know him? Lincoln?"

She caught Grant's quick, faint frown. "No."

"You've heard of him, though."

"Swift Oil. Hard not to."

"Right." She nibbled her cheek again. "The house where Layla was left belongs to Linc."

"Thought you said it belonged to Jaxon."

"Well, it does. They're brothers. They both live there. Inherited it from their grandmother. Ernestine Swift. It's a big place." It was Braden's very own mansion that Ali's mother had once cleaned for Ernestine, but that was beside the point.

"Linc's the one who discovered Layla on the doorstep. Jax was out of town. He knew nothing about the baby being left there. Maddie's a social worker and she ended up on the case. Rather than shuffle the baby around in the system, she got the judge to agree to leave the baby in their care while we try to determine exactly what happened." The entire situation hadn't been quite that simple, but that, too, was beside the point. "Except for a few nights, Layla has been with them from the time she was abandoned." The coffee might have scorched her tongue, but the hot cup nevertheless felt good against her palms as she cradled it. She watched him for a moment and wondered what he was thinking, because his eyes weren't giving away a thing.

But they were causing fresh jolts in her stomach whenever he trained his gaze on her.

"You're our closest connection to your sister, Grant. If you're willing, a DNA test would prove a lot. At the very least, whether Karen's just a person of interest, or that she's Layla's mother for certain. It's a simple test, but it would have to be done in Weaver at the hospital."

"No."

She hesitated. "You refuse?" She wondered if her brother, Archer—also an attorney with a good relationship with Judge Stokes—could get the judge to compel the test. Sometimes DNA testing was court-ordered, though it was usually to prove paternity.

"I'm not refusing. I'm just telling you there's no point to it." He suddenly flipped the menu around so that it was facing him. "Both Karen and I were adopted. There's no common DNA to be found between her and me, much less between me and the baby. Who, by the way, looks nothing like Karen. She's got red hair and green eyes. That kid your mother was holding? Blonde and blue-eyed."

Ali felt like the stuffing was leaking right out of her.

She reached for one of the rolls and started shredding it to pieces. "I didn't even consider the possibility you weren't natural siblings," she muttered.

It was no wonder Chief Kessler kept turning down her request to apply for one of the two detective slots in the department. He recognized her lack of investigative ability.

Josephine had come out from the kitchen and stopped next to their table to get their orders. "Hey, Ali. What'll it be today?"

She had been starving, but finding themselves at another dead end where Layla was concerned put a damper on her appetite. "Just the coffee for me, Josephine." She looked at Grant. "You order whatever you want, though. I meant it when I said lunch was my treat."

"Patty melt," he said, setting aside the menu.

Ali nodded her approval. "Good choice."

He looked at Josephine. "She'll have one, too."

She opened her mouth to protest.

"Double fries and two side salads," Grant added. "What kind of salad dressing you want?"

"She likes the vinaigrette," Josephine told him before Ali could voice her objections.

"Make it happen."

"I like him," Josephine said with a wink before heading back to the kitchen.

Ali looked at him. "I'm not hungry."

"Give it a chance. When'd you eat last? I'm betting it was sometime yesterday."

She narrowed her eyes. It had been, but there was no reason he should know that.

"And don't worry. I went to the bank. I've got cash. I paid my parking ticket to young Timmy while you were probably still getting dressed down by your sergeant, and despite the credit-card business, I'm not quite destitute. I can pay for my own lunch."

Considering the state of his truck and his house, she wasn't sure she believed him. But pride was something she definitely understood, having more than a small helping of it herself. "I told you before, it's on me. As a thank-you for your help last night."

"Okay," he finally said. His gaze came to rest on her face. It was just shy of spine-tingling. "Thanks."

Ali actually felt shaky.

He wrapped his hand around his coffee cup again and she moistened her lips, fussing with the coat and scarf on the seat beside her, waiting for the shakiness to pass.

It didn't.

And she decided that maybe she did need some food.

She took a pinch of the shredded roll and sucked it off her fingers.

Across from her, Grant suddenly shifted and his knee bumped hers beneath the table. "Sorry."

She immediately moved her legs to one side to give him more legroom. Josephine's booths had never struck her as too small, but that's how it felt now. She could feel herself blushing and she never blushed. "No worries."

"Why does your sergeant have it in for you, anyway? Is he like that with everyone, or does he just have a problem with female cops?"

"It doesn't have anything to do with anything."

"You like getting picked on then? Just judging from what I saw, the guy's skirting pretty close to harassment. And these days, *that* don't fly."

The conversation was totally slipping off the rails. "He's not harassing me."

"All sorts of harassment, Officer. I'm sure I don't have to tell you that. What's *his* boss think about it?"

"Chief Kessler believes in the chain of command."

"Gowler ride the other officers like he does you?"

She pinched the bridge of her nose for a moment, and then started shredding the second half of her roll. "If I tell you, will you drop it?"

"I guess that depends."

"I can fight my own battles." She couldn't understand why he even cared.

"So you admit it's a battle."

She sighed noisily. "Fine. Gowler was perfectly normal with me—as normal as he ever is, anyway—until I started dating his son. When I stopped dating Keith, the sergeant took it personally." She made a face. "It's silly and going to sound conceited, but he blames me for breaking Keith's heart."

"Did you?"

"*No!* We only saw each other for a few weeks! That's it. We weren't even serious. I mean we never even—" She managed to put a cork in that admission, but Grant's eyes were suddenly glinting.

"At least I wasn't that serious," she said, more or

less evenly. The truth was, she hadn't been *that* involved with anyone for nearly five years. Not since she'd been with Jack. And that was something she definitely wasn't going to share. "But Keith is Gowler's only child. Raised him on his own after Gowler's wife left them when Keith was a baby. Gowler's hard on everyone." She revised that. "Everyone except Keith." The guy was two years younger than her and spoiled as all get out.

"You're making excuses for your sergeant."

"No, I'm just explaining the situation. Sooner or later, Keith will find someone new and Gowler will get over his snit." She made a face. "Admittedly, that snit has been going on for months." A sudden thought occurred to her.

"I think I should be afraid," Grant drawled. "I can see the wheels turning in your head."

She smiled faintly. "Keith's not *all* bad. I mean, I don't think he has a dishonest bone in his body." Unlike Jack. "Even if he *is* a defense lawyer. He just wasn't exactly my cup of tea." She spread her hands, dropping her voice conspiratorially. "But, I could find someone to set him up with. Help him along in his search for his one true love."

Grant gave her a look. "Sounds like a movie-of-the-week plot. And there's no such thing as one true love."

"I don't know about that." She grinned. "And there's a reason why they make those movies. People *like* them. Same way people like shoot-'em-ups and romantic comedies and military thrillers where the good guy whips the bad guy's butt."

Grant waited a beat, then shook his head as if she was more than a little nuts. "And if this unsuspecting female you find also breaks Keith's tender heart? Gowler's not going to blame you for that, too?"

"How could he if he doesn't know I set it up?"

His lips twitched. "I think I'm sorry I asked."

She sat up straighter, feeling restored to her usual keel.

"What's the judge's plan for Layla?"

And...right back into the fire. "Well," she admitted slowly, "that's kind of a sticky area."

"Because—"

"Because, technically, the department's not supposed to discuss details about any minor under protective services except with those who have an official need to know. And there's no actual proof that you're Layla's uncle."

He grimaced. "Damn bureaucracy."

"It's for the child's protection—"

He cut her off. "I get it. Doesn't mean I have to like it."

She started to shift in her seat, remembered his long legs, and stayed put. "I'm not the, um, the official investigator on the case, either." Truth be told, she was lucky that Gowler hadn't barred her from any involvement at all.

"Who is?"

"Detective Draper. He's the senior investigator with the department."

"Can he tell me anything that you can't?"

"No." She pressed her lips together for a moment. "He's been out of the office for a while with the flu." It was Ali, sneaking department resources when Gowler wasn't looking, who'd managed to create a rough map of Grant's sister's movements after she'd quit working for Jax. It was Ali who'd tracked down people who remembered Daisy. She'd worked with them for a few weeks, or crashed on their couch for a few nights. They'd all talked about her nearly obsessive habit of mailing postcards to her sweet Grant.

At first, Ali had thought he was a boyfriend. Lover. Maybe even Layla's father. But the administrator of a shelter in Oregon where Daisy had spent a few nights told Ali that she believed Grant was Daisy's brother.

"Here you go." Josephine returned with their salads and the coffeepot. "You haven't been in here before," she said to Grant as she topped off their cups with steaming brew.

"No, ma'am."

"You look familiar, though."

"I hear that all the time." He shrugged. "Got one of those everyman faces, I guess."

Ali nearly snorted. Everyman? Please.

She waited until Josephine left before she picked up her fork and jabbed at a crisp slice of cucumber. The second she put it in her mouth, her stomach started growling.

Grant clearly heard and his lips twitched. "I knew I was right."

She ignored him and shoveled a forkful of lettuce after the cucumber.

"So." He leisurely shook pepper over his salad. "Tell me hypothetically how this sort of thing works. No names. No specific child. Just the process. What's usually the next step?"

She swallowed. "Well, the judge has some leeway, but ultimately, the goal is to make sure the needs of the child—physical and emotional—are provided for as quickly and as permanently as possible in the best available setting. The child's biological family takes precedence. If one parent is deemed unsuitable, the other parent is looked at. If that parent is unsuitable, then another family member. And so on. Aunts. Uncles. Grandparents and the like, until an appropriate familial setting *can* be found."

"But if you can't establish the identity of at least one of the parents, you can't establish kinship, either."

"Right. In that case—" she spread her hands "—the judge inevitably rules the child be placed for adoption. And he typically decides that within ninety days. Once he rules there is no acceptable parent-child or kinship relationship, he doesn't like leaving that child in the system any longer than he has to."

Grant paused for a moment. "So there's a ticking clock, too."

She nodded. "Look, I'll be honest here, Grant. Assuming your sister *is* Layla's mom, when we find her, she's not going to automatically get back her daughter. She'll be charged with child endangerment. And maybe once that's been dealt with, she'll be able to work with family services to regain some visitation and parental rights. But that's only if we *find* her before the judge has already severed her rights altogether and if Layla hasn't been adopted."

"Layla's a baby." Grant's voice was even. "Everyone wanting to adopt wants a baby. If things get to that point, it'll happen in the blink of an eye."

Had *he* been a baby when he'd been adopted? Considering his troubled expression, she was inclined to think he hadn't been. Which just made her more curious than ever about him.

She focused on her small salad again—a few more bites and it would be gone. Fortunately, she knew from experience that lunch at Josephine's was never a drawn-out affair. The rest of their meal would be coming soon. "Yes, it will happen fast and that's part of the complication." She glanced toward the door when it jingled. An elderly couple entered and took one of the tables in the middle of the room.

She looked back at Grant. "Let's say the child is presently well cared for in a fostering situation. That this situation has been going on for, at a guess, an entire third of the child's life. Then the child is awarded through adoption to a different family altogether. A family who has been waiting on a long list for a long time for just such a child. Much longer than the foster family, who has fallen in love with the child over the past month and whose name is now added to that long list, but at the very bottom of it. The only thing that can slow down this particular train wreck is bringing forward another biological family member."

He considered that for about a nanosecond. "Your sister and her husband still wouldn't end up with her."

"No, but at least we'll all know that we've done everything we can to get Layla to her rightful family. And maybe, at the very least, her new guardian will be open to letting the foster family stay in touch. If it's a traditional adoption, that's not likely to occur. There're lots of reasons to want her with her rightful family." She studied him. "Assuming that her rightful family wants her and can provide a suitable home."

He pushed aside his now empty salad plate. It was perfect timing, because just then Josephine delivered their meals.

Ali studied him. She was still uncertain how he felt—if he would want Layla, should she turn out to be his niece.

Which was something that she now knew couldn't be proven by something as definitive as a DNA test.

They would have to prove it by other means.

And with as little as they had to go on, they might as well be looking for the proverbial needle in the haystack.

"Seems stupid to pull a kid out of the only consistent environment they've ever had."

Ali propped her elbows on the table, leaning toward him over her plate. "You truly have *no* idea where Karen might be?"

He shook his head. His eyes met hers. "If I did, I'd tell you. My sister's always—" He broke off, shaking his head with a sigh. "I don't know. Searching for something she can't ever seem to find."

When he looked at Ali that way, it was like being touched by a live wire. "What about your parents?"

He shook his head again. "Mom had breast cancer. She survived it twice. She didn't make it the third time. And Dad died a few years after her. And to save you asking, no, there aren't any other family members who might still be in touch with Karen. No other family members, period."

"Why do you think she came to Wyoming? There must be some tie for both of you to land here."

"The ranch I bought. I think she was probably staying there without anyone knowing. She was pretty bad about money."

It was a logical enough explanation, though it didn't tell Ali why he'd bought a ranch in Braden in the first place, only to let it sit there vacant for years before deciding to occupy it. "What about her friends? When she was younger? Before you fell out of contact?" She sat forward again. "Where'd you grow up? Maybe I can reach out to former classmates or—"

"Portland, Oregon. She's ten years younger than me. She wasn't the kind of kid who brought home her school friends—at least not when I was still living there. For that matter, she wasn't the kind who went to school all that regularly. But she did graduate high school."

He picked up his sandwich, only to set it back down again without taking a bite. His expression was grim. "I wasn't there to see it. She didn't go to college at all."

Ali couldn't help herself. She reached out her hand and touched his arm briefly. "It's not your fault, you know."

"Don't be so sure. The last time I saw her, I was pretty pissed." For a moment, he seemed like he would say more. But then he merely nodded toward her untouched plate. "Eat."

She picked up her sandwich. "I will if you will."

His faint smile held no amusement. But he picked up his own sandwich and they ate in silence for a few minutes.

Ali knew her allotted lunch break was drawing to a close. But she was reluctant to end it. Not necessarily because she thought she could divine some relevant nugget about Karen, either.

It was all because of him.

"So. What drew you to Wyoming?" She kept her voice deliberately light. "Work or woman?"

He seemed equally glad to lighten the mood. "Both. But *drove* would be more accurate than *drew*."

"Ah." She nodded sagely. "Escaping a sticky situation?"

"Not sticky. Just unacceptable."

"What did she do? Cheat on you?"

At that, he let out a short laugh and all she could do was sit there, feeling bemused. "Nice to see you can laugh."

He shook his head slightly. "Do you always speak what's on your mind?"

She made a face. "If I did, Growler would have fired me by now for sure."

The fine lines beside his eyes crinkled. "Gowler."

"Right." She smiled. "Well, whatever reason drove you to Wyoming, I'm glad you're here now."

"Because of my supposed niece?"

She waited a beat. "Of course."

His aqua gaze lingered on her face and his smile widened. "Of course," he murmured.

She darn near sighed out loud right then and there.

Chapter Six

Grant pulled the truck off to the side of the highway and parked. Then he got out his cell phone and checked the signal. He'd learned all too quickly that the only places where a decent, solid cell signal existed were in the middle of Braden and in the middle of Weaver. Since his house was not in either town, that had been a problem. He wanted away from his old life, but that didn't mean he could avoid everything altogether.

He'd discovered this particular sweet spot on the highway when his phone had rung while he'd been driving.

The sound had been so foreign since he'd come to Wyoming that he'd damn near run off the road. By the time he found the phone—it had slid under the bench seat between an ancient toolbox and a rat's nest of rope—the call had ended and he'd gotten the little *ping* notifying him that he had a voice mail.

Unfortunately, it hadn't been Karen, suddenly reaching out to him after all this time. The message had been from his agent, Martin.

He'd deleted the message without listening to it, pulled back onto the highway and continued driving into town to hit the library for some plumbing books and earn himself a parking ticket.

Now, he sat here on the side of the road while the truck engine rumbled noisily, tapping the cell phone with his thumb and absently noticing the smear of white paint on the back of his hand.

Then he muttered an oath and quickly dialed. It was Sunday afternoon. It would be two hours ahead in New York. But he knew she'd still be at the office, even on a Sunday. Because she was always at the office. That had been part of the problem. She'd worked too much. And he'd cared more about the air force than her.

No wonder they hadn't lasted.

It rang only twice before his ex-wife picked up. "About time you came to your senses," she barked.

"Hello to you, too, Chels."

She made a faint sound that he knew would be accompanied by a roll of her blue eyes. She'd be pushing back in her expensive-as-hell chair, putting her bare feet on the corner of her expensive-as-hell desk and tugging the expensive-as-hell glasses off her face to dangle them at her side. "Hello, Grant," she finally said. "Where are you? Are you calling me from Nowheresville, USA? You didn't have to bug out of the cabin just because the Rules Rabble had started camping outside your door, you know. All you needed to do was hire a decent security team! And to move without even telling me? Or Martin? You know he's been trying to reach you."

The day that he'd met Ali hovered in his mind. When

he heard her pounding on his door, he'd automatically thought she was just another of the rabid fans who'd invaded his remote Oregon retreat to such a degree that he'd taken the drastic action of escaping to a small Wyoming town where nobody would expect to find him. The only person he'd notified about his move had been Claudia Reid. "Martin doesn't have anything to tell me that I want to hear. And it's obviously not Nowheresville here or you wouldn't have been able to get that box of books to me when it was returned to you. You shouldn't have bothered. Waste of postage."

She snorted softly. "I'm your publisher, darling. I have a contractual obligation to get those copies to you."

She'd been his wife before she'd been his publisher. That particular promotion hadn't come about until after their divorce and his second book. "Don't make me tell you what you can do with your contractual obligation." They both knew good and well that the contract she cared about most was for the next *CCT Rules* installment. The contract he refused to even discuss.

She laughed lightly. "Always the same, dear Grant. I would never put up with you if you weren't such a gifted writer."

He wasn't gifted. After getting out of the air force, he'd written the first *CCT Rules* because it had been cheaper penning the stories that kept him from sleeping at night than paying for counseling. Their marriage might have been crumbling, but that hadn't stopped Chelsea from deciding the handwritten scrawls were worth something. She'd nagged him into putting it in actual story form and then ran it past the editorial team where she worked.

Within months, he had an agent, a book deal and a wife who wanted a divorce. Despite that, she was more responsible for the success of the series than he was. She'd certainly benefited from it more than she'd ever benefited from being married to him. His unexpected catapult up the bestseller list, as the first book was followed by another, and another, had been accompanied by her even more meteoric progress up the ranks at work.

"I'm not calling to talk about *CCT Rules*."

"Pity, when it's the only thing at all that interests me."

"Ever honest, even when it hurts, right, Chels?" It was too easy to fall into nasty old habits. "Have you heard anything from Karen lately?"

"Aside from the occasional piece of mail that ends up getting forwarded from wherever? No. I haven't." Fortunately, the sarcasm left her voice.

Once the gloss of "opposites attract" had worn off, Chelsea had been a witch of a wife. To be fair, he hadn't been much of a husband. But for reasons Grant had never understood, his ex-wife had always had a soft spot for his sister.

"I hope you're not lying to me, Chels. This is important."

"Oh, for God's sake, Grant," she snapped. "Have *I ever* lied to you?"

True. They'd been married for seven years. She'd told him everything that was good and everything that was bad. In excruciating detail. She'd often said that she had a closer relationship with her battery-operated boyfriend than she did with him. And, in the end, that it was preferable to him altogether.

"Just tell me what's happened," she said impatiently.

"Nothing good. When's the last time you *did* talk to her?"

"I didn't actually speak with her, because I was traveling, but when I got back from the Frankfurt Book Fair last October, my assistant told me that she'd called. She didn't leave a number or any particular message, but you know Karen. She rarely does."

"Any hint at all where she was calling from? Like a city? A state?"

"No idea. I did send her some money about six months ago, though."

"Chels—"

"Don't even think about lecturing me. I could always tell whether or not she was sober, and she was. She'd met some guy but it hadn't worked out—"

"Because it never works out."

"And she needed to get out of the situation. So I wired some money to her in Montana. Butte. But given her restlessness, I doubt she was still there when she called me again last October."

It was still more information than he'd had. Maybe the situation his sister had alluded to was her pregnancy. "She happen to say what Butte boy's name was?"

"No, but she gave me the address where she was crashing. I needed it for the wire. I'm sure I've got it somewhere. I'll email it to you."

"I haven't checked my email for months. I don't even have a computer with me here."

She clucked her tongue. "You're taking this no-more-writing thing a little too far, don't you think? If you're holding out for more money for the fifth book—"

"I'm not writing a fifth one, Chelsea. I've told you that a dozen times. I'm done."

She sighed again, even more noisily. "You'll change your mind and sign another contract, just like you changed your mind and signed the last one. The money's just too damn good. We've got momentum on our side, Grant.

You don't want to lose that. The usual networks have been clamoring for interviews…"

He hadn't changed his mind about the last one. Karen's forgery of his signature had. And if Chelsea hadn't enlisted Karen's help to convince Grant to sign by luring her with a shopping spree, Karen wouldn't have cared less about the contract. As much as he wanted to blame Chelsea, though, he blamed himself more. He should have been a better big brother when Karen had been growing up. A person couldn't set an example in someone's life if they just weren't there. He hadn't been there for her when Talia died. And two years later, when Cal followed, instead of leaving the air force when he'd had the opportunity, Grant had just re-upped.

He'd been more concerned with trying to prove he was a real chip off Cal Cooper's block than he'd been with taking care of his wild-child sister.

"No interviews."

"But—"

"I said no, Chelsea. You've got the book. That's all you need."

"You know, for a hard-ass air-force hero, you've turned into quite the prima donna."

"I wasn't a hero," he said flatly. "Text me that address. And if you do hear from her, find out where she is. Or tell her to call me."

"Do I get to know why?"

"Because I think she had a baby and she left her on the doorstep of a stranger, rather than reach out to me for help."

"What?"

"Just text me that address in Montana." Before Chelsea could say anything else, he ended the call.

Then he rubbed his forehead, where the headache always formed when he spoke with his ex-wife.

Prima donna.

Hardly.

But he had no intention of telling her the truth. It wasn't that he didn't *want* to write another *CCT Rules*. He was afraid he *couldn't* write another. For one simple reason.

He had no more words left inside him.

They'd died the same day Seymour had.

"You need to get a phone line," Ali said the next morning when Grant opened his front door to find her once again standing on the porch.

He squinted. The sky was still clear overhead and the sunlight was sharp, particularly after a night spent inside a bottle. "What for?"

"So a person can reach you. Obviously." She gave him a knowing look and, without waiting for an invitation, brushed past him to come inside. "A straight-forward telephone line isn't too expensive," she said. "As long as you don't get any bells and whistles—like voice mail, caller ID. That sort of thing. Everyone around here has landlines. Pretty much have to."

Her hair was up in that god-awful knot, but she wasn't wearing her uniform, which he assumed meant she wasn't on duty. Either she recently had been or would be soon. She was wearing jeans and a puffy red coat that ended just shy enough of her hips that a man— if he was looking—could seriously appreciate the glory of her jean-clad butt.

He told himself not to look. And, of course, he did.

He fastened a few of the buttons on the shirt he'd

yanked on when she'd started pounding on his door. "What're you doing here, Officer?"

"Lord, it's hot in here. How do you stand it?" She peeled out of her coat and dropped it on the couch. The thermal shirt she wore hugged her lithe torso like a lover. And he'd have bet his left hand that there wasn't a thing separating her skin from that clinging gray waffle weave.

"Yeah, well, two days ago, it was freezing in here. If I have to pick a poison, I'll take the hot. Now, what—"

"I got a hit on the missing persons." She lifted her hand, forestalling him. "A woman named Karen Cooper was picked up last night during a drug raid in Seattle. She answers the general description—" Ali broke off when he shook his head.

"It's not her."

"Well—" she spread her palms "—have you turned psychic or do you have information I don't?"

"She's not into drugs. That's not Karen's thing at all. She likes to drink."

"Looks to me like she's not the only one," she murmured, picking up the empty bottle of Jack Daniel's lying on the floor next to the couch he'd finally gotten around to unwrapping. She watched him steadily with her big brown eyes. "Pardon me, but weren't you the one to tell me it's been nearly three years since you last had any contact with her? I'm sure you know that a *lot* can happen in three years." Again without invitation, she went into his kitchen, taking the bottle with her.

A lot could happen in three days. Or five. Which was how many days it had been since Ali had knocked her way into his life.

It seemed longer.

"Wow. Fast work. Did you put in the cupboards yourself?"

He joined her just in time to see her drop the bottle in the trash can under the sink. The work had only been fast because he wasn't sleeping more than a couple hours at a stretch and that left a lot of hours on the clock to fill.

"Yeah."

"Nice." She ran her hand over the butcher-block countertop he'd also added. She smiled. "If you ever get bored, I know the owners of a Victorian who need some real help."

He would have returned her smile if his head wasn't ready to explode. "Karen wouldn't pick up drugs."

"Like she wouldn't leave her baby on someone's doorstep? In the middle of winter? With just a note?"

Point taken.

He pulled out one of the chairs at the table and winced when it screeched against the floor. He sat and scrubbed his hands down his face, pressing the heels of his palms into his eye sockets. "Seattle."

"Mmm-hmm."

He heard her moving around and dropped his hands to see that she'd pulled a can of coffee out of the pantry cupboard. "That can is probably twenty years old."

She peeled off the plastic top and showed it to him. "Never been opened. And it's—" she rolled the can in her hands, looking at the label "—only a couple years old." She looked around. "And I don't exactly see a coffeemaker or coffee pods sitting around anywhere."

He got up and pulled a jar off the top of the fridge. He set it beside her. "Because I've been using instant."

"Instant!" She looked from the jar to him.

"Don't give me that look. It's not a ticket-worthy offense. I get the real stuff when I drive into Weaver." As the crow flew, the ranch was closer to Braden than it was to Weaver. But it took less time to drive to the smaller town than it did to get into Braden. "There's a diner there I like. Great coffee. Great rolls. They remind me of the ones my mom used to make."

She nodded. "Gotta be talking about Ruby's."

"You know it, then."

She smiled wryly and continued opening his cupboards and drawers as if she belonged there. She wouldn't find much. They were more empty than not. What they did contain he'd either found stored in one of the boxes in the barn, or he'd purchased at Shop World in Weaver. "I was born and raised in Braden. I know every nook and cranny in this town and in Weaver." She paused, then pulled an ivory card out of a drawer along with a cheap metal spoon. "This important?"

It was the invitation from Claudia Reid.

He shook his head and Ali shrugged, then set it on the counter before picking right back up where she'd left off. "Used to be what one town didn't possess, the other usually did. Now, Weaver's been growing so much what with Cee-Vid's plant being there, that it's going to be bigger than Braden before long."

"Cee-Vid." He reached out and yanked the cord on the metal blinds hanging in the window over the table until they lowered, sort of. Half of the narrow slats were bent out of shape, and no amount of tugging on the cord got the blinds to hang evenly. He gave up and sat back in his seat. "That's the video gaming deal?" He'd driven by the large complex on the edge of Weaver. "Weird place for the company to be located if you ask me. Not exactly Tech Valley here."

"Cee-Vid makes more than just video games." She gave him a look. "They always have a job opening or two." She waited a beat as if expecting a response, but continued when he gave none. "And the company's located in Weaver because the founder is from Weaver. His son—who just so happens to be one of my cousins—is married to the lady who owns Ruby's." She'd found one of the barn-rescued saucepans and started filling it with water. "But the diner's been there since before I was born. People drive from all over to get Tabby's sticky cinnamon rolls, just like they do to get Josephine's liver and onions." She turned off the water and set the pan on the stove, cranking up the flame beneath it.

Then she turned to face him, leaned against the stove and folded her arms. "The clerk I talked to in Seattle is going to send me the mug shot when Karen's through processing. I didn't get it by the time my shift ended or I'd have printed it and brought it out here with me."

He looked at the cat clock on the wall. "It's nine in the morning."

"I worked graveyard last night."

"How long have you been with the department?"

She looked surprised by the question. "Almost ten years. And before you say anything, I know. I should be a detective by now."

He raised his hands in surrender. "I wasn't going to say anything."

"You were thinking it, though."

He gave her a long look. "Trust me, Officer Ali. You don't want to know what I'm thinking."

She shifted suddenly, turning to jiggle the handle of the pan, as if that would somehow make the water heat faster.

His eyes drifted from the dark strands of hair that had broken free from the knot and rested against the pale skin of her neck, down the length of her spine to her backside.

He'd rather think about anything besides Karen. Or Chelsea. But there was a baby to think about who hadn't asked for any of this. "My ex-wife told me she wired money to Karen about six months ago. She was in Montana. I've got the phone number where she was staying." He'd waited for an hour out at that sweet spot on the highway before the *ping* of Chelsea's text message had come through. Had he not hung up on her first, he figured she wouldn't have waited all that time just to tell him that she was still looking for the address. "If she finds the address, she'll let me know."

"That's great!" Ali turned off the flame and took a clean spoon and mug out of the drainer that he'd bought at Shop World. "Even with just a phone number, we can look into it. If it's not Karen in Seattle—"

"It won't be." Despite everything, he refused to think otherwise. "Spoon the coffee into the cup first. Then add the water. Dissolves better." He got up and retrieved the pencil stub and the notepad he'd been using to keep lists of all the crap that needed repair and wrote out the phone number on the bottom of a sheet and tore it off.

"You're quite the instant-coffee aficionado." She twisted off the lid of the jar and spooned a measure into one of the mugs. "Look about right?"

"Little more." He gave her the slip and went back to sit at the table.

She didn't even glance at the number before sliding it into the back pocket of her jeans. Then she tipped some more of the grounds into the cup. "Teach you the fine art of instant-coffee making in cooking school?"

"Afghanistan." He shrugged when her gaze flew to his. "Air force."

"Is that why you fell out of contact with—"

"No."

She waited, her gaze steady.

"I got out nearly six years ago."

"Were you a pilot?"

"Combat controller."

"First There," she murmured. He saw the way her gaze slid to the ivory card sitting on the counter. The lettering was black and somber. At the top, there was a cross with an eagle over the center and the words *For Valor* printed on a scroll beneath it. "I'll bet you have some stories to tell."

He wasn't touching that with a ten-foot pole.

There was no secret that First There was the CCT motto. But in his experience, it wasn't exactly common vernacular for an ordinary citizen. For that matter, most people didn't even know what a combat controller was. "Your daddy serve? Brother?" He waited a beat. "Boyfriend?"

She shook her head, then immediately backpedaled. "Well, my dad was US Army. But that was a long time ago. And my brother, Archer, was never interested. He was too busy becoming Clarence Darrow." She set down the jar and picked up the pan, pouring water into the mug and then stirring it.

"He's a lawyer?"

She handed him the mug, nodding. "So's Greer. She's with the public defender's office. He's in private practice. Has offices here and Colorado."

"And Maddie's a social worker."

She'd started opening cupboards again, and soon found the jumble of old mugs and new plastic cups. "With a highfalutin psychology degree. Not quite as highfalutin as Hayley's, but close." She managed to extract a mug without sending the whole mess tumbling.

"Hayley's—"

"My oldest sister. Half sister, actually. She's a psychologist. Has a practice in Weaver." Ali didn't bother using the spoon to scoop grounds into the cup this time, just poured straight from the jar. "There's Arch, then Hayley, then Greer and Maddie and me."

"The triplets."

She lifted her eyebrows slightly, but didn't question how he knew that. "Hayley and Arch had a different mom," she went on as if he hadn't said a word. "She died before my dad met my mom."

Meredith. The woman with the wild hair and the blonde baby on her hip.

The baby that could be his niece.

He didn't want to think about that, either.

"And you're the cop," he said.

She focused on pouring water over the grounds and nodded. "Right." Then she stirred the coffee and lifted it to her mouth. "Hmm. Better than the stuff we have at the department, but that's all I'll say about it."

"It's hot and it's caffeine. That's enough for me." He'd had plenty of days when his only java came out of his MRE. He pushed one of the other chairs out with his foot and she sat. "How do you know about CCT?"

"I wanted to enlist out of high school." She grimaced. "Both my parents nearly had strokes. We struck a bargain, though. I had to put in two years of college and if I still wanted to go after that, they wouldn't try to stop me."

"Two years was enough to change your mind."

"Well, I still would have gone." She finally lifted her gaze to his. "College was so *not* my thing. But by then, the BPD was making a concerted effort to add some women to their ranks and by some miracle, I got in. My parents still weren't thrilled, but at least I was sticking close to home." She sipped the coffee again, narrowing her eyes against what he himself had already discovered was its blistering heat. "Now, I can't imagine being anywhere else."

"Itchy feet gone?"

"Totally. Braden may be small and pretty simple, but there's no place else on this earth I want to be."

"Doesn't seem like the department did a great job finding many female officers, though."

"There've been a few others over the years. But nobody local. Nobody who wanted to stay. Sheriff's department has the same problem. Both organizations actively recruit woman, but—" She shook her head, shrugging. "Unfortunately, it gives the impression that neither is an equal opportunity outfit."

She propped her elbows on the table, cupping the mug between her hands. "How about you? Don't have much in the way of airports around here needing an air-traffic controller." She studied him. "And for some reason you don't strike me as a natural-born rancher."

Combat controllers were certified FAA air-traffic controllers. They just generally did their work in downright crummy environments, rather than from a well-equipped airport control tower. They were more than just comm specialists. More than weapons specialists and more than demo. They were the air-to-ground liaisons, establishing assault zones and airfields, calling in air strikes and controlling flights, targeting IEDs and manning artillery pieces, and doing it ahead of everyone else so they could do *their* jobs. In Grant's case, he'd done it alongside Seymour's Special Forces unit. If Sey wasn't watching Grant's back, then Grant was watching Sey's.

And now Seymour was dead.

"I know you bought this place nearly a decade ago." Ali's voice drew him out of his thoughts. It was easier facing the frank curiosity in her eyes than it was to think about Seymour. "But as far as I can tell, you didn't do a single thing with the property. Why did you buy it in the first place? We're a long way away to get noticed by a Portland boy. And I get you were on deployment, but you just said you got out several years ago. So why are you only moving here now?"

He hadn't been a *boy* in a long damn time. "You're full of questions."

"And yet you're not real full of answers. Did you get a settlement from your military service or something? Independently wealthy?" She gestured at the cabinets. "You told me you weren't quite destitute, but stuff like this costs money and as far as I can tell, you don't seem to have a source for any."

"Maybe I charged it all on my credit card that wouldn't work the other day."

"Did you?"

It should have been easy enough to just tell her about *CCT Rules.* But he couldn't make himself do it. Because if he did, he knew everything would change.

He didn't want her to start looking at him differently. Expecting him to be the so-called hero the bio on his book jackets described when he knew he was anything but.

So he said nothing at all. "I'm not a suspect in any crime, am I?"

She raised her eyebrows slightly. "Of course not."

"Then a man's got a right to his privacy, Officer Ali."

"Very true, Mr. Cooper." But the expression in her eyes was openly speculative. With her compact little body and her dark, dark eyes, she was nothing at all like the usual women he went for. They were tall Nordic types, both before Chelsea—who'd fit that description to a T—and after her.

Now, here was this short, skinny, nosy cop with a spectacular butt and shining brown eyes. And he was pretty sure he'd never been more attracted to a woman.

He exhaled roughly. "You're right. I'm not a rancher. I'm a—" *Writer who can't write.*

Her eyebrows rose a little more, disappearing beneath the messy bangs. "Yes?"

He drained the bitter, searing coffee. "A guy who bought up a ranch." He was definitely not a hero, couldn't even tell the truth when he wanted. "It was cheap. And it used to be owned by my grandparents."

Chapter Seven

His grandparents?

Ali studied Grant's closed expression. "The Carmodys were your grandparents?"

"My natural grandparents," he said, as if that explained everything. Considering the discontented twist of his handsome lips, though, she had the feeling that there was a lot more to his story.

And while she was intensely intrigued, there was still the pressing matter of Layla. The baby's welfare had to take precedence. Ali had been so excited to share the news about the hit in Seattle, that she hadn't thought much beyond getting here and telling him. Now that she'd done so, what was next?

"Would you be able to come by the department so you can ID the Karen from Seattle to see if it's your sister?"

"She won't be." He pushed to his feet. "But I'll come

just to prove I'm right." He went to the narrow stairs on the far side of the refrigerator and started climbing. "I need a shower first."

She did *not* need the mental image that announcement conjured. "I, uh—" She had to actually clear a knot in her throat. "Do you want me to wait for you?"

"Unless you're gonna come and join me."

She froze, feeling more than a little like a deer in the headlights when he angled his head so he could see her from his vantage point halfway up the stairs.

"No?" His voice was easy as he straightened and continued up the steps. "Too bad," he said over his shoulder. "Shower's hot water doesn't work. Might've made that a little more bearable."

He'd reached the top of the stairs and she could hear the creak of floorboards overhead as he walked.

She exhaled and her head flopped back weakly against the yellow vinyl padded chair. Obviously, he hadn't been serious, but that didn't stop her imagination from going berserk.

A moment later, she heard the rattle and squeal of water running in the pipes. They sounded even worse than the pipes at her place.

It was too easy imagining him stripping off the blue jeans and the plaid shirt, which had two little buttons that had done nothing—absolutely *nothing*—to hide the magnificent torso beneath. He was obviously tall, and he'd struck her as maybe even a little skinny. And here it turned out he had more muscles and ridges running down his chest than Carter had pills.

She exhaled and wiped the perspiration from her forehead. It was almost as hot in his house as it had been at their Victorian before Christmas, when the furnace had been running amok. Their father had finally dismantled the thing, and then they'd gone from wearing shorts and bikini tops to three layers of clothes just to keep warm.

They had a new furnace now, though.

Which was just one of the reasons why Ali still didn't have the money to fix her pickup's transmission.

The pipes were still rattling but she stood and started up the stairs. At the top, there was a closet door in one direction and a short hallway in the other. She passed the first open door—a room that had nothing in it except a stack of yellowing newspapers—and stopped at the second door. She knocked. "Hey."

The running water stopped. "Yeah?"

She smiled a little, inordinately pleased by the caution in his tone. *Not so cocky after all, are you?* "My father replaced our furnace for us last month. I could talk to him. He's retired and he's always looking for—"

The door suddenly opened and Grant stood there, holding a threadbare white towel at his hip.

The water *was* cold. She could see it in the gooseflesh rippling over his sinewy arms. In the tight nipples on his mind-blowing chest. Droplets were sliding down the dark line of hair, bisecting his ribs, collecting in the indent of his navel—

She snapped her eyes back up where they belonged.

But that meant seeing the devilish amusement in his aqua eyes. "Looking for something?"

"Projects," she blurted, feeling hotter than ever. "Sorry." Didn't matter that she was acting like a virginal schoolgirl. She turned on her heel to get the heck out of Dodge.

His hand grabbed her arm from behind, pulling her to a standstill. "Hold on there."

She didn't know what on earth possessed her. She

caught him in a wristlock and the next thing she knew, she'd flipped him to the ground.

"Jesus H. Christ!" He stared up at her, confounded.

Horrified, she quickly let go of him and backed away, only to bump her head against the wall of the narrow hallway. The towel had entirely gone by the wayside and looking away seemed as impossible as jumping to the moon. Or pretending that she hadn't just lost her marbles entirely.

"I'm sorry," she said, hurriedly crouching down to grab the towel and toss it at him. It did not hit the intended target area, but landed in a ball on his belly.

He jackknifed up, clutching the towel in his big hand in front of him as he stood, but it was a case of way too little and way too late.

She wasn't going to be able to close her eyes anytime soon without seeing him in all his masculine glory on the back of her eyelids.

"What the hell, Ali! I wasn't gonna hurt you."

"I know, I know!" She dragged her fingers through her hair and half the pins in her bun scattered. She scrambled to pick them up, and that only brought her closer to the target she was trying to avoid.

Him.

She quickly decided the bobby pins simply weren't that important. "I just, you just…make me jumpy, okay?"

He muttered an oath, raking his fingers through the wet hair hanging in his face.

He was standing in her path to the staircase and unless he turned himself sideways, there was no way she could slip past without brushing against him.

And *that* wasn't going to happen anymore than she

was going to pick up those two pins right next to the big toe on his right foot.

She backed up a step and hit the damn wall again, this time cracking her elbow. "This place is more treacherous than my house!" She rubbed her elbow.

"Yeah, well, you shouldn't go walking around in strange men's—"

"Hallways?"

His eyes met hers. And they suddenly crinkled. He let out a laugh and shook his head. "Damn," he muttered. "This is a first for me."

Her cheeks were on fire, but she felt a smile tug at her lips, too. "Yeah, well, me, too. I've never actually done that. You know. Outside of practice sparring."

"Yeah, well," he returned. He wiggled his wrist. "Nice job. I think."

She bit the inside of her cheek and dragged her eyes upward again. "You, uh, need to, um, adjust your towel or something."

He cursed and she could have sworn his cheeks actually turned dusky.

"I'm just gonna turn around." She spun on her heel until she was no longer facing him.

"Think that's closing the barn door too late, but okay." She felt more than heard him move. "All right," he said a moment later. "You're safe. All clear."

Her chest hurt from the way her heart was thumping so hard. She cautiously turned.

He'd pulled on a terry-cloth robe.

Not unusual, she supposed.

Except this one was bright red. And it had big white hearts splashed all over it.

"Well," she said after the shock of it passed. "I guess you're set for Valentine's Day."

He spread his palms. The sleeves were at least six inches too short on his long arms. "Someone left it in the closet."

"Maybe your sister when she was squatting here without permission." Ali felt confident it hadn't been left behind by the weed-toking teenagers. "Aside from the fact that it's a little short—" A *little*? She could see nearly every inch of his muscular thighs. "—it's a good color on you."

He cupped the edge of fabric where it crossed over his chest. "You're sure it's not too much? I think it's a little bright, but—"

She rolled her eyes.

He chuckled. Made a point of turning sideways and sweeping his arm out in invitation toward the stairs.

She quickly scooted past him. And it was a wonder she didn't fall over her feet, she skipped down the steps so fast.

"I'm gonna wait in my truck," she yelled over her shoulder as she grabbed her coat and kept right on going until she burst out the front door.

She slammed it behind her and stood on the front porch, hauling in the cold morning air. She was so hot—from the furnace, from embarrassment, from *oh, dear God, he had a perfect body*, that she didn't even bother pulling on her coat once she left the porch to climb up into the SUV.

Then she thumped her head against the headrest. "Alicia, you big dummy."

She turned on the ignition and rolled down the window, because she was *still* too hot.

Only a few minutes passed, though, before the front door opened and Grant came out. And she couldn't help but laugh silently.

He'd changed into jeans. And a brilliant red sweater. He, too, didn't seem to feel the need for a jacket. But he was carrying one bunched in his hand.

He jogged across to the SUV. His hair was still wet and slicked away from his angular face. "I'll follow you into town," he said.

"Are you sure?" She pulled her shoulder belt across her lap and fastened it. She grinned. "You can sit up here with me if being behind the grill is too unnerving." The "grill" was a thick web of metal separating the front seat from the back.

His eyes glinted. "I've ridden in the back of scarier cop cars than this," he assured her. "But if I ride with you into town, you're gonna have to bring me all the way back. No point in making a wasted trip."

She held her grin in place, even though it suddenly felt like it had deflated. "All right then," she agreed, in what she hoped was a creditably easy tone. "I'll see you at the department. I'm sure the mug shot will be there by now." She'd radio ahead just to make sure of it.

"Good enough." He tapped the hood of the SUV as he headed toward the barn. He pushed open the door and disappeared inside and a moment later, the rusted pickup truck was coughing its way through the barn door opening.

Once he was through, he got back out, closed the barn door, climbed back in the truck and sketched a wave toward her as he did.

She pulled the SUV around to head back to Braden.

As soon as she reached the highway, she thumbed the radio. "Timmy, did that fax come in from Seattle that I was waiting for?"

Static greeted her. Then an eventual affirmative.

"On my way." She dropped the mic on the console. Grant's pickup truck was in her rearview mirror.

Nineteen-point-six miles to go, and they'd know whether or not Seattle's Karen was their Karen.

She wasn't.

Dismayed, Ali looked from Grant's face to the fax image. The quality of the picture wasn't great, but it was full color. "Are you sure? I know she's a green-eyed redhead, but ignore the brown hair. Contact lenses these days can make anyone's eyes blue like that." For all she knew *his* aqua beams were a result of contacts.

"It's not her," he said again. "I'd know my own sister's face, Ali."

She sighed. "Of course you would." She dropped the fax onto her desk and led the way out the department's security door.

"See you tomorrow, Timmy," she said as they passed the information desk.

He was their newest recruit, and tended to blush anytime she addressed him. Today was no exception. He nodded, red-faced and Adam's apple bobbing. "See ya, Ali."

"Gonna have a hard time as a police officer if he looks like a beet every time he speaks to a woman," Grant commented once they'd left the building through the rear door.

"He's twenty years old. He'll get over it," she said with more confidence than she felt. "I used to be his babysitter. I think maybe he had a little crush on me back then."

"Back *then*?"

"Well, don't go saying anything too loud about it,"

Ali said. "God knows that Gowler would blame me for that, too."

"Didn't notice him strutting around today."

"He's off."

"Will the mice play?"

"Probably." She grabbed her purse from the SUV and relocked the vehicle. "Mind giving *me* a ride home? I'm off for an entire twenty-four hours. Gowler'll be back in twelve. He won't like it if my ride is parked in front of my house instead of here at the department."

"You don't have a car?"

"Bad transmission. Still in the shop. And it's a pickup." They'd reached *his* pickup and she pulled open the passenger door. It squealed as if it hadn't been opened in a decade. Considering the truck had to be at least twenty years old, she figured that was definitely possible.

He got in beside her and the blanket-covered bench seat seemed to shrink. She started to roll down the window for fresh air, but the handle came right off in her hand. "Uh-oh." She held it up for him to see.

"Yeah, it doesn't work." His fingers brushed hers as he took it from her and tossed it over the back of the seat. Since there was no rear seat, it didn't have far to go and she heard it clang against something when it landed. "Don't worry about it."

She rested her bare knuckles against the window. For some reason the cold sensation seemed to make the interior feel a little less confining.

You don't feel confined. You just can't stop thinking about him being naked.

She chewed the inside of her cheek and trained her attention out the windshield.

He drove out from behind the municipal building to the main street. "Which way?"

She scrabbled her senses together. "Left. Then left again at the light. After that it's just basically up the hill."

The street traffic was light. He turned left with ease and drove down the block. Past the central business district and the bus depot; past the Suds-n-Grill and China Palace. She pointed her thumb at the Chinese restaurant when they stopped at the red traffic signal. "If you like Chinese food, that place is really good." Then she wished she hadn't said anything, because the restaurant was actually a little pricey. "So's the Weaver Town Buffet in Weaver, though. They don't have real tablecloths, but you can get twice the food for half the price." She knew she was babbling. "This is where you turn."

She felt pretty silly stating the obvious, so she clamped her teeth together, determined to just be quiet.

The light changed.

He turned and the truck engine growled a little as they started up Hill Street, not so imaginatively named since the street was, in fact, on a hill.

She glanced over her shoulder, looking out the rear window. At least there was no sign of black exhaust spewing from the tailpipes. She sat forward again. "Got the exhaust fixed, I see. Where'd you take it?"

"Nowhere. Fixed it myself."

"Nice. Wish I could have done the same myself with my transmission. Wouldn't mind not owing money I don't have just *once* in a while. We're totally stalled right now on renovating the house until we can pool together more money." She clamped her fingers under her thigh, as a reminder to stop it from bouncing so nervously. "It's, uh, it's the house at the end of the block."

He pulled up to the curb in front of what had once been a grand lady. Now, it was simply a three-story money pit.

"That is an ambitious house," he said.

"Yep." She eyed it fondly. The snow was piled around it, adding a touch of frost that helped take one's eye away from the peeling paint and the other signs of aging. "Everyone thought we were crazy when we bought it. Particularly my dad. Said we would be throwing good money after bad for the foreseeable and unforeseeable future. I love it, though." She grinned. "Even the ghosts who steal our tools. Greer insists that I'm just too scatterbrained when it comes to keeping track of them, and I know it's not her or Maddie. So, unless it's our neighbor, Mrs. Gunderson, it's got to be—"

"Ghosts." He looked amused.

"Right. Want to come in and see it?" It was the first Monday of the month, so Greer would be at work until that evening, when Ali, Greer and Maddie planned to get together for dinner. "I've got *real* coffee."

His gaze slid over her. "Temptress." But he shook his head and she was more than a little alarmed by the lead balloon that sank in her stomach. "I'll have to meet the ghosts later."

"Sure." She hesitated before pushing open the squealing door. "I'll let you know what I find out about that phone number." She wondered just how involved he still was with his ex-wife. If, like with Jack, the relationship wasn't as finished as the term *divorced* implied.

"You can leave the message on my cell phone."

For some reason, she'd assumed he didn't have one.

"Okay." She pulled out her own phone. "What's the number?"

He recited it and she saved it in her phone, then stuck it back in her purse. "All right." She briskly climbed out of the truck. "I'll be in touch." She started to close the door.

"Ali."

He didn't say her name very loudly, but she still heard it above the screech of metal hinges. She looked at him through the wedge of open space. "Yeah?"

"Is it jumpy in a bad way? Or jumpy in a good way?"

She instantly felt like they were back in his upstairs hallway and her mouth went dry. "Good."

His eyes were steady on her face. "All right then."

She swallowed and moistened her lips. "All right then."

He smiled slightly. Then he reached across the bench seat and pulled the door out of her lax fingers, shutting it the last few inches.

She barely had the presence of mind to step back from the curb before he drove away.

When the sound of his engine faded, she was still standing there, her heart pounding beneath her coat.

"Good morning, Ali." Mrs. Gunderson, bundled in a wool coat that was probably just as ancient as she was, paused on the opposite side of the street while her leashed miniature black poodle, Mignon, did his business in the snow. "Everything all right?"

Ali dropped her hand. "Just fine, Mrs. Gunderson."

"Who was your friend?" Mignon had finished, and now jumped against his mistress's legs until she picked him up. "Oh, you fat little thing. I don't recall seeing that pickup before."

Rather than stand there yelling across the street, Ali crossed to the other side. "His name's Grant," she said when she reached the curb. "He's from Oregon. Moved out to the old Carmody spread."

"I remember the Carmodys." The elderly woman shook her head and the pink scarf tied around her neatly coiffed hair slipped down over her forehead. "That was a nasty business the way they lost their ranch to the bank."

"Mmm." Ali scratched Mignon's head and the dog's button-bright black eyes rolled.

"Can't really blame the economy for it," her neighbor went on. "Though that surely didn't help. But their luck was never good. Particularly after that unsavory business with their daughter."

That got Ali's attention. "Oh?"

"Of course, back in those days, babies born on the wrong side of the blanket still caused a bit of scandal." She dumped Mignon in Ali's hands while she adjusted her scarf and tied it again beneath her chin. "But is a little scandal worth all that trouble?" She clucked her tongue as she took back her little dog and set him on the ground, where he immediately started whining. "Now, Mignon. You have to walk! Dr. Taggart said you *had* to lose some weight!" In her typical way, she barely drew breath between thoughts. "The way they kicked their own daughter out of the house was just shameful, much more shameful than having a baby out of wedlock. Come along, Mignon." She tugged on the leash. "I'm determined that we'll walk to the bottom of the hill and back every day until he loses a couple pounds."

Ali wanted to pump Mrs. Gunderson for more information about the Carmodys, but she was sidetracked by

concern for her neighbor. None of them knew exactly
how old she was, except that she was somewhere north
of eighty and south of a hundred. "It's a pretty steep
hill, Mrs. Gunderson." She slid her purse strap diago-
nally across her body and slipped her arm through her
neighbor's. "How about I walk with you?"

Mrs. Gunderson just laughed and disentangled her
arm before turning her old-fashioned black snow boots
downhill. "You're a sweet girl, Ali. But the day hasn't
come yet when I can't walk my own hill. Go on, now.
I know this is your day off."

Resigned, Ali watched the woman walk away. Mrs.
Gunderson wasn't going to win any speed records, that
was for sure, but she was making steady progress all
the same.

After several minutes, Ali pulled out her cell phone
and called the department, asking that a patrol car run
by the bottom of the hill, just in case Mrs. Gunderson
decided she wanted a ride back up it.

Then she crossed the street, sat down in the rocker
on the front porch and kept watch over her neighbor
from this end.

But that left her thoughts to roam.

And they roamed straight to Grant.

She had resources at the department that she could
use to peek into Grant's personal life. At the very least,
she could find out what happened with his biological
family. It seemed to be fairly common these days for
adopted children to voluntarily seek out their birth families once they were adults, whether it was to have their
questions answered, get a sense of closure or forge a
new relationship. Grant's motives didn't seem to fit any
of those molds.

Maybe there were answers she could find on her own.

But when it came to him, she knew she couldn't do it. Go around his back like that.

She honestly didn't know whether that worried her or not.

Chapter Eight

"Here." Maddie had barely made it into the kitchen later that evening before she plunked Layla in Ali's lap and raced out of the room again, shedding coat and gloves as she went.

Ali looked over the baby's blonde head at Greer, who was also sitting at the table in the unfinished room.

Her sister returned her look with a shrug. "Got me," she murmured, and turned her attention back to the law book she was reading.

It was the first Monday of the month, which meant the three sisters were having dinner together. It was the one time that they all seemed to agree was sacred. Particularly since Maddie had moved in with Linc. Neither work nor husbands nor law books were supposed to get in the way of it. Unfortunately, that was all a fine idea in theory, but they hadn't managed a proper First Monday in months.

But that didn't stop them from trying.

After Ali had finished watching Mrs. Gunderson and Mignon return safely to their home, courtesy of two of Braden's finest, who'd just happened to be driving past the bus bench where a winded Mrs. Gunderson had been sitting, she'd left messages for both Greer and Maddie to remind them what day it was. Then she'd loaded up the slow cooker, remembering to turn it on this time. The one-pot concoction now actually smelled somewhat like what it was supposed to be—teriyaki chicken.

She worked Layla's arms out of her furry white coat and freed her from it, turning the tot to stand on her legs. The baby smiled gummily and Ali's heart just simply squeezed. "You're too sweet, you little chunk." She kissed her round cheek, then her sweet-smelling neck.

Layla chortled.

"Don't eat the baby," Greer drawled. "Give her to me."

Ali made a face. "Oh, I do not think so." She stood up, holding the baby on her hip. "Auntie Greer has always thought she can tell me what to do," she confided to the baby.

"For all the good it's done." Greer's voice followed Ali as she left the kitchen and headed into the living room.

She sat down with the baby on the dated shag rug that partially covered the parquet wood floor. What with all the trips Ali had made chasing "Daisy" Cooper's trail, combined with working nearly every minute when she was home, they'd made absolutely no progress on their restoration project.

The last thing they'd done was agree on a paint color for the kitchen.

Which still hadn't been painted. Not in Svelte Sage or any other hue.

Grant's walls were still unpainted, too.

She reached for the box of the baby's favored toys. She dragged it closer, pulling out the bright blue and red plastic bowls, and laughed softly when the baby immediately grabbed for them both.

"Whew." Maddie came into the living room and threw herself down on the couch that had once resided in their parents' basement. She propped her feet on the coffee table. She looked at the fireplace. "Fire feels good."

"Greer started it just a few minutes ago." Layla threw the red bowl and Ali grabbed it before it could roll too far. "Look at that arm." She wiggled the bowl and the baby snatched it again. She knew from experience that Layla could play this particular game endlessly.

"I'm pouring wine," Greer yelled from the other room.

"Yes," Ali yelled back.

"Pass," Maddie added, equally loudly. She returned Ali's look with an innocent shrug. "What?"

Ali lifted her shoulders. "Nothing." None of them drank a whole lot, but they generally managed to consume a bottle or two on First Monday. "What's the studly husband doing tonight?"

"Having dinner with his mother." Maddie folded her hands over her stomach and her head lolled back against the couch. "How's life with the Growler been?"

Ali shuddered.

Maddie smiled.

"You look tired."

"I am." But her sister sat up and pulled her feet from the coffee table when Greer came into the room carrying wineglasses and an uncorked bottle. She set everything on the coffee table, then pulled the water bottle from where it had been tucked under her arm and dropped it beside Maddie on the couch.

"Hope you showered today," Ali drawled.

Greer made a face back at her.

"Children, children." Maddie uncapped her water and held it out. "To First Monday. Finally."

"Amen to that." Greer and Ali picked up their wineglasses and tapped them against Maddie's water bottle.

After a sip, Ali left the glass well out of Layla's reach and returned to the toss-the-bowl game.

"Keith Gowler was at the courthouse today," Greer said. "Looking as mopey as ever. What *did* you do to the poor guy?"

"Poor guy!" Ali made a face. "The man was talking about marriage and three-point-six kids on our third date. We had barely even kissed. And when we *did* kiss, I knew there wasn't going to be any chance of getting to the baby-making stage. Sloppy kisser."

"Eeeww," Greer said, and grimaced.

"Exactly."

Grant wouldn't be a sloppy kisser. The thought snuck in and Ali hurriedly threw up a mental block against it. "But I *did* have an excellent idea." She reached for the wineglass and pointed the rim of it in Greer's direction. "No smirks, Greer."

Her sister's eyes danced. She hid her smile behind her wineglass. Ali looked toward Maddie. "I just need to get Keith set up with someone new."

"Ahh—" Maddie hesitated, probably hunting for a tactful way of expressing the *"Oh, brother"* that Greer muttered.

It was always that way. Greer and Ali rubbed each

other wrong, and Maddie—the middle sister among the triplets—was the peacemaker.

"I'm serious. Think about it. Keith *so* wants to find a woman that he was willing to think I was the one!"

"Well, that's true," Greer allowed drily. "Maybe if you'd have kept dating him, he'd have come to realize his mistake."

"Oh, hah, Greer. Keith's not a bad guy. I went out with him more times than I should have, just because he's so infernally decent. We just need to think of a single woman who likes—"

"Sloppy kisses?" Maddie shook her head. "I don't know, Ali. Matchmaking? That kind of thing never works out."

"Please. Layla was the matchmaker for you and Linc." She wrapped the baby's hands in hers and clapped them together.

Maddie laughed softly. "Well, that did sort of work out," she agreed.

Greer caught Ali's eye. "Suppose she'll still have that besotted look on her face a year from now?"

"Oh, I expect I will," Maddie answered.

"You look like the cat who's gotten the cream," Ali accused.

"She's a newlywed," Greer said, smiling wryly. "They're probably doing it like rabbits."

"You're just jealous," Maddie returned. "Both of you. When's the last time *you* saw a nekkid man, eh?"

Greer laughed over her wine. "Ooh. Nekkid. Legal meaning? Without clothes and up to no good."

"And it is very, very good no-good," Maddie drawled.

Greer made a face. "Don't rub it in on your poor nunlike sisters. Last man I was with was—" she held her glass to the side as she considered "—criminy. Too long ago to admit even to you two. And Ali—"

"Saw a naked man today." She hadn't really planned to bring that up, but there was just something to be said for being able to make her two sisters sit up and take notice like that.

"No way!" Greer went from looking astonished to suspicious. "Not Keith. Dear God, please not—"

Maddie swatted her with her hand. She was looking at Ali. "You've got a new man? Finally! Why haven't you said something before now? I thought you were never going to let yourself get over Jack's—"

"I haven't *gotten* a man or anything else," Ali explained pointedly. "But I did see a naked man."

"Who?" Greer demanded.

She savored the name for a moment before saying it aloud. "Grant Cooper." Neither one had met Grant in person, but they certainly knew who he was.

Greer's eyebrows skyrocketed.

Maddie's jaw dropped.

Ali fanned her face. "And may I just say...*ooh la.*" Then she laughed and rolled onto her back. She held Layla up in the air above her and the baby gave a big, delicious belly laugh.

Greer scrambled around the coffee table and snatched Layla right out of Ali's hands.

"Hey!"

Her sister kissed the baby's fists and stared down at Ali. "Details, baby sister."

Greer had always lorded her thirty-minute age advantage over Ali.

"You're sleeping with the man who might be Layla's uncle?"

Ali looked at Maddie. "I'm not sleeping with him."

"But you would if you could," Greer said knowingly.

She wasn't going to deny what she wasn't sure she *could* deny.

"But clearly, you're getting…entangled here," Maddie persisted. "Do you think that's wise?"

"She's not worried about wisdom. She's worried about getting some action for her lady bits."

"And you're not," Ali retorted. She sat up and focused on Maddie. "It was a perfectly innocent accident, actually." She didn't elaborate, because if she did, she'd be admitting to the way she'd wristlocked the guy right out of his threadbare towel. Even though she'd flipped him inadvertently, that particular detail would not reflect very well on her. "And we were both embarrassed. Trust me. There is nothing going on between us except where Layla is concerned."

Maddie sighed faintly, but seemed to accept it.

Greer, however, was giving Ali the I-know-better eye.

Which just proved that Greer was better at spotting Ali's lies than Maddie.

"You *are* interested in him." Greer sat down on the coffee table, not seeming to care in the least when Layla butted her in the chin with her head and laughed as if she'd discovered a new game. "Not just sex-terested, either." She grinned. "Alicia likes a bo-oy," she mocked in a singsong voice.

"Grant's definitely no boy." Ali couldn't stop herself.

Greer's eyes danced. "I love it."

"Greer, don't encourage her!"

Greer turned on Maddie. "Why not? You said it yourself a few minutes ago, Maddie my dear. It's about time she got over Jack! Two-timing Ali *with* his ex-wife? He was a total weasel. If Grant *is* Layla's uncle, then we've got a total lock on keeping her in the family!" She bussed the big white heart positioned on the front of Layla's stretchy red sleeper, then made a face and quickly handed her back to Maddie. "Phew alert."

Ali saw the dark shadows under Maddie's eyes and pushed to her feet. Not only was Maddie a newlywed settling into the big old Swift Mansion with Linc, but she was also still working full-time for family services while taking care of the baby. Regardless of how the situation had come about, she'd stepped into the role of new mom without having nine months to get ready. Was it any wonder she looked exhausted?

"I'll do it." Ali ignored both her sisters' surprised expressions as she scooped up the baby and carried her upstairs. They kept diapers and changing supplies as well as a portable crib in Maddie's room for whenever the baby was there.

She grabbed what she needed and set the baby in the middle of the bed, wincing only a little as she changed the messy diaper. "One of these days, I'll get used to it," she promised the infant.

Layla didn't seem to care. She merely kicked her legs merrily and chortled as Ali tried to wrangle her back into a clean diaper and her red-footed onesie. The white heart on the front reminded her of the robe that Grant had pulled on that morning. "I really do hope he *is* your uncle," she whispered as she carried the baby out of the room and headed back down the stairs.

She raised her voice for her sisters' benefit. "If we put our heads together, I'm *sure* we can think of a suitable match for Keith. It's just a matter of setting them up without *seeming* to set them up." She reached the bottom of the stairs.

Greer was once more sipping her wine. Maddie was sipping her water.

And Grant Cooper was sitting on the couch right between them.

Heat filled her face. She probably looked as bright a red as her co-worker Timmy had ever looked, and her sympathy for him went up about a hundred and ten percent.

Jumpy in a good way?

Heaven help her.

She swallowed the nerves suddenly pitching tents in her throat. "Grant. What are you doing here?"

"Got that address finally."

"Oh. Right." She shouldn't be disappointed that he'd come back because of that, particularly when it was one more possible clue to track down Layla's mother, but she was. She was wearing leggings and a Harry Potter sweatshirt and she felt unusually self-conscious as she carried Layla over to Maddie. "Great." She tugged at the hem of the sweatshirt. "I guess you've met my sisters." She gestured to each one in turn. "Greer. Maddie."

They were both smiling at him, though with entirely different tilts to their lips. Greer's expression was knowing, while Maddie's was wary.

Ali curled her hand over the baby's sweet head. "And this, of course, is Layla. Mom had her with her this weekend at the department. Grant happened to be there at the same time," she said to her sisters.

Maddie seemed to brace herself a little as she looked at Grant. Ali doubted that anyone but she or Greer would have noticed. "Would you like to hold her?"

He shook his head, looking as if she'd asked him to hold a land mine. Although, considering his CCT experience, he'd have probably been more comfortable with the land mine. "She doesn't know who I am," he said hurriedly.

Ali had to bite the inside of her lip to keep from smiling. Aside from Maddie, who'd always been good with babies and kids, they'd all had similar reactions to the baby.

At first.

"Come on into the kitchen," she invited. "I'll get that address from you."

He popped up from the couch like an overwound children's toy.

She sincerely wished that Maddie wouldn't look so worried, but she knew there wasn't a thing she could do about it. Maddie needed to take a leaf out of Greer's book. *She* was hiding her smile in her wineglass.

Ali led the way into the kitchen, seeing it through Grant's eyes. Unfinished cabinet frames with missing doors. Plywood countertop. Exposed plumbing. "I know. It's worse than your place." She pulled open the junk drawer and pawed through the mess for the notepad they used for their grocery and supply lists. She gave him a sideways look. "Only now I know you've got skills."

His lips twitched and she felt her cheeks warm.

"*Carpentry* skills."

He laughed softly and shivers danced down her spine. "I don't know about carpentry skills."

She finally latched onto the notepad and yanked it out. "Yeah, well, you say that, but you must be handy with your tools."

His eyes glinted even more. "Haven't had any complaints."

She blushed even harder. What was *wrong* with her? Just because it had been a while, she was no shy virgin.

"Just give me the address. You could have called me, you know. Saved yourself a trip."

"I could have."

She caught her tongue between her teeth, hoping she didn't look as ridiculously pleased as she felt. She might as well have been back in high school, having the senior quarterback ask *her*—not Maddie or Greer—to dance.

He pulled out his cell phone and showed her the text message.

Her schoolgirl euphoria ruptured.

The name of the sender was Chelsea.

She wrote down the Montana address, but left off the "XOXO" and the three hearts that followed it. Then she dropped the pencil back into the drawer and slammed it shut a little harder than necessary. "Chelsea is your ex-wife?" She remembered the first day they'd met. When he'd accused her of being sent by someone named Chelsea.

He stuck the phone back into his pocket. "Very ex," he said as if he knew what she was thinking.

She turned and leaned back against her hands on the drawer. She had to look up a long way to his face. And there seemed like very little space between them. Her heart was suddenly pounding, euphoria sneaking back in. "Are you sure?"

His eyes moved over her face. He slowly lifted his hand and lightly grazed his thumb over her lip. "Positive."

His head started to inch down to hers. "They have little flecks of yellow."

He paused. "What has little flecks of yellow?" he whispered back.

Her mouth felt dry and she swallowed. Moistened her

lips. "Your eyes." Maybe that's why they seemed aqua, rather than merely blue. Laser. Sharp. Blue.

He smiled slightly. "And yours are like chocolate. Dark. Melted. Chocolate. I've got a serious thing for dark chocolate."

She wondered if this was what it felt like to swoon. She heard his name sort of sigh from her lips, even though she hadn't consciously said a word. She swallowed again, leaning toward him—

"Yoo-hoo!" The back door flew open and Ali's mother blew in.

Ali jumped back. Grant merely lifted his head a little.

Feeling entirely cheated out of what she was certain would *not* be a sloppy kiss, she could only stare at her mother. Meredith hadn't really noticed Ali yet at all, since she was busy making sure that her mother-in-law, who was with her, made it safely up the back step. "What's going on?"

Meredith turned then, and seemed to notice Grant for the first time. More specifically, she seemed to notice how close he stood to Ali. Toe-to-toe. Her eyes turned even brighter. "Well, isn't this a nice surprise!" She left Vivian's side to approach them, extending a slender arm that was weighted down with a dozen delicate bracelets. "Grant. I'm Meredith—"

"I remember." He shook her hand. "It's nice to see you."

"What's nice to see is a fresh face around here." Vivian Archer Templeton shut the door with a hand firm enough to guarantee some attention. She was almost as petite as Ali's mom—who was even shorter than Ali and her sisters—but what Vivian lacked in height, she more than made up for in attitude.

Thanks to several wealthy dead husbands and Pennsylvania steel, she was richer than Midas. Ali and her siblings had never even met their grandmother, until a couple years ago when she showed up in Wyoming out of the clear blue sky intent on ending her estrangement with Ali's dad and uncle. Now, Vivian had a decent relationship with most everyone—except her sons. Even though she was opinionated, tended to veer between irreverent and arrogant and had a penchant for sticking her eccentric, aristocratic nose in everyone's business, Ali had become pretty darn fond of her.

Vivian picked her way across the floor as if the worn tiles would damage the soles of her expensive leather boots. She shrugged out of her fur coat and looked up at Grant. "You're a fine specimen, aren't you?" Her brown eyes were as bright as buttons and she patted her stylish silver hair. "Too young for me, but—"

"Vivian," Meredith chided.

Vivian's smile widened. She held out a beringed hand to Grant.

He looked at it for a second. "Do I kiss it or shake it?"

Vivian let out a sharp peal of laughter. She propped her hand on her slender hip. "Maybe you're not too young after all."

"Don't listen to her," Meredith said drily, grabbing Vivian's shoulders and forcibly steering her away from Grant. "She's more bark than bite, I promise."

Grant was smiling. "I think that might be a shame."

Vivian shrugged away from Meredith's hold. She clasped Ali's face between her hands. "If you don't know what to do with him, just tell your old granny, and I'll fill you in. I haven't buried four husbands without learning a thing or two."

Ali laughed wryly. Nobody called Vivian "granny." Hayley—who'd been the first one to show Vivian any welcome when she'd descended upon Wyoming—occasionally called her "Grandmother." To everyone else, she was Vivian. Pure, unadulterated Vivian. "I think I can manage," Ali assured her. And she would have been well on the way to proving it if not for the interruption.

She took Vivian's hands in hers and squeezed them very gently, because—for all of Vivian's larger-than-lifeness—she *was* a little frail. Not necessarily because she was on the high side of her eighties, but because she had an inoperable brain tumor. So far, it was causing only an occasional fainting spell. But they all knew it could cause something much worse. It could happen at any moment. Or it could happen not at all.

Vivian, of course, just took it in stride. She said that the thing had been squatting in her head for more than a few years now, and if the day came when it decided not to squat, well, then she'd finally be able to join "dear Arthur" at last. He'd been the fourth and final of her husbands and to hear her tell it, the only one she'd loved with all her heart.

"What brought you here?"

Vivian lived on the edge of Weaver, in a huge mansion she'd had built. It would have been more fitting for Pittsburgh, where she was from, than anywhere in the state of Wyoming, let alone Weaver.

Meredith unwound her winter scarf from her neck and unfastened her coat. "Vivian insisted."

And when Vivian insisted, woe to anyone who got in her way.

Ali focused on her grandmother again. "Because?"

"Because I'm on the Valentine's ball planning committee, and I wanted some fresh input from you young people."

"Valentine's Day is under two weeks away," Ali said warily. "Aren't the plans already in the works?"

"Yes, but I want to prove a point and there's no time to waste. Everyone on the committee is entirely stodgy." Vivian gestured at Meredith. "Including your bohemian mother, who is generally anything *but* stodgy." She eyed Ali. "Do *you* think the usual potluck in the high-school gymnasium is just fine?" She didn't wait for an answer. "Frankly, calling that a *ball* is a gross reach, if you ask me."

"We don't have a budget for anything else," Meredith reminded her.

"Bah." Vivian waved her hand and settled her fur on one of the kitchen chairs before perching on the edge of it. "I could take care of that with a snap of my fingers if there wasn't a certain dunderhead on the town council who has blocked every idea I bring to it."

"Dunderhead?" Grant asked.

"She means Squire Clay," Greer told him as she came into the kitchen with Layla to check out the fuss. She kissed Vivian's delicately lined cheek and then hugged Meredith, who promptly slipped the baby out of Greer's arms.

Ali couldn't help but notice the way Grant's gaze kept straying to the baby.

"You haven't been here long enough to know," Greer went on, "but Squire Clay—"

"Is intensely annoying."

Greer ignored Vivian. "Owns the largest ranch in the area—the Double C—and now he's also one of Weaver's council members."

"I'm sure he bought the election." Vivian tapped the table and her rings glinted under the bare lightbulb hanging from the ceiling fixture.

"You're still put out because he beat you for the seat last fall," Meredith replied calmly.

Grant looked at Ali. "Sounds like your grandmother has the hots for the guy."

Vivian's finely penciled eyebrows skyrocketed. "You're *obviously* new to the area, so I'll forgive you for that."

"Squire's first wife was our grandfather's sister," Greer disclosed.

"Vivian's first husband," Ali explained. "Vivian and Squire didn't get along then, and they don't get along now."

"What my granddaughter is being too polite to say is that I snubbed my husband's *half* sister ages and ages ago, because she was born on the wrong side of the blanket."

Ali jerked a little at the phrase. Not because it was news to her, but because Mrs. Gunderson had used it that very morning, too. Even if the women were from different locales, it just seemed proof that they were from the same era.

"But the only reason we don't get along *now* is because that old coot refuses to let an old woman apologize." Vivian pointed at Meredith. "He's no different than Carter and David."

"Don't blame me for that," Meredith said mildly. "Carter was your son before he was my husband." She jiggled Layla on her hip and smiled wryly at Grant. "Aren't you glad you brought it up?"

Grant's lips tilted in a smile. He looked at Ali. "Did I?"

"No, you did not."

"Tell me." Vivian looked Grant up and down. "Would *you* like celebrating Valentine's Day by sitting in some school building eating God knows what?"

"Can't say I've celebrated a lot of Valentine's

Days. And as long as the food doesn't come out of a government-issue pouch, I'm pretty good with it."

"That's not the answer I was looking for," Vivian said drily.

"Then you shouldn't have asked the question," Ali pointed out. She took Grant's arm and didn't have to work hard at all to steer him out of the crowded kitchen.

"Hey, I was gonna invite him for dinner," Greer called after them. Laughter was in her voice. "We're not eating out of pouches."

It was immediately apparent to Ali why Maddie hadn't also joined the fray in the kitchen. She was sitting on the couch, feet propped up on the coffee table. Sound asleep.

Ali rubbed her palm over the staircase's newel post. "You *are* welcome to stay for dinner," she told Grant softly. It seemed more than apparent that First Monday was once again derailed.

He shook his head, looking wry. "I mean this with the most respect, Officer Ali, but there's a little too much estrogen in there for comfort."

She grinned. "For me, too. But they are my family. Warts and all."

He glanced toward Maddie. "The three of you really *are* peas in a pod." Then he looked back at Ali and she shivered when his gaze seemed to drop momentarily to her mouth. "Rain check?"

She nodded. "Sure."

He smiled faintly as he grazed his thumb across her lower lip again. Then he plucked his coat from the back of a chair and quietly went out the front door.

Ali's knees had dissolved, and she sat down on the bottom step of the staircase.

"Alicia likes a bo-oy," Greer sang again from the kitchen doorway.

Ali propped her elbows on her knees and stared at the front door. "Yeah," she said on a sigh that was too dreamy for comfort. "Does she ever."

Chapter Nine

Looking into the Montana address Karen Cooper had given Grant's ex-wife to wire her money turned up nothing.

Ali sat at the desk she'd been assigned and stared blindly at the wall in front of her. Every single time they had a possible lead on Grant's sister, it ended up going nowhere.

Gowler dropped a file folder on her desk. "Get over to Braden Drugs. Manager reported a shoplifter. When you get back, type up these reports."

The folder was thick, meaning she'd be typing for some time—which was not her forte. But she wasn't going to complain since at least she got to deal with an actual complaint first. "Yessir." She grabbed her jacket and the keys to her unit before heading toward the door.

"Templeton!"

She paused.

"Take Timmy with you."

Great. She looked across the room at the other officer, who'd looked up from the book he was reading at the sound of his name. "Let's roll, Timmy."

His face turned red, but he grabbed his coat and they went out the back to where the department's vehicles were all parked. Ali drove, wishing there was something she could do to make Timmy relax around her.

"Timmy, you've got a sister, right? Still lives in town here? Single?"

He gave her a quick look. His Adam's apple bobbed. "Tracie. Yeah."

"Tracie got a boyfriend?"

He made a face. "Yeah. He's a jerk."

Keith Gowler wasn't a jerk. Just a sloppy kisser. Which might well be one of those beauty-in-the-eye-of-the-beholder things. "They serious?"

"I hope not," he muttered.

"She teaches over at the elementary school?"

"Yeah." His face was like a beet. "Why?"

"No reason." She smiled at him, wondering how on earth she could maneuver a "meet cute" between an elementary-school teacher and a defense lawyer. "Just making conversation." She turned into the parking lot of the small strip mall where the drugstore was located. The drugstore was at one end. Hardware store at the other. A dress shop and a bakery in between. Timmy called in their location and they went inside.

The girl at the counter jerked her head toward the back. "Manager's got him back in the office."

"Thanks." Ali led the way to the rear of the store. She knocked once on the closed door and then opened it.

The sight of the teenage boy sprawled in a chair made her cluck her tongue. "Trevor Oakes." She hadn't had an encounter with the kid since she'd rousted him out of Grant's vacant ranch house last year. "What's the deal?"

The store manager—a teenager only a few years older than Trevor—gestured at the array of products sitting on his desk. "He was shoveling all of this into his coat pockets. That's what the deal is."

Ali studied the items. Nothing there that he could cook with. Which was a relief. She didn't want to have to call in Trevor's poor mom to tell her that her son had graduated to making meth. "Nothing you can huff or puff here, Trev." She picked up a candy bar from among the other innocuous items. Visually, he didn't appear to be stoned, but that meant nothing. "Or do you just have the munchies?"

He made a face, crossing his arms. He clearly had no intention of answering.

"All right." She looked at Timmy. "Bag up the evidence, Officer. Let's take him in and process him."

To Timmy's credit, he didn't argue, even though they typically dealt with juvenile shoplifters at the scene. They rarely brought them in, even if charges were ultimately filed.

She gestured at Trevor. "Get up. Face the wall. Hands behind your back."

Finally, there was a hint of nervousness in his eyes. He did what she said and she cuffed him. "That your coat on the chair?"

He grunted an answer.

She gave him a look. "What's that?"

His jaw flexed. "Yes."

"Better." She tossed the coat over his shoulders. "You can come in and sign the complaint anytime this afternoon," she told the manager, who was watching with round eyes and slack jaw.

Then she walked Trevor, cuffed for all of Braden Drugs to see, out of the store. She put him in the back of the SUV behind the grill and as she waited for Timmy to catch up, she saw Grant walking out of the hardware store. He had a large bag propped on his shoulder.

Timmy still hadn't come out of the drugstore, but she drove across the parking lot, right in Grant's path.

Her heart wriggled around in her chest a little when he stopped and smiled at her.

She rolled down her window. She saw that he was carrying cement. "Looks like you're moving on from kitchen cabinetry."

"Yup. Spent the morning hunting down water lines. Now I get to repair the mess I made and put down tile again." He angled his head, looking at the occupant in her backseat. "Exciting day for Braden's finest?"

"Something like that." She couldn't seem to get the smile off her face. "No more cold showers?"

He stared into her eyes. His were slightly amused… and entirely mesmerizing. "Not without reason, anyway."

Every day since they'd had the snowstorm had been just a little warmer than the day before. And right then, it felt like the middle of a long hot summer to Ali.

She rolled down the passenger window, letting more winter air in to cool her cheeks. "I checked out the address you gave me." Better to stick to that, than let her imagination run amok. "Turned out to be a boarding-house owned by a woman named Honey Holmes." The name clearly meant nothing to Grant. "She rented a room to your sister for a couple weeks. But she cleared out after only one. The owner didn't have any idea where she was heading." She left out the part that Daisy— which was the name she'd rented the room under—had also left without paying the second week's rent. "Ms. Holmes did confirm that your sister was pregnant at the time. To use Honey's words, 'not quite ready to pop but getting there.'" She'd also called Daisy a tramp, but Ali figured she didn't need to share that detail.

"Maybe she had the baby in Montana."

"Possible. I've got a request in to check the birth records in Butte for the three months following her stay there. It's likely to be a lot, but maybe something will stand out."

Timmy jogged up to the truck then. He was carrying a paper bag that presumably held the confiscated stolen goods. He set it on the floor between his feet when he climbed into the vehicle.

"Talk later?" Grant suggested.

She nodded. It was silly that two words caused such giddiness to flow through her veins. "You could collect your rain check."

"Your kitchen or mine?"

She didn't have to even think about it. "Yours." She waited a beat. "It's in better shape than mine." They'd also be less likely to be interrupted by sisters or mothers or eccentric grandmothers.

His eyes glinted as if he knew exactly what she was thinking. "Come prepared. I have a big appetite."

She felt herself flush. Responding in kind was out of the question. Judging by the look he gave her, he knew it, too.

She waited until he'd crossed to his rusty pickup truck before putting the SUV in gear again.

"Who's that guy again?"

She glanced at Timmy. "Grant Cooper. He bought the Carmody ranch." It was nobody's business but Grant's that the Carmodys had also been his biological grand-parents.

"Oh, right." Timmy clicked his seat belt into place as she turned out of the parking lot and headed back to the department. "Steve said he'll come by and sign the complaint when his shift ends."

"Hey!" Trevor kicked the back of her seat. "I'm supposed to get a phone call or something, aren't I?"

"Sure, Trev. Soon as you're through processing." Which she intended to make as uncomfortable as possible. Maybe if she did the job well enough, Trevor would think twice before pulling his next stunt. "What do you think your mom's going to say when she has to come down and bail you out of jail?"

"You're not gonna put me in jail," he scoffed. "Stuff wasn't worth nothin'."

"Stuff worth nothin' can still get you up to six months, Trevor. Store manager caught you red-handed. We also got the surveillance tape, right, Timmy?"

"Right." Timmy made a face at her, which Trevor fortunately couldn't see. Because there was no surveillance tape. Not unless the drugstore had replaced their equipment since their last shoplifting episode, and she doubted it. The owner of the store was too cheap. Despite their recommendations, he maintained that the sight alone of a security camera was enough to deter would-be thieves. "Watched it myself." Timmy said it so convincingly that Ali was impressed. "Got him dead to rights."

She braked at the stop light and looked over the seat at Trevor. "Your mom's a pretty lady. She'll be really popular when she goes to visit you down at the prison in—"

"Prison!" Trevor's young face paled.

She faced forward again, leaving him to stew on that for a while.

When they got back to the department, she turned him over to Jerry. The older officer was a dad to two teenage boys about Trevor's age. He'd do a good job finishing what they'd started, and with any luck Trevor would see the value of returning to the straight and narrow.

Then she sat back down at her desk and flipped open Gowler's thick file of handwritten reports. But even the unappealing task of typing them up didn't bother her too much.

Not when she had Grant's big appetite awaiting her.

The sight of Ali on his doorstep that evening caused more pleasure than Grant expected.

If the winsome smile she was giving him was anything to go by, he figured the feeling was at least a little mutual. "I come bearing dinner." She held up a wide, flat pan with a blue-and-white-striped towel folded on top of it.

He started to take it from her but she looked down and nodded toward something. "Why don't you get that instead?" She didn't wait for an answer, but scooted past him into the house.

Another box sat on his porch.

More books.

Dammit, Chelsea.

He brought the box inside and shoved it in a closet. He'd lit a fire in the newly inspected fireplace and the box would have made good fuel. But it also would likely garner more curiosity from Ali than he wanted.

"When'd you paint in here?" She stood in the doorway to the kitchen, unfastening her puffy red coat. "Looks great."

"Last night." After he'd tired of staring at his ceiling while sleep eluded him. He took her coat from her and tossed it on top of the packing crates he still hadn't dealt with. "Needs another layer of paint, though. I can still see the shadow of graffiti showing through."

"If you say so. Personally, I can't see it, but—" She shrugged. Since he'd run into her that afternoon, she'd changed out of her uniform into jeans and another waffle-weave shirt—black, this time—and taken down her hair. The streaky locks waved around her neck. Her shoulders. Her breasts. "Did you get your cement work done?"

"I got it poured. It'll be a while before it's ready for me to tile. Meanwhile, I have a butt-load of painting still to do." He looked past her to see the blue-and-white-striped towel sitting on the counter. "What's in the pan?"

"Nothing fancy. Just a casserole. I stuck it in the oven to keep warm. Hope you like chicken, because if you don't, I'm not sure the pizza place will deliver this far outside of town. I do have these, though." She lifted a plastic bag full of cookies. "Almond-fudge drops. Best ever." She set it down on top of the towel.

"Cookies're always welcome." He held out his hand. "Hand 'em over."

"Didn't your mother tell you that dessert comes *after* dinner?"

He grinned. "Some situations call for different rules." He pulled out a cookie. They were small. It took three of them just to make up a proper bite. "Not bad," he said when he swallowed the delicious little bits. They had a dollop of frosting and little bits of almonds on top. "Who made 'em?"

"I beg your pardon?" She snatched the bag away from him like a punishment. "I did!"

Her indignation made him smile even more. Regardless of what brought her to his door, he knew he'd smiled more since he met her than he had in the last year. At least. "That stuff in the oven'll keep a while, then?"

"Should." Her eyes sparkled. "Why? You want to put a paint roller in my hand first?"

He slid his hand meaningfully around her waist and pulled her close, enjoying the way sparkle turned to melted chocolate. He took the cookie bag from her and tossed it onto the counter. "Maybe later."

Her hands flattened against the front of his sweatshirt. But she didn't push him away and the corners of her lips rose in a slight smile. "I don't sleep with strange men," she warned softly.

"Neither do I." He lowered his head toward hers. "You smell good. What is it?"

"Soap." Her voice dropped. Turned husky in a way that would have had all his nerve endings standing at attention if they weren't already. "You smell good, too." Her hands moved up his chest and linked behind his neck.

He brushed his lips over her temple, then skimmed down along her cheek. "Soap," he murmured against her ear. He kissed her shoulder and her heat radiated through the soft, textured shirt.

"Grant—"

He lifted his head and linked his hands behind her back. "Yes?"

She sighed a little, then suddenly melted into him.

"Hell with it." She pulled on his head, lifting her mouth toward his. "Kiss me, already."

"That was my intention. Good to know we're on the same page," he murmured and lightly grazed one corner of her lips with his. Little more than a whisper.

She made a sound and her fingers slid from his neck into his hair. "I don't know what page you're on, but I'm a little further into the book."

He laughed softly and teased the other corner of her mouth.

She tugged lightly at his hair, making another impatient sound. "Come on now," she complained. "Don't make me get rough."

He spread his fingers against her spine, feeling every little ridge. "Gonna flip me on my back again?"

Her eyes met his. "You on your back does have merit." Then she dragged his head back to hers, boldly fastening her mouth to his.

He hadn't intended on getting her into bed. Not exactly.

But at that moment, it was the only thing he could think of. He lifted her straight off the ground and she twined those deceptively long, lithe legs around his hips, lips still fastened to his.

He turned and bumped his way through the doorway. "Sorry," he mumbled against the smile he could feel on her mouth.

Her answer was to slide one hand down the back of his sweatshirt. Bare palm against his spine, fingertips pressing into his skin. "Not sloppy at all."

He could barely think for the fire licking at his veins. "What?"

She dragged his mouth to hers again. "Hurry."

The top of his head felt like it was ready to blow.

Instead of heading toward the stairs, he just turned and pressed her up against the wall, managing in the process to send the stack of paint cans and supplies careening.

She gasped, half-laughing, when he yanked up her thermal shirt and thrust his hands beneath, making direct contact with that silky smooth source of heat. She wasn't wearing a bra and he filled his hands with her slight curves. Her hips cradled his where he pinned her against the wall, rocking against him. Inviting more.

He tore his mouth away, breathing hard. "I wasn't prepared for this."

She tugged her shirt over her head and tossed it aside, then started yanking at his sweatshirt. "Definitely not a Boy Scout," she said breathlessly and pulled his hand back to her breast after he finished the job and pitched his sweatshirt in the general direction of hers. "Fortunately, I was. Am."

"A Boy Scout?"

"Prepared," she said throatily, and reached between them, fumbling with his belt. "I'm on the pill and I have a clean bill of health, so unless you—"

She was a whirlwind, decimating his few remaining brain cells that were still functioning. "I'm good," he responded.

She let out an exhilarated laugh. "Well, we'll see, won't we?" She finally got the belt undone. His fly. Freeing him. She wrapped her hand around him.

Need was roaring inside him but he latched his fingers around her wrists, catching them both and pulling them away. "Wait."

"I can't wait." She pressed her open mouth against his throat. Her hips worked against his and she wriggled her hands free. "I don't want to wait." As if to prove it, she reached between them again, somehow managing to unfasten her own jeans. Then she was guiding him to her, shuddering out a greedy sound that was hands-down the most erotic thing he'd ever heard.

Muttering a breathless oath, he caught her hips, sliding his hands beneath her thighs.

"Hurry," she whispered again. "Hurry, hurry."

How could he do anything else when she was gloving him so tightly? She was hot and wet and her need for speed was a good thing because he didn't have a hope in hell of lasting for long. "The couch."

She groaned, shook her head. "Too far—" She broke off and her fingers raked down his spine as she clung even tighter. He could feel the shudders in the very center of her working their way outward, wave upon wave upon wave. She cried out and he slammed his hand against the wall above her head. His only sane thought was not to crush her, while the rest of him raced headlong straight into the storm.

"Tsunami," he muttered when he could finally form words again.

They were sprawled on the couch, which he vaguely remembered stumbling to.

"Hmm?" She rubbed the top of her head against his chin. She was lying across his chest, her hands on his heart, her cheek on her hands.

"Tsu-Ali," he joked.

She lifted her head a few inches, giving him a look from drowsy eyes. "I think *tsu* means *sea* and *nami* means *wave*." She lowered her head again, sighing deeply, which just pressed all her pretty curves more firmly against him. "Or something like that. I saw it on the internet, and goodness knows everything on the internet is *always* accurate."

"Ali-nami."

She laughed softly. "Macho CCT not only knows how to laugh, but he also has a silly sense of humor."

He kissed the top of her head. He'd laughed more around Ali than he had in years. Rather than admit it, though, he slid his palm slowly down her bare back. "Not very macho with my jeans twisted around my ankles," he said.

"Don't hear me complaining." She stretched again, slipping her thigh between his.

He wasn't sure he'd felt this randy even when he'd been a teenager. "How'd we manage to get all your clothes off, but not mine?"

"Dunno." She rubbed her head against his chin again. "Does it matter?" She shimmied a little against him. "Oh. Right there. Scratch right there."

He obediently scraped his fingertips lightly against her spine.

She practically purred. "Perfect."

The wood in the fireplace popped and flung a spray of sparks against the black mesh of the screen. "This is pretty perfect."

She lifted her head again. "I meant the scratching—" She broke off, her eyes softening. "Oh." She lifted her hand and slowly rubbed her fingertip over his lower lip. "Yes." Then she hauled in another deep breath and let it out, causing all sorts of interesting sensations along the length of him.

She noticed and, once again, she looked up at him. Her eyebrows rose a little. A smile that was fifty-percent satisfied female and one-hundred-percent sexy flirted around her lips. "Already?"

He slowly dragged his finger along her spine, watching the way her eyes flickered in response. "Evidently, I'm properly inspired."

"I'll say." She slid the rest of the way over him, making a good imitation of a clinging blanket. "That casserole in the oven isn't gonna keep forever," she warned. "It'll dry out if we're not careful." She arched just right, and he slid home.

Her lips parted slightly and she exhaled, long and slow.

It occurred to him that he could watch that expression on her face for a life of Sundays and not tire of it. "Darlin', let it turn to dust. I can wait. I've eaten a lot worse. And there's always the cookies." Holding her in place, he jackknifed up until they were sitting.

She hissed a little between her teeth, holding on to the back of the couch while he managed to extricate himself from the jeans without extricating himself from her.

And then he flipped her over, onto her back. He slid his fingers through hers and lifted her arms over her head while he pressed even deeper and watched her eyes go wide, then flutter closed while she let out that shaky, husky sigh.

Even though it would be so easy to race back into the wind-tossed sea with her, he made himself go slow. He gently kissed her lips. Kissed the thick, dark lashes against her creamy cheeks. Lashes that lifted after he stopped.

She stared up at him. "This is going to get complicated," she whispered. "Isn't it." It wasn't a question.

He thought about the box of books.

About his sister.

Layla.

"Life's always complicated," he murmured.
And then he kissed her again.
This time, there was no rush.
Just a long, slow trip to the inevitable.

Chapter Ten

"Much as I appreciate the sentiment, this is not going to work." This time, Ali was the one wearing the red robe with the big white hearts. Though she'd enjoyed the sight of Grant wearing it the other day, it truly did fit *her* much better.

"What're you saying?"

She eyed Grant, who was pretty much folded in half in the bathtub. He'd filled it with enough hot water to fog up the cracked mirror above the sink, but not enough to reach above his knees, all bent the way they were. It was hard to pretend she wasn't melting inside. "I'm saying there ain't no way you and I are both fitting inside that tub. Not at the same time." She leaned over and pressed a fast kiss on his lips, then cupped some hot water and tossed it over his head before straightening.

He looked so disappointed that she almost laughed. With water dripping down his thick, dark hair into his face and that pouty expression pulling on his ridiculously perfect lower lip, she had an instant image of him as a little boy.

The longing that struck inside her came out of nowhere. And frankly, it scared the stuffing right out of her.

Being lovers would be complicated enough, considering Layla. The last thing she needed to be doing was imagining little Grants with aqua-colored eyes running around.

So she waved her hand at him. "Come on. I'm the one who has to get her butt into work this morning."

"Speaking of butts." His hand snuck up beneath the terry-cloth robe and cupped her rear. "Have I told you just how much I appreciate yours?"

She sidled away from him, slapping at his hand, even though delight was coating the knot of want suddenly throbbing inside her. "I believe you made that apparent around three this morning." The chicken casserole hadn't been quite dust when they'd finally gotten to it the night before. But it had been more of a shovel-it-in-for-fuel than fine-dining experience. Then he'd wolfed down her cookies and tugged her up the stairs and into his bedroom.

When he pulled her down onto his bed, she'd discovered that the kisses he bestowed on every other part of her body besides her mouth weren't sloppy, either. She'd finally fallen exhaustedly asleep only to be awakened by the insistent nudge of his erection against her backside.

They'd had enough sex in the last twelve hours to fill her five-year drought, and then some.

She could hardly walk.

And she needed to get to work.

"I *need* the bath," she told him sternly. A shower would have been faster, but they couldn't use the one upstairs because the cement on the bathroom floor was still curing.

"Fine." Still endearingly pouty, he stood and water sluiced lovingly down his body, the level inside the bathtub dropping several inches.

She reminded herself that her body ached in places that it hadn't ached in ages. A delicious ache.

"Did you have to do a lot of swimming to qualify for combat control?"

He grabbed a thin, faded blue towel from the rack. "Enough," he said warily. "Combat diving. Parachuting. We did a lot of stuff. Why?"

"I read an article the other day about the men's Olympic swimmers. You've got the same kind of body. Perfect for swimming." Long arms. Roping muscles. Wide, flaring shoulders and a narrow waist, and those ripped abs.

She swallowed before she started drooling and shucked the robe. Carefully keeping a safe foot between them, she stepped over the side of the tub and sat down gingerly.

She didn't know whether to gasp or groan when the hot water hit her tender regions.

She glanced up at Grant. He was watching her with an expression she couldn't decipher. "What?"

He kneeled on the plain towel that Ali had spread on the floor in place of a bath mat. "You're sore."

She blamed the sudden heat in her cheeks on the temperature of the water.

"Hand me the washcloth," he said.

She warily handed him the cloth, which matched the towel he'd wrapped around his hips both in faded color and thinness. When he thrust it down into the water beside her hip, she jumped a little. "What—"

"Don't be so suspicious. Relax." He pulled the cloth back out and soaped it up, then slowly ran it over her shoulders and down her back.

Her resistance dissolved as her bones melted. She hugged her knees to her chest and rested her forehead on them while he repeated the process. "Nobody's ever washed my back." She smiled faintly. "Except my mother."

"I'm not your mother."

She turned her cheek until she could see him. "I'm well aware."

His aqua eyes darkened. "Lean back."

How—*how* could she be so easily aroused by him? When every muscle inside her had already been wrung with so much pleasure that she could have wept from it?

She stretched out her legs. Unlike Grant, she fit in the tub comfortably. She pressed her toes against the foot of the tub and lay back. The white enamel was chilly behind her neck and despite the water lapping at them, her nipples tightened.

Or maybe that was from the way Grant's gaze ran over her in the moment before he glided the soapy cloth over her shoulders and down the valley between her breasts. Then back up and over them, lightly dragging the vaguely scratchy terry cloth, making her skin feel even more deliciously sensitized.

Her mouth went dry as he tugged the cloth back into the water, then along her hip. Her thigh. Knee. He soaped her feet. Her toes. Smiled slightly when she curled her toes against the tickle of the rough cloth.

"You're frighteningly good at this," she murmured

when he'd reached across her to bestow the same attention on the left side of her body.

He sat back a little and touched the cloth to the base of her throat. The water had become cloudy from soap. It was more lukewarm than hot. "Is that a problem?"

She pressed her tongue against the inside of her teeth for a moment. "I don't know. Is it from practice?"

"Using soap and water? Been doing it all my life."

His hand had guided the cloth downward again. She caught his wrist before he reached her belly. "You know that's not what I mean."

"Have I ever washed a woman's back?" His eyes met hers. "Yes."

She couldn't blame him for answering the question that *she* had asked.

"Have I ever washed a woman's front? Yes."

She swallowed.

"I'm thirty-seven, Ali. I was married. And when I wasn't, there were others." His intense gaze was disturbingly steady. "Not going to pretend I was a saint and not going to brag that I wasn't. I'm not your first, either." He released the cloth and it sank in the water. He turned his hand and pressed his wet palm against hers. "But there hasn't been anyone in a long while. I haven't wanted anyone. Until now. Until you."

She shivered. And it wasn't because of the cooling water. It was because of him. His words. "Grant—" She broke off, not sure what exactly she wanted to say. She wasn't a verbal expert like Greer. Nor a relationship expert like Maddie. She just knew that there were things about Grant that drew her in. Physically. Emotionally.

And he was still waiting for her to finish.

She exhaled shakily and drew his hand into the

water. Toward her. Physical was easier than emotional. Always had been. "I'm going to be late for work."

He didn't smile. "Then we'd better make it worth it, right?"

And they did.

"Templeton!"

Gowler was yelling her name the very second she showed her nose at work.

She rolled her eyes at Timmy and hurried to the door of the sergeant's office. "Yessir?"

He was holding a file folder in the air. "What the hell're you doing messing with Draper's investigation about that abandoned baby your sister's fostering?"

She hesitated. "I, uh—"

"You're lucky I'm feeling magnanimous today." He tossed the file across his desk at her. "Next time you're late reporting, don't bother showing up at all."

She quickly retrieved the file folder. "I won't, sir."

He grunted. "Close the door on your way out."

She scurried out and closed the door.

Then she quickly flipped open the file folder.

Inside were her notes about births in Montana within the estimated time frame of Layla's birthday and she realized she must have gotten it mixed in with the reports she'd typed up for Gowler.

It seemed a lot longer ago than just the previous afternoon.

"What's wrong with you?" Timmy asked when she headed back to her desk.

She stopped short. "What do you mean?"

"You're walking all stiff-like. You hurt yourself working out again?"

Her cheeks went hot. "Um, yeah. Working out."

She slipped into her chair and jabbed her computer keyboard, bringing the blank screen to life. She went through her emails, which were all fairly routine. Then she checked the missing persons on Grant's sister. It had only been a week since she'd broadened the search to include Daisy's real name. She didn't really expect any results, and in that regard, she wasn't disappointed.

Her cell phone pinged, and she glanced at it, making a face when she read the brief note from Greer.

She swiveled around to look at Timmy. "Prosecutor's filed against Trevor Oakes."

"Yeah." Her coworker didn't look up from the book he was reading. "So?"

She threw an eraser at him and it bounced off his head.

"What?" He leaned over and grabbed the pink eraser and tossed it back at her.

She caught it. "Did you know about it?"

"Yeah. When Jerry was with him, Trevor hauled off and decked him."

All she did was stare at Timmy in shock. "That's what he's charged with? Assaulting a peace officer? Not petty theft?"

"Yep." Jerry walked into the squad room. He'd obviously overheard. "I tried to talk Gowler out of it, but half a dozen people saw it."

She sighed. He was already sporting a shiner. "I should have taken him home to his mother instead of bringing him here."

"It's not your fault, Ali." Jerry shrugged. "Kid just hasn't hit bottom yet. But he will."

"Hopefully sooner rather than later," she muttered. There were degrees of *bottom*, and for everyone's sake, she hoped Trevor's wouldn't be much deeper. He was still a minor, but an assault charge wasn't one they could just sweep under the rug.

"My sister didn't say when he was supposed to appear." Time was rarely slow in juvenile court cases. At least not in Braden, which was her only field of experience.

"Tomorrow morning at nine," Jerry said. He sat down at his desk, two over from Ali's, and tossed her a pink notepad. "Got a call yesterday after you left from some lady in Montana. Number's there."

Excitement warred with her concern over Trevor as she looked at the handwritten phone message. Jerry was old-school. He never texted and he used email only as a very last resort. He even refused to carry his cell phone with him, because he was adamant that they caused brain cancer. Instead, the thing sat—usually with a dead battery—on his desk. "Thanks." She swiveled around to face her own desk again and quickly picked up the phone, returning Honey Holmes's call.

"Mrs. Holmes!" Ali sat up straighter when the woman answered on the third ring. "This is Ali Templeton from the Braden Police Department in Wyoming. You phoned me yesterday?"

Honey sounded breathless. "Sorry, Detective. I've been changing sheets."

Ali didn't bother correcting the title. "What, uh, what can I do for you?"

"Come here and change the sheets for me?" Honey laughed ruefully. "You said I should call if I remembered anything else about that poor sad Daisy."

"Poor and sad" was an upgrade from "tramp." "Yes, I did." Ali automatically grabbed a sharp pencil from the cup of them she kept on her desk. "What do you have for me?"

"Well, one morning, she came down to breakfast. I serve breakfast every morning, you see. Nothing fancy, mind you. My people here are mostly hard workers who appreciate good, wholesome fare. You know. Oatmeal. And scrambled eggs. Good thick slices of toast. I make two loaves of country bread every day and—"

"That sounds really delicious, ma'am." Ali tapped the eraser end of her yellow pencil against her desk. "If I'm ever in Montana, I'll have to look you up. But about Dai—"

"Oh, my, yes. Well, as I said, she came down to breakfast late one morning and I was already starting to clean up."

Ali tapped her pencil a few more times, reining in her impatience.

"She must've been in a mood to talk," Honey went on, "because she started helping me clear the serving dishes. She mentioned that she used to waitress someplace in Wyoming. *Magic Mike.* Oh—" the woman tittered "—that's that racy movie about those dancing men. My daughter took me to it some time ago when it was playing in the movie house, and oh, my stars and body. What a show that is! Did you happen to see it?"

"Mrs. Holmes, please. Was the place she mentioned called Magic Jax?"

"Well, yes. Yes, I believe it was!"

Ali's shoulders sank. No new information at all. Which certainly wasn't Honey Holmes's fault. "Daisy was a cocktail waitress at Magic Jax over a year ago. It's a business here in Braden."

"Oh. You already knew that."

"That's okay. Remember, I said anything that you recall would be important to me. And maybe you'll think of something else she happened to mention when she was staying there. Maybe about the baby. Or even the baby's father."

"Well, she just said that Grant would really hate her if he ever found out what she'd done."

Ali stiffened. "Grant?"

"I assumed he was her baby daddy. Isn't that the term they use nowadays? Young people having babies out of wedlock left and right. Not that it's anything new..." Ali closed her eyes, letting the woman rattle on, figuring that sooner or later, Honey would peter out.

And when she finally did, Ali's ear felt hot from the plastic receiver pressed against it for so long. "I really do appreciate your time, ma'am," she assured her. "Don't hesitate to call again."

"Well, I sure won't," Honey answered. "If you ever find that rapscallion Grant person, you tell him he needs to pay the week's rent that she still owes. You take care now, Detective."

Ali pinched the bridge of her nose. "You, too, Mrs. Holmes." Grateful that was over, she dropped the receiver onto the cradle and proceeded to drop her head onto her desk.

"What the devil's wrong with you?" Gowler stopped next to her desk, and she lifted her head in time to see him dump another pile of handwritten reports into her in-basket.

She sighed faintly and reached for the top one.

"Traffic first," he barked.

Her fingers curled.

In a contest between the dreaded typewriter and reading parking meters, she wasn't sure which was worse.

She waited until he returned to his office and slammed the door behind him.

Maybe Sgt. Gowler needed a woman in his life even more than his son did.

She swiveled around to look at Timmy again. As usual, he was still nose-deep into his book. "Timmy, honest to God, you read more than anyone I know." Except maybe Grant. He had boxes of books getting delivered right to his front door. Although she hadn't seen any evidence that he was actually reading in between installing kitchen cabinets, painting walls and loving her into a near coma.

Timmy's face was its usual shade of scarlet. But he held up the book so she could see the dark red cover. "Cal Reid," he said. "He's a great character. Right up there with Marlowe and Bosch and Rapp and—"

She lifted her hand. "The last book I read was a do-it-yourself on drywalling. I don't even know *who* you're talking about." She got up, knowing that she was moving stiffly but not able to do a darn thing about it. Lifting weights and doing chin-ups in her basement was one thing.

Nonstop hotter-than-Hades sex with Grant was on a different scale altogether.

She grabbed her coat and gloves, made sure her radio had fresh batteries and headed out to do traffic.

She supposed it could be worse.

It could be snowing.

She was still consoling herself with that fact two hours later as she trudged along the slushy streets, willfully ignoring most of the expired meters. When she spotted an ostentatious car parked crookedly at the curb in front of Sally's Treasures, though, she groaned. One of the wheels had jumped the curb and the corner bumper was kissing the meter post.

"Oh, Vivian," she muttered. Because, unless someone *else* in the area had taken to driving around a Rolls-Royce Phantom—which she highly doubted— the terrible parking job was owed to none other than her indomitable grandmother.

She checked out the meter post and decided it had survived the impact better than the bumper, which wasn't quite crumpled, but definitely bore a new scratch, and then headed toward the antique shop.

To this day, Ali wasn't sure how Sally stayed in business. As far as she'd ever been able to tell, the antiques that were crowded nose-to-toe inside the overly warm shop never seemed to change. But year-in and year-out, the shop remained, with Sally Enders sitting at the ancient cash register, usually hunched over while she carefully cleaned some ugly piece of jewelry she'd triumphantly found at an estate sale.

"Hi, Sally," she greeted when she went inside, quickly unfastening her coat. "My grandmother here?"

Sally barely looked up. She had a loupe clipped to her eyeglasses. "In the back."

"Thanks." She went straight to the rear of the store and pushed through the door that sported a Keep Out sign square in the middle of it.

And there was Vivian, poking her way around a jumble of chairs that were only fit for a bonfire. "Looking for more furniture for the palace?"

Vivian jumped a little. She pressed her lined hand against the front of her pink Chanel suit. "Lord, Ali. If this thing squatting in my head doesn't kill me, a heart attack will."

"Sorry." Ali kissed her cheek. "What *are* you doing?"

Evidently mollified, her grandmother quickly went back to her poking. "I need chairs," she said. "Lots and lots of chairs."

"For—"

"The Valentine's ball."

"The gym has chairs. Well," she amended, "benches, I guess."

Vivian gave a derisive snort and kept poking.

"It didn't look like you put any change in the parking meter outside."

"Parking shmarking."

Ali had to bite her lip. "You also came pretty *close* to the meter when you parked." There'd been a time shortly after Vivian moved to Wyoming when she'd paid a teenager to drive for her. Not a single member of her family didn't still wish that someone else was behind the wheel of the Rolls whenever Vivian wanted to go for a spin.

Her grandmother shrugged. "It's still standing, isn't it?" She'd managed to free one of the chairs from the tangle. "What do you think?"

At a loss, Ali looked at the chair. "I think whatever rear end sits on it is going to be touching the ground."

Vivian laughed. "You need to look beyond the obvious, darling."

"Vivian, you're talking over my head. The chair has two arms, four legs and part of a back. No spot to sit in. So to me, it's not much of a chair."

"It will be." Looking eminently satisfied, she gestured at the rest of the jumble. "When I'm finished, they all will be. And it will be simply grand."

"What will be grand?"

"The Valentine's ball, of course. Do try and keep up, dear." Vivian picked up her handbag from where she'd left it on a dusty bureau and tucked it in the crook of her elbow. She led the way back out to the shop, giving Ali a look. "Are you saddle sore or something?"

Ali nearly choked. "What?"

"You're walking like—oh, never mind. Sally—" Vivian raised her voice "—I want them all. Tell your son they need to be upholstered in that red velvet I gave you a sample of, and I'll want them delivered to my estate by next Saturday. How many did you say there were?"

Sally set aside her loupe and the ugly necklace she was working on. "Thirty-two."

"I'd hoped for more, but it'll have to do for now." Vivian smiled. "You know where to send the bill."

"Absolutely." Sally handed Vivian her fur coat, which had been hanging on a standing coatrack carved to look like elephant tusks. "Always a pleasure, Mrs. Templeton."

Ali hurried out the door after her grandmother. "Vivian, I'd dearly love to keep up with you. Did you get the planning committee to agree to this?"

"Please." She waved her hand dismissively.

Ali took that as a *no*. Knowing her grandmother, that was enough cause for concern. Vivian could spend money like nobody's business. Of course, that habit was mitigated somewhat by the fact that she was richer than sin. If Vivian wanted to throw her money away, it was hers to throw. "So...*you* are having a ball instead."

"Well, not a formal ball in the traditional sense." Her grandmother clasped her hands together and leaned against the side of her car. Parked among pickup trucks and SUVs, it looked particularly outrageous.

"I'm not exactly sure what a formal ball is in the traditional sense," Ali said drily, "but go on."

Vivian gave her a look. "Don't play dumb. You're merely trembling in those awful man-boots you wear, afraid that I'll require you to wear a ball gown."

Ali made a point of glancing down at her so-called

man-boots. They were entirely department-issue. But she still took a little issue. At Christmastime, her grandmother had thrown what was becoming her usual fancy-dress party. Ali had had to borrow a dress from her mother, but she'd done it and shown up more or less appropriately attired. "Just because I'm a cop doesn't mean I don't like to wear pretty things," she said defensively. "I just can't afford—"

"Bah. You could afford plenty if you'd just let me get that hovel you live in fixed up for you."

"I'm not taking money from you, Vivian." It was an old argument—Vivian wanting to give Ali and her sisters money to fix the place up right. And by that, Vivian meant right now.

"Instead, you insist on pouring what meager money you *do* have right down leaking pipes."

She let the "meager" part slide, since it was more than a little accurate. "In that, you and Dad agree."

"Well, that would be the *only* thing your father would agree with me about. And David is nearly as bad."

Ali hurriedly changed the subject. Carter and David's feud with their mother had been going on longer than she'd been alive. While it wasn't entirely open warfare between them, the way it had been in the beginning, the rest of the family had pretty much accepted that it wouldn't end anytime soon. "Back to the untraditional nonformal ball."

Vivian's expression immediately brightened. "Oh, yes. A ball on ice."

"Pardon?"

"Ice skating." She clasped her fur collar closer beneath her chin and her eyes danced. "Arthur took me ice skating the first time he proposed to me. Oh, it was magical."

Ali couldn't help but smile at the image that brought to mind. When her grandmother married Arthur Finley, she'd been in her seventies. Ali figured most people would be worried about falling and breaking a hip or something. But not Vivian.

"We'll have an ice rink. And a warming tent, of course, with every refreshment that Montrose can think of. He's in his element, I can tell you that."

Montrose was her grandmother's chef, brought with her from Pennsylvania. He was bald as a cue ball and as snooty as a dowager. Nevertheless, the things that came out of his kitchen were a taste bud's treasure.

"That's a lot to get underway in very little time, Vivian. Are you sure you're not taking on too much?"

"Delia's helping. She doesn't have the natural abilities that Penny had, of course, but she's coming along quite nicely, actually."

Delia was one of Ali's cousins. She'd never particularly been known for her consistency in life. But she'd been acting as their grandmother's personal assistant since before Christmas, ever since Penny, Vivian's previous assistant, had married Delia's big brother, Quinn. "Is Penny returning to work for you once she and Quinn are back from Texas?"

"They're already back. Good Lord, child. Don't you keep up with your own cousin and his wife?"

Ali wasn't going to get sidetracked. "Back to the chairs, Vivian. What are the chairs for?"

"Just because it's a Valentine's ball on ice doesn't mean guests won't need a place to sit." She plucked a pair of gloves from inside her handbag and started pulling them on. "It'll be a lovely sight. Women in old-fashioned dresses. Men in their ties and tails. It'll look like a Victorian postcard."

"In an area where dressing up basically means kicking the cow pies off your boots before going inside." Ali knew she sounded doubtful and couldn't help it. "That kind of fancy dress might be hard for some people to come by, you know. Particularly on such short notice."

"I know. Which is why I'm making sure that *some*—" she gave Ali a pointed look "—*are* accurately attired. I've already arranged for costumes to be sent out from Pennsylvania. My former dressmaker is handling it. The rest of my guests will simply make do. I'm certainly not going to turn them away from the event just because they aren't dressed right. The old me might have wanted to, but not anymore. All I'm asking for is that everyone who comes consider making a small donation to the Fielding Memorial Library Fund."

Ali felt a pain in her forehead. "I didn't know there was such a fund."

"There is now," Vivian assured her blithely. "Arthur was a strong believer in the public library system, and Weaver's is entirely inadequate. I mean to see that changed, starting with building a new library. And I could pay for it myself, but Hayley keeps reminding me that it's important for people to feel invested in their community. So." She clapped her gloved hands together. "I'm making this the start."

"What about the potluck that's already in the works?"

"It's the following day. It'll be fine. Delia has begun posting signs around town and she's already getting interest."

Vivian had all her bases covered. "I haven't been on ice skates in years, Vivian," Ali warned. As a girl, she'd played hockey with the boys and always figured she'd had more fun than the girls prancing around in their white figure skates. "And never while wearing some froufrou skating dress, much less some old-fashioned outfit straight out of a Dickens novel."

"Skating'll come back to you."

"I'm glad *you* think so," she said drily. "Where is this postcard rink supposed to be? Weaver has a skating rink already."

"Yes, and they play *hockey* on it. Dreadful sport." Oblivious to Ali's reaction, she plowed on. "The rink will be created behind my house. I already have it worked out with my landscape architect. It'll be like nothing Weaver has ever seen."

Ali nodded. "That's for sure."

"And you'll bring your handsome Grant. He'll be a fine escort, I'm certain."

Ali's lips parted. "I don't know if that's something he'll be particularly interested in, Vivian."

Vivian gave her a sidelong look. "I'm sure you'll find a way to convince him." She had her keys out now and they jangled as she waved gaily and hurried around to the driver's side of the car.

"Vivian, *please* be careful driving."

"I'm always careful, darling." She got inside and a moment later, revved the engine. The window on the passenger side rolled down.

Ali stepped closer, looking inside the car. "What?"

"Try Epsom salts in the bath," Vivian advised, looking crafty. Then she rolled up the window, bumped off the curb and shot down the street.

Chapter Eleven

"How far did you get reading that *Plumbing for Dummies* book?"

Grant looked up from the liver and onions he'd ordered for lunch and felt something lift inside him. It was barely more than twenty-four hours since he and Ali had sloshed bathwater all over his bathroom floor. "If it isn't Officer Ali. Young Timmy told me you were over at the courthouse when I stopped in." He lifted his fork. "I'd offer you some, but I know how you feel about this stuff."

She grinned and slid into the booth opposite him. Without asking, she did, however, reach for his cup of coffee and take a sip, squinting a little over the steam rising from it. "As a matter of fact, I was at the courthouse."

"You look pretty happy about it."

"Only because of the ironies of fate."

He raised his eyebrows.

She laughed softly and leaned toward him across the table. "I told you about Keith."

"Yeah. You also told me your movie-of-the-week plot."

"Which you scoffed at," she reminded him. "And yet…" She sat back, spreading her slender palms wide. Her dark eyes sparkled.

"You actually set him up with someone."

"That's the beauty of it." She was practically wriggling in her seat with excitement. "I didn't have to!"

"Hey there, Ali. Bring you some lunch?"

Ali looked up at Josephine. "Um, sure. The French dip. But only if it's fast. I've got to get back to the department before Gowler notices I'm not still at court."

"Coming right up," Josephine assured her before hustling back to the kitchen.

"You didn't have to set him up."

"Nope. Keith's pulling public-defender duty this week and got assigned a juvenile we hauled in a couple days ago. He took one look at the boy's mama and—" she spread her fingers "—*poof.* Love was in the air."

"Just like that."

"Hey. It happens."

She didn't need to tell him. Once Cal and Talia had scooped him out of the bowels of perpetual unwantedness, Grant had listened dozens of times to their love-at-first-sight story.

Even then, he'd never been a particular believer. He'd always figured that lust at first sight was probably closer to the truth of it.

And *that* he could seriously believe in.

"Maybe," he said. "So long as it helps get Gowler off your back, why not?"

"Oh, I promise you. I recognized the signs on Keith's face." She fluttered her lashes. "By the time Judge Stokes cracked his gavel on the case, Keith was giving Lydia Oakes the most besotted looks you've ever seen."

"Besotted?"

She nodded. "Besotted. Sarge is *definitely* going to be hearing about his boy's latest love interest." Her knee brushed against Grant's beneath the table. "So about that plumbing."

He eyed her, genuinely amused. "That's some pretty seductive talk there, Officer."

She leaned across the table again. "It's not a euphemism!"

He laughed, drawing glances from the other diners.

She grinned and sat back again. Her eyes clung to his and he wondered if the onlookers would describe *them* as besotted. Then he wondered if he even cared. "Isn't Stokes the judge in charge of Layla's case?"

She nodded. "And speaking of Layla, I learned there were roughly forty female births in the general area during the three months after your sister was at the boardinghouse in Butte. If I want statistics more recent than that, it's going to take a trip to the recorder's office there."

"And?"

"None of the mothers' names was Karen Cooper or Daisy Miranda. But if she used one alias, she could have used another. It's a matter of tracking all the families down and, well…" She made a face. "You know how it is. Not enough hours in the day."

"Situation calls for a private investigator."

"Yeah, and I'd need a mint to print some money to pay one, too."

The truth sat coiled inside him. If he was any sort

of decent brother at all, he would have contacted John
Fletcher to track down his sister when he'd first learned
about Layla. John had done plenty of other work for
him. "Your brother-in-law's got money. And a vested
interest."

"Yeah, but because Linc *does* have a vested interest, they need to avoid the appearance of trying to manipulate the situation. It was touchy enough for him to
foot the bill for the trips I've already made. Same thing
with my grandmother. She'd do anything she could to
help Maddie and Linc. She'd even consider bribing a
judge. She didn't, thank God." She rolled her eyes ex-
pressively. "But that's why the detectives are handling
the investigation."

"Who haven't done squat. You're the one who tracked
Karen to me."

"And that's as *far* as I've gotten, which hasn't helped
much. We still don't know for sure that Karen is Layla's
mother, and we have absolutely *no* idea who the father
might actually be. The lady in Butte remembered your
sister mentioning your name, and she assumed *you* were
the dad."

He grimaced. "I'm from a twisted family, but not
that twisted."

Ali eyes rested on his face and he wished he hadn't
said that. Fortunately, she seemed to sense his discomfort and after a second, she went right on. "She
also relayed that Daisy said you would really hate her
if you found out what she'd done. Do you suppose she
meant getting pregnant?"

"Who knows?"

"There are just so many blanks that need filling in."

"Anyway." She took another sip of his coffee. Setting
the cup back next to his hand, her fingertips brushed

against his. "The investigation has gone beyond what's normal in this situation. It's a miracle that Stokes hasn't already placed Layla for adoption. Truthfully, I think he's got a soft spot for Maddie."

"But not soft enough to put your sister's name at the top of the adoption waiting list."

"Not if he wants to keep getting reelected. It's one thing to push the envelope and another thing to toss it out entirely."

"Here you go." Josephine had returned in record time. She set a loaded plate and a tall glass of water in front of Ali. Then she was off again.

Ali immediately picked up the roast-beef sandwich and dunked it deeply into the cup of juice nestled in a mountain of crispy French fries. "Great French dips here," she murmured, and shoved the dripping sandwich into her mouth, taking a huge bite. She swallowed quickly, barely seeming to chew first. "So about the kitchen faucet. Totally flipped its lid this morning. Water was spewing everywhere, which makes me glad we *haven't* gotten the cupboards finished, or we'd have that mess to deal with all over again. Maddie knows how to replace the faucet and the pipes leading to it, but she's so busy with Layla and Linc and her job, I don't want to bug her."

"Do all social workers know how to plumb a sink?"

"I think if they work around these parts they do," Ali said. "I can manage it myself, I think, but I don't have the tools."

"Ah. The crux of the matter." He was glad to change subjects to something else besides Karen having her baby alone in Montana. If he'd been there for her, none of this would be happening. But did that mean he wouldn't have met Ali?

He dismissed the thought as soon as it hit.

Braden was a small town. One way or another, they'd have met.

And if you'd never decided to hide out in this small town in the first place?

He shoved the question to the back of his mind and pressed *his* knee against hers. "It's my tools that you're really wanting."

She grinned and took another whopping bite of her sandwich, as if she was starving.

Maybe she was. God knew he wanted to take some whopping bites of *her.*

"When do you want to do this? I'll have to run out to the ranch to get 'em."

"I've already promised Marty I'd pull a shift at Magic Jax tonight, so maybe after work tomorrow? I get off at five." The tip of her pink tongue snuck out and caught a drop of au jus from the corner of her lip, causing his mind to immediately jump off the tracks.

He shifted and cleared his throat. "Then I'll meet you at your place a little after five tomorrow. Tools at the ready."

She pointed her sandwich at him. "Real tools. Not… you know."

He gave her a steady look and watched her pupils flare a little. "Pretty sure I can talk you into *you know* as well."

She leaned across the table again, lowering her voice "My grandmother asked if I was saddle sore! Can you believe it?" She shook her head. "I nearly died." She took another hefty bite of her sandwich.

His encounter with her grandmother had been brief but somehow he wasn't surprised. "If you don't slow down, you're gonna choke."

She shook her head, chasing the bite with a gulp of water. "Seriously, I'm supposed to be en route from the courthouse. Which is only a whopping ten-minute walk from the department. But I saw your truck in front of the diner and couldn't resist." She grabbed some French fries in one hand and slid out of the booth. She hadn't even taken off her coat in the few minutes she'd been there. She pulled out some crumpled currency and dropped it on the table.

His conscience stirred. "I can get it."

"Don't go all macho on me. Someday when you want to tell me where you get your money to buy cement and paint, you can pay. But for now? It's payday and I like to pay my own way." She quickly swiped her mouth with her napkin and wrapped the French fries in it. Then in front of God and all of Josephine's customers, she leaned over and kissed him boldly on the mouth, her lips all salty and enticing. "I'll see you tonight."

"See you tonight," he said, but she was already hurrying across the diner, stopping short at one of the nearby tables where an old man sat alone, nursing a cup of coffee.

"Well, hello there, handsome! I didn't even notice you were here!"

"Probably 'cause you were a mite busy kissin' that fella." The man's steely gaze traveled to Grant.

But Ali just laughed. "Come in for the liver and onions?"

"You bet."

She looked over her shoulder at Grant. Her eyes were sparkling and she gave him a saucy wink. "Well, you enjoy it." She patted the man's shoulder. "I have to get back on duty."

"Be careful, child."

Both Grant and the old man watched her hurry out of the restaurant. And then the iron-haired guy was looking back at Grant. "She's a good little lady."

That's when Grant placed him. "Squire Clay. From Magic Jax."

"Yep. You're new around here." Squire was definitely taking Grant's measure.

He didn't flinch. "Yes. And she doesn't like being called 'little lady.'"

"No, she does not," he agreed. "She's not quite blood, but she's close, so I'm interested all the same."

"So am I, Mr. Clay."

A smile curled the old guy's lips. Then he lifted his cup in salute. "Good luck to you, then. You're gonna need it with that one."

"Here you go, Squire." Josephine unloaded her tray on the man's table. "While I appreciate you comin' all the way from Weaver for my liver and onions, I *know* Gloria wouldn't approve."

Squire cackled softly. "Man can't live on the leaves and twigs she wants to feed me these days, Josie. Hell, I'm lucky if she feeds me some of my own damn beefsteak once a month!"

Not bothering to hide his amusement, Grant turned to look out the window. He could see Ali jogging across the street, eating her fries and cutting around vehicles moving slowly along the street. The few strands of hair escaping her bun bounced around the shoulders of her coat.

Someday.

History had proven to Grant that thinking of somedays—of futures—was the quickest way to disappointment. If not outright pain. In the service, he'd had to think on his feet. Yeah, there was a lot of planning. But that was always about the mission. About the job.

When it came to his personal life?

"Top off your coffee for you?"

He shook his head, also shaking off the things he didn't want to think about. "No thanks, Josephine." Sleeping at night was hard enough without feeding the caffeine monster all afternoon. The only night since moving into Roger Carmody's house that he'd actually slept without a nightmare had been the one he'd spent with Ali.

He pulled out his wallet, added some cash to Ali's and slid it inside the red vinyl folder Josephine had placed near the edge of the table.

"Need change?"

He shook his head. "All yours."

She slid the folder into the pocket on her apron. "Take your time now. Just let me know if you need anything else."

"Thanks."

She picked up Ali's plate and started to turn away, but hesitated. He automatically braced himself, assuming the worst when she gave him a close look.

"You know, you really *do* remind me of someone," she said. "It's your eyes."

It was his own damn fault for returning to the diner.

"Sorry. Couldn't tell you." He poked at the liver and onions. It was good. But not as good as what Talia used to make back in the day. Before she'd ever gotten sick.

Josephine smiled and shrugged and finally moved away from his booth.

Grant set down his fork, wiped his mouth and slid out of the booth. Before Josephine came back out of the kitchen, he left.

Did she recognize him as T. C. Grant or as Ralph Carmody's bastard grandson?

He didn't know, and didn't have any desire to stick around and find out.

The next night, Ali put on the cocktail-waitress uniform and the dreaded high heels and worked a shift at Magic Jax. But she didn't mind it too much, because Grant sat at the bar nearly the whole time.

"That guy's got it bad for you," Charlene murmured halfway through their shift.

"No, he doesn't." She barely waited a beat before she stole a look at Grant, who was talking with Marty over the soda he'd been drinking all night. "Does he?" Good Lord, she was turning into a teenager.

Charlene just nodded knowingly. "Watch yourself," she warned. "Last guy looking at me like that put babies in my belly and there went all my plans to go to college and get outta this dang town."

Ali had done her stint in college and had no desire to go back. And Charlene was just being Charlene.

She carried the tray of empties she'd been collecting back to the bar and exchanged them for fresh drinks.

Grant caught her eye and smiled slowly.

She swallowed a sudden knot as she lifted the tray.

Babies in her belly…

She didn't want to admit what a tempting thought *that* was. Not even to herself.

Maybe it was just the Layla effect.

She delivered the drinks and returned to the bar. "Don't suppose you ever played hockey, did you?"

His eyes narrowed. "Why do I feel like I should ask for some context before I answer?"

"Because you're a smart man." She leaned her hip

against the empty bar stool next to him and absently wriggled her toes inside her shoes. "My grandmother's solution to her annoyance with the Valentine's committee is to throw her own event."

"Hockey?"

She laughed. "Ice skating, actually. She's calling it a Valentine's ball on ice." She felt strangely diffident all of a sudden. "Would you, uh, like to go? You know. With me?"

His lips tilted upward. "You asking me on a date, Officer Ali?"

"I guess I am, Mr. Cooper." She lifted her chin a little. She felt flustered and didn't much care for it. "Well?"

"Maybe he has to check his calendar," Marty interjected from where he stood behind the taps, pulling a beer.

The starch in Ali's shoulders softened.

She rolled her eyes, tucked the round tray beneath her arm and straightened away from the stool.

Grant caught her hand before she could take a step, though. He ran his thumb slowly over the back of her hand and heat climbed sweetly through her veins. "I haven't worn hockey skates in a long damn time. And I've never worn figure skates."

"That makes two of us."

"You played hockey?" His thumb paused over the pulse throbbing in her wrist.

"For a couple years."

"Were you any good?"

"I was all of ten and I could bodycheck with the best of my teammates."

He smiled. "Why am I not surprised?"

"Good grief." Charlene reached between them in

order to grab the basket of peanuts sitting in front of Grant. "Either get on with it, or get a room." She stomped away on her high heels and deposited the basket on a table.

Grant's eyes returned to Ali's. "What's her problem?" His thumb was still pressed against her pulse, which seemed to be speeding up with each breath she took.

"She didn't get to go to college."

His eyes narrowed slightly, hunting for the joke.

"So, you up for a spin around the ice rink or not?"

His eyes drifted to her lips. Then down her body, his glance as warming as a physical touch. "Definitely up."

Ali nearly choked. She tugged her hand away from him and moistened her lips. Then she leaned over and whispered in his ear, "If you still feel that way in an hour, meet me in the storeroom. I've got a fifteen-minute break and the door locks."

His head reared back. Shock, surprise and interest were all in his piercing, aqua eyes. "Officer Ali."

She smiled slightly and turned on her heel, sashaying away.

Chapter Twelve

"Tool man at your service."

Ali knew she had a crazy happy smile on her face, but she didn't care. She opened the front door wider so that Grant could enter. She hadn't seen him since the night before at Magic Jax.

When they'd locked themselves in the storeroom for fifteen glorious minutes.

He was carrying a large red toolbox. And though it was a welcome sight, because it meant she wouldn't have to cave in and call her dad to come to the rescue, it wasn't what caused her to feel so giddy.

That was all on Grant.

"I ordered pizza," she said. "It'll be here in an hour. I hope you like pepperoni and sausage."

He closed the door behind him and set the toolbox on the table near the door. "Only thing I don't like are green peppers." His gaze swept over the empty living room, ending on the clothes draped over their couch. "What's all that?"

"My grandmother's idea of skating attire. She's got this whole Victorian image in her head, I guess. Wants to make sure some of us look the part." She went over and picked up the dark blue coat first. "I can maybe see wearing this. It's sort of cool in a vintage kind of way." She held the wool coat to her shoulders. It had puffy sleeves and nipped in tightly at the waist, then flared out to end below the knee in a wide band of white fur. Fake, she hoped, but when it came to her grandmother, it was dangerous to assume.

She tossed it down and picked up the finely striped yellow-and-white dress that was so long she'd probably catch her skate blades in it and land on her butt. "This, though? There's no way." She spread out the fancily ruffled fabric. "I think it's got a bustle!"

He was grinning as he stopped next to her. He touched the dress. "And I think you'd look real cute in this."

"Oh, come on." She dumped the dress in a heap. "If I'm going to wear that, then you can wear a top hat and…and spats!"

"Might get a little cold without anything covering the areas between. Wear the coat. Make your grandma happy. At least she cares. As for me, I'll skip the spats if you don't mind." He gave her a long look. "We alone?"

Her stomach swooped. "Greer's got a date. She'll be late."

Then he pulled Ali into his arms and kissed her.

Excitement built oh, so fast and oh, so sweetly. But she made herself press her hands against his wide shoulders, and broke the kiss. "No, you don't." She sounded just as breathless as she felt. "I've got a kitchen-fauce situation going nowhere. You can kiss me senseless *after*."

"You're the one leaving me senseless." Amusement filled his deep voice. But he let her go and retrieved the toolbox. "All right. Lead the way, sweetheart."

Sweetheart.

She was afraid she might actually be floating two inches above the floor as she headed into the kitchen.

The towels she'd used to mop up the flood were sitting out of sight in the washing machine. She'd also put away the mop and bucket. Aside from the damp patches still remaining on the unpainted walls, there wasn't a lot of visible damage left. "I shut the water off at the main this morning before I went on duty. On my way home, I stopped at the hardware store. Bobby Don sold me all those parts in the bag there. Said whatever we didn't need, I could return."

"Good deal." Grant set his tools on the floor and glanced in the bag before kneeling down to look under the sink. It wasn't hard, since the cupboard below it possessed no door. "Looks like you've patched this pipe a time or two." He pulled his head out to look at her. "Would've been easier to change out the pipes."

"Yes, yes. You went to the same school that my father did. Point is, we're doing it now." She hugged her elbows. "If I let you play doctor with me later will you save the lecture that I *know* my father would deliver?"

He slanted a look her way and she shivered. "That's a pretty hard bargain you drive, little lady."

She propped her hands on her hips. "Oh. My. God. Do *not* start that up. Squire can get away with it because he's sort of related and he's older than dirt." She jabbed her finger in the air at him. "You, however, are neither."

He chuckled and pulled off his coat, handing it to her.

Then he rolled up the long sleeves of his T-shirt and lay down on his back, working his head and upper torso as far as possible into the sink cabinet. Then he stuck his hand out blindly. "Scalpel, Nurse Ali."

She giggled and flipped open the toolbox. "How'd you learn this home-repair stuff, anyway? It can't possibly all come from books." She handed him a pipe wrench and his hand disappeared beneath the cabinet. He bent one knee as he worked and she swallowed, enjoying the sight of him sprawled there. Her very own Mr. Fix-it.

"Learned a lot from Cal. My dad. And in the service I learned even more. Not just the tech stuff, but how to creatively make an unlivable place a little more livable." He clanged a pipe and a moment later tossed a piece onto the floor by her feet. "There's your problem," he said. "Pipe's rusted right through."

She could see that. She was a long way away from being squeamish, but she picked up the gross pipe with two fingers and pitched it in the trash, then returned to crouch near his knees. "What did your dad do?"

"Retired air force."

Ahh. She smiled, glancing at his midsection where his shirt had ridden up an intriguing inch. It was all she could do not to trail her finger along that wedge of bare skin. She already knew he had a few ticklish spots. And she knew exactly where they were. "You followed in his footsteps?"

"Something like that. I enlisted after 9/11."

"A lot of people did."

He tossed her two more pieces of pipe and came out from the cupboard long enough to grab some new ones from the bag. "He was an honest-to-God hero, though," he said after he'd ducked back beneath the sink. "A PJ."

"Pararescueman? No kidding? I have a cousin who—" She broke off at the sound of the front door opening. "Hold on. Greer's date must have tanked." She pushed to her feet and went to the doorway.

But it wasn't Greer who'd come in. It was Maddie, carrying Layla on her hip.

"Hi!" Ali went over and divested her sister of the baby. "What're you doing here? Where's Linc?"

Maddie peeled out of her coat, then deftly worked off Layla's. "He's outside talking to Mrs. Gunderson. We just came from dinner with Judge Stokes."

Ali froze. "And…?"

"And what do you think? I see you got a delivery from Vivian, too. You going to wear it?" Maddie kicked off her shoes and padded into the kitchen, only to stop short. No doubt because of the sight of half a man sticking out from the kitchen cabinet. "Um, hello?"

"Hello."

Ali slid between Maddie and the doorjamb in time to see Grant sketch a wave with the wrench in his hand.

She sat at the table with the baby on her lap and smiled into Layla's face. The baby was wearing a stretchy footed thing with a green monster on the belly that Ali had bought for her before Christmas. It already looked like it was getting too small. "Grant's replacing the pipes and the faucet."

"That's great." Maddie stepped around his long legs and pulled open the refrigerator. "Got anything edible in here?"

"Pizza'll be here in less than an hour. Manetti's. You know there'll be plenty." The pizzeria only made one size—gargantuan.

Her sister made a face.

"Oh, and since *when* do you not like pizza?"

"Well." Maddie closed the refrigerator door and turned to look at Ali. Her palm settled on her flat stomach.

And just like that, Ali knew. She knew, and delight filled her, along with a sharp little pang that she feared might be envy. "You're pregnant!"

Maddie nodded.

"No *wonder* you've looked like a worn-out rag lately!"

Her sister sputtered a laugh. "Geez, Ali. So flattering."

Envy be damned. She leaned over and set Layla on the floor, with Grant's legs providing a suitable barrier between her and the toolbox, then darted to her sister, pulling her in for a boisterous hug. "Oh, my God. We're getting a baby!"

"Well, don't squeeze it out of her just yet."

Ali looked over to see her brother-in-law in the kitchen doorway. She let go of Maddie to hug Linc, too. "This is *such* great news!"

Grant had pulled himself out from the cabinet and was giving Layla a wary look. "Congratulations." He extended his hand.

"Thanks, man." Linc's eyes were watchful as the two of them shook.

Ali had to remind herself that even though it felt like Grant had been in their lives—*her* life—for a very long time, the reality was something quite different. She quickly introduced them. "Grant Cooper. Lincoln Swift. Maddie's husband."

"You're Layla's uncle."

Grant's expression looked a little tight to Ali. Maybe it was because Layla had decided to explore his legs and was rocking back and forth on his stomach as if she wanted to climb over them. Which would have been a feat, since she hadn't even started crawling yet.

"That's the working theory," he said. He glanced at Ali. "You should probably pick her up, shouldn't you?"

The worn floor had never been so clean, because of the flood from the kitchen pipes yesterday. She briefly entertained the notion of plopping the baby on his belly, just to see what he would do, but ultimately, she leaned down and plucked Layla off the ground to nuzzle her sweet-smelling neck. "Better?"

"Yep." He stuck his head back beneath the cabinet and started clanging around the pipes again.

She was determined not to read too much into his apparent disinterest. It had taken her a while to get comfortable around a baby, too.

She turned her attention back to Maddie. "Have you told Greer yet?"

"I thought she'd be here, too."

"She's got a date."

Ali caught the look that passed between Maddie and Linc and a knot formed inside her stomach. "All right. So we know the good news. Now what's the bad? What did Judge Stokes say?"

Her question seemed to hover in the tense air and the knot doubled in size.

Maddie cupped her hand tenderly over Layla's blonde head. "He said that unless new information about her real mother surfaces, he's going to rule on Layla's final status before the end of the month."

"And what's that mean?" Grant's voice sounded hollow from inside the cabinet.

Ali could see the truth in her sister's eyes. "It means we're all going to lose her," she said huskily. "Just admit it, Maddie. That's what you're saying!"

Maddie bit her lip. Her eyes were damp. She reached for Linc's hand and cleared her throat. "The, uh, the family that's next on the list is being reviewed. My boss is handling it himself. He warned me that they are eminently qualified to adopt. They live over in Jackson, but they have plans to move to Florida, where they have other family. They would have gone already, except that they learned there's a baby who might be available for placement soon."

Ali's eyes burned. "This is *such* bull. Layla should be staying here. We all know it. Aren't you going to fight Stokes, Maddie?"

"How?" Maddie spread her hands. "Everywhere we've turned has brought us to a dead end, Ali."

"But Grant's her uncle! We *know* he is."

Grant slid out from beneath the sink. He sat up. His aqua eyes were unreadable. "Knowing isn't proof."

"And we can't *get* proof. Not until we find your sister. And look what a bang-up job I've done of that!" Frustration twisted inside her. "There's only one thing left to do."

"We're not running off with Layla," Maddie warned.

"And that's the difference between you and me," Ali retorted. "Because I would."

Maddie just looked at her.

Her shoulders fell. "Okay, so I wouldn't. But I'd *want* to."

"You think we don't?" Linc closed his arm around Maddie and she leaned into him.

"I don't care what it looks like to the court," Ali said flatly. "Time is running out. We need—"

"A private investigator," Grant interrupted.

Ali nodded. "Vivian will pay for it. She's offered often enough—"

"Layla's *my* niece." Grant pushed to his feet. "I'll pay for it."

Ali opened her mouth to challenge him. Where on earth would he get the money?

"There's not a court around who would argue with my legitimate right to find my own missing sister." His voice was even. "It doesn't have a damn thing to do with the baby and who has the best claim to her."

"You do have that right," Maddie whispered huskily. "She's your family."

He looked grim. "And I'm probably the worst one for her."

"Grant. That's not true." Ali reached for his hand but he shook her off. And the knot inside her stomach got a whole lot tighter.

"Yeah? Nobody with *my blood* has ever wanted me. Not my mom. She spent years trying to pass me off on guys she'd slept with as their kid, just to get money that she'd usually snort up her nose. And her dad—well, good ol' Roger Carmody said he'd rot in hell before he'd see his family name smeared by a little bastard like me. That's the kind of blood that runs in my veins.

"I'll find Karen and she can answer for what she did—abandoning her own baby. But for Layla's sake, she'd be better off with almost anyone other than me." He dropped his wrench in the toolbox and kicked the lid closed. He looked at Ali; his expression was closed. "Pipes are replaced. All you need to do is fit the new faucet in place and tighten the bolts and connect the supply line." He left the kitchen.

"Wait!" She hurriedly transferred Layla to her sister's arms and followed him. "Where are you going?"

He'd already grabbed his coat and was reaching for the front door. "I need to get out of here."

"But I—" She broke off. Swallowed hard. Her mind was still spinning. Not only because of Layla, but also because of everything he'd said. "I'll come with you, then."

"That's not a good idea."

"Grant, I just… I don't want you to be by yourself."

"I've been by myself nearly my whole damn life, Ali. It's what I'm good at." His eyes skated over her. "And frankly, it's what I prefer."

Then he yanked open the door and went out into the dark.

And all she could do was stand there, watching him go.

"Here." A hand came out of nowhere and set a short, squat glass partially filled with amber liquid in front of her.

Ali wrinkled her nose against the smell of the whiskey and looked up at Greer. "I didn't hear you come in. When did you get home?"

"Little while ago. Maddie called me."

She and Linc had left shortly after Grant had bolted. But that had been hours ago. "What time is it?"

"Little after eleven." Greer pulled out the chair opposite her and sat. She looked at the faucetless sink, but made no comment. "Want to talk about it?"

"Nothing to talk about. There's a ninety-nine-point-nine percent chance that Layla will be adopted by a couple who're moving to *Florida*." She'd never been to the state. Never had reason to hate it. But she did now.

"About Grant."

"Why? So you can tease me for liking a bo-oy?"

Greer just watched her.

Ali groaned. She dropped her head onto her arms atop the table. "I'm sorry. I'm a bitch."

"You're in love."

She whipped her head up so fast it was a wonder she didn't get whiplash. "No, I'm not."

"Anyone denying something that fast is guilty."

"They teach you that in law school?"

Her sister smiled slightly. "You sleep with him?"

She dropped her head back onto her arms. "Like you would not believe."

"Well. I think I'm envious."

"Because this is *so* much fun." She lifted her head again. "I fall for the wrong guy. Every time."

"Every time. As if there have been *so* many." Greer tsked. "Ali. Come on. Who's to say Grant's the wrong guy, anyway?"

"He told me he didn't want me!"

"In those exact words?"

"Yes! Well, no. But it's what he meant."

"Yup. Okay. I see."

"You weren't there. You don't know."

"Maddie was there. She heard. And if she weren't feeling so blasted sick being newly pregnant, she'd be here thumping your head instead of me." Suiting action to words, Greer flicked Ali's head with her finger. Hard.

And it smarted now the same way it had when they were ten. Ali sat up again, rubbing her head. "Maddie doesn't thump anyone's head. She's too nice."

"Unlike me," Greer said tartly.

"Oh, you're nice," Ali said grouchily. "You just hide it under that laywer layer you got going. Maddie's nice on the surface. And you're both brilliant. And I'm—" She made a face. "I'm a glorified meter maid. And not all that glorified, when it comes down to it. I let more people slide on expired meters than not. If the town's budget was dependent on parking fines, Braden would go bankrupt."

"Good grief," Greer muttered. "Exaggerate much?" She reached for the drink and took a sip of it herself. "What I am is too impatient with people who are feeling sorry for themselves."

"I'm not feeling sorry for myself. I'm just facing the truth." She slid the glass out of Greer's hand and tossed it back, wincing when the liquor hit the back of her throat like a blowtorch. "I started thinking maybe we were onto something special." She blamed her hoarseness on the fire burning down her esophagus.

Not that she was in love with him.

"You know what I admire about you, Ali?"

Ali fluffed her streaky brown hair. "My incredible taste in hair color?" She knew Greer had thought she was nuts when she'd done it.

"I have never understood the chip you have on your shoulder." Greer's eyes were annoyed. "The fact that you never quit. Never. You don't give up. On anything. And God knows you don't back down. Even when it would be more advantageous in the long run for you to do so."

Ali jerked back, genuinely surprised.

"So why are you giving up on Grant just because he spewed some claptrap about being better off alone?"

She opened her mouth to argue. But nothing came out.

She stood and went over to the counter. The fancy gooseneck faucet they'd bought months ago was still in its box. She pulled it out and started assembling it.

"You don't have anything to say?"

She fed the faucet line through the hole in the sink and then crouched down. Nuts and bolts. Supply line.

"Alicia!"

She finally sat down on the floor and looked at her sister. "What if he really meant it, Greer? What if he turns me away?"

Greer leaned over and grabbed her hands, squeezing them. "Ali. What if he doesn't?"

Chapter Thirteen

"You need a phone line."

Grant eyed Ali, standing on his porch beneath the bare, flickering lightbulb, and wondered if he'd finally fallen asleep to dream. She was wearing her uniform and coat, but her hair streamed loosely over her shoulders. "Haven't we been here before?"

She watched him. It had started snowing again, and the occasional snowflake floated into the sphere of flickering light. "Are you going to invite me in?"

Last time she hadn't waited for an invitation.

He stepped out of the doorway and she came inside.

There were two more boxes sitting near the door. They'd been there when he came home tonight.

Chelsea's biting idea of humor. Bury him in shipments of his own damn book.

Ali stepped around them. She unfastened her coat but didn't take it off. "You get a lot of books. I never see you read."

"It's two in the morning, Ali. What do you want?"

"Yeah. It's two in the morning. I didn't have to pound on your door to wake you up or anything."

"Waking would require sleeping."

Her lashes were lowered, keeping him from truly seeing what she was thinking. "I wasn't going to come."

He threw himself down on the couch and pinched his eyes shut. "That would have been a good choice."

"What's your story, Grant?"

"I didn't give you enough of it back at your house?" He opened his eyes to see her slowly pace across the floor.

"From what I've been able to piece together," she said in an even tone, "Roger Carmody was a puritanical bastard. Helen Carmody, Roger's wife, appeared to be equally puritanical, though it was common knowledge that Roger was abusive. When she died, their daughter, Denise, was just sixteen. There was a brief investigation into Helen's death and it was ruled suicide." Ali turned to pace the other way. "A few years later, when Denise, now eighteen, came to tell her father that she'd been raped, Roger blamed her. Kicked her out of the house. When Denise learned she was pregnant as a result of that rape and once more went to her father, he turned her away yet again."

His stomach churned. "Guess you've been doing some homework, Officer Ali."

"I wish you would have told me."

"So you can feel sorry for me?"

"So I would have understood you more. Instead, I had to spend the last several hours pumping poor Mrs. Gunderson for details and once again use departmental resources for a personal matter." She stopped pacing. Pushing one of Chelsea's oversize boxes in front of him, she sat on the edge of it, clasping her hands in front of her. "None of what happened with the Carmodys was your fault. You must know that, Grant. Roger's failure as a father *and* a grandfather is not your failure." She hesitated. Waiting.

But he had nothing to say.

"He's dead, you know. After the bank took back the ranch, he went to Minnesota, where he had grown up. Died alone and penniless, living on the street just like he'd condemned his daughter and grandson to do some thirty years earlier."

"I know."

She didn't question how he knew. She merely pulled a piece of paper from her pocket and held it out. "My grandmother gave me the name of an investigator that she's had reason to use before. She says his retainer is pretty high but he always gets results. And she says that now isn't the time for pride. She's happy to pay—"

"I already have an investigator."

Ali slowly returned the paper to her pocket.

"It's the same investigator who told me the glad tidings about Roger. I don't need anyone's money when I've got plenty of my own."

She pushed to her feet, looking disbelieving.

"It's all under the corporation."

"What's all under what corporation?"

"Rules, Inc. My corporation."

He got up and went into the kitchen, returning with a knife.

Her eyebrows rose slightly.

"Don't worry. I'm not gonna use it on you." He sliced open the box and pulled out one of the slick hardbacks stacked tightly inside. He handed it to her and went back to the couch, waiting for the puzzlement in he eyes to shift inevitably to comprehension. Blame would be soon to follow.

She stared at the gold lettering on the glossy black background. "You tried to give me this the day I first came here." She flipped over the book. And there on the back jacket was his photograph. "T. C. Grant." She looked pained. "Right there in front of me this whole time." Instead of heaving the book at his head, which is what he'd have wanted to do if their positions were reversed, she flipped it open and started paging through it. "What's the T.C. stand for?"

"Talia and Cal."

She closed the book and held it against the front of her coat. "Your adoptive parents. That's another blank I couldn't fill in. How did your paths cross? Mrs. Gunderson said when Roger turned away Denise that last time, she didn't stick around here. Rumor had it she hitched a ride out with a trucker heading north. After that—" Ali spread her arms, shaking her head "—all Mrs. Gunderson heard was an occasional rumor that Denise was in Florida. Texas. California. Everyone figured she'd either lost the baby or had an abortion. Not surprisingly, Roger never said anything more about either one of you. So why Oregon?"

"Why not Oregon? We'd been every place else. Denise had a one-nighter with Cal once. Before he and Talia were married. We were in Portland and she was broke. She looked him up, prepared for her usual con. Only this time it didn't work like either one of us expected. He knew I wasn't his kid, but he still offered her twice her normal asking price. In order to get it, though, she had to leave me there."

She sucked in an audible breath.

"She jumped at it. Took the money, told me 'so long' and ran. I never saw her again."

"Grant—"

"I don't want your pity."

"No, you just want to be left alone. So you can... what? Feel sorry for yourself while you make this house habitable again? Is it working? Are you erasing Roger Carmody from this place with every pass of a paint roller?" She spread her arms wide. "Or are you just here to keep reminding yourself that the Carmodys didn't want you?"

"Dammit, Ali—"

"No! Dammit, Grant!" She tossed the book aside. "Their failures aren't *your* failures!"

"Then why did I tell my own sister to stay the hell out of my life!"

Grant's shout seemed to echo around the walls, and Ali sucked in a breath.

He swore and kicked over the box and dozens of black-covered books slid out onto the floor. "I did the same damn thing to her that Roger did to my...to Denise. I shut her out. Cut her off. And she ended up so freaking desperate she dumped her kid off on someone else, too."

Ali slid her arms around his waist and pressed her head against his heart. It was pounding hard.

"Don't."

She linked her fingers together even tighter.

"Goddammit, Ali. I said don't." He tried to push her away, but she hung on like a limpet.

Finally, he stopped pushing and held her back. And only then, when his heart wasn't pounding like a wild beast's and his breath wasn't whistling between his teeth, did she finally ease her grip. "Tell me about Cal and Talia. You said he was a PJ?"

He gave a huge sigh, and it took only a small nudge from her before he dropped unresistingly onto the couch. "It's not gonna work," he said. "Getting me to talk about them doesn't make me forget the rest."

"I have the feeling getting you to talk at all is an accomplishment."

He frowned. "Cal couldn't have kids. That's how he knew Denise's claim was crap. And evidently Talia had a soft spot in her heart for nine-year-old boys who could barely read or write thanks to their upbringing. They hadn't even had Karen a year when I entered the picture."

Ali pulled off her coat and sat next to him. "Obviously you overcame the reading and writing challenges."

"She was an English teacher." He leaned his head back against the couch. "But she quit work once I entered the picture. I did *not* appreciate all of her attention. They had rules I was expected to follow. The only rules I knew up until then were to keep the clerks distracted in stores while Denise shoplifted our next meal and to keep my head down if the cops were too close. With Cal and Talia it was keeping my room clean. I'd never even *had* a room before. I had to say please and thank you. I had to go to school on weekdays. Church on Sundays. It was a helluva change."

"I can only imagine."

"Cal didn't put up with any crap, either. I don't know if I was more afraid of getting kicked out by them or of not getting kicked out by them. I think I pulled every stunt in the book during those first six months."

"You were a boy. You were testing boundaries you'd never had before."

"That's what the therapist they made me see said, too."

As far as Ali was concerned, that didn't take any specialized knowledge. It was obvious.

"Anyway, Cal just got tougher. But no matter what I did, he never threatened to kick me out. I'd been with them eleven months and three days when they sat me down and told me they wanted to adopt me. The court had already made them my guardians. But this was more. They were giving me their name." He looked at her and the color of his eyes was even starker against the shadows under them. "There were no long lists of families anxious to adopt a ten-year-old. Particularly one with a history like mine. Less than a month later, I was officially Grant Cooper. I got a brand-new birth certificate with Cal and Talia listed as my parents." He made a low sound. "They gave me a copy of it and I made a frame for it in school and hung it on my wall. It's still hanging on my wall back in Oregon."

She had to push the words past the lump in her throat. "They sound like they were really good people."

He leaned his head back against the couch and closed his eyes. He nodded once.

"Did they know about T. C. Grant? About your writing?"

"No."

"I'm sure they'd have been very proud."

"Maybe. My mom wasn't particularly happy when I quit college to enlist."

"What were you studying?"

"English education."

The lump got bigger. "You wanted to be an English

teacher?" Like his adoptive mother. The woman who'd helped him learn to read and write.

"Hard to imagine."

She rested her head against his shoulder. "Not so hard," she whispered. Instead of teaching, he'd turned to the military. Like his father. "What was the air force like?"

"Like I'd found another family. Particularly after they were both gone."

"Why didn't you stay in?"

"I left to try to save my marriage. That was a bust."

She remembered his text message from his ex-wife all too vividly. The hearts. The lovey-dovey. "Are you sure?"

He opened his eyes then and looked at her. He gestured at the books. "The only thing Chelsea still wants out of me are words. And I don't have any."

"She likes the books, then."

"She publishes the books," he revealed in a tired voice. "All these boxes she sends me? Her idea of making a point."

"About what?"

"She wants another *CCT Rules* novel. Wants me out on book tours. Look-ee here. Real-life hero, writing about the true-to-life exploits of fictional hero Cal Reid. And it's all bull." He pushed off the couch and kicked one of the books. It skidded wildly across the floor. "She keeps sending 'em just to prove that no matter where I run, I can't get away from *CCT Rules*. She doesn't get that no matter where I am, I can't write. I've tried. And there's nothing there. Not. One. Word. There hasn't been since Seymour died." He kicked another book. And another.

They shot across the floor like weapons.

"Grant."

"He shouldn't have died. *He* was the hero. He stayed with his wife. He loved his kids. But I got out and what happened?"

He kicked yet another book and Ali hastily jumped out of the way.

"I perform what's supposed to be cathartic exercise, and Chelsea's off and running. Suddenly, there's a book and people start thinking *I'm* the hero." He clawed his fingers through his hair. "They start coming out of the woodwork, showing up at my door, telling me about their dads and their moms and their sons and daughters who've paid the ultimate price and think there's some magical way I can make that *better* by knowing their stories. Or writing about 'em. Have Cal Reid, fictional war hero, save their lives at least between the pages of a book. And if it's not those poor souls, it's the women thinking I'm worth a notch on their bedpost just because I've hit a bestseller list or two! Sneaking in my house. Showing up in my bed." He kicked another entire box of books and the cardboard snapped, sounding like a shot. The books poured out of it like an exploding volcano.

He finally went still, wrapping his fingers around the back of his neck. His shoulders were slumped. "All I wanted to do was be able to *sleep* at night," he said gruffly. "That's all I ever wanted to do. After the first book, it was okay. For a long time. But then—" He broke off, shaking his head.

"Seymour died," she ventured softly. She remembered the ivory invitation she'd found in his kitchen drawer that first day. He hadn't made a big deal about it, but that hadn't kept her from reading what it said. *Seymour Reid. Valorous Actions. Award Ceremony.*

He didn't answer and she ached inside. For the little boy he'd been. For the man he'd become.

"I can't do what Cal and Talia did. I can't be a parent to Layla. I don't have what it takes to do the job right."

"How do you know that until you try?"

"Every time I've found something to love, I've lost it. And if I didn't lose it, I kicked it away. Layla deserves more."

"So do you."

He shook his head. He dropped his hands and finally looked at her. His eyes were dark. "Go home, Ali. There's nothing here for you."

She remembered getting thrown by a horse once when she was little. The way her breath had been knocked out of her. The feeling of trying to pull in air and not being able to.

This was worse.

She bent down and picked up one of the books from the floor. The glossy black jacket had been torn and was slipping off the hardback's spine. "I'm an ordinary woman, Grant." The words felt raw. As raw as oxygen sneaking out of stunned lungs. "Living an ordinary life in a small, ordinary town." She held the book up in front of his face. "This sort of thing freaks me out. The hearts and hugs and kisses that your ex-wife texts to you freak me out. The fact that I'm falling in love with you freaks me out. But that doesn't keep me from knowing that everything here is for me. You are for me."

"Ali," he said, his jaw clenching.

"I can't make you believe a thing until you stop looking at what was and allow yourself to hope for what could be. It doesn't have to be with me. It doesn't even have to be with Layla. But please, if only to honor the ones who did get to love you while they could, don't close yourself off from the possibility of having that again. Whether you want to admit it or not, you deserve to be loved. You deserve to be able to love."

"I can't—"

"You mean you won't." She tossed aside the book and picked up her coat. "What do you think a real hero is? Some mythical, perfect, larger-than-life figure? This Cal Reid character you write about? Is it someone who never falters? Is never afraid?" Her voice went raw all over again. "I think a real hero is someone who shows courage despite the odds." Her eyes burned and she pulled open the door. If he saw her cry, he'd blame himself for that, too. "I think a hero is someone who'll face the fear behind *can't* and at least *try*."

Then, without even pulling on her coat, she hurried out into the snowy night.

She made it all the way to the highway before she had to pull over. Not from the snow. But from the tears blinding her. From the fact that he hadn't changed his mind and asked her to stay. From the fear that it was entirely likely that he never would.

Ali dipped the paint roller into the pan and rolled it back and forth, coating it with Svelte Sage. The paint was vaguely green. Vaguely gray. Vaguely brown.

It had taken her and her sisters weeks to agree on the color.

Now, as she lifted the roller from the paint and ran it in a long swathe against the kitchen wall, carefully avoiding the cabinets that one day would be a lovely off-white, she couldn't even remember why that decision had been so darn hard to make.

It had been nearly a week since she'd seen Grant. Since she'd told him she was falling in love with him.

"Falling." Her lips twisted in a frown. "Too late."

"Talking to yourself?"

She looked at Greer, who'd padded barefoot into the kitchen. "I thought you were still at the office. I didn't hear you come in."

"Walked right past you thirty minutes ago, sweetie. Obviously, you were preoccupied."

"Paint will do that to a person." She ran the roller up and down.

"Yeah. Paint." Greer picked up a clean paintbrush and toyed with the bristles. "I'm thinking about quitting my job."

The paint roller jumped right over the edge of the cabinets. "*What?* Why?" Somehow, she'd managed to get paint all over her hands, too.

"Because I feel like I'm not accomplishing anything useful!" Greer tossed down the brush and grabbed a rag, wetting it under the gooseneck faucet before swiping the side of the cabinets. "Shoplifters and drunk drivers and bad-check writers. It seems so pointless. I can't help the people I want to help." She dropped the rag on the plastic sheet that Ali had spread over the table to protect it from paint spatters.

"So what do you want to do? Start working for the prosecutor?"

Greer's lips compressed. "I don't know."

"Join Archer's practice?"

"I don't know," she said again.

Ali didn't know what was worse. Her own personal pity party or the disconcerting sight of her sister not knowing what to do. "You'll figure it out," she said. "You always do." The phone on the wall rang and she automatically reached out to get it, forgetting the paint on her hand. "Hello?"

Greer rolled her eyes and tossed the paint rag toward her.

"Templeton." Sgt. Gowler's voice was abrupt and so unexpected that she automatically feared she'd gotten her days off messed up. "You're gonna want to get in here."

Her shoulders sank. That's what she got for allowing her own misery to so preoccupy her. "I'm sorry, sir. I'll be there as soon as I can."

"Got a hit in Minneapolis on that missing persons for the Cooper woman."

"What?"

"It's not good, Ali."

Her stomach clenched. Gowler never called her by her first name.

"Woman now identified as Karen Cooper was killed in a multivehicle collision on New Year's Eve."

She sank weakly onto a chair, vaguely aware of Greer's concerned face. "That was over a month ago."

"She died as a Jane Doe."

"How do we know it's actually Karen?"

"Friend of hers—roommate—came in to report she'd gone missing. She'd evidently been staying there but the friend was out of town until now. Came back and Karen's stuff was all there, but there was no sign of Karen. Two reports meshed."

"Disposition?"

"Unidentified Doe. County's storing the remains. Collision involved a gas explosion and the fire was pretty damaging."

Ali's stomach churned. "Was there any DNA recovered?"

"Should have been, but there was some complication with it. I don't know what exactly. You can find that out when you come in. She didn't have much in the way of personal effects. From what I understand, the friend has what there is boxed up and ready if there's someone who'll want it."

"There is," Ali said quietly. "I'll be there as soon as I can. Sergeant, thank you for calling me."

"Sort of thing doesn't make any of us happy," he said, sounding gruff. Then he hung up.

Ali slowly did the same.

"What is it?"

"Now I know why it's been so hard to find Karen."

Chapter Fourteen

The memorial service was five days later.

It was held at the Braden cemetery even though there was no body to bury. Just a wooden box of ashes that Ali handed to Grant after the service. She'd wanted to get it to him sooner, but red tape and bureaucracy had gotten in the way. In the end, she'd flown to Minnesota herself to retrieve and transport Karen's remains back to Grant. What should have been simple in theory had involved nearly twenty-four hours of travel.

She'd barely made it back to town in time for the service.

"I'm very sorry for your loss." Her voice was husky. It was only the second time she'd seen him since she'd had the unfortunate task of notifying him of his sister's gruesome death. In all her time with the department, she'd had to make a handful of death notifications. They were never easy.

His had been nearly impossible.

Not even the fact that he'd already received the same news from his private investigator had lessened the burden.

Now, his fingers brushed against hers as he took his sister's ashes.

"Thank you."

The words didn't come from Grant.

They came from the tall, strikingly beautiful blonde standing next to him.

Chelsea. His ex-wife. Of the hearts and kissy-kissy text message and the seemingly endless boxes of *CCT Final Rules*. She'd spoken briefly during the service. Talked about Karen in such a way that Ali hadn't even had the heart to hate her too badly.

But that was then. And now, Chelsea's arm was linked with Grant's, as if she still had that right. That wasn't the worst part. The worst part was Grant allowing it.

Ex-wife for the win.

She didn't know why she didn't just move along. There were other people milling around who clearly expected to extend their condolences to Grant. Jaxon was there, along with more than half the staff at Magic Jax, and there were others. Folks Ali didn't even recognize. "A lot of people came."

"More than we expected," Chelsea answered.

Ali's teeth were set on edge. She imagined herself wearing blinders, where all she could see was Grant, not the woman glued to his side. "I noticed that Judge Stokes came, too."

Grant finally spoke. "Not in an official capacity." He looked at Chelsea. "Would you excuse us, Chels?"

The woman's perfectly painted red lips curved downward. "Of course." She unwound her arm, but before she

walkcd away, she pressed her lips to his cheek. As tall
as she was and with the expensive high-heeled leather
boots she wore, she didn't even have to stretch up to
reach him. Together, the two of them looked like they
belonged in a magazine.

Ali watched her walk away. Then she looked back
at Grant. At the lipstick his ex-wife had left on him.
"How are you doing?"

He looked down at the box he held. "I've had better
days."

Despite everything, her heart squeezed. "I'm so sorry
it ended this way." She pressed her gloved hand against
the wooden box. It had started out as a cardboard one.
Much like a shoebox. She'd charged the finely carved
wooden urn on her credit card. As far as she was concerned, Grant never needed to know about the shoebox.

"She was on her way back here." His eyes were more
blue than aqua today. Maybe they were reflecting the
pale blue sky. "That's what John—my investigator—
thinks, anyway. I'm not so sure, considering she left
what few belongings she had behind."

"I wasn't able to speak with her friend who reported
her as missing." Ali had tried, but hadn't been able to
reach her. If she'd pursued it any further, she wouldn't
have made it back in time for the service. "Did you?"

"John did. The friend wasn't all that much of a friend.
She had only known Karen for a couple of months.
Didn't know anything about her past or whether she'd
had a baby. They met because they were both waitress-
ing at the same place. Mostly, she was concerned about
collecting the rent that Karen owed. She wouldn't re-
lease Karen's stuff until John paid her."

Charming. "You received her belongings, though?"

"Two days ago. She had a few childhood pictures."

"Anything of Layla?"

He shook his head.

Short of a birth certificate, photos of Layla would have helped. Even though they had now located Karen, they were no better off legally establishing her identity as the baby's mother. No better off establishing Grant as her uncle. Even though the medical examiner's office had retained some of Karen's DNA after her terrible end, their bad luck had persisted. The samples had been accidentally damaged, to such a degree that they were useless in trying to match Karen to Layla. Ali would have had a hard time believing it, if she hadn't spoken with the medical examiner's office herself.

"She had a Wyoming driver's license. Nobody knows why she wasn't carrying it with her, but it probably would have burned up in the crash, anyway. A few rings. John thinks one of 'em looks like a wedding ring."

She looked at him sharply. "If she was married, maybe we can find out to whom."

"Sure. Because looking for one needle in the haystack isn't enough."

He was right, but that didn't mean she wouldn't start searching. "Anything else in her things?"

"A couple of rodeo magazines." His lips formed a thin line for a moment. "A couple of novels."

She folded her arms over her chest, shivering. Not from cold. "T. C. Grant novels?" He didn't have to answer when she could see the truth on his face.

It was so painful to see that she had to look away.

But that only brought Chelsea back into her line of sight. She was speaking with a much shorter, plump woman who had two gawky teenagers with her. The fact that Chelsea hugged the other woman made Ali

206 *SHOW ME A HERO*

think she was more likely a friend from their shared past than a friend of Karen's.

"How long were the two of you married?"

"Seven years. Six and a half too long."

She raised her eyebrows. "Yet you worked with her on the books. And she's here now."

"I told you," he said, his expression darkening. "She thinks she can twist another book out of me."

"She sounded like she genuinely cared about Karen."

"She did. Maybe enough to want to be here today, but Chelsea's nothing if not practical. Come to a memorial service. Try and bribe a man into her publishing clutches at the same time."

Chelsea was heading back their way and Ali had no desire to come up short—literally—next to her. "If you ask me, she looks like she's got an interest in keeping her clutches on you in all sorts of ways." Ali pulled off her glove to wipe her finger against his sharp, angular jaw. She showed him the red color that she came away with. "She's certainly leaving her mark." She rubbed the lipstick away on her glove and pulled it back on. "I should go. Vivian's Valentine's ball is tomorrow."

A whisper of a smile lit his face for just a moment. "Going to wear the bustle?"

Her throat tightened. "Still debating that," she responded in a credibly dry tone. Then she gave Chelsea what she thought was a polite nod and she walked away.

"That's her."

Grant barely listened to Chelsea. He was too busy watching Ali walk away.

"Her grandmother is Vivian Archer Templeton," Chelsea went on.

"So?"

His ex-wife huffed a little. "So, she's one of the wealthiest women in the country."

"Good for her."

"She asked if my company would consider donating to the library she's trying to get built."

He looked down at the box. At Karen. He should feel more grief. Except that he'd been preparing himself for this moment for years. "You knew Karen as well as I did. Do you think she was capable of abandoning her baby?"

Chelsea didn't hesitate. "Yes." She squeezed his arm. "I also think she was capable of immediately regretting it, but as usual didn't have a clue about how to make it right. Karen was an adult, Grant. She was always responsible for her own decisions. Including forging your name on that contract."

He gave her a sharp look. "You *knew*? And never said squat?"

"I didn't know at first. And I stayed quiet for the same reason you did."

"Another *CCT Rules* book."

Her lips tightened. "To protect Karen. You know, I'm happy to ride the money train, but if you don't want to write another, then don't. Write something else. Or finish your teaching degree. Or pretend you actually want to live in your grandfather's house. Whatever. I'd actually rather see you happy for once." She nodded toward Ali, who'd nearly reached her departmental SUV. "Her grandmother told me how much she went through to get Karen back to you. Above and beyond, if you ask me."

"What are you talking about?"

So she told him.

"I didn't think she could do it, but I was wrong." Meredith stood next to Ali and Greer on the short end of the oval ice-skating rink, where at least two dozen skaters were circling the perimeter to the old-timey music playing from a loudspeaker. The sound quality was somewhat scratchy, which only seemed to add to the ambiance.

"What I don't get," Greer added, "is why so many people were willing to get dolled up in clothes like these." She plucked at her outfit, which was equally as fussy as Ali's. "Look at Archer." She gestured at their big brother, who was wearing a long coat—a frock coat, according to Vivian—narrow trousers and a top hat. He carefully escorted Vivian around the edge of the ice. "Even he got into the spirit."

"He just wanted to make Vivian happy," Ali murmured. But Greer had a point. There were more skaters who were dressed in old-fashioned outfits than in jeans and jackets.

"Well, I like to dress up now and then, but this is ridiculous. Maddie should be glad she's feeling so crummy with morning sickness and had a good reason to be able to stay home." Greer grabbed handfuls of her dress, making sure it was clear of her skates, and stomped off toward the warming hut, which was actually an extremely large heated party tent, where even more people were hanging out, drinking and eating and having a grand time if the decibel level of the conversation was anything to go by.

"Does Greer seem particularly edgy to you?"

"I think she's as frustrated as we all are with Layla's situation," she murmured. "I'm going to get some hot chocolate. Can I bring you one?"

Meredith beamed. She looked especially lovely with a dark purple coat that was similar to Ali's and a furry white muff. "I'd love some, sweetie. Oh, I wish you dad was here. He would've seen that his mother isn't a terrible as he still wants to believe." She stepped onto the edge of the ice and waved her hand toward Archer as he and Vivian approached.

Ali waited a moment, smiling at the sight of her mother and brother and grandmother all skating together. She wished she could feel the smile deeper than just the surface, though.

She followed the path to the warming hut and walked inside. She was wearing the white figure skates that her grandmother had provided along with the clothing, and walking around in them was making her ankles hurt. Maybe she wouldn't notice so much if she was skating, but since Grant was supposed to have been her date before everything had exploded around them, she didn't really have the heart or the desire to get on the ice.

She joined the people in line at the closest refreshment station. There were four such stations, all positioned in the corners of the tent like open bars at a wedding reception. And next to each one, there was a tall standing mirror, along with more piles of costumes and an old-fashioned photo booth, where people could get their pictures taken. She knew that had been Delia's idea. Her cousin was flitting around from corner to corner, making certain that everyone was having a grand time.

From what Ali could see, most were. She even spotted Hayley and Seth in the far corner, mugging for the camera. Her eldest sister didn't have skates on her feet, Ali noted. Probably because she was a million months pregnant and Seth had an overprotective streak about two miles wide.

As she waited in line, her thoughts drifted to Grant. And to his sister. It had been years since he'd spoken with Karen and that left a lot of time in which she could have married someone. Of course, it was a big if that she had been married in the first place. But if there'd been a husband, maybe even at the time of Layla's birth—

"I like the bustle."

Ali's wandering thoughts screeched to a standstill.

She slowly turned to see Grant behind her. "Hi." The word sort of oozed out of her, more breath than voice. She looked past him, more than a little certain that Chelsea wouldn't be too far away. "I didn't expect to see you here."

"I don't think we ever officially canceled our date."

She chewed the inside of her cheek on that one. "I figured after what we said the other night, it was pretty official." She rocked slightly on her ice skates. The floor inside the tent was made of thick, firm rubber that couldn't be damaged by skate blades.

"Well, regardless. Eva and Emi wanted to come. They saw the signs in the window at Josephine's when we went there after the service yesterday." He lifted his shoulder. He was in the minority when it came to dress. First off, he had boots on his feet rather than skates. He wore dark blue jeans, a tan sweater that looked as soft as cashmere—and probably was—and a black leather jacket.

He looked delicious and handsome and entirely out of her reach.

"Who are Eva and Emi?"

"My goddaughters." He gestured toward the thick transparent tent panels on the sides of the tent that kept it from feeling too closed-in. "They're out there skating somewhere with Claudia."

"That's nice." She had no clue exactly who he was talking about. "Goddaughters, though. That's a little surprising."

"They're Seymour's kids."

She went still.

"Even though they never met Karen, they came to pay their respects. Because it was what Seymour would've done. They're staying with me out at the ranch."

Her chest felt tight. "That's… I'm glad. Glad you're not alone."

"Seymour was my best friend. Someday I'll tell you all about him. But he wasn't what you would call particularly smart with money."

"I'm not sure where you're going with this," she said faintly, "but okay."

"I'm going to give his family the ranch."

She inhaled. "Oh."

"They'll never need to worry about a roof over their heads. And it's long past time I did more than send them money at Christmas and birthdays. Once the ceremony's over, when they give Claudia Sey's Distinguished Service Cross, I'll make the arrangements to move them. I'll have to get the rest of the house fixed up for them, but—"

She slid her arms around his neck and kissed him. His lips were cool. Firm. He was unquestionably surprised by her move.

Just as abruptly, she backed away again. Her face felt hot. "I think that's a wonderful idea," she said softly. He'd be putting Roger Carmody's ghost to rest for sure.

She realized the line in front of her had disappeared and quickly stepped forward to fill two cups with hot cocoa. "My mother's waiting for me," she said huskily when she tried to move away from the table only to find him standing in her way.

"Did you mean it? What you said the other night?"

She'd said a lot of things the other night. But there

was no question what he meant. Lying was impossible. "Yes."

He lifted the cups out of her hand and set them on the table, then pulled her to the side. Toward the tall mirror. His eyes met hers in the reflection. "What do you see?"

Heartbreak. "I don't know what you want me to say, Grant."

"I want you to say that you see it."

"See *what*?"

He lowered his head until his lips were near her ear. "The mark."

"What are you talking about?"

"The mark," he said again. "You've left it all over me."

She went still.

"Chelsea isn't here," he said quietly. "Not in Braden. Not in my heart. And when she was, she was never as deep as you've gotten since you first pounded your fist on my front door. Your mark is all over me, Officer Ali. And I don't want to rub it off, even if I could. I want to be the man that you think I am. I want to at least try."

Her eyes flooded.

"I'm still a writer with no words, sweetheart. Still a guy who has nightmares more often than not. I'm so far from being the kind of man you deserve that you should walk away and keep going, but the thought of you actually doing that is the one thing I don't think I can survive. Not now. Not after everything that's happened. I know how hard you worked to bring Kare back to me. And I want an ordinary life with an extraordinary woman." His husky voice dropped a notch. "So tell me. Can you see the mark now?"

She exhaled shakily and lifted her fingers to graze

his jaw where Chelsea's lipstick had been. "I think I see it here."

He caught her fingers in his and kissed them. "It's here." He pressed her hand against his chest. His heart.

Tears slid over her lashes. She stared into his aqua eyes. "What do we do now?"

"I don't know," he murmured, lowering his mouth toward hers. "But as long as we do it together, I know we're on the right track. I know it's fast, but my dad always said that just because something was fast didn't mean it wasn't real." He slid his arms around her and pulled her close. "And nothing has ever felt more real than this. I love you, Ali. I never thought I'd say those words again, much less feel them, and I'll spend the rest of my life trying to prove that I deserve you."

Her heart cracked wide. Right then and there. Just fell right open to him. "You don't have to prove anything," she said softly. "You just have to love me."

He slowly smiled. "I think I can manage that."

"Well, can you manage to move it off to the side so some of us who want to use the photo booth *can*?"

Ali and Grant looked over to see Charlene from Magic Jax.

"Better watch yourself," she went on, giving Ali a broad wink. "Babies in the belly." Hauling on the arm of her gangly tall husband, she dragged him toward the photo booth.

Grant pressed his lips against Ali's ear. "What was that about babies?"

She smiled and tightened her arms around him. "I'll tell you all about it later," she promised. "For now…"

His eyebrows went up as he waited for her to finish.

She looked past him to the skating rink beyond the tent. "For now, I want to meet these goddaughters of yours. And then I want to get on the ice and skate with you. My grandmother assures me it's *magical*."

He laughed softly, wrapping his hand with hers. "Well, then. Let's go make some magic."

Epilogue

The glow of the bonfire could be seen for half a mile.

Grant sat huddled on the porch with his arm around Ali and watched it burn.

"I'm glad you decided to donate the books to the local veteran organizations," Ali commented. "I would've felt wasteful burning them all. I mean, Cal Reid seemed to deserve more."

"Yeah, well, he's getting more. I'm also donating to our grandmother's library fund." He linked his fingers with hers. He still couldn't believe he wasn't burning the books. For that matter, he still couldn't believe he had this particular woman at his side.

Just went to prove that miracles could happen.

Maybe enough miracles to get him writing again.

"What do you know about Cal Reid, anyway?"

"He's named after your dad and your best friend. He always gets his man." She bumped her shoulder against his. "Or woman." She gave him a look. "Timmy loaned me his copies of the whole series. I had to swear an oath that I'd return them in perfect condition. They're good, Grant. Really good. Particularly *Final Rules*, even though I know how you felt about writing it." She looked out at the bonfire again. They were burning the wall he'd taken down upstairs to make two small bedrooms into a larger bedroom for Eva and Emi. They'd built the fire well away from the barn so that even if the sparks should fly, they wouldn't do any damage.

Until he'd decided to give the ranch to Claudia and her daughters, he wouldn't have cared if the whole thing went up in flames.

Now, he cared.

He lifted the last item to toss on the fire. "Do you want to do the honors, or shall I?"

She cautiously took the thick, catalog-style envelope and looked inside. She lifted out the junk mail and circulars inside and he felt her relax. "I thought I was going to find an unfinished manuscript in here or something."

"Just Karen's mail that Chelsea had been collecting. She told me there was nothing important in it, so don't know why she didn't get rid of it herself. But—" He shrugged. "More fuel for the bonfire."

Ali was still pouring stuff out on her lap, occasionally holding a piece of mail up to the light to read. "Some of these things go back years!" She upended the envelope entirely and a last thin piece of mail floated out. She caught it in her hand. "I should have thought to get marshmallows," she said. "A bonfire without marshmallows is kind of a sad thing."

"Next time."

"Why *do* you suppose Karen used the name Dais

Miranda instead of her own?" She tore open the envelope and looked inside.

"She liked old Carmen Miranda movies. Daisy was the name of the cat she had when we were kids. Why she put the two together is anyone's guess."

"You put Cal and Reid together. She put two things she loved together..." Her voice trailed off. "Grant. This is Karen." She held up a small color photograph of his sister and a man wearing a cowboy hat.

He glanced at the picture. "Yep." He slid his hand beneath her sweater. "What do you say we take this inside?"

"You don't know who the man is with her?"

He sighed faintly and looked more closely at the photograph. "Nope."

"You see what he's doing?"

"Kissing her hand."

"He's kissing the *ring* on her hand." She flipped the photograph over and went still.

He looked.

"So much for vows" had been scrawled on the back.

She pawed through the pieces of mail strewn over the porch beside her. "Here!" She pounced on one and lifted it to the light. "This was postmarked last February. The return address is right here." She stood and the mail scattered as she waved the envelope at him. "Your sister *was* married. Her husband—" she stopped waving to peer at the envelope again— "*Ryder Wilson* mailed this from right here! A year ago. You know what this means?"

"The haystack just got a lot smaller."

She smiled brilliantly and kissed his lips. "The haystack doesn't even exist. This Wilson guy is surely Layla's father! Judge Stokes needs to see this. I know he'll hold off ruling on Layla a little longer while we track down Wilson."

"You're crediting my wild sister with pretty traditional behavior," he cautioned. "Being married to the father of her child."

"At least it's a possibility. Even you must admit that." Her eyes were sparkling. She was extraordinary, and he couldn't believe his good luck.

"Thank you," he said.

"For what?"

"For believing in possibilities. For pounding on my door." He wrapped his arms around her. "For never giving up. I love you, Ali Templeton."

She softened against him. "And I love you, Grant Cooper."

* * * * *

COMING SOON!

We really hope you enjoyed reading this book. If you're looking for more romance, be sure to head to the shops when new books are available on

Thursday
23rd August

MILLS & BOON

Coming next month

THE MILLION POUND MARRIAGE DEAL
Michelle Douglas

Sophie had had good sex before, but what she shared with Will wasn't just good. It was *spectacular*. She hadn't known it could be like this.

Not that she said that to Will, of course. It smacked too much of a neediness that would send him running for the hills. She didn't want him running for the hills. Not yet.

Not that they spent all their time in bed. They spent hours riding Magnus and Annabelle as he showed her all the places he'd loved when he was young. They explored the glens and the hills, traversed lochs and cantered through crystal-clear streams. They spent hours playing board games and watching musicals with Carol Ann.

But when they retired to their room each night — they made love as if they never wanted to stop. Not just once, but again and again. As if they couldn't get enough of each other. As if they were addicted.

It wasn't until Thursday, though, that Sophie finally realised how much trouble she was in. When Will told her he had to go back to London the next day. The depth of the protest that rose through her had her clutching the wedding folder she held to her chest. As casually as she could, she leant a shoulder against the bedroom doorframe to counter the sensation of falling, of dizziness. Loss, anguish and despair all pounded through her.

Will sat on the side of the bed, his back to her, pulling on his shoes, so she allowed herself precisely three seconds to close her eyes and drag in a breath, to pull herself together. 'No rest for the wicked?' she forced herself to ask, with award-winning composure.

He didn't move and she tried to paste what she hoped was a cheeky grin into place. 'I suppose I should be focusing on the wedding anyway. Nine days, Will. The month has flown!'

He turned, a frown in his eyes. 'Do you want to back out?'

'Of course not.' It was just... She hadn't known when she'd agreed to this paper marriage that she'd be marrying the man she *loved*. 'Do you?'

Continue reading
THE MILLION POUND MARRIAGE DEAL
Michelle Douglas

Available next month
www.millsandboon.co.uk

LET'S TALK
Romance

For exclusive extracts, competitions
and special offers, find us online:

f facebook.com/millsandboon

◯ @millsandboonuk

✖ @millsandboon

Or get in touch on 0844 844 1351*

For all the latest titles coming soon, visit
millsandboon.co.uk/nextmonth

Want even more
ROMANCE?

Join our bookclub today!

'Mills & Boon books, the perfect way to escape for an hour or so.'

Miss W. Dyer

'Excellent service, promptly delivered and very good subscription choices.'

Miss A. Pearson

'You get fantastic special offers and the chance to get books before they hit the shops'

Mrs V. Hall

Visit millsandbook.co.uk/Bookclub and save on brand new books.

MILLS & BOON